John Bunyan (1628–88) was born at Elstow near Bedford. The son of a brazier, he learned to read and write at the village school and prepared to follow his father's trade. But in 1644, the Civil War changed the course of events and, at the age of sixteen, he was drafted into the Parliamentary army and was stationed at Newport Pagnell, from 1644 to 1646. In 1649, he married his first wife, by whom he had four children. She died c. 1656, and about three years later he married his second wife, Elizabeth.

It was in 1648 that Bunyan suffered a severe religious crisis which lasted for several years. He emerged with the resolution to convert others and help them in their spiritual problems. In 1653 he joined a Nonconformist church in Bedford, where he came into contact with the Quakers, against whom he published his first writings, *Some Gospel Truths Opened* (1656) and *A Vindication* (1657). In November 1660, he was arrested while preaching in the fields. He refused to cease preaching and spent most of the next twelve years in Bedford gaol. During the first half of this period, he wrote nine books and among them were *The Holy City, or the New Jerusalem* (1665), which was inspired by a passage in the book of Revelation, and his most well-known book of this period, *Grace Abounding to the Chief of Sinners* (1666), his spiritual autobiography. It centres almost wholly on the development of his inner religious feelings and in it he also describes his religious crisis of 1648. During the latter years of his imprisonment, Bunyan also began *The Pilgrim's Progress*, the work for which he is most famous, and which renders the personal spiritual experience of the earlier *Grace Abounding* into the more objective form of a universal myth, where all Christians who seek the truth are embodied within the figure of the solitary man pursuing his pilgrimage. In 1672, after his release from prison, he became pastor of the Bedford separatist church, but was imprisoned again in 1676 for a shorter period of about six months, during which he probably finished the first part of *The Pilgrim's Progress*, which was published in 1678. The second part, together with the whole work, was published in 1684. His other works include *The Life and Death of Mr Badman* (1680) and *The Holy War* (1682). He died just when the period of religious persecution was coming to an end.

Roger Sharrock is Emeritus Professor of English in the University of London where he held the chair at King's College; he has been Chairman of the English Association. Among other books and articles he is the author of the critical study *John Bunyan* and of *Saints, Sinners and Comedians*, on the novels of Graham Greene; he is the editor of the first volume of *The Pelican Book of English Prose* and general editor of the Oxford edition of *The Miscellaneous Works of John Bunyan*.

THE PILGRIM'S PROGRESS

THE
PILGRIM'S PROGRESS

JOHN BUNYAN

Edited with an introduction and notes by
Roger Sharrock

PENGUIN BOOKS

PENGUIN BOOKS

Published by the Penguin Group
Penguin Books Ltd, 27 Wrights Lane, London W8 5TZ, England
Viking Penguin, a division of Penguin Books USA Inc.
375 Hudson Street, New York, New York 10014, USA
Penguin Books Australia Ltd, Ringwood, Victoria, Australia
Penguin Books Canada Ltd, 2801 John Street, Markham, Ontario, Canada L3R 1B4
Penguin Books (NZ) Ltd, 182–190 Wairau Road, Auckland 10, New Zealand

Penguin Books Ltd, Registered Offices: Harmondsworth, Middlesex, England

This edition first published by Penguin English Library 1965
Reprinted in Penguin Classics 1986
Reprinted with revisions 1987
7 9 10 8 6

Printed in England by Clays Ltd, St Ives plc
Set in Monotype Bembo

CONTENTS

INTRODUCTION

THE PILGRIM'S PROGRESS is a book which in the three hundred years of its existence has crossed most of those barriers of race and culture that usually serve to limit the communicative power of a classic. It has penetrated into the non-Christian world; it has been read by cultivated Moslems during the rise of religious individualism within Islam, and at the same time in cheap missionary editions by American Indians and South Sea Islanders. Its uncompromising evangelical Protestantism has not prevented it from exercising an appeal in Catholic countries. But to English readers it is bound to appear as the supreme classic of the English Puritan tradition. John Bunyan, its author, wrote about sixty other evangelical and controversial tracts; only three of his books are works of fiction, and of these only *The Pilgrim's Progress* has carried the heroic image of militant Puritanism to a vastly wider public than Bunyan's original Nonconformist audiences.

In literature, no less than in religion, Bunyan has always offended the establishment. The appeal of his coarse, speech-patterned English is not polite; he breaks the canon, and in a period which has become aware of the social limitations of the canon and the need to revise it, it is not surprising that there is a renewal of interest in his work. Indeed there is in progress an outburst of critical and scholarly activity comparable to that called forth in the Romantic age. The first complete edition of his writings is under way. The anniversary of his masterpiece occasioned a volume of essays on his narrative methods (*The Pilgrim's Progress: Critical and Historical Essays*, ed. Vincent Newey, Liverpool University Press, 1980);

7

he has been subjected to an early brand of the technique of deconstruction (Stanley Fish, *Self-Consuming Artifacts*, 1972); not unnaturally, for one in so sensitive a relation to his public, as preacher and fabulist, he has caught the attention of the founder of reader-response criticism (Wolfgang Iser, *The Implied Reader from Bunyan to Beckett*, 1974). The Marxists have begun to pay attention to his insights into a working-class world. But the predominantly and avowedly feminine world of the Second Part of *The Pilgrim's Progress* still awaits adequate attention. Meanwhile Christopher Hill and others have been exploring the background of radical Puritanism, flowering between 1640 and 1660, which formed the seed-bed for all his work.

The life of the author was as much a classic witness to that heroic Puritan faith as was the book; and though the book is a religious allegory in form, it grew naturally out of the circumstances of his life. Bunyan was born at Elstow near Bedford in 1628; he came of yeoman stock, but the family fortunes had declined and his father was a brazier or travelling tinker. He learned to read and write at a local grammar school and prepared to follow his father's trade. But in 1644 the Civil War swept him up into its course: at the age of sixteen he was mustered in the county levy, or militia, on the Parliamentary side, and spent some years on garrison duty before his discharge. Soon after this he married. His wife and he set up house 'as poor as poor might be, with not so much household-stuff as a dish or spoon betwixt us both'. About 1648 he was plunged into a religious crisis which lasted for several years and which brought him to the brink of despair. His vivid imagination was possessed in a simple and terrible form by the Calvinist doctrine that all men were predestined either to salvation or to damnation; he battled with doubts of his own faith. In *Grace Abounding to the Chief of Sinners* he has left an account of the fearful dreams and visions of this period: they took on the almost tangible form of voices, blows, and buffets, and he records the sensation of being pulled and pinched by the demons sent to torment him and the menacing texts of Scripture that filled his thoughts.

Weathering the storm, he emerged a new man after conversion, directed outwards to converting others and comforting them in their spiritual problems. He attached himself to a Nonconformist group in Bedford and began to preach. His new strength and resolution were soon put to the test, for in November 1660, a few months after Charles II's Restoration, he was arrested by a local magistrate while preaching in the fields. He refused to give an undertaking not to preach and was imprisoned off and on for the next twelve years. It seems that at any time he might have obtained his release: he had only to enter into a bond giving assurance that he would cease from preaching and evangelizing and conform to the worship of the Church of England. It is a measure of the personal integrity he had achieved that he refused to do this. His confinement was not brutal by twentieth-century standards, but like Boethius in the dungeon of the Gothic King, or like a modern political prisoner, he was put to the supreme existential test; isolated among people who believed that his conduct was foolish or criminal or both, he had to give a reason for the faith that was in him. This involved an examination of his past experience and a translation of it into a form which would

9

provide a recognizable pattern of hope for other Christians. Out of this grew his spiritual autobiography, *Grace Abounding to the Chief of Sinners*, and later *The Pilgrim's Progress* which renders the personal spiritual experience of the earlier book into the objective form of a universal myth. All types of Christians searching for the truth and prepared to reject a hostile society are comprehended under the figure of the wayfaring man earnestly pursuing his pilgrimage.

After his twelve years' imprisonment and another, shorter period of confinement, Bunyan became the pastor of the Bedford separatist church. He earned the nickname of 'Bishop Bunyan' for his zeal in travelling throughout Bedfordshire and into Cambridgeshire, both to preach and to attempt to solve the personal problems of his scattered congregation. He died in 1688 just when the period of religious persecution was drawing to an end and Nonconformists were becoming more fully integrated into the life of the nation.

The legend persisted down to recent times that Bunyan wrote *The Pilgrim's Progress* in the little town lock-up which stood in Bedford on the bridge over the Ouse till 1765. This was no place for a long imprisonment; in any case, Bunyan's was a county offence and would be punished in the county jail.* However, that he wrote the allegory in his prison is supported by the text: the book begins: 'As I walked through the wilderness of this world, I lighted on a certain place, where was a den; and I laid me down in that place to sleep'; and a note in the margin glosses 'den' as 'the gaol'. The sleeper recounts his dream,

---

* See Joyce Godber, *Transactions of the Congregational Historical Society*, vol. xvi (1949).

and half way through it he says, 'Then I awoke and dreamed again'. This suggests that Bunyan had obtained his release from prison before completing the book. Earlier students of Bunyan, like John Brown,* believed that *The Pilgrim's Progress* had been partly composed during the second shorter imprisonment of about six months. But a balance of recent opinion has inclined to the view that the work was begun during the first imprisonment, immediately after *Grace Abounding* was finished. It has the urgency, the air of absorbed self-discovery, that hangs about a prison book; and it is easy to see how its allegory builds on the first-hand experience of the autobiography.

Grace Abounding deals almost wholly with the development of his inner religious feelings; there are hardly any references to persons or places. Bunyan discards any attempts at literary adornment in order to achieve an absolutely naked rendering of his spiritual history. When there is an image it is drawn naturally from his life as a countryman: 'Down I fell as a bird that is shot from the tree,' he says when describing his surrender to the temptation of despair. But the effort to describe with complete honesty his inner psychological terrors, and his subsequent triumph over them, led him to the bold use of personification, since his terrors were so real and palpable. Voices urge him to blasphemy; threatening texts of Scripture 'do pinch him very sore' or 'lay like a mill-post upon his back'. *The Pilgrim's Progress* gives a further turn to this drive towards personification: Bunyan, the sole character of the autobiography, is now Christian, the spiritual pilgrim, but

* *John Bunyan: His Life, Times and Work* (1885, revised edition 1928).

instead of the empty introspective space of *Grace Abounding*, there is a peopled world for the hero to move through. The menacing texts become real demons to threaten his progress, the temptation to despair of his faith, which seems to have been the weakness Bunyan feared most, becomes a Giant Despair who locks him in his dungeon, and the reliance on the literal text of the Bible which is the prime motive of the autobiography is rendered by a character called Evangelist who reappears from time to time to guide a bewildered Christian back on to the road to the Celestial City.

The movement into allegory serves to naturalize and familiarize Bunyan's religious perceptions to us. As men and women and spiritual beings encountered along the road, his doubts and assurances lose some of the almost psychopathic intensity with which they are endowed in the autobiography; they cease to be peculiarities of Bunyan's temperament and become the doubts and assurances of the spirit that all of us feel from time to time. The process of changing his experience into fiction had led him to a less personal and more universal truth. But *The Pilgrim's Progress* still retains the sense of personal urgency: it is his tremendous need to find a righteousness not his own by which to be saved that we encounter in the very first paragraph, and which is the force irresistibly driving Christian along the road to his final entry into the Celestial City:

As I walked through the wilderness of this world, I lighted on a certain place, where was a den; and I laid me down in that place to sleep: and as I slept I dreamed a dream. I dreamed, and behold I saw a man clothed with rags, standing in a certain place, with his face from his own house, a book in his hand, and a great burden upon his back. I looked, and saw him open the book, and read therein; and as he read, he wept and trembled: and not being able longer to contain, he brake out with a lamentable cry saying, 'What shall I do?'

The naturalness of *The Pilgrim's Progress* springs from the fact that, while stressing the supreme importance of religious salvation according to the tenets of Bunyan and his immediate public, the book contrives to describe the familiar behaviour of people as we know them. This is not so paradoxical as it seems. Man is a creature who finds his own greatness in conforming to projects that lie beyond the attainment of material well-being. *The Pilgrim's Progress* describes in living examples the depths of hypocrisy and self-deceit and the splendours of martyrdom, and both are demonstrated in other creeds as well as Calvinism.

Coleridge could not grant that Calvinist theology had anything to do with Bunyan's success; he declared that 'His piety was baffled by his genius; and Bunyan the dreamer overcame the Bunyan of the conventicle'. Calvinism has gained an ill reputation for intolerance and bigotry, but it provided Bunyan and other Puritan Englishmen of his time with a powerful and dramatic myth: life was a confrontation between the powers of light and the powers of darkness, or, to change the metaphor, the adventurous journey of the armed and vigilant Christian through hostile country. As a pamphlet writer of the time, John Geree, says of the typical Puritan:

His whole life he accounted a warfare wherein Christ was his Captaine, his armes, prayers and teares, the Crosse his Banner . . .

Coleridge may indeed have underestimated the psychological dynamic of Calvinism and the manner in which its dramatic character could contribute something to a work of the imagination. But on the other hand it was undoubtedly valuable for Bunyan that he had not been born into a sectarian group, but had grown up as a typical member of an early seventeenth-century village community, not marked off from his fellows by any special claims to piety. Baulked in their bid for ecclesiastical power, the Puritan party had, between the Elizabethan Church Settlement and the Civil Wars, achieved a different kind of success: through their Calvinistic preaching and commenting on the English Bible they had effected a cultural revolution and created a new type of Englishman, endowed with an earnestness and a sense of mission not present in his medieval ancestor but familiar in the evangelical rebels and pioneers of the eighteenth and nineteenth centuries. Puritanism has been misconceived as restrictive moral prohibitions, weighed down by sexual guilt; in the mid seventeenth century it was a fiery religious and social dynamic resembling contemporary Marxism more than modern Fundamentalism. Bunyan's advantage was that as a convert he could draw both on the spirit of militant Puritanism and on the older traditions of figurative sermon and moral anecdote that linked the nineteenth-century village pulpit with medieval habits of preaching; for example with the personified 'Deadly Sins' in the preaching of the friars.

The keynote of the whole First Part of the book is this lonely integrity of the ideal Puritan; Christian is the central figure. The story begins when, at the prompting of Evangelist, he puts wife and children and security behind him and flies from their pleading with his fingers in his ears, crying, 'Life, life, eternal life'. His sole desire is to be on the right road to the Celestial City: 'he went like one that was all the while treading on forbidden ground, and could by no means think himself safe, till again he was got into the way'. From the start we are made to see everything from Christian's point of view, so that his desperate plight is humanly touching and convincing: we accept even his abandonment of his family because in the terms of the allegory their city is the City of Destruction, and Christian does his best to persuade them to leave it with him. As in Kafka's novels, we are placed in the situation of the central character and accept the world around him with complete objectivity whatever intensity of nightmare it inflicts. An overhanging mountain (Mount Sinai representing the old law of sin and death) threatens to fall upon Christian with peals of thunder; a little later he has to endure foul smoke, demons, whisperings, and blasphemies in the Valley of the Shadow of Death (recalling Bunyan's own worst temptations). But this allegory of the darker side of Calvinist spiritual experience is not allowed to become morbidly subjective; Bunyan sets his own experience in an inhabited world, and by so doing draws it nearer to the experience of other Christian people so that it appears less as a special and obsessed phenomenon than it does in the revelations of *Grace Abounding*.

For instance, early on his pilgrimage Christian encounters Worldly-Wiseman who meets him with pompous self-assurance: 'How now, good fellow, whither away after this burdened manner?' Wiseman attempts to convince him that he will save himself a great deal of trouble by adopting a merely nominal and respectable form of Christianity. This is expressed in the allegory by an invitation to take up residence in the village of Morality under the care of Legality and his son Civility: 'Provision is there also cheap and good, and that which will make thy life the more happy, is, to be sure there thou shalt live by honest neighbours, in credit and good fashion.' In the strict terms of the allegory Mr Worldly-Wiseman stands for the temptation of the World and provides a satirical comment on the attractions of a merely conformist, 'Establishment' type of Christianity. But he appears in the narrative as a living personality, talking and acting for himself the role of a pompous humbug, the eternal bourgeois trying to tell a social inferior the way he should go ('Hast thou a wife and children?').

The strength of the work and the sense of reality it communicates to readers of widely differing varieties of belief depend on this combination of religious vision with loving, exact observation of human character.

The presentation of characters is often most lively in the studies of hypocrites and villains met along the way; By-Ends is a near relation of Worldly-Wiseman and his corruption is suggested by a similar air of social importance with which he invests himself.

My wife is a very virtuous woman, the daughter of a virtuous woman. She was my Lady Faining's daughter, therefore she came of a very honourable family, and is arrived to such a pitch of breeding, that she knows how to carry it to all, even to prince and peasant. 'Tis true, we somewhat differ in religion from those of the stricter sort ...

But insight into the natural processes of human intercourse is not confined to the satirical portraits. Christian's companions along the road, Faithful and, after his martyrdom, Hopeful, tend to be less strongly characterized than the tempters; they do however afford an opportunity for some moving instances of the beauty of friendship; again, all of them ring psychologically true. Before ever he meets Faithful, Christian knows that he is going before him through the Valley of the Shadow of Death, and is encouraged in his own lonely ordeal when he hears the unknown friend-to-be singing out, 'Though I walk through the Valley of the Shadow of Death, I will fear none ill, for thou art with me'. Before the heroic endurance of his martyrdom at Vanity Fair, Faithful is little more than a peg on which to hang a doctrinal summary of the action in the form of dialogue between him and Christian; later the relationship of Christian with Hopeful is developed with more subtlety. Hopeful is young and untried, the tyro to Christian, now an experienced pilgrim. But Christian is always falling through unpreparedness and it is at his careless instigation that Hopeful lets himself be persuaded to take a short cut by By-Path Meadow which leads them eventually into the hands of Giant Despair. At first Hopeful cannot help the universal human urge to say 'I told you so': 'I was afraid on't at very first ... I would have spoke plainer, but that you are older than I'. Christian apologizes handsomely; so far, both moral lesson and realistic observation of character are straightforward. But then each strives to excel the other in a bravery that is also sensitive. Christian wishes to go first on the dangerous path because it is on his account they are in it; Hopeful, with a fine sense of discretion, declares he must not do so, 'for your mind being troubled may lead you out of the way again'. This is clearly a realism that can explore human affection as well as human faith.

For the same reasons the allegory of *The Pilgrim's Progress* is not intellectual or highly organized as in the sophisticated religious allegory of Dante or

Spenser. Many of the figures and incidents that spring up along the route are created for the sake of an immediate effect and then passed over when a fresh incident occurs in Christian's progress; they are not closely related to the main structure of the allegory. Such are many of the personages who are simply mentioned for the effect of their names. (Bunyan is extremely skilful with names: consider those of the packed jury at Faithful's trial: 'Mr Blindman, Mr No-good, Mr Malice, Mr Love-lust, Mr Live-loose, Mr Heady, Mr High-mind, Mr Enmity, Mr Liar, Mr Cruelty, Mr Hate-light, and Mr Implacable'.) In the same way the allegory is not consistently maintained; realism is always breaking in, because the one truly binding element in the structure of the narrative is Christian's drive onward through dangerous country to the Celestial City, and the stream of adventures that he encounters as a pilgrim. Thus the metaphor of warfare against the powers of darkness is generally kept up ('put on you the whole armour of God'): Christian fights Apollyon, the demon of spiritual doubt, with sword in hand and armour on his back. But as he goes on with drawn sword through the demon-haunted valley we are told that 'he was forced to put up his sword, and betake himself to another weapon called All-prayer; so he cried, in my hearing, "O Lord I beseech thee deliver my soul".' Bunyan has simply slipped out of the allegorical mode and declared directly that prayer is the chief weapon against temptation. Such apparent clumsiness does not result in any failure of interest, still less in any breakdown of the primary illusion of fiction. This is not solely due to the often real charm of Bunyan's naïveté when he is making such *gaffes*. If Bunyan is blundering here, he is blundering with his eye on the object and avoiding the mistakes of an over-classified and mechanical spiritual allegory. The thrill of struggle remains, and with it the illusion of a dramatic fiction, because though there may be a departure from a uniform allegorical framework, the metaphors are still there embedded in all human thinking about this type of experience. Prayer is still 'another weapon'. In the same way, characters appear not as the perfect, digested essences of a certain quality, but as that quality in action in a human being. The simple and modest veteran Honest in the Second Part says, 'Not honesty in the abstract, but Honest is my name, and I wish that my nature shall agree to what I am called'.

For the modern reader, the human working compromise between realism and allegory is likely to conceal the firm outlines of the theological structure which were much more obvious to Bunyan's contemporaries and especially to his fellow-Nonconformists. What is on the surface an episodic series of adventures, a narrative of folk-tale ups and downs such as Bunyan himself enjoyed in the popular romances of his unregenerate youth, has a tough skeleton of which each articulated joint, precisely indicates a stage in the Puritan psychology of conversion. There is conviction of sin, classically accepted as the first awakening of the soul; this is represented by Christian's leaving the City of Destruction at the beginning, only to fall into the Slough of Despond. The episode of Worldly-Wiseman deals briefly and effectively with the next stage: the attempt to found the religious life on moral righteousness, inevitably doomed to failure. Then comes the gradual education of the convert through Bible-study and meditation; Christian is entertained at the House of the Interpreter by a series of emblematic pictures. As with the popular romances like *The Seven Champions of Christendom*, Bunyan here draws imaginative life from another folk form, the emblem books with their combined mottoes, verses, and symbolic illustrations (it was originally a learned form, but by the late seventeenth century had come down in the world, from the cabinet of the Renaissance humanist to the children's reading book aimed at a middle-class public).

Christian then comes to the Cross where the burden (of his original sin) that he has been carrying falls from his shoulder and is buried in the open sepulchre below. Again there is a mixture of fresh allegorical invention with the traditional symbols of the Redemption, and indeed with the dramatic features of the Gospel story. Christian is clothed in white raiment, a mark is set on his forehead, and he is given the roll of his salvation. It might seem, with two-thirds of the story to go, that the narrative was here in danger of succumbing to the remorseless mechanics of the Calvinist doctrine of conversion. Christian has received an assurance of grace; he is numbered among the elect, among those who are to be saved from damnation. But many of the most desperate adventures with the forces of doubt and despair lie ahead: this is not the end of the drama but the beginning. God may have chosen Christian, but the reader sees this only as something seen by Christian, an assurance strong at the time but likely to become weaker under fresh assaults of temptation and when the moment of grace is past. However simple his techniques and attitudes, in this respect Bunyan writes as a man of the new post-Cartesian age for whom the world of religious fact, like the physical world, is something lying apart from his own consciousness and having to be perceived through it.

The narrative now proceeds by alternating scenes of exciting action and static recuperation at various houses of resort for pilgrims along the road. Sometimes the quiet rests in the story are provided by doctrinal and moral conservation between Christian and the other pilgrims. Thus the story-teller's need for action and relief from action is combined with the need to incorporate some overtly didactic matter into a fable that must have seemed extraordinarily daring in its time (it offended many members of Bunyan's sect). In the House Beautiful there is more education through symbols and preparation for future dangers; but the chief impression conveyed by the women who tend Christian there is of the human dignity of the best English Puritan household rather than of vague female allegorical personages: Piety and Prudence they may be called, but these very names take us into the middle-class families of Bunyan's time. After this Christian is ready to meet the terrors of the Valley of Humiliation and the Valley of the Shadow of Death.

United for a time with Faithful, Christian and he engage in a long argument with Talkative. Talkative can give a plausible imitation of having undergone the sort of religious experience shared by the two pilgrims. But their interrogation reveals that this is a façade: 'the soul of religion is the practic part'; the most evident sign of grace is the transformation of the ordinary moral life, and of this Talkative knows nothing. He is one of several types of hypocrite encountered on the pilgrimage; their exposure does more than provide comic relief since it serves to base Christian's aspirations on the firm ground of daily living.

The pilgrims go on to Vanity-Fair. Here again the purely allegorical conception of a city to represent the attractions of worldly power and sensuality is strongly modified by contemporary reference and a complex of unconscious allusions; the Fair with its separate rows for the merchants of different nationalities recalls the great summer fairs of eastern England like that at Stourbridge, probably known to Bunyan. Once Christian and Faithful fall foul of the authorities, and are persecuted and then brought to trial, the atmosphere is that of a seventeenth-century English court applying the penal laws against Dissenters, but shot through with nightmarish evocations of the martyrdom of the early Christians as recounted in Foxe's *Acts and Monuments*. The bullying judge and the packed jury, the crowds mocking at the strange clothes of the prisoners, all these features speak straight to the problems of the English Nonconformist in the age of Judge Jeffreys; by so doing they give the grim episode an authenticity and hardness of outline that could never be obtained by pure allegorizing.

Christian escapes the fate of Faithful. After another static episode of conversation with backsliders from the town of Fair-speech, he and Hopeful, his new companion, fall into the hands of Giant Despair and are imprisoned in Doubting-Castle. The episode has a dramatic importance corresponding to the significance attached by Bunyan to the sin of spiritual despair; he had suffered himself from this gnawing doubt, the medieval *accidie*, and therefore ranked it above all the other dangers of the spiritual life. Christian is always falling through unpreparedness: immediately after a stroll by the River of the Water of Life, which has given him new ease of mind, he wanders into By-Path Meadow. Bunyan excels in depicting the particular price one pays for advantages gained.

INTRODUCTION

After sojourning briefly with the shepherds among the evocatively named Delectable Mountains, Christian and Hopeful go on their way. The pilgrimage continues at a more leisurely pace; after all, the best narratives do not retain a constant momentum but sink away serenely towards the close. A series of static episodes of argument and conversation introduce some more hypocrites and backsliders, the glib and callow youth Ignorance and a group of time-servers, By-Ends and his companions. The skill with which whole depths of self-deception are suggested by a short answer to a question is masterly:

Ignorance. But my heart and life agree together, and therefore my hope is well grounded.
Christian. Who told thee that thy heart and life agrees together?
Ignorance. My heart tells me so.

After this, these quieter episodes shade gradually to the arrival of Hopeful and Christian in the land of Beulah, where the air is sweet and pleasant, and every day the flowers appear in the earth. Here is their resting place before their passage over the River of Death, and the finale. Though 'much stounded' at the River, they pass through its waters to the Celestial City, and the trumpets sound for them on the other side.

The Second Part of *The Pilgrim's Progress* was written six years after the first (1684) and is really an independent work. Christiana and her children decide to go on pilgrimage; she is sorry not to have accompanied her husband in the first place. They are escorted by the warrior Great-heart, an archetype of the ideal Puritan pastor. The pace is leisurely; sometimes it seems almost like a conducted tour of the battlefields where Christian vanquished giants and

23

demons. Occasionally there is a giant-fight, but Great-heart now has sturdy supporters from the different houses of resort along the way, and the resulting combats resemble an afternoon's hunting rather than the life-and-death struggles of the First Part. There are even monumental inscriptions of Christian's triumphs to read along the way. But the work is no forced sequel: it is a different book, a bustling social novel. Christiana and her beloved friend Mercy may seem to be moving in the afterglow of her husband's heroism, but they have their own vitality. Mercy wards off an unwelcome suitor; the children grow up and get married; Christiana fusses, is tender, and endures to the end of the pilgrimage. The interest has shifted from the lonely epic of the individual to the problems of the small urban community of Nonconformists: problems of mixed marriages, the need for cohesion, and the difficulty certain members have (Fearing, Feeblemind) in fitting into the life of the church. Bunyan had now been many years an administrator and a pastor of souls. Like Fielding in his days as a Bow Street magistrate writing fiction about the real nature of justice and crime in contemporary society, he now has a professional point of view from which to pass judgement. As most novelists do, he has passed from an autobiographical first novel to an external, more calculated subject.

The Pilgrim's Progress is soaked in the imagery of the Bible and deeply pervaded by the Puritan belief that the Bible provided a key to every problem of life and thought. But it would be a careless reading of the book that gave the impression that the Authorized Version was the main influence on Bunyan's style. His language has the life of speech, salted with proverbs and vigorous provincial turns of phrase; it is the plain colloquial manner that he no doubt also employed in the pulpit: 'his house is as empty of religion as the white of an egg is of savour'; 'we were as merry as the maids'; 'he all to-befooled me'. It is the manner of generations of popular preachers using parables to point their case, but in *The Pilgrim's Progress* it is wrought to the pitch of art. Many proverbs and phrases have gained a new life and continued in circulation on account of their use in the allegory.

The achievement of Bunyan in *The Pilgrim's Progress* which gives the work its continuing vitality is the creation, not of allegory, but of myth. Allegory is dependent on an intellectual scheme: we can connect symbol and significance neatly with an 'equals' sign, and for a purely allegorical work it should always be possible to compile a table of characters and meanings in two columns which should perform the whole work of commentary. Christian, young Ignorance, Great-heart, and the country through which they go, are not like this. Their moral significance cannot be neatly pared away from the sensuous form in which they are presented. This is something which is far easier to realize than to discuss, but there is one striking demonstration of the authenticity of Bunyan's fiction: each main episode has carried over into the sensibility of English-speaking people, many of whom have not read the book but have met its ideas through the floating mythology by which the life of a people is lived—Vanity-Fair, the Slough of Despond, the Delectable Mountains. The conception of Vanity-Fair is an imaginative shorthand for all the pride and show of the acquisitive life; its notion of a raree-show of human pride was the working model on which Thackeray could build his contemporary illustration of the myth. Sometimes

Bunyan's imagination is illuminating or recasting traditional symbols; the Christian warfare, waged with the protection of 'the whole armour of God', is one of these. The figure of the lonely wayfaring man, the simple, honest foot-traveller with his pack on his back, goes back to the middle ages; Langland's Piers Plowman sets out thus on pilgrimage to find Truth after he has ploughed his half-acre. The modern imagination perhaps tends to see man more as a prisoner than as a traveller, but the image of the purposeful journey through life still has great evocative power; it is reflected in all those long fictions of which the main theme is individual growth, from Proust to Anthony Powell and C. P. Snow.

Sometimes Bunyan develops a very slight metaphorical hint in Scripture into a fully-realized allegorical episode: the Valley of the Shadow of Death, with its deep ditch on one side and mire on the other, haunted by the same voices and noises as preyed on Bunyan in the days of his obsession with personal guilt, is an example of such free interpretation. The hint of a single figure of speech has been daringly expanded. Similarly, the friendliness and dignity of the houses of resort along the road owe much to the entertainment of Christians in apostolic times, as it is described in the Acts of the Apostles; again, hints have been exapnded into full-grown fictions. Clearly, if the Bible has not influenced the language of *The Pilgrim's Progress*, Bunyan's intense, peculiar reading of Scripture has guided the very structure of his narrative.

Literary criticism in our time has shown a refined preoccupation with the art of narrative. Among the reasons for the increase of interest in Bunyan may be the fact that most of the devices and problems of narrative come up in the course of *The Pilgrim's*

Progress. Every time Bunyan, in his sublime uncon-sciousness, breaks the pattern of his own allegory, or breaks the fiction by talking directly to the reader, we see the mysteriousness of the fictional thing by thus being distanced from it.

In his prefatory verses Bunyan uses a metaphor from flax-spinning to suggest how effortlessly the whole story came to him once he had started:

> Still as I pull'd, it came.

It is this sheer creative spontaneity of *The Pilgrim's Progress*, drawing on the deepest resources of the popular tradition and the unconscious mind, that makes the book fascinating. A seventeenth-century Calvinist sat down to write a tract and produced a folk-epic of the universal religious imagination.

ROGER SHARROCK

A NOTE ON THE TEXT

THE PILGRIM'S PROGRESS was first published in 1678 by Nathaniel Ponder, 'at the Peacock in the Poultrey'; later as Bunyan's regular publisher he became known as 'Bunyan Ponder'. Second (1678) and third (1679) editions followed; these contained several additions including the whole episode of By-Ends and his companions. There were twelve editions in all in Bunyan's lifetime. The Second Part first appeared in 1684, and since then both parts have been published together.

A critical text was edited by J. B. Wharey (Oxford, 1928). In my revision of that edition (Oxford, 1960) a return was made to the first edition, restoring the original vigorous colloquial forms which were later modified by the printing-house. A similar plan has been followed in this edition, though spelling and punctuation have been modernized to meet the needs of the general reader. The use of capitals in the early editions was generous; in this edition capitals have been retained only in the case of personification and where their use is otherwise essential to the allegorical sense.

Chronology of Bunyan's Life

1628　John Bunyan was born at Elstow near Bedford, the eldest of three sons of Thomas Bunyan and his wife Margaret Bentley. The father was a brazier or tinker, poor but not a vagabond, sinced he owned a cottage between Elstow and Bedford.

c.1638　He attended for a time Bedford grammar school or that at Houghton Conquest nearby. He was taken from school to follow his father's trade.

1644　His mother died and his father married again within the year. In November he was mustered in a county levy of the Parliamentary army (the Civil War had been in progress for two years) and was assigned to the garrison at Newport Pagnell.

1645–6　He seems to have spent most of his military service in garrison duty and there is little support for the theory that he was present at the siege of Leicester in 1645.

1647　His company was disbanded and he returned to Elstow to practise his trade.

1649　He married his first wife 'whose Father was counted godly'.

1650　His blind daughter Mary was born. Three other children of the first marriage followed.

1650–4　He underwent the spiritual crisis described in *Grace Abounding*; in the course of it he came into contact with the Open Communion church in Bedford and its pastor John Gifford, an ex-Royalist officer.

1655　Having joined the Bedford church he discovered his gift in speaking to the brethren.

1656   He began to preach the Word in the neighbourhood. He became involved in disputes with the local Quakers under Edward Burrough; these led to his first book, *Some Gospel-Truths Opened*.

1658   His first wife died. In *A Few Sighs from Hell* he projected his recent terrors into an arousing sermon treatise.

1659   He married his second wife Elizabeth. *The Doctrine of the Law and Grace Unfolded*, his most ambitious theological work, was published.

1660   He is arrested for preaching to a conventicle (unauthorized religious service) at Lower Samsell. The persecution of Nonconformists had only just begun and the penal legislation of the Clarendon Code was yet to be enacted.

1661   He is tried and sentenced to three months' imprisonment in the county jail. Since he refused to give an assurance not to preach, he remained in prison for twelve years, but there were some short periods of parole and he attended some meetings of the Bedford church. During imprisonment he supported his family by making 'long tagged laces' for shoes.

1663   *Christian Behaviour*.

1665   *The Holy City*.

1666   *Grace Abounding*, his spiritual autobiography.

1667–72 In this period Bunyan probably wrote the First Part of *The Pilgrim's Progress*.

1672   He was elected pastor of the Bedford church and, in March, released from prison under Charles II's first Declaration of Indulgence. From this point until his death he led a busy life preaching, directing the affairs of the church, and visiting outlying congregations outside Bedford and sister churches in London. It is now that he earned the nickname 'Bishop Bunyan'.

1677   He was imprisoned for six months early in the year.

1678   *The Pilgrim's Progress* (First Part).

1680   *The Life and Death of Mr Badman*.

1682   *The Holy War*.

1684   *The Pilgrim's Progress* (Second Part).

1685   He made a deed of gift of his property to his wife, probably to avoid confiscation during the period of renewed persecution.

1688   He died in London at the house of a friend, 31 August, after contracting a fever during a journey by horse from Reading to offer reconciliation in a family dispute. Buried in Bunhill Fields.

Suggestions for Further Reading

Works by Bunyan

The Works of That Eminent Servant of Christ Mr. John Bunyan, edited by Charles Doe (1692). This first collected edition in a single folio volume, by a printer who was a friend of Bunyan, is incomplete.

The Works of That Eminent Servant of Christ, Mr. John Bunyan, edited by Samuel Wilson (2 vols., 1736–7). The completion of the 1692 edition, often reprinted.

The Works of John Bunyan, edited by George Offor (3 vols., London and Edinburgh, 1806–2). The extensive commentary is unscholarly and stridently pious, but this is the last complete edition, and it is full of information.

The Miscellaneous Works of John Bunyan, edited by Roger Sharrock (Oxford University Press, 1976–). A complete text based on the earliest editions and with full introductions, critical apparatus, and historical and explanatory notes. Thirteen volumes, of which six have appeared. Uniform with the personal and allegorical works in four volumes.

Grace Abounding to the Chief of Sinners, edited by Roger Sharrock (Clarendon Press, 1962).

The Holy War, edited by Roger Sharrock and James F. Forrest (Clarendon Press, 1980).

The Life and Death of Mr Badman, edited by Roger Sharrock and James F. Forrest (Clarendon Press, to appear shortly).

The Pilgrim's Progress From This World To That Which Is To Come, edited by James Blanton Wharey and revised by Roger Sharrock (Clarendon Press, 1960, and subsequent reprints).

Grace Abounding and The Pilgrim's Progress, edited by Roger Sharrock (Oxford University Press, 1966).

The Puritan Background

Richard Baxter, *Reliquiae Baxterianae*, edited by Matthew Sylvester (1696; selections edited by J. M. Lloyd Thomas, Dent, 1925, etc.).

The Narrative of the Persecution of Agnes Beaumont in 1674, edited with an introduction by G. B. Harrison (Constable, 1929).

A Biographical Dictionary of British Radicals in the Seventeenth Century, edited by Richard L. Greaves and Robert Zaller (Harvester Press, 1981).

Calamy Revised, edited by A. G. Matthews (Oxford University Press, 1934). The lives of Puritan ministers ejected after the Restoration in 1662.

The Journeys of Celia Fiennes, edited by Christopher Morris (Cresset Press, 1947).

George Fox, *Journal*, revised edition by John L. Nickalls (Cambridge University Press, 1952).

Lucy Hutchinson, *Memoirs of Colonel Hutchinson*, edited by James Sutherland (Oxford University Press, 1973).

Revolutionary Prose of the English Civil War, edited by Howard Erskine-Hill and Graham Storey (Cambridge University Press, 1983).

The Puritans, edited by Perry Miller and T. H. Johnson (American Book Company, 1938). A useful collection of texts.

Modern Studies

Historical and Theological

Robert Barclay, *The Inner Life of the Religious Societies of the Commonwealth* (1876).

SUGGESTIONS FOR FURTHER READING

L. F. Brown, *Baptists and Fifth Monarchy Men during the Interregnum* (Clarendon Press, 1912).

Edward Dowden, *Puritan and Anglican* (Kegan Paul, 1900).

William Haller, *The Rise of Puritanism* (Columbia University Press, 1938).

William Haller, *Liberty and Reformation in the Puritan Revolution* (Columbia University Press, 1953).

Christopher Hill, *The Century of Revolution, 1603–1714* (Thomas Nelson, 1961).

Christopher Hill, *Puritanism and Revolution: Studies in Interpretation of the English Revolution of the Seventeenth Century* (Secker & Warburg, 1958).

N. H. Keeble, *Richard Baxter: Puritan Man of Letters* (Clarendon Press, 1982).

Geoffrey F. Nuttall, *The Holy Spirit in Puritan Faith and Experience* (Basil Blackwell, 1946).

Geoffrey F. Nuttall, *Visible Saints: The Congregational Way, 1640–1660* (Basil Blackwell, 1957).

Puritans and Revolutionaries: Essays on Seventeenth-Century History Presented to Christopher Hill, edited by Donald Pennington and Keith Thomas (Oxford University Press, 1978).

Robert S. Paul, *The Lord Protector: Religion and Politics in the Life of Oliver Cromwell* (Lutterworth Press, 1955).

Wilhelm Schenk, *The Concern for Social Justice in the Puritan Revolution* (Longmans, 1948).

R. H. Tawney, *Religion and the Rise of Capitalism* (John Murray, 1926, etc.).

Ernst Troeltsch, *The Social Teaching of the Christian Churches*, translated by Olive Wyon (Allen & Unwin, 1931).

Murray Tolmie, *The Triumph of the Saints* (Cambridge University Press, 1978).

G. S. Wakefield, *Puritan Devotion: Its Place in the Development of Christian Piety* (Epworth Press, 1957).

Owen C. Watkins, *The Puritan Experience* (Routledge & Kegan Paul, 1972). On spiritual autobiographies in the seventeenth century.

Michael Watts, *The Dissenters* (Oxford University Press, 1978).

C. E. Whiting, *Studies in English Puritanism, 1660–1688* (Society for Promoting Christian Knowledge, 1931).

Keith Wrightson, *English Society 1580–1680* (Longman, 1982).

Biographical and Literary

Jacques Blondel, *Allégorie et réalisme dans le Pilgrim's Progress* (Archives des Lettres Modernes, 1959).

John Brown, *John Bunyan: His Life, Times and Work* (1885; revised by F. M. Harrison, Hulbert Publishing Company, 1928).

Sir Charles Firth, *Essays Historical and Literary* (Clarendon Press, 1938).

R. M. Frye, *God, Man and Satan* (Princeton University Press, 1960).

Joyce Godber, 'The Imprisonments of John Bunyan', *Transactions of the Congregational Historical Society* vol. xvi (1949).

Richard L. Greaves, *John Bunyan* (Abingdon, 1969). A study of Bunyan's theology.

Sir Herbert Grierson, *Cross Currents in English Literature of the Seventeenth Century* (Chatto & Windus, 1927).

Gwilym O. Griffith, *John Bunyan* (Hodder & Stoughton, 1927).

F. M. Harrison, 'A Bibliography of the Works of

John Bunyan' *Supplement No. 6 to the Transactions of the Bibliographical Society* (Oxford, 1932).

G. B. Harrison, *John Bunyan: A Study in Personality* (Dent, 1928).

Maurice Hussey, in *The Pelican Guide to English Literature Vol. 3: From Donne to Marvell* (Penguin, 1956).

Wolfgang Iser, 'Bunyan's *Pilgrim's Progress*: die kalvinistische Heilsgewissheit und die Form des Romans', in *Festschrift für Walther Bülst* (Heidelberg, 1960).

U. M. Kaufmann, *The Pilgrim's Progress and Traditions in Puritan Meditation* (Yale University Press, 1966).

Arnold Kettle, in *The English Novel* (Hutchinson, 1951, etc.).

John R. Knott, Jr., in *The Sword of the Spirit: Puritan Responses to the Bible* (Chicago University Press, 1980).

F. R. Leavis, in *The Common Pursuit* (Chatto & Windus, 1952).

Bunyan's *The Pilgrim's Progress: Essays Historical and Literary*, edited by Vincent Newey (Liverpool University Press, 1980).

Roy Pascal, 'The Present Tense in *The Pilgrim's Progress*', *Modern Language Review* vol. lx (1965).

Mark Rutherford (William Hale White), *John Bunyan* (1905; new edition, Nelson, 1933).

Roger Sharrock, 'Personal Vision and Puritan Tradition in Bunyan', *Hibbert Journal* (1957).

Roger Sharrock, *The Pilgrim's Progress* (Arnold, 1966). Critical study.

The Pilgrim's Progress: A Casebook, edited and selected by Roger Sharrock (Macmillan, 1976).

George Bernard Shaw, from the Preface to *Man and*

Superman, in *Dramatic Opinions and Essays* (Constable, 1970).

Robert Southey, Introduction to his edition of *The Pilgrim's Progress* (1830; reprinted in *Select Biographies*, 1844).

Henri A. Talon, *John Bunyan, the Man and his Works* (Paris, 1948; English translation, Rockcliff, 1951).

Henri A. Talon, *John Bunyan* (Longman, 1956).

William York Tindall, *John Bunyan: Mechanick Preacher* (Columbia University Press, 1934).

Dorothy Van Ghent, in *The English Novel: Form and Function* (Rinehart, 1953).

Joan Webber, in *The Eloquent I: Style and Self in Seventeenth-Century Prose* (University of Wisconsin Press, 1968).

J. B. Wharey, *The Sources of Bunyan's Allegories* (J. H. Furst Company, 1904).

O. L. Winslow, *John Bunyan* (Macmillan, New York, 1961). A straightforward biography.

THE
Pilgrim's Progress
FROM
THIS WORLD,
TO
That which is to come:

Delivered under the Similitude of a

DREAM

Wherein is Discovered,
The manner of his setting out,
His Dangerous Journey; And safe
Arrival at the Desired Countrey.

I have used Similitudes, Hos. 12. 10.

By *John Bunyan.*

Licensed and Entred according to Order.

LONDON,
Printed for *Nath. Ponder* at the *Peacock*
in the *Poultrey* near *Cornhil,* 1678.

THE AUTHOR'S APOLOGY FOR
HIS BOOK

WHEN at the first I took my pen in hand,
Thus for to write, I did not understand
That I at all should make a little book
In such a mode; nay, I had undertook
To make another, which when almost done,
Before I was aware, I this begun.

And thus it was: I writing of the way
And race of saints' in this our Gospel-day,
Fell suddenly into an <u>allegory</u>
About their journey, and the way to glory,
In more than twenty things, which I set down;
This done, I twenty more had in my crown,
And they again began to multiply,
Like sparks that from the coals of fire do fly.
Nay then, thought I, if that you breed so fast,
I'll put you by yourselves, lest you at last
Should <u>prove *ad infinitum,*</u> and eat out
The book that I already am about.

Well, so I did; but yet I did not think
To show to all the world my pen and ink
In such a mode; I only thought to make
I knew not what, nor did I undertake
Thereby to please my neighbour; no, not I,
I did it mine own self to gratify.

Neither did I but vacant seasons spend
In this my scribble, nor did I intend
But to divert myself in doing this,
From worser thoughts which make me do amiss.

Thus I set pen to paper with delight,
And quickly had my thoughts in black and white.
For having now my method by the end,
Still as I pulled it came,² and so I penned
It down, until it came at last to be

For length and breadth the bigness which you see.
Well, when I had thus put mine ends together,
I show'd them others that I might see whether
They would condemn them, or them justify:
And some said, 'let them live'; some, 'let them die':
Some said, 'John, print it'; others said, 'not so':
Some said, 'it might do good'; others said, 'no'.

Now was I in a strait, and did not see
Which was the best thing to be done by me:
At last I thought, since you are thus divided,
I print it will, and so the case decided.

For, thought I, some I see would have it done,
Though others in that channel do not run.
To prove then who advised for the best,
Thus I thought fit to put it to the test.

I further thought, if now I did deny
Those that would have it thus, to gratify,
I did not know, but hinder them I might,
Of that which would to them be great delight.

For those that were not for its coming forth,
I said to them, offend you I am loth;
Yet since your brethren pleased with it be,
Forbear to judge, till you do further see.

If that thou wilt not read, let it alone;
Some love the meat, some love to pick the bone:
Yea, that I might them better palliate,
I did too with them thus expostulate.

May I not write in such a style as this?
In such a method too, and yet not miss
Mine end, thy good? why may it not be done?
Dark clouds bring waters, when the bright bring
    none;
Yea, dark, or bright, if they their silver drops
Cause to descend, the earth by yielding crops
Gives praise to both, and carpeth not at either,
But treasures up the fruit they yield together:

Yea, so commixes both, that in her fruit
None can distinguish this from that, they suit
Her well when hungry, but if she be full
She spews out both, and makes their blessings null.

   You see the ways the fisherman doth take
To catch the fish, what engines doth he make?
Behold! how he engageth all his wits
Also his snares, lines, angles, hooks and nets.
Yet fish there be, that neither hook, nor line,
Nor snare, nor net, nor engine can make thine;
They must be groped for, and be tickled too,
Or they will not be catched, what e'er you do.

   How doth the fowler seek to catch his game?
By divers means, all which one cannot name.
His gun, his nets, his lime-twigs, light and bell:
He creeps, he goes, he stands; yea, who can tell
Of all his postures? Yet there's none of these
Will make him master of what fowls he please.
Yea, he must pipe, and whistle to catch this,
Yet if he does so, that bird he will miss.

   If that a pearl may in a toad's head dwell,[3]
And may be found too in an oyster-shell;
If things that promise nothing, do contain
What better is than gold, who will disdain
(That have an inkling of it) there to look,
That they may find it? Now my little book
(Though void of all those paintings that may make
It with this or the other man to take)
Is not without those things that do excel,
What do in brave but empty notions dwell.

   'Well, yet I am not fully satisfied,
That this your book will stand, when soundly
      tried.'
   Why, what's the matter? 'It is dark', What tho'?
'But it is feigned', What of that I trow?
Some men by feigning words as dark as mine,

<u>Make truth to spangle, and its rays to shine.</u>
  'But they want solidness.' Speak man thy mind.
'They drowned the weak; metaphors make us
      blind.'
  Solidity, indeed becomes the pen
Of him that writeth things divine to men:
But must I needs want solidness, because
By metaphors I speak; was not God's laws,
His Gospel-laws in olden time held forth
By types, shadows and metaphors?[4] Yet loth
Will any sober man be to find fault
With them, lest he be found for to assault
The highest wisdom. No, he rather stoops,
And seeks to find out what by pins and loops,
By calves, and sheep, by heifers, and by rams,
By birds and herbs, and by the blood of lambs
God speaketh to him: and happy is he
That finds the light, and grace that in them be.

  Be not too forward therefore to conclude
That I want solidness, that I am rude:
All things solid in show not solid be;
All things in parables despise not we
Lest things most hurtful lightly we receive;
And things that good are, of our souls bereave.

  My dark and cloudy words they do but hold
The truth, as cabinets enclose the gold.

  The prophets used much by metaphors
To set forth truth; yea, who so considers
Christ, his Apostles too, shall plainly see,
That truths to this day in such mantles be.

  Am I afraid to say that Holy Writ,
Which for its style and phrase puts down all wit,
Is everywhere so full of all these things,
(Dark figures, allegories), yet there springs
From that same book that lustre and those rays
Of light that turns our darkest nights to days.

Come, let my carper to his life now look,
And find there darker lines than in my book
He findeth any. Yea, and let him know
That in his best things there are worse lines too.

May we but stand before impartial men,
To his poor one, I durst adventure ten
That they will take my meaning in these lines
Far better than his lies in silver shrines.
Come, truth, although in swaddling-clouts, I find
Informs the judgement, rectifies the mind,
Pleases the understanding, makes the will
Submit; the memory too it doth fill
With what doth our imagination please,
Likewise, it tends our troubles to appease.

Sound words I know Timothy is to use,[5]
And old wives' fables he is to refuse,
But yet grave Paul him nowhere doth forbid
The use of parables; in which lay hid
That gold, those pearls, and precious stones that
    were
Worth digging for, and that with greatest care.

Let me add one word more, O man of God!
Art thou offended? Dost thou wish I had
Put forth my matter in another dress,
Or that I had in things been more express?
Three things let me propound, then I submit
To those that are my betters (as is fit).

1. I find not that I am denied the use
Of this my method, so I no abuse
Put on the words, things, readers, or be rude
In handling figure, or similitude,
In application; but all that I may
Seek the advance of Truth this or that way.
Denied did I say? Nay, I have leave
(Example too, and that from them that have
God better pleased by their words or ways

Than any man that breatheth nowadays),
Thus to express my mind, thus to declare
Things unto thee that excellentest are.

2. I find that men (as high as trees) will write
Dialogue-wise;[6] yet no man doth them slight
For writing so: indeed if they abuse
Truth, cursed be they, and the craft they use
To that intent; but yet let truth be free
To make her sallies upon thee, and me,
Which way it pleases God. For who knows how,
Better than he that taught us first to plough,
To guide our mind and pens for his design?
And he makes base things usher in divine.

3. I find that Holy Writ in many places
Hath semblance with this method, where the cases
Doth call for one thing to set forth another:
Use it I may then, and yet nothing smother
Truth's golden beams, nay, by this method may
Make it cast forth its rays as light as day.

And now, before I do put up my pen,
I'll show the profit of my book, and then
Commit both thee, and it unto that hand
That pulls the strong down, and makes weak ones
    stand.

This book it chalketh out before thine eyes
The man that seeks the everlasting prize:
It shows you whence he comes, whither he goes,
What he leaves undone, also what he does:
It also shows you how he runs, and runs,
Till he unto the Gate of Glory comes.

It shows too who sets out for life amain,
As if the lasting crown they would attain:
Here also you may see the reason why
They lose their labour, and like fools do die.

This book will make a traveller of thee,
If by its counsel thou wilt ruled be;

It will direct thee to the Holy Land,
If thou wilt its directions understand:
Yea, it will make the slothful active be,
The blind also delightful things to see.
— Art thou for something rare, and profitable?
Would'st thou see a truth within a fable?
Art thou forgetful? Wouldest thou remember
From New Year's Day to the last of December?
Then read my fancies, they will stick like burrs, — plain
And may be to the helpless, comforters.

This book is writ in such a dialect
As may the minds of listless men affect:
It seems a novelty, and yet contains
Nothing but sound and honest gospel-strains.

Would'st thou divert thyself from melancholy?
Would'st thou be pleasant, yet be far from folly?
Would'st thou read riddles and their explanation,
Or else be drownded in thy contemplation?
Dost thou love picking-meat?[7] Or would'st thou see
A man i' the clouds, and hear him speak to thee?
Would'st thou be in a dream, and yet not sleep?
Or would'st thou in a moment laugh and weep?
Wouldest thou lose thyself, and catch no harm
And find thyself again without a charm?
Would'st read thyself, and read thou know'st not
      what
And yet know whether thou art blest or not,
By reading the same lines? O then come hither,
And lay my book, thy head and heart together.

                                    JOHN BUNYAN

THE PILGRIM'S PROGRESS
in the similitude of a
DREAM

As I walked through the wilderness of this world, I lighted on a certain place, where was a den; *The goal*[8] and I laid me down in that place to sleep: and as I slept I dreamed a dream. I dreamed, and behold I saw a man clothed with rags, standing in a certain place, with his face from his own house, a book in his hand, and a great burden upon his back. I looked, and saw him open the book, and read therein; and as he read, he wept and trembled: and not being able longer to contain, he brake out with a lamentable cry; saying, 'What shall I do?' *His out-cry*

In this plight therefore he went home, and restrained himself as long as he could, that his wife and children should not perceive his distress; but he could not be silent long, because that his trouble increased: wherefore at length he brake his mind to his wife and children; and thus he began to talk to them: 'O my dear wife,' said he, 'and you the children of my bowels, I your dear friend[9] am in myself undone, by reason of a burden that lieth hard upon me: moreover, I am for certain informed that this our city will be burned with fire from Heaven, in which fearful overthrow, both myself, with thee, my wife, and you my sweet babes, shall miserably come to ruin; except (the which yet I see not) some way of escape can be found, whereby we may be delivered.' At this his relations were sore amazed; not for that they believed that what he said to them was true, but because they thought that some frenzy distemper had got into his head: therefore, it drawing towards night, and they hoping that sleep might settle his brains, with all haste they got him to bed; but the night was as troublesome to him as the day: wherefore instead of sleeping, he spent it in sighs and tears. So when the morning was come, they would know how he did and he told them worse and worse. He also set to talking to them again, but they began to be hardened; *Carnal* they also thought to drive away his distemper by *physic for* harsh and surly carriages to him: sometimes they *a sick soul* would deride, sometimes they would chide, and sometimes they would quite neglect him: wherefore he began to retire himself to his chamber to pray for, and pity them; and also to condole his own misery: he would also walk solitarily in the fields,[10] sometimes reading, and sometimes praying: and thus for some days he spent his time.

Now, I saw upon a time, when he was walking in the fields, that he was (as he was wont) reading in his book, and greatly distressed in his mind; and as he read, he burst out, as he had done before, crying, *What shall I do to be saved?*

I saw also that he looked this way, and that way, as if he would run; yet he stood still, because, as I perceived, he could not tell which way to go. I looked then, and saw a man named Evangelist[11] coming to him, and asked, 'Wherefore dost thou cry?' He answered, 'Sir, I perceive, by the book in my hand, that I am condemned to die, and after that to come to judgement; and I find that I am not willing to do the first, nor able to do the second.'

Then said Evangelist, 'Why not willing to die? since this life is attended with so many evils?' The man answered, 'Because I fear that this burden that is upon my back will sink me lower than the grave; and I shall fall into Tophet.[12] And, Sir, if I be not fit to go to prison, I am not fit (I am sure) to go to

hell

judgement, and from thence to execution; and the thoughts of these things make me cry.'

Then said Evangelist, 'If this be thy condition, why standest thou still?' He answered, 'Because I know not whither to go.' Then he gave him a parchment roll, and there was written within, *Fly from the wrath to come.* *Conviction of the necessity of flying*

The man therefore read it, and looking upon Evangelist very carefully, said, 'Whither must I fly?' Then said Evangelist, pointing with his finger over a very wide field, 'Do you see yonder Wicket Gate?'[13] The man said, 'No.' Then said the other, 'Do you see yonder shining light?' He said, 'I think I do.' Then said Evangelist, 'Keep that light in your eye, and go up directly thereto, so shalt thou see the Gate at which, when thou knockest, it shall be told thee what thou shalt do.' *straight gate* *Christ and the way to him cannot be found without the Word*

So I saw in my dream that the man began to run. Now he had not run far from his own door, but his wife and children perceiving it began to cry after him to return: but the man put his fingers in his ears, and ran on crying, 'Life, life, eternal life.' So he looked not behind him, but fled towards the middle of the plain.

The neighbours also came out to see him run, and as he ran some mocked, others threatened; and some cried after him to return. Now among those that did so, there were two that were resolved to fetch him back by force. The name of the one was Obstinate, and the name of the other Pliable. Now by this time the man was got a good distance from them, but however they were resolved to pursue him, which they did and in little time they overtook him. Then said the man, 'Neighbours, wherefore are you come?' They said, 'To persuade you to go back with us.' But he said, 'That can by no means be. You dwell,' *They that fly from the wrath to come, are a gazing-stock to the world* *Obstinate and Pliable follow him* said he, 'in the City of Destruction (the place also where I was born), I see it to be so; and dying there, sooner or later, you will sink lower than the grave, into a place that burns with fire and brimstone; be content, good neighbours, and go along with me.'

'What!' said Obstinate, 'and leave our friends and our comforts behind us!'

'Yes,' said Christian (for that was his name), 'because, that all which you shall forsake is not worthy to be compared with a little of that that I am seeking to enjoy, and if you will go along with me, and hold it, you shall fare as I myself; for there where I go is enough and to spare; come away, and prove my words.'

Obstinate. What are the things you seek, since you leave all the world to find them?

Christian. I seek an inheritance, incorruptible, undefiled, and that fadeth not away; and it is laid up in Heaven, and fast there, to be bestowed at the time appointed, on them that diligently seek it. Read it so, if you will, in my book.

Obstinate. Tush, said Obstinate, away with your book; will you go back with us, or no?

Christian. No, not I, said the other; because I have laid my hand to the plough.

Obstinate. Come then, neighbour Pliable, let us turn again, and go home without him; there is a company of these crazed-headed coxcombs that when they take a fancy by the end are wiser in their own eyes than seven men that can render a reason.

Pliable. Then said Pliable, Don't revile; if what the good Christian says is true, the things he looks after are better than ours; my heart inclines to go with my neighbour.

Obstinate. What! more fools still? Be ruled by me and go back. Who knows whither such a brain-sick fellow will lead you? Go back, go back, and be wise.

Christian. Come with me neighbour Pliable, there are such things to be had which I spoke of, and many more glories besides. If you believe not me, read here in this book; and for the truth of what is expressed therein, behold, all is confirmed by the blood of him that made it.

Christian and Obstinate pull for Pliable's soul

Pliable. Well neighbour Obstinate (said Pliable) I begin to come to a point; I intend to go along with this good man, and to cast in my lot with him. But my good companion, do you know the way to this desired place?

Pliable consented to go with Christian

Christian. I am directed by a man whose name is Evangelist, to speed me to a little Gate that is before us, where we shall receive instruction about the way.

Pliable. Come then, good neighbour, let us be going. Then they went both together.

Obstinate. And I will go back to my place, said Obstinate; I will be no companion of such misled fantastical fellows.

Now I saw in my dream, that when Obstinate was gone back, Christian and Pliable went talking over the plain; and thus they began their discourse:

Talk between Christian and Pliable

Christian. Come neighbour Pliable, how do you do? I am glad you are persuaded to go along with me, and had even Obstinate himself but felt what I have felt of the powers and terrors of what is yet unseen, he would not thus lightly have given us the back.

Pliable. Come neighbour Christian, since there is none but us two here, tell me now further, what the things are, and how to be enjoyed, whither we are going.

Christian. I can better conceive of them with my mind, than speak of them with my tongue; but yet since you are desirous to know, I will read of them in my book.

Pliable. And do you think that the words of your book are certainly true?

Christian. Yes verily, for it was made by him that cannot lie.

Pliable. Well said; what things are they?

Christian. There is an endless Kingdom to be inhabited, and everlasting life to be given us; that we may inhabit that Kingdom for ever.

Pliable. Well said, and what else?

Christian. There are crowns of glory to be given us; and garments that will make us shine like the sun in the firmament of heaven.

Pliable. This is excellent; and what else?

Christian. There shall be no more crying, nor sorrow; for he that is owner of the place will wipe all tears from our eyes.

Pliable. And what company shall we have there?

Christian. There we shall be with Seraphims, and Cherubins, creatures that will dazzle your eyes to look on them. There also you shall meet with thousands, and ten thousands that have gone before us to that place; none of them are hurtful, but loving, and holy, every one walking in the sight of God and standing in his presence with acceptance for ever: in a word, there we shall see the elders with their golden crowns; there we shall see the holy virgins with their golden harps. There we shall see men that by the world were cut in pieces, burnt in flames, eaten of beasts, drownded in the seas, for the love that they bare to the Lord of the place, all well, and clothed with immortality, as with a garment.

Pliable. The hearing of this is enough to ravish one's heart; but are these things to be enjoyed? How shall we get to be sharers hereof?

Christian. The Lord, the governor of that country, hath recorded that in this book, the substance of which is, if we be truly willing to have it, he will bestow it upon us freely.

Pliable. Well, my good companion, glad am I to hear of these things: come on, let us mend our pace.

Christian. I cannot go so fast as I would, by reason of this burden that is upon my back.

Now I saw in my dream, that just as they had ended this talk, they drew near to a very miry Slough that was in the midst of the plain, and they, being heedless, did both fall suddenly into the bog. The name of the Slough was <u>Despond</u>.[14] Here there- *despair ofsn* fore they wallowed for a time, being grievously bedaubed with the dirt, and Christian, because of the burden that was on his back, began to sink in the mire.

Pliable. Then said Pliable, Ah, neighbour Christian, where are you now?

Christian. Truly, said Christian, I do not know.

Pliable. At that Pliable began to be offended, and angerly, said to his fellow, Is this the happiness you have told me all this while of? If we have such ill speed at our first setting out, what may we expect, 'twixt this and our journey's end? May I get out *It is not* again with my life you shall possess the brave *enough to be* country alone for me. And with that he gave a *pliable* desperate struggle or two, and got out of the mire on that side of the Slough which was next to his own house. So away he went, and Christian saw him no more.

Wherefore Christian was left to tumble in the *Christian in* Slough of Despond alone; but still he endeavoured to *trouble, seeks* struggle to that side of the Slough that was still *still to get* further from his own house, and next to the Wicket *further from* Gate; the which he did, but could not get out, *house* because of the burden that was upon his back; but I beheld in my dream, that a man came to him, whose name was Help, and asked him what he did there.

Christian. Sir, said Christian, I was bid go this way, by a man called Evangelist, who directed me also to yonder Gate, that I might escape the wrath to come; and as I was going thither, I fell in here.

The Promises

Help. But why did you not look for the steps?

Christian. Fear followed me so hard, that I fled the next way, and fell in.

Help lifts him out

Help. Then, said he, Give me thy hand; so he gave him his hand, and he drew him out, and set him upon sound ground, and bid him go on his way.

Then I stepped to him that plucked him out, and said, 'Sir, wherefore, since over this place is the way from the City of Destruction, to yonder Gate, is it, that this plat[15] is not mended, that poor travellers might go thither with more security?' And he said unto me, 'This miry Slough is such a place as cannot be mended; it is the descent whither the scum and filth that attends conviction for sin doth continually run, and therefore is it called the Slough of Despond: for still as the sinner is awakened about his lost condition, there ariseth in his soul many fears, and doubts, and discouraging apprehensions, which all of them get together, and settle in this place; and this is the reason of the badness of this ground.

What makes the Slough of Despond

'It is not the pleasure of the King that this place should remain so bad; his labourers also, have, by the direction of His Majesty's surveyors, been for above this sixteen hundred years,[16] employed about this patch of ground, if perhaps it might have been mended; yea, and to my knowledge,' saith he, 'here hath been swallowed up at least twenty thousand cart loads; yea, millions of wholesome instructions, that have at all seasons been brought from all places of the King's dominions (and they that can tell, say they are the best materials to make good ground of the place); if so be it might have been mended, but it is the Slough of Despond still, and so will be when they have done what they can.

'True, there are by the direction of the law-giver, certain good and substantial steps, placed even through the very midst of this Slough; but at such time as this place doth much spew out its filth, as it doth against change of weather, these steps are hardly seen; or if they be, men through the dizziness of their heads step besides; and then they are bemired to purpose, notwithstanding the steps be there; but the ground is good when they are once got in at the Gate.' *The promises of forgiveness and acceptance to life by faith in Christ*

Now I saw in my dream, that by this time Pliable was got home to his house again. So his neighbours came to visit him; and some of them called him wise man for coming back; and some called him fool for hazarding himself with Christian; others again did mock at his cowardliness, saying, 'Surely since you began to venture, I would not have been so base to have given out for a few difficulties.' So Pliable sat sneaking among them. But at last he got more confidence, and then they all turned their tales, and began to deride poor Christian behind his back. And thus much concerning Pliable. *Pliable got home, and is visited of his neighbours. His entertainment by them at his return*

Now as Christian was walking solitary by himself, he espied one afar off come crossing over the field to meet him; and their hap was to meet just as they were crossing the way of each other. The gentleman's name was Mr Worldly-Wiseman,[17] he dwelt in the town of Carnal-Policy, a very great town, and also hard by from whence Christian came. This man then meeting with Christian, and having some inkling of *Mr Worldly-Wiseman meets with Christian* him, for Christian's setting forth from the City of Destruction was much noised abroad, not only in the town where he dwelt, but also it began to be the town-talk in some other places, Master Worldly-Wiseman therefore, having some guess of him, by beholding his laborious going, by observing his sighs and groans and the like, began thus to enter into some talk with Christian.

Talk betwixt Mr Worldly-Wiseman and Christian

Worldly-Wiseman. How now, good fellow, whither away after this burdened manner?

Christian. A burdened manner indeed, as ever I think poor creature had. And whereas you ask me, 'Whither away,' I tell you, sir, I am going to yonder Wicket Gate before me; for there, as I am informed, I shall be put into a way to be rid of my heavy burden.

Worldly-Wiseman. Hast thou a wife and children?

Christian. Yes, but I am so laden with this burden, that I cannot take that pleasure in them as formerly: methinks, I am as if I had none.

Worldly-Wiseman. Wilt thou hearken to me, if I give thee counsel?

Christian. If it be good, I will; for I stand in need of good counsel.

Mr Worldly-Wiseman's counsel to Christian

Worldly-Wiseman. I would advise thee then that thou with all speed get thyself rid of thy burden; for thou wilt never be settled in thy mind till then: nor canst thou enjoy the benefits of the blessing which God hath bestowed upon thee till then.

Christian. That is that which I seek for, even to be rid of this heavy burden; but get it off myself I cannot: nor is there a man in our country that can take it off my shoulders; therefore am I going this way, as I told you, that I may be rid of my burden.

Worldly-Wiseman. Who bid thee go this way to be rid of thy burden?

Christian. A man that appeared to me to be a very great and honourable person; his name, as I remember, is Evangelist.

Worldly-Wiseman. I beshrew him for his counsel; there is not a more dangerous and troublesome way in the world than is that unto which he hath directed thee, and that thou shalt find if thou wilt be ruled by his counsel. Thou hast met with something (as I perceive) already; for I see the dirt of the Slough of Despond is upon thee; but that Slough is the beginning of the sorrows that do attend those that go on in that way; hear me, I am older than thou! Thou art like to meet with in the way which thou goest, wearisomeness, painfulness, hunger, perils, nakedness, sword, lions, dragons, darkness, and in a word, death, and what not? These things are certainly true, having been confirmed by many testimonies. And why should a man so carelessly cast away himself by giving heed to a stranger. *Mr Worldly-Wiseman condemned Evangelist's counsel*

Christian. Why, sir, this burden upon my back is more terrible to me than are all these things which you have mentioned: nay, methinks I care not what I meet with in the way, so be I can also meet with deliverance from my burden. *The frame of the heart of young Christians*

Worldly-Wiseman. How camest thou by thy burden at first?

Christian. By reading this book in my hand.

Worldly-Wiseman. I thought so; and it is happened unto thee as to other weak men, who meddling with things too high for them, do suddenly fall into thy distractions; which distractions do not only unman men (as thine I perceive has done thee), but they run them upon desperate ventures, to obtain they know not what. *Worldly-Wiseman does not like that men should be serious in reading the Bible*

Christian. I know what I would obtain; it is ease for my heavy burden.

Worldly-Wiseman. But why wilt thou seek for ease this way, seeing so many dangers attend it, especially, since (hadst thou but patience to hear me) I could direct thee to the obtaining of what thou desirest, without the dangers that thou in this way wilt run thyself into: yea, and the remedy is at hand. Besides, I will add, that instead of those dangers, thou shalt meet with much safety, friendship, and content.

Christian. Pray, sir, open this secret to me.

Worldly-Wiseman. Why, in yonder village (the village is named Morality) there dwells a gentleman, whose name is Legality, a very judicious man (and a man of a very good name) that has skill to help men off with such burdens as thine are, from their shoulders: yea, to my knowledge he hath done a great deal of good this way: ay, and besides, he hath skill to cure those that are somewhat crazed in their wits with their burdens. To him, as I said, thou mayest go, and be helped presently. His house is not quite a mile from this place; and if he should not be at home himself, he hath a pretty young man to his son, whose name is Civility, that can do it (to speak on) as well as the old gentleman himself. There, I say, thou mayest be eased of thy burden, and if thou art not minded to go back to thy former habitation, as indeed I would not wish thee, thou mayest send for thy wife and children to thee to this village, where there are houses now stand empty, one of which thou mayest have at reasonable rates; provision is there also cheap and good, and that which will make thy life the more happy, is, to be sure there thou shalt live by honest neighbours, in credit and good fashion.

Now was Christian somewhat at a stand, but presently he concluded; if this be true which this

Whether Mr Worldly-Wiseman prefers Morality before the Strait Gate

Christian snared by Mr Worldly-Wiseman's word

gentleman hath said, my wisest course is to take his advice, and with that he thus further spoke.

Christian. Sir, which is my way to this honest man's house?

Worldly-Wiseman. Do you see yonder high Hill?[18] *Mount Sinai*

Christian. Yes, very well.

Worldly-Wiseman. By that Hill you must go, and the first house you come at is his.

So Christian turned out of his way to go to Mr Legality's house for help: but behold, when he was got now hard by the Hill, it seemed so high, and also that side of it that was next the way side, did hang so much over, that Christian was afraid to venture *Christian* further, lest the Hill should fall on his head: where- *afraid that* fore there he stood still, and wotted not what to do. *would fall on* Also his burden, now, seemed heavier to him, than *his head* while he was in his way. There came also flashes of fire out of the Hill, that made Christian afraid that he should be burned: here therefore he sweat, and did quake for fear. And now he began to be sorry that he had taken Mr Worldly-Wiseman's counsel; and with that he saw Evangelist coming to meet him; at *Evangelist* the sight also of whom he began to blush for shame. *findeth* So Evangelist drew nearer, and nearer, and coming *under Mount* up to him, he looked upon him with a severe and *Sinai and* dreadful countenance, and thus began to reason with *looketh* Christian. *severely upon* *him*

Evangelist. What doest thou here? said he; at which *Evangelist* word Christian knew not what to answer: where- *reasons afresh* fore, at present he stood speechless before him. Then *with Christian* said Evangelist further, Art not thou the man that I found crying, without the walls of the City of Destruction?

Christian. Yes, dear sir, I am the man.

Evangelist. Did not I direct thee the way to the little Wicket Gate?

Christian. Yes, dear sir, said Christian.

Evangelist. How is it then that thou art so quickly turned aside, for thou art now out of the way?

Christian. I met with a gentleman, so soon as I had got over the Slough of Despond, who persuaded me that I might in the village before me find a man that could take off my burden.

Evangelist. What was he?

Christian. He looked like a gentleman, and talked much to me, and got me at last to yield; so I came hither: but when I beheld this Hill, and how it hangs over the way, I suddenly made a stand, lest it should fall on my head.

Evangelist. What said that gentleman to you?

Christian. Why, he asked me whither I was going, and I told him.

Evangelist. And what said he then?

Christian. He asked me if I had a family, and I told him: but, said I, I am so loaden with the burden that is on my back that I cannot take pleasure in them as formerly.

Evangelist. And what said he then?

Christian. He bid me with speed get rid of my burden and I told him 'twas ease that I sought; and, said I, I am therefore going to yonder Gate to receive further direction how I may get to the place of deliverance. So he said that he would show me a better way, and short, not so attended with difficulties as the way, sir, that you set me; 'which way,' said he, 'will direct you to a gentleman's house that hath skill to take off these burdens.' So I believed him, and turned out of that way into this, if haply I might be soon eased of my burden: but when I came to this place, and beheld things as they are, I stopped for fear (as I said) of danger: but I now know not what to do.

Evangelist. Then (said Evangelist) stand still a little, that I may show thee the words of God. So he stood trembling. Then (said Evangelist) See that ye refuse not him that speaketh; for if they escaped not who refused him that spake on earth, much more shall *Evangelist* not we escape, if we turn away from him that *convinces* speaketh from Heaven. He said moreover, <u>*Now the*</u> *Christian of* <u>*just shall live by faith; but if any man draw back, my soul*</u> *his error* <u>*shall have no pleasure in him.*</u>[19] He also did thus apply them, Thou art the man that art running into this misery, thou hast began to reject the counsel of the most high, and to draw back thy foot from the way of peace, even almost to the hazarding of thy perdition.

Then Christian fell down at his foot as dead, crying, 'Woe is me, for I am undone', at the sight of which Evangelist caught him by the right hand, saying, '<u>All manner of sin and blasphemies shall be</u> <u>forgiven unto men; be not faithless, but believing.</u>' Then did Christian again a little revive, and stood up trembling, as at first, before Evangelist.

Then Evangelist proceeded, saying, 'Give more earnest heed to the things that I shall tell thee of. I will now show thee who it was that deluded thee, and who 'twas also to whom he sent thee. The man *Mr Worldly-* that met thee is one Worldly-Wiseman, and rightly *Wiseman* is he so called; partly, because he favoureth only the *described by* doctrine of this world (therefore he always goes to *Evangelist* the town of Morality to church) and partly because he loveth that doctrine best, for it saveth him from the Cross; and because he is of this carnal temper, therefore he seeketh to prevent my ways, though right. Now there are three things in this man's counsel that *Evangelist* thou must utterly abhor. *discovers the* *deceit of*

1. His turning thee out of the way. *Mr Worldly-*
2. His labouring to render the Cross odious to thee. *Wiseman*

3. And his setting thy feet in that way that leadeth unto the administration of death.

'First, thou must abhor his turning thee out of the way; yea, and thine own consenting thereto: because this is to reject the counsel of God, for the sake of the counsel of a Worldly-Wiseman. The Lord says, *Strive to enter in at the strait gate, the Gate to which I sent thee; for strait is the gate that leadeth unto life, and few there be that find it.* From this little Wicket Gate, and from the way thereto hath this wicked man turned thee, to the bringing of thee almost to destruction; hate therefore his turning thee out of the way, and abhor thyself for hearkening to him.

'Secondly, thou must abhor his labouring to render the Cross odious unto thee; for thou art to prefer it before the treasures in Egypt: besides the King of Glory hath told thee, that he that will save his life shall lose it: and *he that comes after him, and hates not his father and mother, and wife, and children, and brethren, and sisters; yea, and his own life also, he cannot be my disciple.* I say therefore, for a man to labour to persuade thee, that that shall be thy death, without which the truth hath said, thou canst not have eternal life, this doctrine thou must abhor.

'Thirdly, thou must hate his setting of thy feet in the way that leadeth to the ministration of death. And for this thou must consider to whom he sent thee, and also how unable that person was to deliver thee from thy burden.

'He to whom thou wast sent for ease, being by name Legality, is the son of the bond-woman which now is, and is in bondage with her children, and is in *The bond-woman* a mystery this Mount Sinai, which thou hast feared will fall on thy head. Now if she with her children are in bondage, how canst thou expect by them to be made free? This Legality therefore is not able to set thee free from thy burden. No man was as yet ever rid of his burden by him, no, nor ever is like to be: ye cannot be justified by the works of the law; for by the deeds of the law no man living can be rid of his burden: therefore Mr Worldly-Wiseman is an alien, and Mr Legality a cheat, and for his son Civility, notwithstanding his simpering looks, he is but an hypocrite, and cannot help thee. Believe me, there is nothing in all this noise that thou hast heard of this sottish man, but a design to beguile thee of thy salvation, by turning thee from the way in which I had set thee.' After this Evangelist called aloud to the Heavens for confirmation of what he had said; and with that there came words and fire out of the mountain under which poor Christian stood, that made the hair of his flesh stand. The words were thus pronounced, *As many as are of the works of the law, are under the curse; for it is written, Cursed is every one that continueth not in all things which are written in the book of the law to do them*.

Now Christian looked for nothing but death, and began to cry out lamentably, even cursing the time in which he met with Mr Worldly-Wiseman, still calling himself a thousand fools for hearkening to his counsel: he also was greatly ashamed to think that this gentleman's arguments, flowing only from the flesh, should have that prevalency with him as to cause him to forsake the right way. This done, he applied himself again to Evangelist in words and sense as follows.

Christian. Sir, what think you? Is there hopes? May I now go back and go up to the Wicket Gate, shall I not be abandoned for this, and sent back from thence ashamed. I am sorry I have hearkened to this man's counsel, but may my sin be forgiven.

Evangelist. Then said Evangelist to him, Thy sin is

Christian inquired if he may yet be happy

very great, for by it thou hast committed two evils; thou hast forsaken the way that is good, to tread in *Evangelist* forbidden paths: yet will the man at the Gate receive *comforts him* thee, for he has good will for men; only, said he, take heed that thou turn not aside again, lest thou perish from the way when his wrath is kindled but a little. Then did Christian address himself to go back, and Evangelist, after he had kissed him, gave him one smile, and bid him godspeed; so he went on with haste, neither spake he to any man by the way; nor if any man asked him, would he vouchsafe them an answer. He went like one that was all the while treading on forbidden ground, and could by no means think himself safe, till again he was got into the way which he left to follow Mr Worldly-Wiseman's counsel: so in process of time Christian got up to the Gate. Now over the Gate there was written, *Knock and it shall be opened unto you.* He knocked therefore, more than once or twice, saying,

> *May I now enter here? Will he within*
> *Open to sorry me, though I have been*
> *An undeserving rebel? Then shall I,*
> *Not fail to sing his lasting praise on high.*

At last there came a grave person to the Gate named Good Will, who asked who was there, and whence he came, and what he would have.

Christian. Here is a poor burdened sinner, I come from the City of Destruction, but am going to Mount Sion, that I may be delivered from the wrath to come; I would therefore, sir, since I am informed that by this Gate is the way thither, know if you are *The gate* willing to let me in.

will be *Good Will.* I am willing with all my heart, said he; *opened to* *broken-hearted* and with that he opened the Gate.[20]

sinners So when Christian was stepping in, the other gave

him a pull: Then said Christian, 'What means that?' The other told him, 'A little distance from this Gate, there is erected a strong castle, of which Beelzebub[21] is the captain: from thence both he, and them that are with him, shoot arrows at those that come up to this Gate, if happily they may die before they can enter in.' 'Then,' said Christian, 'I rejoice and tremble.' So when he was got in, the man of the Gate asked him who directed him thither.

leader of the devil

Satan envies those that enter the Strait Gate

Christian entered the Gate with joy and trembling

Christian. Evangelist bid me come hither and knock (as I did). And he said that you, sir, would tell me what I must do.

Talk between Good Will and Christian

Good Will. An open door is set before thee, and no man can shut it.

Christian. Now I begin to reap the benefits of my hazards.

Good Will. But how is it that you came alone?

Christian. Because none of my neighbours saw their danger as I saw mine.

Good Will. Did any of them know of your coming?

Christian. Yes, my wife and children saw me at the first, and called after me to turn again. Also some of my neighbours stood crying, and calling after me to return; but I put my fingers in mine ears, and so came on my way.

Good Will. But did none of them follow you to persuade you to go back?

Christian. Yes, both Obstinate and Pliable; but when they saw that they could not prevail, Obstinate went railing back, but Pliable came with me a little way.

Good Will. But why did he not come through?

Christian. We indeed came both together, until we came at the Slough of Despond, into the which we also suddenly fell. And then was my neighbour Pliable discouraged, and would not adventure fur-

A man may have company when he sets out for Heaven, and yet go thither alone ther. Wherefore getting out again, on that side next to his own house, he told me I should possess the brave country alone for him; so he went his way, and I came mine. He after Obstinate, and I to this Gate.

Good Will. Then said Good Will, Alas, poor man, is the celestial glory of so small esteem with him that he counteth it not worth running the hazards of a few difficulties to obtain it?

Christian. Truly, said Christian, I have said the truth of Pliable, and if I should also say all the truth *Christian accuseth himself before the man at the gate* of myself, it will appear there is no betterment 'twixt him and myself. 'Tis true, he went back to his own house, but I also turned aside to go in the way of death, being persuaded thereto by the carnal arguments of one Mr Worldly-Wiseman.

Good Will. Oh, did he light upon you! What, he would have had you a sought for[22] ease at the hands of Mr Legality; they are both of them a very cheat: but did you take his counsel?

Christian. Yes, as far as I durst, I went to find out Mr Legality, until I thought that the Mountain that stands by his house would have fallen upon my head: wherefore there I was forced to stop.

Good Will. That Mountain has been the death of many, and will be the death of many more: 'tis well you escaped being by it dashed in pieces.

Christian. Why, truly I do not know what had become of me there, had not Evangelist happily met me again as I was musing in the midst of my dumps: but 'twas God's mercy that he came to me again, for else I had never come hither. But now I am come, such a one as I am, more fit indeed for death by that Mountain, than thus to stand talking with my Lord. But oh, what a favour is this to me, that yet I am *Christian is comforted again* admitted entrance here.

Good Will. We make no objections against any,

notwithstanding all that they have done before they come hither, they in no wise are cast out; and therefore, good Christian, come a little way with me, and I will teach thee about the way thou must go. Look before thee; dost thou see this narrow way? That is the way thou must go. It was cast up by the patriarchs, prophets, Christ, and his apostles, and it is as straight as a rule can make it. This is the way thou must go.

Christian directed yet on his way

Christian. But said Christian, Is there no turnings nor windings, by which a stranger may lose the way?

Good Will. Yes, there are many ways butt down upon[23] this; and they are crooked, and wide; but thus thou may'st distinguish the right from the wrong, that only being straight and narrow.

Christian afraid of losing his way

Then I saw in my dream that Christian asked him further if he could not help him off with his burden that was upon his back; for as yet he had not got rid thereof, nor could he by any means get it off without help.

Christian weary of his burden

He told him, 'As to the burden, be content to bear it, until thou comest to the place of deliverance; for there it will fall from thy back itself.'

Then Christian began to gird up his loins, and to address himself to his journey. So the other told him that by that he was gone some distance from the Gate he would come at the House of the Interpreter,[4] at whose door he should knock; and he would show him excellent things. Then Christian took his leave of his friend, and he again bid him godspeed.

There is no deliverance from the guilt and burden of sin, but by the death and blood of Christ

Then he went on, till he came at the House of the Interpreter,[24] where he knocked, over and over; at last one came to the door, and asked who was there.

Christian comes to the House of the Interpreter

Christian. Sir, here is a traveller, who was bid by an acquaintance of the good man of this House, to call here for my profit: I would therefore speak with the master of the House. So he called for the master of the House, who after a little time came to Christian and asked him what he would have.

Christian. Sir, said Christian, I am a man that am come from the City of Destruction, and am going to the Mount Sion, and I was told by the man that stands at the Gate, at the head of this way that if I called here, you would show me excellent things, such as would be an help to me in my journey.

He is entertained *Interpreter.* Then said the Interpreter, Come in, I will show thee that which will be profitable to thee.

Illumination So he commanded his man to light the candle, and bid Christian follow him; so he had him into a private room, and bid his man open a door, the which

Christian sees a brave picture when he had done, Christian saw a picture of a very grave person[25] hang up against the wall, and this was

The fashion of the picture the fashion of it: it had eyes lift up to Heaven, the best of books in its hand, the law of truth was written upon its lips, the world was behind its back; it stood as if it pleaded with men, and a crown of gold did hang over its head.

Christian. Then said Christian, What means this?

Interpreter. The man whose picture this is is one of a thousand; he can beget children, travail in birth with children, and nurse them himself when they are born. And whereas thou seest him with his eyes lift up to Heaven, the best of books in his hand, and *preacher* the law of truth writ on his lips, it is to show thee that his work is to know, and unfold dark things to

The meaning of the picture sinners even as also thou seest him stand as if he pleaded with men; and whereas thou seest the world as cast behind him, and that a crown hangs over his head, that is to show thee that slighting and despising the things that are present, for the love that he hath to his Master's service, he is sure in the world that comes next to have glory for his reward. Now, said the Interpreter, I have showed thee this picture first, because the man whose picture this is, is the only man whom the Lord of the Place whither thou art going hath authorized to be thy guide in all difficult places thou mayest meet with in the way; wherefore take good heed to what I have showed thee, and bear well in thy mind what thou hast seen, lest in thy journey thou meet with some that pretend to lead thee right, but their way goes down to death. *Why he showed him the picture first*

Then he took him by the hand, and led him into a very large parlour that was full of dust, because never swept; the which, after he had reviewed a little while, the Interpreter called for a man to sweep: now when he began to sweep, the dust began so abundantly to fly about, that Christian had almost therewith been choked. Then said the Interpreter to a damsel that stood by, 'Bring hither water, and sprinkle the room', which when she had done, was swept and cleansed with pleasure.

Christian. Then said Christian, What means this?

Interpreter. The Interpreter answered: This parlour is the heart of a man that was never sanctified by the sweet grace of the Gospel; that dust is his original sin, and inward corruptions that have defiled the whole man. He that began to sweep at first is the Law, but she that brought water, and did sprinkle it, is the Gospel. Now, whereas thou sawest that so soon as the first began to sweep, the dust did so fly about that the room by him could not be cleansed, but that thou wast almost choked therewith, this is to show thee that the Law, instead of cleansing the heart (by its working) from sin, doth revive, put strength into, and increase it in the soul, even as it doth discover and forbid it, for it doth not give power to subdue.

Again, as thou sawest the damsel sprinkle the room

73

with water, upon which it was cleansed with pleasure: this is to show thee that when the Gospel comes in the sweet and precious influences thereof to the heart, then I say, even as thou sawest the damsel lay the dust by sprinkling the floor with water, so is sin vanquished and subdued, and the soul made clean, through the faith of it; and consequently fit for the King of Glory to inhabit.

He showed him Passion and Patience. Passion will have all now

I saw moreover in my dream, that the Interpreter took him by the hand, and had him into a little room, where sat two little children, each one in his chair: the name of the eldest was Passion, and of the other, Patience; Passion seemed to be much discontent, but Patience was very quiet. Then Christian asked, 'What is the reason of the discontent of Passion?' The Interpreter answered, 'The Governor of them would have him stay for his best things till the beginning of the next year, but he will have all now:

Patience is for waiting, Passion has his desire

but Patience is willing to wait.'

Then I saw that one came to Passion, and brought him a bag of treasure, and poured it down at his feet; the which he took up, and rejoiced therein, and withal, laughed Patience to scorn. But I beheld but a while, and he had lavished all away, and had nothing left him but rags.

And quickly lavishes all away

The matter expounded

Christian. Then said Christian to the Interpreter, Expound this matter more fully to me.

Interpreter. So he said, These two lads are figures, Passion, of the men of this world, and Patience, of the men of that which is to come; for as here thou seest, Passion will have all now, this year; that is to say, in this world; so are the men of this world: they must have all their good things now, they cannot stay till next year; that is, until the next world, for their portion of good. That proverb, 'A bird in the hand is worth two in the bush', is of more authority

The worldly man for a bird in the hand

74

with them, than are all the divine testimonies of the good of the world to come. But as thou sawest, that he had quickly lavished all away, and had presently left him nothing but rags; so will it be with all such men at the end of this world.

Christian. Then said Christian, Now I see that Patience has the best wisdom, and that upon many accounts. 1. Because he stays for the best things. 2. And also because he will have the glory of his, when the other hath nothing but rags.

Patience had the best wisdom

Interpreter. Nay, you may add another; to wit, the glory of the next world will never wear out; but these are suddenly gone. Therefore Passion had not so much reason to laugh at Patience because he had his good things first, as Patience will have to laugh at Passion because he had his best things last; for first must give place to last, because last must have his time to come, but last gives place to nothing, for there is not another to succeed; he therefore that hath his portion first, must needs have a time to spend it, but he that has his portion last must have it lastingly. Therefore it is said of Dives, *In thy life thou received'st thy good things, and likewise Lazarus evil things; but now he is comforted, and thou art tormented.*[26]

Things that are first must give place, but things that are last are lasting

Dives had his good things first

Christian. Then I perceive, 'tis not best to covet things that are now, but to wait for things to come.

Interpreter. You say the truth, *For the things that are seen, are temporal; but the things that are not seen, are eternal.* But though this be so, yet since things present and our fleshly appetite are such near neighbours one to another, and again, because things to come, and carnal sense, are such strangers one to another, therefore it is that the first of these so suddenly fall into amity, and that distance is so continued between the second.

The first things are but temporal

Then I saw in my dream that the Interpreter took

Christian by the hand, and led him into a place where was a fire burning against a wall, and one standing by it always, casting much water upon it to quench it: yet did the fire burn higher and hotter.

Then said Christian, 'What means this?'

The Interpreter answered, 'This fire is the work of grace[27] that is wrought in the heart; he that casts water upon it, to extinguish and put it out, is the Devil: but in that thou seest the fire, notwithstanding, burn higher and hotter, thou shalt also see the reason of that. So he had him about to the backside of the wall, where he saw a man with a vessel of oil in his hand, of the which he did also continually cast, but secretly, into the fire. Then said Christian, 'What means this?' The Interpreter answered, 'This is Christ, who continually with the oil of his grace maintains the work already begun in the heart, by the means of which, notwithstanding what the Devil can do, the souls of his people prove gracious still. And in that thou sawest that the man stood behind the wall to maintain the fire, this is to teach thee that it is hard for the tempted to see how this work of grace is maintained in the soul.'

I saw also that the Interpreter took him again by the hand, and led him into a pleasant place where was builded a stately palace, beautiful to behold; at the sight of which, Christian was greatly delighted; he saw also upon the top thereof certain persons walked who were clothed all in gold. Then said Christian, 'May we go in thither?' Then the Interpreter took him, and led him up toward the door of the palace; and behold, at the door stood a great company of men as desirous to go in, but durst not. There also sat a man, at a little distance from the door, at a table-side, with a book, and his inkhorn before him, to take the name of him that should enter therein.

He saw also that in the doorway stood many men in armour to keep it, being resolved to do to the man that would enter what hurt and mischief they could. Now was Christian somewhat in a muse; at last, when every man started back for fear of the armed men, Christian saw a man of a very stout countenance[28] *Armour of God* come up to the man that sat there to write, saying, 'Set down my name, Sir,' the which when he had *The valiant* done, he saw the man draw his sword, and put an *man* helmet upon his head, and rush toward the door upon the armed men, who laid upon him with deadly force; but the man, not at all discouraged, fell to cutting and hacking most fiercely; so after he had received and given many wounds to those that attempted to keep him out, he cut his way through them all, and pressed forward into the palace; at which there was a pleasant voice heard from those that were within, even of the three[29] that walked upon the top of the palace, saying, *? Peto Moses, Enoch Elijah*

> Come in, come in;
> Eternal Glory thou shalt win.

So he went in, and was clothed with such garments as they. Then Christian smiled, and said, 'I think verily I know the meaning of this'.

'Now,' said Christian, 'let me go hence.' 'Nay, stay,' said the Interpreter, 'till I have showed thee a little more, and after that, thou shalt go on thy way.' So he took him by the hand again, and led him into a very dark room, where there sat a man in an iron cage. *Despair like an iron cage*

Now the man, to look on, seemed very sad: he sat with his eyes looking down to the ground, his hands folded together, and he sighed as if he would break his heart. Then said Christian, 'What means this?' At which the Interpreter bid him talk with the man.

Christian. Then said Christian to the man, What art thou? The man answered, 'I am what I was not once.'

Christian. What wast thou once?

Man. The man said, I was once a fair and flourishing professor,[30] both in mine own eyes, and also in the eyes of others: I once was, as I thought, fair for[31] the Celestial City, and had then even joy at the thoughts that I should get thither.

Christian. Well, but what art thou now?

Man. I am now a man of despair,[32] and am shut up in it, as in this iron cage. I cannot get out, O now I cannot.

Christian. But how camest thou in this condition?

Man. I left off to watch, and be sober; I laid the reins upon the neck of my lusts; I sinned against the light of the word, and the goodness of God: I have grieved the Spirit, and he is gone; I tempted the Devil, and he is come to me; I have provoked God to anger, and he has left me; I have so hardened my heart, that I cannot repent.

Then said Christian to the Interpreter, 'But is there no hopes for such a man as this?' 'Ask him,' said the Interpreter.

Christian. Then said Christian, Is there no hope but you must be kept in this iron cage of despair?

Man. No, none at all.

Christian. Why? The Son of the Blessed is very pitiful.

Man. I have crucified him to myself afresh, I have despised his person, I have despised his righteousness, I have counted his blood an unholy thing, I have done despite to the spirit of grace: therefore I have shut myself out of all the promises; and there now remains to me nothing but threatenings, dreadful threatenings, fearful threatenings of certain judgement and fiery indignation, which shall devour me as an adversary.

Christian. For what did you bring yourself into this condition?

Man. For the lusts, pleasures, and profits of this world; in the enjoyment of which I did then promise myself much delight: but now even every one of those things also bite me and gnaw me like a burning worm.

Christian. But canst thou not now repent and turn?

Man. God hath denied me repentance; his word gives me no encouragement to believe; yea, himself hath shut me up in this iron cage: nor can all the men in the world let me out. O eternity! eternity! how shall I grapple with the misery that I must meet with in eternity?

Interpreter. Then said the Interpreter to Christian, Let this man's misery be remembered by thee, and be an everlasting caution to thee.

Christian. Well, said Christian, this is fearful; God help me to watch and be sober; and to pray, that I may shun the cause of this man's misery. Sir, is it not time for me to go on my way now?

Interpreter. Tarry till I shall show thee one thing more, and then thou shalt go on thy way.

So he took Christian by the hand again, and led him into a chamber, where there was one a rising out of bed; and as he put on his raiment he shook and trembled. Then said Christian, 'Why doth this man thus tremble?' The Interpreter then bid him tell to Christian the reason of his so doing: so he began, and said, 'This night as I was in my sleep, I dreamed, and behold the heavens grew exceeding black; also it thundered and lightened in most fearful wise, that it put me into an agony. So I looked up in my dream, and saw the clouds rack* at an unusual rate, upon which I heard a great sound of a trumpet, and saw also a man sit upon a cloud, attended with the thousands of Heaven; they were all in flaming fire, also the heavens was on a burning flame. I heard then a voice, saying, 'Arise ye dead, and come to judgement,' and with that the rocks rent, the graves opened, and the dead that were therein came forth; some of them were exceeding glad, and looked upward, and some sought to hide themselves under the mountains. Then I saw the man that sat upon the cloud open the book and bid the world draw near. Yet there was by reason of a fiery flame that issued out and came from before him a convenient distance betwixt him and them, as betwixt the judge and the prisoners at the bar. I heard it also proclaimed to them that attended on the man that sat on the cloud, 'Gather together the tares, the chaff, and stubble, and cast them into the burning lake,' and with that the bottomless pit opened, just whereabout I stood; out of the mouth of which there came in an abundant manner smoke, and coals of fire, with hideous noises. It was also said to the same persons 'Gather my wheat into my garner.' And with that I saw many catched up and carried away into the clouds, but I was left behind. I also sought to hide myself, but I could not; for the man that sat upon the cloud still kept his eye upon me: my sins also came into mind, and my conscience did accuse me on every side. Upon this I awaked from my sleep.

Christian. But what was it that made you so afraid of this sight?

Man. Why, I thought that the Day of Judgement

* Move.

was come, and that I was not ready for it: but this frighted me most, that the angels gathered up several, and left me behind; also the pit of Hell opened her mouth just where I stood; my conscience too within afflicted me; and as I thought, the Judge had always his eye upon me, showing indignation in his countenance.

Then said the Interpreter to Christian, 'Hast thou considered all these things?'

Christian. Yes, and they put me in hope and fear.

Interpreter. Well, keep all things so in thy mind, that they may be as a goad in thy sides, to prick thee forward in the way thou must go. Then Christian began to gird up his loins, and to address himself to his journey. Then said the Interpreter, The Comforter be always with thee good Christian, to guide thee in the way that leads to the City.

So Christian went on his way, saying,

> *Here I have seen things rare, and profitable;*
> *Things pleasant, dreadful, things to make me stable*
> *In what I have begun to take in hand:*
> *Then let me think on them, and understand*
> *Wherefore they showed me was, and let me be*
> *Thankful, O good Interpreter, to thee.*

Now I saw in my dream, that the highway up which Christian was to go, was fenced on either side with a Wall, and that Wall is called Salvation. Up this way therefore did burdened Christian run, but not without great difficulty, because of the load on his back.

He ran thus till he came at a place somewhat ascending; and upon that place stood a Cross,[33] and a little below in the bottom, a sepulchre. So I saw in my dream, that just as Christian came up with the Cross, his burden loosed from off his shoulders, and fell from off his back; and began to tumble, and so continued to do till it came to the mouth of the sepulchre, where it fell in, and I saw it no more.

When God releases us of our guilt and burden, we are as those that leap for joy

Then was Christian glad and lightsome, and said with a merry heart, 'He hath given me rest, by his sorrow, and life, by his death.' Then he stood still a while, to look and wonder; for it was very surprising to him that the sight of the Cross should thus ease him of his burden. He looked therefore, and looked again, even till the springs that were in his head sent the waters down his cheeks. Now as he stood looking and weeping, behold three Shining Ones[34] came to him, and saluted him, with 'Peace be to thee.' So the first said to him, 'Thy sins be forgiven.' The second stripped him of his rags, and clothed him with change of raiment. The third also set a mark on his forehead, and gave him a roll with a seal upon it, which he bid him look on as he ran, and that he should give it in at the Celestial Gate: so they went their way. Then Christian gave three leaps for joy, and went on singing,

A Christian can sing though alone, when God doth give him the joy of his heart

Thus far did I come loaden with my sin,
Nor could aught ease the grief that I was in,
Till I came hither. What a place is this!
Must here be the beginning of my bliss?
Must here the burden fall from off my back?
Must here the strings that bound it to me, crack?
Blessed Cross! Blessed Sepulchre! Blessed rather be
The man that there was put to shame for me.

I saw then in my dream that he went on thus, even until he came at a bottom,[35] where he saw, a little out of the way, three men fast asleep, with fetters

Simple, Sloth, and Presumption

upon their heels. The name of the one was Simple, another Sloth, and the third Presumption.

Christian then seeing them lie in this case went to them, if peradventure he might awake them. And cried, 'You are like them that sleep on the top of a mast, for the Dead Sea is under you, a gulf that hath no bottom; awake therefore, and come away; be willing also, and I will help you off with your irons.' He also told them, 'If he that goeth about like a roaring lion comes by, you will certainly become a prey to his teeth.' With that they looked upon him, and began to reply in this sort: Simple said, 'I see no danger'; Sloth said, 'Yet a little more sleep'; and Presumption said, 'Every fat[36] must stand upon his own bottom, what is the answer else that I should give thee?' And so they lay down to sleep again, and Christian went on his way.

There is no persuasion will do, if God openeth not the eyes

Yet was he troubled to think that men in that danger should so little esteem the kindness of him that so freely offered to help them, both by awakening of them, counselling of them, and proffering to help them off with their irons. And as he was troubled thereabout, he espied two men come tumbling over the wall on the left hand of the narrow way; and they made up a pace to him. The name of the one was Formalist, and the name of the other Hypocrisy. So, as I said, they drew up unto him, who thus entered with them into discourse.

Christian. Gentlemen, whence came you, and whither do you go?

Christian talked with them

Formalist and Hypocrisy. We were born in the land of Vainglory, and are going for praise to Mount Sion.

Christian. Why came you not in at the Gate which standeth at the beginning of the way? Know you not that it is written that, *He that cometh not in by the door, but climbeth up some other way, the same is a thief and a robber.*

Formalist and Hypocrisy. They said, that to go to the Gate for entrance, was by all their countrymen counted too far about; and that therefore their usual way was to make a short cut of it, and to climb over the wall as they had done.

Christian. But will it not be counted a trespass against the Lord of the City whither we are bound, thus to violate his revealed will?

They that come into the way, but not by the door, think that they can say something in vindication of their own practice

Formalist and Hypocrisy. They told him, that as for that, he needed not to trouble his head thereabout, for what they did they had custom for; and could produce, if need were, testimony that would witness it for more than a thousand years.

Christian. But said Christian, Will your practice stand a trial at law?

Formalist and Hypocrisy. They told him that custom, it being of so long a standing as above a thousand years,[37] would doubtless now be admitted as a thing legal, by any impartial judge. And besides, said they, so be we get into the way, what's matter which way we get in; if we are in, we are in: thou art but in the way, who, as we perceive, came in at the Gate; and we are also in the way that came tumbling over the wall: wherein now is thy condition better than ours?

Christian. I walk by the rule of my master, you walk by the rude working of your fancies. You are counted thieves already by the Lord of the way, therefore I doubt you will not be found true men at the end of the way. You come in by yourselves without his direction, and shall go out by yourselves without his mercy.

To this they made him but little answer; only they bid him look to himself. Then I saw that they went on every man in his way, without much conference one with another; save that these two men told

Christian, that, as to laws and ordinances, they doubted not, but they should as conscientiously do them as he. 'Therefore,' said they, 'we see not wherein thou differest from us, but by the coat that is on thy back,[38] which was, as we trow, given thee by some of thy neighbours to hide the shame of thy nakedness.'

Christian. By laws and ordinances you will not be saved, since you came not in by the door. And as for this coat that is on my back, it was given me by the Lord of the place whither I go; and that, as you say, to cover my nakedness with. And I take it as a token of his kindness to me, for I had nothing but rags before; and besides, thus I comfort myself as I go, surely, think I, when I come to the Gate of the City, the Lord thereof will know me for good, since I have his coat on my back; a coat that he gave me freely in the day that he stripped me of my rags. I have moreover a mark in my forehead, of which perhaps you have taken no notice, which one of my Lord's most intimate associates fixed there in the day that my burden fell off my shoulders. I will tell you moreover, that I had then given me a roll sealed to comfort me by reading, as I go in the way; I was also bid to give it in at the Celestial Gate in token of my certain going in after it: all which things I doubt you want, and want them because you came not in at the Gate.

Christian has got his Lord's coat on his back, and is comforted therewith, he is comforted also with his mark, and his roll

To these things they gave him no answer, only they looked upon each other, and laughed. Then I saw that they went on all, save that Christian kept before, who had no more talk but with himself, and that sometimes sighingly, and sometimes comfortably: also he would be often reading in the roll that one of the Shining Ones gave him, by which he was refreshed.

I believe then, that they all went on till they came *He comes to* to the foot of a Hill, at the bottom of which was a *the Hill* spring. There was also in the same place two other *Difficulty* ways besides that which came straight from the Gate; one turned to the left hand, and the other to the right, at the bottom of the Hill: but the narrow way lay right up the Hill (and the name of the going up the side of the Hill is called Difficulty). Christian now went to the spring and drank thereof to refresh himself, and then began to go up the Hill, saying,

> This Hill, though high, I covet to ascend,
> The difficulty will not me offend,
> For I perceive the way to life lies here;
> Come, pluck up, heart; let's neither faint nor fear:
> Better, though difficult, the right way to go,
> Than wrong, though easy, where the end is woe.

The other two also came to the foot of the Hill. But when they saw that the Hill was steep and high, and that there was two other ways to go; and supposing also that these two ways might meet again with that up which Christian went, on the other side of the Hill; therefore they were resolved to go in those ways. (Now the name of one of those ways was Danger, and the name of the other Destruction.) *The danger* So the one took the way which is called Danger, *of turning out* which led him into a great wood, and the other took *of the way* directly up the way to Destruction, which led him into a wide field full of dark mountains,[39] where he stumbled and fell, and rose no more.

I looked then after Christian, to see him go up the Hill, where I perceived he fell from running to going, and from going to clambering upon his hands and his knees, because of the steepness of the place. Now *Award of* about the midway to the top of the Hill was a *grace* pleasant Arbour, made by the Lord of the Hill, for the refreshing of weary travellers. Thither therefore Christian got, where also he sat down to rest him. Then he pulled his roll out of his bosom, and read therein to his comfort; he also now began afresh to take a review of the coat or garment that was given him as he stood by the Cross. Thus pleasing himself a while, he at last fell into a slumber, and thence into a fast sleep, which detained him in that place until it was almost night, and in his sleep his roll fell out of *He that sleeps* his hand. Now as he was sleeping, there came one *is a loser* to him and awaked him, saying 'Go to the ant, thou sluggard, consider her ways, and be wise,'[40] and with that Christian suddenly started up, and sped him on his way, and went apace till he came to the top of the Hill.

Now when he was got up to the top of the Hill, there came two men running against him amain; the name of the one was Timorous, and the name of *Christian* the other Mistrust. To whom Christian said, 'Sirs, *meets with* what's the matter you run the wrong way?' Timorous *Mistrust and* answered that they were going to the City of Sion, *Timorous* and had got up that difficult place; 'But,' said he, 'the further we go, the more danger we meet with, wherefore we turned, and are going back again.'

'Yes,' said Mistrust, 'for just before us lie a couple of lions in the way, whether sleeping or waking we know not and we could not think, if we came within reach, but they would presently pull us in pieces.'

Christian. Then said Christian, You make me afraid, but whither shall I fly to be safe? If I go back to mine own country, that is prepared for fire and brimstone, and I shall certainly perish there. If I can get to the Celestial City, I am sure to be in safety there. I must *Christian* venture: to go back is nothing but death, to go *shakes off fear* forward is fear of death, and life everlasting beyond it. I will yet go forward. So Mistrust and Timorous ran down the Hill, and Christian went on his way. But thinking again of what he heard from the men, he felt in his bosom for his roll[41] that he might read *Christian* therein and be comforted; but he felt, and found it *missed his* not. Then was Christian in great distress, and knew *roll,* not what to do, for he wanted that which used to *wherein he* relieve him, and that which should have been his *used to take* pass into the Celestial City. Here therefore he began *comfort* to be much perplexed, and knew not what to do; at *He is* last he bethought himself that he had slept in the *perplexed* Arbour that is on the side of the Hill: and falling *for his roll* down upon his knees, he asked God forgiveness for that his <u>foolish fact</u>,[42] and then went back to look for his roll. But all the way he went back, who can sufficiently set forth the sorrow of Christian's heart? Sometimes he sighed, sometimes he wept, and often-times he chid himself, for being so foolish to fall asleep in that place which was erected only for a little refreshment from his weariness. Thus therefore he went back, carefully looking on this side and on that, all the way as he went, if happily he might find his roll, that had been his comfort so many times in his journey. He went thus till he came again within sight of the Arbour, where he sat and slept; but that *Christian* sight renewed his sorrow the more, by bringing *bewails his* again, even afresh, his evil of sleeping unto his mind. *foolish* Thus therefore he now went on, bewailing his <u>sinful</u> *sleeping* <u>sleep</u>, saying, 'O wretched man that I am, that I should sleep in the day-time! That I should sleep in the midst of difficulty! That I should so indulge the flesh as to use that rest for ease to my flesh which the Lord of the Hill hath erected only for the relief of the spirits of pilgrims! How many steps have I took in vain! (Thus it happened to Israel for their sin, they were sent back again by the way of the Red Sea.)

And I am made to tread those steps with sorrow which I might have trod with delight, had it not been for this sinful sleep. How far might I have been on my way by this time! I am made to tread those steps thrice over which I needed not to have trod but once: Yea, now also I am like to be benighted, for the day is almost spent. O that I had not slept!' Now by this time he was come to the Arbour again, where for a while he sat down and wept, but at last (as Christian would have it) looking sorrowfully down under the settle, there he espied his roll; the which he with trembling and haste catched up, and put it into his bosom; but who can tell how joyful this man was, when he had gotten his roll again! For this roll was the assurance of his life, and acceptance at the desired haven. Therefore he laid it up in his bosom, gave thanks to God for directing his eye to the place where it lay, and with joy and tears betook himself again to his journey. But oh how nimbly now did he go up the rest of the Hill! Yet before he got up, the sun went down upon Christian; and this made him again recall the vanity of his sleeping to his remembrance, and thus he again began to condole with himself: 'Ah thou sinful sleep! How for thy sake am I like to be benighted in my journey! I must walk without the sun, darkness must cover the path of my feet, and I must hear the noise of doleful creatures, because of my sinful sleep!' Now also he remembered the story that Mistrust and Timorous told him of, how they were frighted with the sight of the lions. Then said Christian to himself again, 'These beasts range in the night for their prey, and if they should meet with me in the dark, how should I shift them? How should I escape being by them torn in pieces? Thus he went on his way, but while he was thus bewailing his unhappy miscarriage, he lift

Christian findeth his roll where he lost it

[handwritten margin note: Church relations]

up his eyes, and behold there was a very stately palace before him, the name whereof was Beautiful,[43] and it stood just by the highway side.

So I saw in my dream that he made haste and went forward, that if possible he might get lodging there. Now before he had gone far, he entered into a very narrow passage, which was about a furlong off of the porter's lodge, and looking very narrowly before him as he went, he espied two lions[44] in the way. Now,

[handwritten margin note: persecution civil + ecclesiastical]

thought he, I see the dangers that Mistrust and Timorous were driven back by (the lions were chained, but he saw not the chains). Then he was afraid, and thought also himself to go back after them, for he thought nothing but death was before him. But the porter at the lodge, whose name is Watchful, perceiving that Christian made a halt, as if he would go back, cried unto him saying, 'Is thy strength so small? Fear not the lions, for they are chained, and are placed there for trial of faith where it is; and for discovery of those that have none: keep in the midst of the path, and no hurt shall come unto thee.'

Then I saw that he went on, trembling for fear of the lions, but taking good heed to the directions of the porter; he heard them roar, but they did him no harm. Then he clapped his hands, and went on till he came and stood before the gate where the porter was. Then said Christian to the porter, 'Sir, what House is this? and may I lodge here tonight?' The porter answered, 'This House was built by the Lord of the Hill, and he built it for the relief and security of pilgrims.' The porter also asked whence he was, and whither he was going.

Christian. I am come from the City of Destruction, and am going to Mount Sion; but because the sun is now set, I desire, if I may, to lodge here tonight.

Porter. What is your name?

Christian. My name is, now, <u>Christian</u>; but my name at the first was <u>Graceless</u>; I came of the race of Japhet, whom God will persuade to dwell in the tents of Shem.

Porter. But how doth it happen that you come so late? The sun is set.

Christian. I had been here sooner, but that, wretched man that I am! I slept in the Arbour that stands on the hillside; nay, I had notwithstanding that, been here much sooner, but that in my sleep I lost my evidence, and came without it to the brow of the Hill; and then feeling for it, and finding it not, I was forced with sorrow of heart, to go back to the place where I slept my sleep, where I found it, and now I am come.

Porter. Well, I will call out one of the virgins of this place, who will, if she likes your talk, bring you in to the rest of the family, according to the rules of the House. So Watchful the porter rang a bell, at the sound of which came out at the door of the House, a grave and beautiful damsel named <u>Discretion</u>, and asked why she was called.

The porter answered, 'This man is in a journey from the City of Destruction to Mount Sion, but being weary and benighted, he asked me if he might lodge here tonight; so I told him I would call for thee, who after discourse had with him, mayest do as seemeth thee good, even according to the law of the house.'

Then she asked him whence he was, and whither he was going, and he told her. She asked him also, how he got into the way and he told her. Then she asked him what he had seen, and met with in the way, and he told her; and last, she asked his name, so he said, 'It is Christian; and I have so much the more a desire to lodge here tonight, because, by what I perceive, this place was built by the Lord of the Hill for the relief and security of pilgrims.' So she smiled, but the water stood in her eyes. And after a little pause, she said, 'I will call forth two or three more of the family.' So she ran to the door, and called out <u>Prudence, Piety and Charity</u>,[45] who after a little more discourse with him, had him in to the family; and many of them meeting him at the threshold of the House, said, 'Come in thou blessed of the Lord; this House was built by the Lord of the Hill on purpose to entertain such pilgrims in.' Then he bowed his head, and followed them into the House. So when he was come in, and set down, they gave him something to drink; and consented together that until supper was ready, some one or two of them should have some particular discourse with Christian, for the best improvement of time: and they appointed Piety and Prudence and Charity to discourse with him; and thus they began.

Piety discourses him

Piety. Come, good Christian, since we have been so loving to you, to receive you in to our House this night; let us, if perhaps we may better ourselves thereby, talk with you of all things that have happened to you in your pilgrimage.

Christian. With a very good will, and I am glad that you are so well disposed.

Piety. What moved you at first to betake yourself to a pilgrim's life?

How Christian was driven out of his own country

Christian. I was driven out of my native country by a dreadful sound that was in mine ears, to wit, that unavoidable destruction did attend me, if I abode in that place where I was.

Piety. But how did it happen that you came out of your country this way?

Christian. It was as God would have it; for when

I was under the fears of destruction I did not know whither to go; but by chance there came a man, even to me (as I was trembling and weeping), whose name is Evangelist, and he directed me to the Wicket Gate, which else I should never have found; and so set me into the way that hath led me directly to this House.

How he got into the way to Sion

Piety. But did you not come by the House of the Interpreter?

Christian. Yes, and did see such things there, the remembrance of which will stick by me as long as I live; specially three things; to wit, how Christ, in despite of Satan, maintains his work of grace in the heart; how the man had sinned himself quite out of hopes of God's mercy; and also the dream of him that thought in his sleep the Day of Judgement was come.

A rehearsal of what he saw in the way

3 things

Piety. Why? Did you hear him tell his dream?

Christian. Yes, and a dreadful one it was, I thought. It made my heart ache as he was telling of it, but yet I am glad I heard it.

Piety. Was that all that you saw at the House of the Interpreter?

Christian. No, he took me and had me where he showed me a stately palace, and how the people were clad in gold that were in it; and how there came a venturous man, and cut his way through the armed men that stood in the door to keep him out; and how he was bid to come in, and win eternal glory. Methought those things did ravish my heart; I could have stayed at that good man's House a twelve-month, but that I knew I had further to go.

Piety. And what saw you else in the way?

Christian. Saw! Why, I went but a little further, and I saw one, as I thought in my mind, hang bleeding upon the tree; and the very sight of him made

✻
Christ

93

my burden fall off my back (for I groaned under a weary burden), but then it fell down from off me. 'Twas a strange thing to me, for I never saw such a thing before: Yea, and while I stood looking up (for then I could not forbear looking), <u>three Shining Ones</u> came to me: one of them testified that my sins were forgiven me: another stripped me of my rags, and gave me this broidered coat which you see; and the third set the mark which you see on my forehead, and gave me this sealed roll (and with that he plucked it out of his bosom).

Piety. But you saw more than this, did you not?

Christian. The things that I have told you were the best: yet some other matters I saw, as namely I saw three men, <u>Simple, Sloth, and Presumption,</u> lie asleep a little out of the way as I came, with irons upon their heels; but do you think I could awake them! I also saw <u>Formalist and Hypocrisy</u> come tumbling over the wall, to go, as they pretended, to Sion, but they were quickly lost; even as I myself did tell them, but they would not believe: but, above all, I found it hard work to get up this Hill, and as hard to come by the lions' mouths, and truly if it had not been for the good man, the porter that stands at the gate, I do not know but that after all, I might have gone back again: but now I thank God I am here, and I thank you for receiving of me.

Prudence discourses him

Then Prudence thought good to ask him a few questions, and desired his answer to them.

Prudence. Do you not think sometimes of the country from whence you came?

Christian's thoughts of his native country

Christian. Yes, but with much shame and detestation; *Truly, if I had been mindful of that country from whence I came out, I might have had opportunity to have returned; but now I desire a better country; that is, an heavenly.*

94

Prudence. Do you not yet bear away with you some of the things that then you were conversant withal?

Christian. Yes, but greatly against my will; especially my inward and carnal cogitations with which all my countrymen, as well as myself, were delighted; but now all those things are my grief, and might I but choose mine own things I would choose never to think of those things more; but when I would be doing of that which is best, that which is worst is with me.

Prudence. Do you not find sometimes, as if those things were vanquished, which at other times are your perplexity?

Christian. Yes, but that is but seldom; but they are to me golden hours, in which such things happens to me.

Prudence. Can you remember by what means you find your annoyances at times as if they were vanquished?

Christian. Yes, when I think what I saw at the Cross, that will do it; and when I look upon my broidered coat, that will do it; also when I look into the roll that I carry in my bosom, that will do it; and when my thoughts wax warm about whither I am going, that will do it.

Prudence. And what is it that makes you so desirous to go to Mount Sion?

Christian. Why, there I hope to see him alive, that did hang dead on the Cross; and there I hope to be rid of all those things that to this day are in me an annoyance to me; there they say there is no death, and there I shall dwell with such company as I like best. For to tell you truth, I love him, because I was by him eased of my burden, and I am weary of my inward sickness; I would fain be where I shall die no

Christian distasted with carnal cogitations

Christian's choice

Christian's golden hours

How Christian gets power against his corruptions

Why Christian would be at Mount Sion

more, and with the company that shall continually
cry, *Holy, Holy, Holy.*

Charity discourses him

Then said Charity to Christian, 'Have you a family? Are you a married man?'

Christian. I have a wife and four small children.[46]

Charity. And why did you not bring them along with you?

Christian's love to his wife and children

Christian. Then Christian wept, and said, Oh how willingly would I have done it, but they were all of them utterly averse to my going on pilgrimage.

Charity. But you should have talked to them, and have endeavoured to have shown them the danger of being behind.

Christian. So I did, and told them also what God had showed to me of the destruction of our City; but I seemed to them as one that mocked, and they believed me not.

Charity. And did you pray to God that he would bless your counsel to them?

Christian. Yes, and that with much affection; for you must think that my wife and poor children were very dear unto me.

Charity. But did you tell them of your own sorrow and fear of destruction? For I suppose that destruction was visible enough to you?

Christian's fears of perishing might be read in his very countenance

Christian. Yes, over and over and over. They might also see my fears in my countenance, in my tears, and also in my trembling under the apprehension of the judgement that did hang over our heads; but all was not sufficient to prevail with them to come with me.

Charity. But what could they say for themselves why they came not?

The cause why his wife and children did not go with him

Christian. Why, my wife was afraid of losing this world, and my children were given to the foolish delights of youth: so what by one thing, and what by

96

another, they left me to wander in this manner alone.

Charity. But did you not with your vain life, damp all that you by words used by way of persuasion to bring them away with you?

Christian. Indeed I cannot commend my life; for I am conscious to myself of many failings: therein, I know also that a man by his conversation, may soon overthrow what by argument or persuasion he doth labour to fasten upon others for their good. Yet, this I can say, I was very wary of giving them occasion, by any unseemly action, to make them averse to going on pilgrimage. Yea, for this very thing, they would tell me I was too precise, and that I denied myself of things (for their sakes) in which they saw no evil. Nay, I think I may say, that, if what they saw in me did hinder them, it was my great tenderness in sinning against God, or of doing any wrong to my neighbour. *Christian's good conversation before his wife and children*

Charity. Indeed Cain hated his brother, because his own works were evil, and his brother's righteous; and if thy wife and children have been offended with thee for this they thereby show themselves to be implacable to good; and thou hast delivered thy soul from their blood. *Christian clear of their blood if they perish*

Now I saw in my dream that thus they sat talking together until supper was ready. So when they had made ready they sat down to meat. Now the table was furnished with fat things and with wine that was well refined, and all their talk at the table was about the Lord of the Hill; as namely about what he had done, and wherefore he did what he did, and why he had builded that House; and by what they said I perceived that he had been a great warrior, and had fought with and slain him that had the power of death, but not without great danger to himself, which made me love him the more. *What Christian had to his supper. Their talk at supper-time*

For, as they said, and as I believe (said Christian), he did it with the loss of much blood; but that which put glory of grace into all he did was, that he did it of pure love to his country. And besides, there were some of them of the household that said they had seen, and spoke with him since he did die on the Cross; and they have attested that they had it from his own lips, that he is such a lover of poor pilgrims that the like is not to be found from the east to the west.

They moreover gave an instance of what they affirmed, and that was: he had stripped himself of his glory that he might do this for the poor; and that they heard him say and affirm that he would not dwell in the Mountain of Sion alone. They said *Christ makes* moreover that he had made many pilgrims princes *princes of* though by nature they were beggars born, and their *beggars* original had been the dunghill.

Thus they discoursed together till late at night; and after they had committed themselves to their Lord for protection, they betook themselves to rest. *Christian's* The pilgrim they laid in a large upper chamber, *bed-chamber* whose window opened towards the sun rising; the name of the chamber was <u>Peace</u>, where he slept till break of day; and then he awoke and sang,

> *Where am I now? Is this the love and care*
> *Of Jesus, for the men that pilgrims are?*
> *Thus to provide ! That I should be forgiven !*
> *And dwell already the <u>next door to Heaven.</u>*

So in the morning they all got up, and after some more discourse they told him that he should not *Christian* depart, till they had showed him the rarities of that *had into the* place. And first they had him into the <u>study</u> where *study, and* *what he saw* they showed him records of the greatest antiquity; *there* in which, as I remember my dream, they showed him first the pedigree of the Lord of the Hill, that he was the Son of the Ancient of Days, and came by an eternal generation. Here also was more fully recorded the acts that he had done, and the names of many hundreds that he had taken into his service; and how he had placed them in such habitations that could neither by length of days, nor decays of nature, be dissolved.

Then they read to him some of the worthy acts that some of his servants had done, as how they had subdued kingdoms, wrought righteousness, obtained promises, stopped the mouths of lions, quenched the violence of fire, escaped the edge of the sword, out of weakness were made strong, waxed valiant in fight, and turned to flight the armies of the aliens.

Then they read again in another part of the records of the House where it was showed how willing their Lord was to receive into his favour any, even any, though they in time past had offered great affronts to his person and proceedings. Here also were several other histories of many other famous things; of all which Christian had a view, as of things both ancient and modern, together with prophecies and predictions of things that have their certain accomplishment, both to the dread and amazement of enemies, and the comfort and solace of pilgrims.

The next day they took him, and had him into the armoury,[47] where they showed him all manner of furniture, which their Lord had provided for pilgrims, as sword, shield, helmet, breastplate, All-Prayer, and shoes that would not wear out. And there was here enough of this, to harness out as many men for the service of their Lord as there be stars in the heaven for multitude.

military metaphor

Christian had into the armoury

They also showed him some of the engines with which some of his servants had done wonderful

Christian is made to see ancient things things. They showed him Moses' rod, the hammer and nail with which Jael slew Sisera, the pitchers, trumpets, and lamps too, with which Gideon put to flight the armies of Midian. Then they showed him the ox's goad wherewith Shamger slew six hundred men. They showed him also the jaw-bone with which Sampson did such mighty feats; they showed him moreover the sling and stone with which David slew Goliath of Gath: and the sword also with which their Lord will kill the man of sin, in the day that he shall rise up to the prey. They showed him besides many excellent things, with which Christian was much delighted. This done, they went to their rest again.

Then I saw in my dream, that on the morrow he got up to go forwards, but they desired him to stay till the next day also. 'And then,' said they, 'we will *Christian showed the Delectable Mountains* (if the day be clear) show you the <u>Delectable Mountains</u>,'[48] which they said would yet further add to his comfort, because they were nearer the desired haven than the place where at present he was. So he consented and stayed. When the morning was up they had him to the top of the House, and bid him look south; so he did, and behold, at a great distance he saw a most pleasant mountainous country, beautified with woods, vineyards, fruits of all sorts; flowers also, with springs and fountains, very delectable to behold. Then he asked the name of the country; they said it was <u>Immanuel's Land</u>: 'And it is as common,' said they, 'as this Hill is to and for all the pilgrims. And when thou comest there, from thence, thou mayest see to the <u>Gate of the Celestial City</u>, as the shepherds that live there will make appear.

Christian sets forward Now he bethought himself of setting forward, and they were willing he should: 'But first,' said they, 'let us go again into the armoury'; so they did; and when he came there, they harnessed him from head *Christian* to foot with what was of proof, lest perhaps he should *sent away* meet with assaults in the way. He being therefore *armed* thus accoutred walketh out with his friends to the gate, and there he asked the porter if he saw any pilgrims pass by; then the porter answered, 'Yes.'

Charity. Pray, did you know him?

Porter. I asked his name, and he told me it was Faithful.

Christian. O, said Christian, I know him, he is my townsman, my near neighbour, he comes from the place where I was born: how far do you think he may be before?

Porter. He is got by this time below the Hill.

Christian. Well, said Christian, good porter, the *How* Lord be with thee, and add to all thy blessings much *Christian* increase, for the kindness that thou hast showed to *and the porter* me. *greet at parting*

Then he began to go forward, but Discretion, Piety, Charity, and Prudence would accompany him down to the foot of the Hill. So they went on together, reiterating their former discourses till they came to go down the Hill. Then said Christian, 'As it was difficult coming up, so (so far as I can see) it is dangerous going down.' 'Yes,' said Prudence, 'so it is; for it is an hard matter for a man to go down into the Valley of Humiliation, as thou art now, and to catch no slip by the way; therefore,' said they, 'are we come out to accompany thee down the Hill.' So he began to go down, but very warily, yet he caught a slip or two.

Then I saw in my dream that these good companions (when Christian was gone down to the bottom of the Hill) gave him a loaf of bread, a bottle of wine, and a cluster of raisins; and then he went on his way.

Greek
destroyer

But now in this Valley of Humiliation poor Christian was hard put to it, for he had gone but a little way before he espied a foul fiend coming over the field to meet him; his name is Apollyon.[49] Then did Christian begin to be afraid, and to cast in his mind whether to go back, or to stand his ground. But he considered again that he had no armour for his back, and therefore thought that to turn the back to him might give him greater advantage with ease to pierce him with his darts; therefore he resolved to venture, *Christian's* and stand his ground. For, thought he, had I no more *resolution at* in mine eye, than the saving of my life, 'twould be *the approach* *of Apollyon* the best way to stand.

So he went on, and Apollyon met him; now the monster was hideous to behold, he was clothed with scales like a fish[50] (and they are his pride) he had wings *dragon* like a dragon, feet like a bear, and out of his belly came fire and smoke, and his mouth was as the mouth of a lion. When he was come up to Christian he beheld him with a disdainful countenance and thus began to question with him.

Apollyon. Whence come you, and whither are you bound?

Christian. I come from the City of Destruction, *Discourse* which is the place of all evil, and am going to the *betwixt* City of Sion. *Christian* *and Apollyon* *Apollyon.* By this I perceive thou art one of my subjects, for all that country is mine; and I am the prince and god of it. How is it then that thou hast ran away from thy king? Were it not that I hope thou mayest do me more service, I would strike thee now at one blow to the ground.

Christian. I was born indeed in your dominions, but your service was hard, and your wages such as a man could not live on, *for the wages of sin is death*; therefore when I was come to years, I did as other considerate persons do, look out if perhaps I might mend myself.

Apollyon. There is no prince that will thus lightly lose his subjects, neither will I as yet lose thee. But since thou complainest of thy service and wages, be content to go back; what our country will afford I do here promise to give thee.

Apollyon's flattery

Christian. But I have let myself to another, even to the King of Princes, and how can I with fairness go back with thee?

Apollyon. Thou hast done in this, according to the proverb, changed a bad for a worse: but it is ordinary for those that have professed themselves his servants, after a while to give him the slip; and return again to me: do thou so too, and all shall be well.

Apollyon undervalues Christ's service

Christian. I have given him my faith, and sworn my allegiance to him; how then can I go back from this, and not be hanged as a traitor?

Apollyon. Thou didst the same to me and yet I am willing to pass by all, if now thou wilt yet turn again, and go back.

Apollyon pretends to be merciful

Christian. What I promised thee was in my none-age; and besides, I count that the Prince under whose banner now I stand is able to absolve me; yea, and to pardon also what I did as to my compliance with thee: and besides (O thou destroying Apollyon), to speak truth, I like his service, his wages, his servants, his government, his company, and country better than thine: and therefore leave off to persuade me further, <u>I am his servant, and I will follow him.</u>

Apollyon. Consider again when thou art in cool blood what thou art like to meet with in the way that thou goest. Thou knowest that for the most part his servants come to an ill end, because they are transgressors against me and my ways: how many of them have been put to shameful deaths! And

Apollyon pleads the grievous ends of Christians, to dissuade Christian from persisting in his way

besides, thou countest his service better than mine, whereas he never came yet from the place where he is, to deliver any that served him out of our hands; but as for me, how many times, as all the world very well knows, have I delivered, either by power or fraud, those that have faithfully served me, from him and his, though taken by them; and so I will deliver thee.

Christian. His forbearing at present to deliver them is on purpose to try their love, whether they will cleave to him to the end: and as for the ill end thou sayest they come to, that is most glorious in their account: for, for present deliverance, they do not much expect it; for they stay for their glory, and then they shall have it, when their Prince comes in his, and the glory of the angels.

Apollyon. Thou hast already been unfaithful in thy service to him, and how dost thou think to receive wages of him?

Christian. Wherein, O Apollyon, have I been unfaithful to him?

Apollyon. Thou didst faint at first setting out, when thou wast almost choked in the Gulf of Despond. Thou didst attempt wrong ways to be rid of thy burden, whereas thou shouldest have stayed till thy Prince had taken it off. Thou didst sinfully sleep, and lose thy choice thing: thou wast also almost persuaded to go back at the sight of the lions; and when thou talkest of thy journey, and of what thou hast heard and seen, thou art inwardly desirous of vainglory in all that thou sayest or doest.

Apollyon pleads Christian's infirmities against him

Christian. All this is true, and much more, which thou hast left out; but the Prince whom I serve and honour is merciful and ready to forgive: but besides, these infirmities possessed me in thy country, for there I sucked them in, and I have groaned under them, been sorry for them, and have obtained pardon of my Prince.

Apollyon. Then Apollyon broke out into a grievous rage, saying, I am an enemy to this Prince: I hate his person, his laws, and people: I am come out on purpose to withstand thee.

Apollyon in a rage falls upon Christian

Christian. Apollyon, beware what you do, for I am in the King's highway, the way of holiness, therefore take heed to yourself.

Apollyon. Then Apollyon stroddled[51] quite over the whole breadth of the way, and said, I am void of fear in this matter, prepare thyself to die, for I swear by my infernal den that thou shalt go no further, here will I spill thy soul: and with that he threw a flaming dart at his breast; but Christian had a shield in his hand, with which he caught it, and so prevented the danger of that. Then did Christian draw, for he saw 'twas time to bestir him; and Apollyon as fast made at him, throwing darts as thick as hail by the which, notwithstanding all that Christian could do to avoid it, Apollyon wounded him in his head, his hand and foot; this made Christian give a little back: Apollyon therefore followed his work amain, and Christian again took courage, and resisted as manfully as he could. This sore combat lasted for above half a day, even till Christian was almost quite spent. For you must know, that Christian, by reason of his wounds, must needs grow weaker and weaker.

Christian wounded in his understanding, faith and conversation

Then Apollyon, espying his opportunity, began to gather up close to Christian, and wrestling with him, gave him a dreadful fall; and with that Christian's sword flew out of his hand. Then said Apollyon, 'I am sure of thee now,' and with that he had almost pressed him to death, so that Christian began to despair of life. But as God would have it, while Apollyon was fetching of his last blow thereby to

Apollyon casteth down to the ground Christian

Christian's make a full end of this good man, Christian nimbly
victory over reached out his hand for his sword, and caught it,
Apollyon saying '*Rejoice not against me, O mine enemy! when I
fall I shall arise,*' and with that gave him a deadly
thrust, which made him give back as one that had
received his mortal wound: Christian perceiving that,
made at him again, saying, '<u>*Nay, in all these things we
are more than conquerors through him that loved us.*</u>' And
with that Apollyon spread forth his dragon's wings,
and sped him away, that Christian saw him no more.

A brief In this combat no man can imagine, unless he had
relation of seen and heard as I did, what yelling, and hideous
the combat roaring Apollyon made all the time of the fight; he
by the spake like a dragon: and on the other side, what sighs
spectator and groans brast[52] from Christian's heart. I never saw
him all the while give so much as one pleasant look,
till he perceived he had wounded Apollyon with his
two-edged sword; then indeed he did smile, and
look upward, but 'twas the dreadfullest sight that
ever I saw.

Christian So when the battle was over, Christian said, 'I
gives God will here give thanks to him that hath delivered me
thanks for out of the mouth of the lion, to him that did help me
deliverance against Apollyon.' And so he did, saying,

> *Great Beelzebub, the captain of this fiend,*
> *Designed my ruin; therefore to this end*
> *He sent him harnessed out, and he with rage*
> *That hellish was did fiercely me engage;*
> *But blessed Michael helped me, and I*
> *By dint of sword did quickly make him fly;*
> *Therefore to him let me give lasting praise,*
> *And thank and bless his holy name always.*

Then there came to him an hand with some of the
leaves of the <u>Tree of Life</u>, the which Christian took,

and applied to the wounds that he had received in the battle, and was healed immediately. He also sat down in that place to eat bread, and to drink of the bottle that was given him a little before; so being refreshed, he addressed himself to his journey, with his sword drawn in his hand; for he said, I know not *Christian* but some other enemy may be at hand. But he met *goes on his* with no other affront from Apollyon quite through *his sword* this valley. *drawn in his*

Now at the end of this Valley, was another, called *hand* the Valley of the <u>Shadow of Death</u>, and Christian must needs go through it because the way to the Celestial City lay through the midst of it: now this Valley is a very solitary place. The prophet Jeremiah thus describes it, *A wilderness, a land of deserts, and of pits, a land of drought, and of the shadow of death, a land that no man* (but a Christian) *passeth through, and where no man dwelt.*

Now here Christian was worse put to it than in his fight with Apollyon, as by the sequel you shall see.

I saw then in my dream, that when Christian was got to the borders of the Shadow of Death there met him two men, children of them that brought up an *The children* evil report of the good land, making haste to go back: *of the spies*[53] to whom Christian spake as follows. *go back*

Christian. Whither are you going?

Men. They said, Back, back; and would have you to do so too, if either life or peace is prized by you.

Christian. Why? what's the matter? said Christian.

Men. Matter! said they; we were going that way as you are going, and went as far as we durst; and indeed we were almost past coming back, for had we gone a little further, we had not been here to bring the news to thee.

Christian. But what have you met with? said Christian.

Men. Why we were almost in the Valley of the Shadow of Death, but that by good hap we looked before us, and saw the danger before we came to it.

Christian. But what have you seen? said Christian.

Men. Seen! Why the Valley itself, which is as dark as pitch; we also saw there the hobgoblins, satyrs, and dragons of the pit: we heard also in that Valley a continual howling and yelling, as of a people under unutterable misery who there sat bound in affliction and irons: and over that Valley hangs the discouraging clouds of confusion; death also doth always spread his wings over it: in a word, it is every whit dreadful, being utterly without order.

Christian. Then said Christian, I perceive not yet, by what you have said, but that this is my way to the desired haven.

Men. Be it thy way, we will not choose it for ours. So they parted, and Christian went on his way, but still with his sword drawn in his hand, for fear lest he should be assaulted.

I saw then in my dream so far as this Valley reached, there was on the right hand a very deep ditch;[54] that ditch is it into which the blind have led the blind in all ages, and have both there miserably perished. Again, behold on the left hand there was a very dangerous quag,[55] into which, if even a good man falls he can find no bottom for his foot to stand on. Into that quag King David once did fall, and had no doubt therein been smothered, had not he that is able plucked him out.

The pathway was here also exceeding narrow, and therefore good Christian was the more put to it; for when he sought in the dark to shun the ditch on the one hand, he was ready to tip over into the mire[56] on the other; also when he sought to escape the mire, without great carefulness he would be ready to fall into the ditch. Thus he went on, and I heard him here sigh bitterly, for, besides the dangers mentioned above, the pathway was here so dark that oft times when he lift up his foot to set forward he knew not where, or upon what, he should set it next.

About the midst of this Valley, I perceived the mouth of Hell to be, and it stood also hard by the wayside. Now, thought Christian, what shall I do? And ever and anon the flame and smoke would come out in such abundance, with sparks and hideous noises (things that cared not for Christian's sword, as did Apollyon before) that he was forced to put up his sword, and betake himself to <u>another weapon called All-Prayer</u>: so he cried in my hearing, '*O Lord I beseech thee deliver my Soul.*' Thus he went on a great while, yet still the flames would be reaching towards him: also he heard doleful voices, and rushings too and fro, so that sometimes he thought he should be torn in pieces, or trodden down like mire in the streets. This frightful sight was seen, and these dreadful noises were heard by him, for several miles together: and coming to a place where he thought he heard a company of fiends coming forward to meet him, he stopped, and began to muse what he had best to do. Sometimes he had half a thought to go back. Then again he thought he might be halfway through the Valley; he remembered also how he had already vanquished many a danger: and that the danger of going back might be much more than for to go forward; so he resolved to go on. Yet the fiends seemed to come nearer and nearer, but when they were come even almost at him, he cried out with a most vehement voice, '<u>I will walk in the strength of the Lord God</u>'; so they gave back, and came no further.

Christian put to a stand, but for a while

One thing I would not let slip, I took notice that now poor Christian was so confounded that he did not know his own voice, and thus I perceived it: just when he was come over against the mouth of the burning pit, one of the wicked ones got behind him, and stepped up softly to him, and whisperingly suggested many grievous blasphemies to him[57] which *Christian* he verily thought had proceeded from his own mind. *made believe* This put Christian more to it than anything that he *that he spoke* met with before, even to think that he should now *blasphemies,* blaspheme him that he loved so much before; yet, *when 'twas* could he have helped it, he would not have done it: *Satan that* but he had not the discretion neither to stop his ears, *suggested them* nor to know from whence those blasphemies came. *into his mind*

When Christian had travelled in this disconsolate condition some considerable time, he thought he heard the voice of a man, as going before him, saying, '*Though I walk through the Valley of the Shadow of Death, I will fear none ill,*[58] *for thou art with me.*'

Then was he glad, and that for these reasons:

First, because he gathered from thence, that some who feared God were in this Valley as well as himself.

Secondly, for that he perceived God was with them, though in that dark and dismal state; and why not, thought he, with me, though by reason of the impediment that attends this place I cannot perceive it.

Thirdly, for that he hoped (could he overtake them) to have company by and by. So he went on, and called to him that was before; but he knew not what to answer, for that he also thought himself to be alone: and by and by, the day broke; then said *Christian* Christian, '*He hath turned the shadow of death into the* *glad at break* *morning.*' *of day*

Now morning being come he looked back, not of desire to return, but to see by the light of the day what hazards he had gone through in the dark. So he saw more perfectly the ditch that was on the one hand, and the quag that was on the other; also how narrow the way was which lay betwixt them both; also now he saw the <u>hobgoblins, and satyrs</u>,[59] and dragons of the pit, but all afar off; for after break of day they came not nigh; yet they were discovered to him, according to that which is written, *He discovereth deep things out of darkness, and bringeth out to light the shadow of death*.

Now was Christian much affected with his deliverance from all the dangers of his solitary way, which dangers, though he feared them more before, yet he saw them more clearly now, because the light of the day made them conspicuous to him; and about this time the sun was rising, and this was another mercy to Christian: for you must note, that though the first part of the Valley of the Shadow of Death was dangerous, yet this second part which he was yet to go, was, if possible, far more dangerous: for from the place where he now stood, even to the end of the Valley, the way was all along set so full of snares, traps, gins, and nets here, and so full of pits, pitfalls, deep holes, and shelvings down there, that had it now been dark, as it was when he came the first part of the way, had he had a thousand souls, they had in reason been cast away; but, as I said, just now the sun was rising. Then said he '*His candle shineth on my head, and by his light I go through darkness*.'

The second part of this valley very dangerous

In this light therefore he came to the end of the Valley. Now I saw in my dream that at the end of this Valley lay blood, bones, ashes, and mangled bodies of men, even of pilgrims that had gone this way formerly: and while I was musing what should be the reason, I espied a little before me a cave, where two giants, <u>Pope and Pagan</u>, dwelt in old time, by whose power and tyranny the men whose bones, blood, ashes, etc., lay there, were cruelly put to death. But by this place Christian went without much danger, whereat I somewhat wondered; but I have learnt since that Pagan has been dead many a day; and as for the other, though he be yet alive he is by reason of age, and also of the many shrewd brushes that he met with in his younger days, grown so crazy and stiff in his joints[60] that he can now do little more than sit in his cave's mouth, grinning at pilgrims as they go by, and biting his nails, because he cannot come at them.

Papal powers

So I saw that Christian went on his way, yet at the sight of the old man that sat in the mouth of the cave, he could not tell what to think, specially because he spake to him, though he could not go after him, saying, 'You will never mend till more of you be burned': but he held his peace, and set a good face on't, and so went by, and catched no hurt. Then sang Christian,

> *O world of wonders! (I can say no less)*
> *That I should be preserved in that distress*
> *That I have met with here! O blessed be*
> *That hand that from it hath delivered me!*
> *Dangers in darkness, devils, Hell, and sin,*
> *Did compass me, while I this Vale was in;*
> *Yea, snares, and pits, and traps, and nets did lie*
> *My path about, that worthless silly I*
> *Might have been catched, entangled, and cast down:*
> *But since I live let* JESUS *wear the Crown.*

Now as Christian went on his way he came to a little ascent, which was cast up on purpose that pilgrims might see before them: up there therefore Christian went, and looking forward he saw Faithful before him, upon his journey. Then said Christian aloud, 'Ho, ho, so-ho, stay, and I will be your companion.' At that Faithful looked behind him, to whom Christian cried again, 'Stay, stay, till I come up to you'; but Faithful answered, 'No, I am upon my life, and the avenger of blood[61] is behind me.' At this Christian was somewhat moved, and putting to all his strength, he quickly got up with <u>Faithful</u>, and did also over-run him, so the last was first. Then did Christian vain-gloriously smile, because he had gotten the start of his brother: but not taking good heed to his feet, he suddenly stumbled and fell, and could not rise again, until Faithful came up to help him. *Christian overtakes Faithful*

Christian's fall makes Faithful and he go lovingly together

Then I saw in my dream they went very lovingly on together, and had sweet discourse of all things that had happened to them in their pilgrimage: and thus Christian began.

Christian. My honoured and well beloved brother Faithful, I am glad that I have overtaken you and that God has so tempered our spirits that we can walk as companions in this so pleasant a path.

Faithful. I had thought, dear friend, to have had your company quite from our town, but you did get the start of me; wherefore I was forced to come thus much of the way alone.

Christian. How long did you stay in the City of Destruction, before you set out after me on your pilgrimage?

Faithful. Till I could stay no longer; for there was great talk presently after you was gone out that our city would in short time with fire from Heaven be burned down to the ground.

Christian. What? Did your neighbours talk so?

Faithful. Yes, 'twas for a while in everybody's mouth. *Their talk about the country from whence they came*

Christian. What, and did no more of them but you come out to escape the danger?

Faithful. Though there was, as I said, a great talk thereabout, yet I do not think they did firmly believe it. For in the heat of the discourse I heard some of them deridingly speak of you, and of your desperate journey (for so they called this your pilgrimage), but I did believe, and do still, that the end of our City will be with fire and brimstone from above, and therefore I have made mine escape.

Christian. Did you hear no talk of neighbour Pliable?

Faithful. Yes, Christian, I heard that he followed you till he came at the <u>Slough of Despond</u>; where, as some said, he fell in, but he would not be known to have so done: but I am sure he was soundly be-dabbled with that kind of dirt.

Christian. And what said the neighbours to him?

How Pliable was accounted of when he got home *Faithful.* He hath since his going back been had greatly in derision, and that among all sorts of people: some do mock and despise him, and scarce will any set him on work. He is now seven times worse than if he had never gone out of the city.

Christian. But why should they be so set against him, since they also despise the way that he forsook?

Faithful. Oh, they say, 'Hang him; he is a turn-coat, he was not true to his profession.' I think God has stirred up even his enemies to hiss at him and make him a proverb, because he hath forsaken the way.

Christian. Had you no talk with him before you came out?

Faithful. I met him once in the streets, but he leered away[62] on the other side, as one ashamed of what he had done; so I spake not to him.

Christian. Well, at my first setting out, I had hopes of that man; but now I fear he will perish in the overthrow of the City, for it is happened to him

according to the true proverb, *The dog is turned to his* *The dog and*
vomit again, and the sow that was washed to her wallowing *sow*
in the mire.[63]

Faithful. They are my fears of him too: but who
can hinder that which will be?

Christian. Well, neighbour Faithful, said Christian,
let us leave him, and talk of things that more immediately concern ourselves. Tell me now, what you
have met with in the way as you came. For I know
you have met with some things, or else it may be
writ for a wonder.

Faithful. I escaped the Slough that I perceive you
fell into, and got up to the Gate without that danger;
only I met with one whose name was <u>Wanton</u>, that *Faithful*
had like to have done me a mischief. *assaulted by*
Wanton

Christian. 'Twas well you escaped her net: Joseph
was hard put to it by her,[64] and he escaped her as you
did, but it had like to have cost him his life. But what
did she do to you?

Faithful. You cannot think (but that you know
something) what a flattering tongue she had; she lay
at me hard to turn aside with her, promising me all
manner of content.

Christian. Nay, she did not promise you the content
of a good conscience.

Faithful. You know what I mean, all carnal and
fleshly content.

Christian. Thank God you have escaped her: the
abhorred of the Lord shall fall into her ditch.

Faithful. Nay, I know not whether I did wholly
escape her, or no.

Christian. Why, I trow you did not consent to her
desires?

Faithful. No, not to defile myself; for I remembered
an old writing that I had seen which saith, *Her steps*
take hold of Hell. So I shut mine eyes, because I

would not be bewitched with her looks: then she railed on me, and I went my way.

Christian. Did you meet with no other assault as you came?

Faithful. When I came to the foot of the Hill called Difficulty, I met with a very aged man, who asked me what I was, and whither bound? I told him that I was a pilgrim, going to the Celestial City. Then said the old man, 'Thou lookest like an honest fellow; wilt thou be content to dwell with me, for the wages that I shall give thee?' Then I asked him his name, and where he dwelt. He said his name was 'Adam the First,[65] and I dwell in the town of Deceit.' I asked him then, What was his work? And what the wages that he would give? He told me, That his work was many delights and his wages, that I should be his heir at last. I further asked him what house he kept, and what other servants he had. So he told me that his house was maintained with all the dainties in the world, and that his servants were those of his own begetting. Then I asked how many children he had; he said, that he had but three daughters, The Lust of the Flesh, The Lust of the Eyes, and The Pride of Life, and that I should marry them all if I would. Then I asked how long time he would have me live with him. And he told me, as long as he lived himself.

Christian. Well, and what conclusion came the old man and you to at last?

Faithful. Why, at first I found myself somewhat inclinable to go with the man, for I thought he spake very fair; but looking in his forehead as I talked with him I saw there written, 'Put off the old man with his deeds.'

Christian. And how then?

Faithful. Then it came burning hot into my mind, whatever he said and however he flattered when he got me home to his house he would sell me for a slave. So I bid him forbear to talk, for I would not come near the door of his house. Then he reviled me, and told me that he would send such a one after me, that should make my way bitter to my soul. So I turned to go away from him: but just as I turned myself to go thence, I felt him take hold of my flesh, and give me such a deadly twitch back that I thought he had pulled part of me after himself. This made me cry, 'O wretched Man!' So I went on my way up the Hill.

Now when I had got about half way up, I looked behind me, and saw one coming after me, swift as the wind; so he overtook me just about the place where the settle stands.

Christian. Just there, said Christian, did I sit down to rest me; but being overcome with sleep I there lost this roll out of my bosom.

Faithful. But good brother, hear me out: so soon as the man overtook me, he was but a word and a blow: for down he knocked me and laid me for dead. But when I was a little come to myself again, I asked him wherefore he served me so. He said, 'Because of my secret inclining to Adam the First'; and with that he struck me another deadly blow on the breast, and beat me down backward; so I lay at his foot as dead as before. So when I came to myself again, I cried him mercy; but he said, 'I know not how to show mercy', and with that knocked me down again. He had doubtless made an end of me, but that one came by and bid him forbear.

Christian. Who was that, that bid him forbear?

Faithful. I did not know him at first, but as he went by, I perceived the holes in his hands, and his side; then I concluded that he was our Lord. So I went up the Hill.

The temper *Christian.* That man that overtook you was <u>Moses</u>,
of Moses he spareth none, neither knoweth he how to show
mercy to those that transgress his law.

Faithful. I know it very well, it was not the first
time that he has met with me. 'Twas he that came to
me when I dwelt securely at home, and that told me
he would burn my house over my head, if I stayed
there.

Christian. But did not you see the House that stood
there on the top of that Hill on the side of which
Moses met you?

Faithful. Yes, and the lions too, before I came at it;
but for the lions, I think they were asleep, for it was
about noon; and because I had so much of the day
before me I passed by the porter, and came down the
Hill.

Christian. He told me indeed that he saw you go by,
but I wish you had called at the House; for they would
have showed you so many rarities, that you would
scarce have forgot them to the day of your death.
But pray tell me, did you meet nobody in the <u>Valley
of Humility</u>?

Faithful *Faithful.* Yes, I met with one <u>Discontent</u>, who
assaulted by would willingly have persuaded me to go back
Discontent again with him: his reason was, for that the Valley
was altogether without honour; he told me more-
over, that there to go, was the way to disobey all
my friends, as <u>Pride, Arrogancy, Self-conceit,
Worldly-Glory</u>, with others, who he knew, as he
said, would be very much offended, if I made such a
fool of myself, as to wade through this Valley.

Christian. Well, and how did you answer him?

Faithful's *Faithful.* I told him that although all these that he
answer to named might claim kindred of me, and that rightly
Discontent (for indeed they were my relations, according to the
flesh), yet since I became a pilgrim they have dis-

owned me, as I also have rejected them; and therefore they were to me now no more than if they had never been of my lineage; I told him moreover that as to this Valley, he had quite misrepresented the thing: *for before honour is humility, and a haughty spirit before a fall.* 'Therefore,' said I, 'I had rather go through this Valley to the honour that was so accounted by the wisest, than choose that which he esteemed most worth our affections.'

Christian. Met you with nothing else in that Valley?

Faithful. Yes, I met with Shame, but of all the men that I met with in my pilgrimage, he, I think, bears the wrong name: the other would be said nay after a little argumentation (and somewhat else) but this bold-faced Shame would never have done.

He is assaulted with Shame

Christian. Why, what did he say to you?

Faithful. What! Why he objected against religion itself; he said it was a pitiful, low, sneaking business for a man to mind religion; he said that a tender conscience was an unmanly thing, and that for man to watch over his words and ways, so as to tie up himself from that hectoring liberty that the brave spirits of the times accustom themselves unto would make him the ridicule of the times. He objected also that but few of the mighty, rich, or wise, were ever of my opinion; nor any of them neither, before they were persuaded to be fools, and to be of a voluntary fondness, to venture the loss of all, for nobody else knows what. He moreover objected the base and low estate and condition of those that were chiefly the pilgrims; also their ignorance of the times in which they lived, and want of understanding in all natural science.[66] Yea, he did hold me to it at that rate also about a great many more things than here I relate; as, that it was a shame to sit whining and mourning under a sermon, and a shame to come sighing and groaning home. That it was a shame to ask my neighbour forgiveness for petty faults, or to make restitution where I had taken from any: he said also that religion made a man grow strange to the great, because of a few vices (which he called by finer names) and made him own and respect the base, because of the same religious fraternity. And is not this, said he, a shame?

Christian. And what did you say to him?

Faithful. Say! I could not tell what to say at the first. Yea, he put me so to it, that my blood came up in my face, even this Shame fetched it up, and had almost beat me quite off. But at last I began to consider, that *that which is highly esteemed among men, is had in abomination with God.* And I thought again, this Shame tells me what men are, but it tells me nothing what God or the Word of God is. And I thought moreover, that at the day of doom we shall not be doomed to death or life, according to the hectoring spirits of the world, but according to the wisdom and law of the Highest. Therefore thought I, what God says is best, though all the men in the world are against it. Seeing then that God prefers his religion, seeing God prefers a tender conscience, seeing they that make themselves fools for the Kingdom of Heaven are wisest; and that the poor man that loveth Christ is richer than the greatest man in the world that hates him, Shame, depart, thou art an enemy to my salvation: shall I entertain thee against my sovereign Lord? How then shall I look him in the face at his coming? Should I now be ashamed of his ways and servants, how can I expect the blessing? But indeed this Shame was a bold villain; I could scarce shake him out of my company; yea, he would be haunting of me, and continually whispering me in the ear, with some one or other of the infirmities that attend religion: but at last I told him, 'twas but in vain to attempt further in this business; for those things that he disdained, in those did I see most glory: and so at last I got past this importunate one.

And when I had shaken him off, then I began to sing.

> The trials that those men do meet withal
> That are obedient to the heavenly call,
> Are manifold and suited to the flesh,
> And come, and come, and come again afresh;
> That now, or sometime else, we by them may
> Be taken, overcome, and cast away.
> O let the pilgrims, let the pilgrims then
> Be vigilant, and quit themselves like men.

Christian. I am glad, my brother, that thou didst withstand this villain so bravely; for of all, as thou sayest, I think he has the wrong name: for he is so bold as to follow us in the streets, and to attempt to put us to shame before all men; that is, to make us ashamed of that which is good; but if he was not himself audacious, he would never attempt to do as he does, but let us still resist him: for notwithstanding all his bravadoes, he promoteth the fool, and none else. *The wise shall inherit glory,*[67] said Solomon, *but shame shall be the promotion of fools*.

Faithful. I think we must cry to him for help against shame, that would have us be valiant for truth upon the earth.

Christian. You say true. But did you meet nobody else in that Valley?

Faithful. No not I, for I had sunshine all the rest of the way, through that, and also through the Valley of the Shadow of Death.

Christian. 'Twas well for you; I am sure it fared far otherwise with me. I had for a long season, as soon almost as I entered into that Valley, a dreadful combat with that foul fiend Apollyon. Yea, I thought verily he would have killed me; especially when he got me down, and crushed me under him as if he would have crushed me to pieces. For as he threw me, my sword flew out of my hand; nay he told me he was sure of me, but I cried to God, and he heard me, and delivered me out of all my troubles. Then I entered into the Valley of the Shadow of Death and had no light for almost half the way through it. I thought I should a been killed there, over, and over: but at last, day brake, and the sun rise, and I went through that which was behind with far more ease and quiet.

Moreover I saw in my dream, that as they went on, Faithful, as he chanced to look on one side, saw a man whose name is Talkative,[68] walking at a distance besides them (for in this place there was room enough *Talkative* for them all to walk). He was a tall man, and some- *described* thing more comely at a distance than at hand. To this man, Faithful addressed himself in this manner.

Faithful. Friend, whither away? Are you going to the Heavenly Country?

Talkative. I am going to that same place.

Faithful. That is well: then I hope we may have your good company.

Talkative. With a very good will, will I be your companion.

Faithful and *Faithful.* Come on then, and let us go together, and *Talkative* let us spend our time in discoursing of things that are *enter* *discourse* profitable.

Talkative. To talk of things that are good to me is very acceptable, with you or with any other; and I am glad that I have met with those that incline to so good a work. For to speak the truth, there are but few that care thus to spend their time (as they are in their travels) but choose much rather to be speaking *Talkative's* of things to no profit, and this hath been a trouble *dislike of bad* to me. *discourse*

Faithful. That is indeed a thing to be lamented; for what things so worthy of the use of the tongue and mouth of men on earth, as are the things of the God of Heaven?

Talkative. I like you wonderful well, for your saying is full of conviction; and I will add, what thing so pleasant, and what so profitable, as to talk of the things of God?

What things so pleasant, that is, if a man hath any delight in things that are wonderful, for instance, if a man doth delight to talk of the history or the mystery of things; or if a man doth love to talk of miracles, wonders, or signs, where shall he find things recorded so delightful, and so sweetly penned, as in the holy Scripture?

Faithful. That's true: but to be profited by such things in our talk should be that which we design.

Talkative. That is it that I said; for to talk of such things is most profitable, for by so doing, a man may get knowledge of many things; as of the vanity of earthly things, and the benefit of things above: thus in general, but more particularly, by this a man may learn the necessity of the new birth, the insufficiency of our works, the need of Christ's righteousness, etc. *Talkative's* Besides, by this a man may learn by talk, what it is *fine discourse* to repent, to believe, to pray, to suffer, or the like: by this also a man may learn what are the great promises and consolations of the Gospel, to his own comfort. Further, by this a man may learn to refute false opinions, to vindicate the truth, and also to instruct the ignorant.

Faithful. All this is true, and glad am I to hear these things from you.

Talkative. Alas! the want of this is the cause that so few understand the need of faith, and the necessity of a work of grace in their soul, in order to eternal life, but ignorantly live in the works of the law, by which a man can by no means obtain the Kingdom of Heaven.

Faithful. But by your leave, heavenly knowledge of these is the gift of God; no man attaineth to them by human industry, or only by the talk of them.

Talkative. All this I know very well. For a man can receive nothing except it be given him from *O brave* Heaven; all is of grace, not of works: I could give *Talkative* you an hundred scriptures for the confirmation of this.

Faithful. Well then, said Faithful; what is that one thing that we shall at this time found our discourse upon?

O brave *Talkative.* What you will: I will talk of things *Talkative* heavenly, or things earthly; things moral, or things evangelical; things sacred, or things profane; things past, or things to come; things foreign, or things at home; things more essential, or things circumstantial, provided that all be done to our profit.

Faithful *Faithful.* Now did Faithful begin to wonder; and *beguiled by* stepping to Christian (for he walked all this while *Talkative* by himself), he said to him (but softly), What a brave companion have we got! Surely this man will make *Christian* a very excellent pilgrim.

makes a *discovery of* *Christian.* At this Christian modestly smiled, and *Talkative,* said, This man with whom you are so taken will *telling* beguile with this tongue of his twenty of them that *Faithful* *who he was* know him not.

Faithful. Do you know him then?

Christian. Know him! Yes, better than he knows himself.

Faithful. Pray what is he?

Christian. His name is <u>Talkative</u>, he dwelleth in our town; I wonder that you should be a stranger to him, only I consider that our town is large.

Faithful. Whose son is he? And whereabout doth he dwell?

Christian. He is the son of one <u>Saywell,</u> he dwelt in <u>Prating-row</u>; and he is known of all that are acquaint-<u>ed with him</u>, by the name of Talkative in Prating-row, and notwithstanding his fine tongue, he is but a sorry fellow.

Faithful. Well, he seems to be a very pretty man.

Christian. That is, to them that have not thorough acquaintance with him, for he is best abroad; near home he is ugly enough: your saying, that he is a pretty man, brings to my mind what I have observed in the work of the painter whose pictures shows best at a distance, but very near, more unpleasing.

Faithful. But I am ready to think you do but jest, because you smiled.

Christian. God forbid that I should jest (though I smiled), in this matter, or that I should accuse any falsely; I will give you a further discovery of him: this man is for any company, and for any talk; as he talketh now with you, so will he talk when he is on the ale-bench; and the more drink he hath in his crown, the more of these things he hath in his mouth: religion hath no place in his heart, or house, or conversation; all he hath lieth in his tongue, and his religion is to make a noise therewith.

Faithful. Say you so! Then I am in this man greatly deceived.

Christian. Deceived? you may be sure of it. Re-

Talkative talks, but does not member the proverb, *They say and do not: but the Kingdom of God is not in word, but in power*. He talketh of prayer, of repentance, of faith, and of the new birth: but he knows but only to *talk* of them. I have been in his family, and have observed him both at home and abroad; and I know what I say of him is the truth. His house is as empty of religion, as the white of an egg is of savour. There is there neither prayer nor sign of repentance for sin: yea, the brute in his kind serves God far better than he.

His house is empty of religion

He is a stain to religion He is the very stain, reproach, and shame of religion to all that know him; it can hardly have a good word in all that end of the town where he dwells, through him. Thus say the common people that know him,

The proverb that goes of him A saint abroad and a devil at home. His poor family finds it so, he is such a churl, such a railer at, and so unreasonable with his servants, that they neither know how to do for or speak to him. Men that have any

Men shun to deal with him dealings with him, say 'tis better to deal with a Turk than with him, for fairer dealing they shall have at their hands. This Talkative, if it be possible, will go beyond them, defraud, beguile, and overreach them. Besides, he brings up his sons to follow his steps; and if he findeth in any of them a foolish timorousness (for so he calls the first appearance of a tender conscience), he calls them fools and blockheads, and by no means will employ them in much, or speak to their commendations before others. For my part I am of opinion that he has, by his wicked life, caused many to stumble and fall; and will be, if God prevent not, the ruin of many more.

Faithful. Well, my brother, I am bound to believe you; not only because you say you know him, but also because like a Christian, you make your reports of men. For I cannot think that you speak these things of ill will, but because it is even so as you say.

Christian. Had I known him no more than you, I might perhaps have thought of him as at the first you did. Yea, had he received this report, at their hands only, that are enemies to religion, I should have thought it had been a slander, a lot that often falls from bad men's mouths upon good men's names and professions. But all these things, yea, and a great many more as bad, of my own knowledge I can prove him guilty of. Besides, good men are ashamed of him, they can neither call him brother nor friend: the very naming of him among them, makes them blush, if they know him.

Faithful. Well, I see that saying and doing are two things, and hereafter I shall better observe this distinction.

Christian. They are two things indeed, and are as diverse as are the soul and the body: for as the body *The carcass* without the soul is but a dead carcass; so, saying, if *of religion* it be alone, is but a dead carcass also. The soul of religion is the practic part: *pure religion and undefiled, before God and the Father, is this, to visit the fatherless and widows in their affliction, and to keep himself unspotted from the world.*[69] This Talkative is not aware of, he thinks that hearing and saying will make a good Christian and thus he deceiveth his own soul. Hearing is but as the sowing of the seed; talking is not sufficient to prove that fruit is indeed in the heart and life; and let us assure ourselves, that at the day of doom, men shall be judged according to their fruits. It will not be said then, 'Did you believe?' but, 'Were you *doers,* or *talkers* only?' and accordingly shall they be judged. The end of the world is compared to our harvest, and you know men at harvest regard nothing but fruit. Not that anything can be accepted that is not of faith: but I speak this to show you how insignificant the profession of Talkative will be at that day.

Faithful. This brings to my mind that of Moses, by which he describeth the beast that is clean. He is such an one that parteth the hoof, and cheweth the cud; not that parteth the hoof only, or that cheweth the cud only. The hare cheweth the cud, but yet is unclean, because he parteth not the hoof. And this truly resembleth Talkative; he cheweth the cud, he seeketh knowledge, he cheweth upon the Word, but he divideth not the hoof, he parteth not with the way of sinners; but as the hare he retaineth the foot of a dog, or bear, and therefore he is unclean.

Christian. You have spoken, for aught I know, the true Gospel sense of those texts; and I will add another thing. Paul calleth some men, yea, and those great talkers too, *sounding brass, and tinkling cymbals;*[70] that is, as he expounds them in another place, *Things without life, giving sound.* Things without life, that is, without the true faith and grace of the Gospel; and consequently, things that shall never be placed in the Kingdom of Heaven among those that are the children of life, though their sound by their talk, be as if it were the tongue, or voice of an angel.

Faithful. Well, I was not so fond of his company at first, but I am as sick of it now. What shall we do to be rid of him?

Christian. Take my advice, and do as I bid you, and you shall find that he will soon be sick of your company too, except God shall touch his heart and turn it.

Faithful. What would you have me to do?

Christian. Why, go to him, and enter into some serious discourse about the power of religion; and ask him plainly (when he has approved of it, for that he will) whether this thing be set up in his heart, house, or conversation.

Faithful. Then Faithful stepped forward again and said to Talkative, Come, what cheer? how is it now?

Margin notes:
- *Faithful convinced of the badness of Talkative*
- *Talkative, like to things that sound without life*

Talkative. Thank you, well. I thought we should have had a great deal of talk by this time.

Faithful. Well, if you will, we will fall to it now; and since you left it with me to state the question, let it be this: how doth the saving grace of God discover itself, when it is in the heart of man?

Talkative. I perceive then that our talk must be about the power of things; well, 'tis a very good question, and I shall be willing to answer you. And take my answer in brief thus: first, where the grace of God is in the heart, it causeth there a great outcry against sin. Secondly –

Talkative's false discovery of a work of grace

Faithful. Nay, hold, let us consider of one at once: I think you should rather say, it shows itself by inclining the soul to abhor its sin.

Talkative. Why, what difference is there between crying out against and abhorring of sin?

Faithful. Oh! a great deal; a man may cry out against sin, of policy; but he cannot abhor it but by virtue of a godly antipathy against it. I have heard many cry out against sin in the pulpit, who yet can abide it well enough in the heart, and house, and conversation. Joseph's mistress cried out with a loud voice, as if she had been very holy; but she would willingly, notwithstanding that, have committed uncleanness with him. Some cry out against sin even as the mother cries out against her child in her lap, when she calleth it slut and naughty girl, and then falls to hugging and kissing it.

To cry out against sin, no sign of Grace

Talkative. You lie at the catch,[71] I perceive.

Faithful. No, not I, I am only for setting things right. But what is the second thing whereby you would prove a discovery of a work of grace in the heart?

Talkative. Great knowledge of Gospel mysteries.

Faithful. This sign should have been first, but first

Great knowledge no sign of grace or last it is also false; knowledge, great knowledge may be obtained in the mysteries of the Gospel, and yet no work of grace in the soul. Yea, if a man have all knowledge, he may yet be nothing, and so consequently be no child of God. When Christ said, 'Do you know all these things?' And the disciples had answered, 'Yes', he addeth, 'Blessed are ye if ye do them.' He doth not lay the blessing in the knowing of them, but in the doing of them. For there is a knowledge that is not attended with doing: he that knoweth his master's will and doth it not. A man may know like an angel and yet be no Christian: therefore your sign is not true. Indeed to know is a thing that pleaseth talkers and boasters, but to do is that which pleaseth God. Not that the heart can be good without knowledge; for without that the heart is naught: there is therefore knowledge, and know-

Knowledge and knowledge ledge. Knowledge that resteth in the bare speculation of things, and knowledge that is accompanied with the grace of faith and love, which puts a man upon doing even the will of God from the heart: the first

True knowledge attended with endeavours of these will serve the talker, but without the other the true Christian is not content. *Give me understanding, and I shall keep thy Law, yea, I shall observe it with my whole heart.*[72]

Talkative. You lie at the catch again, this is not for edification.

Faithful. Well, if you please propound another sign how this work of grace discovereth itself where it is.

Talkative. Not I, for I see we shall not agree.

Faithful. Well, if you will not, will you give me leave to do it?

Talkative. You may use your liberty.

One good sign of grace *Faithful.* A work of grace in the soul discovereth itself, either to him that hath it, or to standers-by.

To him that hath it, thus. It gives him conviction

of sin, especially of the defilement of his nature, and the sin of unbelief (for the sake of which he is sure to be damned, if he findeth not mercy at God's hand by faith in Jesus Christ). This sight and sense of things worketh in him sorrow and shame for sin; he findeth moreover revealed in him the Saviour of the World, and the absolute necessity of closing with him for life, at the which he findeth hungerings and thirstings after him, to which hungerings, etc. the promise is made. Now according to the strength or weakness of his faith in his Saviour, so is his joy and peace, so is his love to holiness, so are his desires to know him more, and also to serve him in this world. But though I say it discovereth itself thus unto him yet it is but seldom that he is able to conclude that this is a work of grace, because his corruptions now, and his abused reason makes his mind to misjudge in this matter; therefore in him that hath this work there is required a very sound judgement before he can with steadiness conclude that this is a work of grace.

To others it is thus discovered:

1. By an experimental confession of his faith in Christ. 2. By a life answerable to that confession, to wit, a life of holiness: heart-holiness, family-holiness (if he hath a family) and by conversation-holiness[73] in the world; which in the general teacheth him inwardly to abhor his sin and himself for that in secret, to suppress it in his family, and to promote holiness in the world; not by talk only, as an hypocrite or talkative person may do: but by a practical subjection in faith and love to the power of the Word. And now, sir, as to this brief description of the work of grace, and also the discovery of it, if you have aught to object, object: if not, then give me leave to propound to you a second question.

Another good sign of grace

Talkative. Nay, my part is not now to object, but to hear; let me therefore have your second question.

Faithful. It is this: do you experience the first part of this description of it? and doth your life and conversation testify the same? or standeth your religion in word, or in tongue, and not in deed and truth: pray, if you incline to answer me in this, say no more than you know the God above will say amen to; and also, nothing but what your conscience can justify you in. *For not he that commendeth himself is approved, but whom the Lord commendeth*. Besides, to say I am thus and thus when my conversation and all my neighbours tell me I lie, is great wickedness.

Talkative not pleased with Faithful's question

Talkative. Then Talkative at first began to blush, but recovering himself, thus he replied, You come now to experience, to conscience, and God; and to appeals to him for justification of what is spoken. This kind of discourse I did not expect, nor am I disposed to give an answer to such questions, because I count not myself bound thereto, unless you take upon you to be a catechizer; and, though you should so do, yet I may refuse to make you my judge: but I pray will you tell me why you ask me such questions?

Faithful. Because I saw you forward to talk, and because I knew not that you had aught else but notion. Besides, to tell you all the truth, I have heard of you that you are a man whose religion lies in talk, and that your conversation gives this your mouth-profession the lie. They say you are a spot among Christians, and that religion fareth the worse for your ungodly conversation, that some already have stumbled at your wicked ways, and that more are in danger of being destroyed thereby; your

The reasons why Faithful put to him that question

Faithful's plain dealing to Talkative

religion and an ale-house, and covetousness, and uncleanness, and swearing, and lying, and vain company-keeping, etc. will stand together. The proverb is true of you which is said of a whore; to wit, that she is a shame to all women; so you are a shame to all professors.

Talkative. Since you are ready to take up reports, and to judge so rashly as you do, I cannot but conclude you are some peevish, or melancholy man not fit to be discoursed with, and so adieu. *Talkative flings away from Faithful*

Christian. Then came up Christian and said to his brother, I told you how it would happen, your words and his lusts could not agree; he had rather leave your company than reform his life: but he is gone as I said; let him go; the loss is no man's but his own; he has saved us the trouble of going from him: for he continuing, as I suppose he will do, as he is, he would have been but a blot in our company: besides, the apostle says, *From such withdraw thyself.* *A good riddance*

Faithful. But I am glad we had this little discourse with him, it may happen that he will think of it again; however, I have dealt plainly with him; and so am clear of his blood if he perisheth.

Christian. You did well to talk so plainly to him as you did; there is but little of this faithful dealing with men nowadays, and that makes religion so stink in the nostrils of many, as it doth: for they are these talkative fools, whose religion is only in word, and are debauched and vain in their conversation, that being so much admitted into the fellowship of the godly do stumble the world, blemish Christianity, and grieve the sincere. I wish that all men would deal with such, as you have done, then should they either be made more conformable to religion, or the company of saints would be too hot for them. Then did Faithful say,

How Talkative at first lifts up his plumes!
How bravely doth he speak! how he presumes
To drive down all before him! but so soon
As Faithful talks of heart-work, like the moon
That's past the full, into the wane he goes;
And so will all, but he that heart-work knows.

Thus they went on talking of what they had seen by the way; and so made that way easy, which would otherwise, no doubt, have been tedious to them: for now they went through a wilderness.

Now when they were got almost quite out of this wilderness, Faithful chanced to cast his eye back, and espied one coming after them, and he knew him. 'Oh!' said Faithful to his brother, 'who comes yonder?' Then Christian looked, and said, 'It is my good friend Evangelist.' 'Ay, and my good friend too,' said Faithful; 'for 'twas he that set me the way to *Evangelist* the Gate.' Now was Evangelist come up unto them, *overtakes* and thus saluted them.
them again

Evangelist. Peace be with you, dearly beloved, and peace be to your helpers.

They are *Christian.* Welcome, welcome, my good Evangel-
glad at the ist, the sight of thy countenance brings to my
sight of him remembrance thy ancient kindness and unwearied labouring for my eternal good.

Faithful. And a thousand times welcome, said good Faithful; thy company, O sweet Evangelist, how desirable is it to us, poor pilgrims!

Evangelist. Then, said Evangelist, How hath it fared with you, my friends, since the time of our last parting? what have you met with, and how have you behaved yourselves?

Christian. Then Christian and Faithful told him of all things that had happened to them in the way; and how, and with what difficulty they had arrived to that place.

Evangelist. Right glad am I, said Evangelist; not that you met with trials, but that you have been victors; and for that you have, notwithstanding many weaknesses, continued in the way to this very day.

His exhortation to them

I say, right glad am I of this thing, and that for mine own sake and yours; I have sowed, and you have reaped, and the day is coming when both he that sowed, and they that reaped shall rejoice together; that is, if you hold out: for, in due time ye shall reap, if you faint not. The crown is before you, and it is an incorruptible one; so run that you may obtain it. Some there be that set out for this crown, and after they have gone far for it, another comes in and takes it from them; hold fast therefore that you have, let no man take your crown; you are not yet out of the gun-shot of the Devil: you have not resisted unto blood, striving against sin: let the Kingdom be always before you, and believe steadfastly concerning things that are invisible. Let nothing that is on this side the other world get within you; and above all, look well to your own hearts, and to the lusts thereof; for they are deceitful above all things, and desperately wicked: set your faces like a flint, you have all power in heaven and earth on your side.

Christian. Then Christian thanked him for his exhortation, but told him withal that they would have him speak further to them for their help the rest of the way; and the rather for that they well knew that he was a prophet, and could tell them of things that might happen unto them; and also how they might resist and overcome them. To which request Faithful also consented. So Evangelist began as followeth.

They do thank him for his exhortation

He predicteth what troubles they shall meet with in Vanity-Fair, and encourageth them to steadfastness

Evangelist. My sons, you have heard in the words

of the truth of the Gospel, that you must through many tribulations enter into the Kingdom of Heaven. And again, that in every city, bonds and afflictions abide in you; and therefore you cannot expect that you should go long on your pilgrimage without them, in some sort or other. You have found something of the truth of these testimonies upon you already, and more will immediately follow: for now, as you see, you are almost out of this wilderness, and therefore you will soon come into a town that you will by and by see before you, and in that town you will be hardly beset with enemies who will strain hard but they will kill you: and be you sure that one or both of you must seal the testimony which you hold, with blood: but be you faithful unto death, and *He whose lot* the King will give you a crown of life. He that *it will be there* shall die there, although his death will be unnatural, *to suffer, will* and his pain perhaps great, he will yet have the better *have the* of his fellow; not only because he will be arrived at *better of his* the Celestial City soonest, but because he will escape *brother* many miseries that the other will meet with in the rest of his journey. But when you are come to the town, and shall find fulfilled what I have here related, then remember your friend and quit yourselves like men; and commit the keeping of your souls to your God, as unto a faithful Creator.

Then I saw in my dream that when they were got out of the wilderness they presently saw a town before them, and the name of that town is Vanity; and at the town there is a fair kept called Vanity-Fair.[74] It is kept all the year long; it beareth the name of Vanity-Fair, because the town where 'tis kept is lighter than vanity; and also, because all that is there sold, or that cometh thither, is Vanity. As is the saying of the wise, *All that cometh is vanity*.

This Fair is no new erected business, but a thing

of ancient standing; I will show you the original of it.

Almost five thousand years agone, there were pilgrims walking to the Celestial City, as these two honest persons are; and Beelzebub, Apollyon, and Legion, with their companions, perceiving by the path that the Pilgrims made that their way to the City lay through this town of Vanity, they contrived here to set up a fair; a fair wherein should be sold of all sorts of vanity, and that it should last all the year long. Therefore at this Fair are all such merchandise sold, as houses, lands, trades, places, honours, preferments, titles, countries, kingdoms, lusts, pleasures, and delights of all sorts, as whores, bawds, wives, husbands, children, masters, servants, lives, blood, bodies, souls, silver, gold, pearls, precious stones, and what not. *The antiquity of this Fair* *The merchandise of this Fair*

And moreover, at this Fair there is at all times to be seen jugglings, cheats, games, plays, fools, apes, knaves, and rogues, and that of all sorts.

Here are to be seen too, and that for nothing, thefts, murders, adulteries, false-swearers, and that of a blood-red colour.

And as in other fairs of less moment there are the several rows and streets[75] under their proper names, where such and such wares are vended: so here likewise, you have the proper places, rows, streets (*viz.* countries and kingdoms), where the wares of this Fair are soonest to be found: here is the Britain Row, the French Row, the Italian Row, the Spanish Row, the German Row, where several sorts of vanities are to be sold. But as in other fairs, some one commodity is as the chief of all the fair, so the ware of Rome and her merchandise is greatly promoted in this Fair: only our English nation, with some others, have taken a dislike thereat. *The streets of this Fair*

Now, as I said, the way to the Celestial City lies just through this town, where this lusty Fair is kept; and he that will go to the City, and yet not go through this town, must needs go out of the world.

Christ went through this Fair The <u>Prince of Princes</u> himself, when here, went through this <u>Town</u> to his own country, and that upon a fair-day too. Yea, and as I think it was <u>Beelzebub, the chief lord of this Fair, that invited him to buy of his vanities</u>; yea, would have made him lord of the Fair, would he but have done him reverence as he went through the town. Yea, because he was such a person of honour, Beelzebub had him from street to street, and showed him all the kingdoms of the world in a little time, that he might if possible allure that Blessed One, to cheapen and *Christ bought nothing in this Fair* buy some of his vanities. But he had no mind to the merchandise, and therefore left the town without laying out so much as one farthing upon these vanities. This Fair therefore is an ancient thing, of long standing, and a very great Fair.

The pilgrims enter the Fair Now these pilgrims, as I said, must needs go through this Fair: well, so they did; but behold, even as they entered into the Fair, all the people in the Fair were *The Fair in a hubbub about them* moved, and the town itself as it were in a <u>hubbub</u> about them; and that for several reasons: for,

The first cause of the hubbub First, the pilgrims were clothed with such kind of raiment as was diverse from the raiment of any that traded in that Fair. The people therefore of the Fair made a great gazing upon them: Some said they were fools, some they were <u>bedlams</u>,[76] and some 'They are outlandish-men.' *lunatics*

The second cause of the hubbub Secondly, and as they wondered at their apparel so they did likewise at their speech; for few could understand what they said; they naturally spoke the <u>language of Canaan</u>;[77] but they that kept the Fair, were the men of this world: so that from one end of the Fair to the other, they seemed barbarians each to the other.

Thirdly, but that which did not a little amuse [bewilder] the merchandisers was that these pilgrims set very light by all their wares, they cared not so much as to look upon them; and if they called upon them to buy, they would put their fingers in their ears, and cry, *Turn away mine eyes from beholding vanity*; and look upwards, signifying that their trade and traffic was in Heaven.

Third cause of the hubbub

One chanced mockingly, beholding the carriages of the men, to say unto them, 'What will ye buy?' but they, looking gravely upon him, said, 'We buy the truth.' At that there was an occasion taken to despise the men the more; some mocking, some taunting, some speaking reproachfully, and some calling upon others to smite them. At last things came to an hubbub and great stir in the Fair; insomuch that all order was confounded. Now was word presently brought to the great one of the Fair, who quickly came down and deputed some of his most trusty friends to take these men into examination about whom the Fair was almost overturned. So the men were brought to examination; and they that sat upon them asked them whence they came, whither they went, and what they did there in such an unusual garb? The men told them that they were pilgrims and strangers in the world, and that they were going to their own country, which was the heavenly Jerusalem; and that they had given none occasion to the men of the town, nor yet to the merchandisers, thus to abuse them, and to let them in their journey, except it was for that when one asked them what they would buy, they said they would buy the truth. But they that were appointed to examine them did not believe them to be any other than bedlams and mad,

Fourth cause of the hubbub

They are mocked

The Fair in a hubbub

They are examined

They tell who they are and whence they came

They are not believed

or else such as came to put all things into a confusion in the Fair. Therefore they took them, and beat them, and besmeared them with dirt, and then put them *They are put* into the cage, that they might be made a spectacle to *in the cage* all the men of the Fair. There therefore they lay for some time, and were made the objects of any man's *Their* sport, or malice, or revenge, the great one of the *behaviour in* Fair laughing still at all that befell them. But the men *the cage* being patient, and not rendering railing for railing, but contrariwise blessing, and giving good words for *The men of* bad, and kindness for injuries done, some men in the *the Fair do* Fair that were more observing, and less prejudiced *fall out* than the rest, began to check and blame the baser sort *among* for their continual abuses done by them to the men. *themselves* *about these* They therefore in angry manner let fly at them again, *two men* counting them as bad as the men in the cage, and telling them that they seemed confederates, and should be made partakers of their misfortunes. The other replied that for aught they could see, the men were quiet, and sober, and intended nobody any harm; and that there were many that traded in their Fair that were more worthy to be put into the cage, yea, and pillory too, than were the men that they had abused. Thus, after divers words had passed on both sides (the men behaving themselves all the while very wisely and soberly before them), they fell to some blows among themselves and did harm one to *They are* another. Then were these two poor men brought *made the* before their examiners again, and there charged as *authors of* being guilty of the late hubbub that had been in the *this* *disturbance* Fair. So they beat them pitifully, and hanged irons *They are led* upon them, and led them in chains up and down the *up and down* Fair, for an example and a terror to others, lest any *the Fair in* should further speak in their behalf, or join them- *chains, for a* selves unto them. But Christian and Faithful behaved *terror to* themselves yet more wisely, and received the igno- *others* miny and shame that was cast upon them with so much meekness and patience, that it won to their side (though but few in comparison of the rest) several of the men in the Fair. This put the other party yet into a greater rage, insomuch that they concluded the death of these two men. Wherefore they threatened that the cage, nor irons, should serve their turn, but that they should die for the abuse they had done and for deluding the men of the Fair. *Some of the men of the Fair won to them* *Their adversaries resolve to kill them*

Then were they remanded to the cage again, until further order should be taken with them. So they put them in, and made their feet fast in the stocks. *They are again put into the cage and after brought to trial*

Here also they called again to mind what they had heard from their faithful friend Evangelist, and was the more confirmed in their way and sufferings by what he told them would happen to them. They also now comforted each other that whose lot it was to suffer, even he should have the best on't; therefore each man secretly wished that he might have that preferment: but committing themselves to the all-wise dispose of him that ruleth all things, with much content they abode in the condition in which they were, until they should be otherwise disposed of.

Then a convenient time being appointed, they brought them forth to their trial in order to their condemnation. When the time was come, they were brought before their enemies and arraigned; the Judge's name was Lord Hategood.[79] Their indictment was one and the same in substance, though somewhat varying in form; the contents whereof was this:

That they were enemies to, and disturbers of their trade; that they had made commotions and divisions in the town, and had won a party to their own most dangerous opinions, in contempt of the law of their prince. *Their indictment*

Then Faithful began to answer that he had only set himself against that which had set itself against *Faithful's answer for himself* him that is higher than the highest. 'And,' said he, 'as for disturbance, I make none, being myself a man of peace; the party that were won to us were won by beholding our truth and innocence, and they are only turned from the worse to the better. And as to the king you talk of; since he is Beelzebub, the enemy of our Lord, I defy him and all his angels.'

Then proclamation was made, that they that had aught to say for their lord the King against the prisoner at the bar, should forthwith appear, and give in their evidence. So there came in three witnesses, to wit, Envy, Superstition, and Pickthank.[80] flatter. They was then asked if they knew the prisoner at the bar and what they had to say for their lord the King against him.

Envy begins   Then stood forth Envy, and said to this effect: 'My lord, I have known this man a long time, and will attest upon my oath before this honourable bench, that he is –

Judge. Hold, give him his oath. So they sware him. Then he said, 'My lord, this man, notwithstanding his plausible name, is one of the vilest men in our country; he neither regardeth prince nor people, law nor custom, but doth all that he can to possess all men with certain of his disloyal notions, which he in the general calls principles of faith and holiness. And in particular, I heard him once myself affirm that Christianity, and the customs of our town of Vanity were diametrically opposite, and could not be reconciled. By which saying, my Lord, he doth at once not only condemn all our laudable doings, but us in the doing of them.'

Judge. Then did the Judge say to him, Hast thou any more to say?

Envy. My lord, I could say much more, only I would not be tedious to the court. Yet if need be, when the other gentlemen have given in their evidence, rather than anything shall be wanting that will dispatch him, I will enlarge my testimony against him. So he was bid stand by. Then they called Superstition, and bid him look upon the prisoner; they also asked what he could say for their lord the King against him. Then they sware him, so he began.

Superstition. My lord, I have no great acquaintance *Superstition* with this man, nor do I desire to have further know- *follows* ledge of him; however this I know, that he is a very pestilent fellow, from some discourse that the other day I had with him in this town; for then talking with him, I heard him say that our religion was naught, and such by which a man could by no means please God: which sayings of his, my lord, your lordship very well knows what necessarily thence will follow, to wit, that we still do worship in vain, are yet in our sins, and finally shall be damned; and this is that which I have to say.

Then was Pickthank sworn, and bid say what he knew, in behalf of their lord the King against the prisoner at the bar.

Pickthank. My lord, and you gentlemen all, this *Pickthank's* fellow I have known of a long time, and have heard *testimony* him speak things that ought not to be spoke. For he hath railed on our noble Prince Beelzebub, and hath spoke contemptibly of his honourable friends, whose *Sins are all* names are the Lord Old Man, the Lord Carnal *lords and* Delight, the Lord Luxurious, the Lord Desire of *great ones* Vain-glory, my old Lord Lechery, Sir Having-Greedy, with all the rest of our nobility; and he hath said moreover, that if all men were of his mind, if possible, there is not one of these noblemen should have any longer a being in this town. Besides, he hath not been afraid to rail on you, my lord, who are now appointed to be his judge, calling you an ungodly villain, with many other such like vilifying terms, with which he hath bespattered most of the gentry of our town. When this Pickthank had told his tale, the Judge directed his speech to the prisoner at the bar, saying, 'Thou runagate, heretic, and traitor, hast thou heard what these honest gentlemen have witnessed against thee?'

Faithful. May I speak a few words in my own defence?

Judge. Sirrah, sirrah, thou deservest to live no longer, but to be slain immediately upon the place; yet that all men may see our gentleness towards thee, let us hear what thou hast to say.

Faithful's defence of himself *Faithful.* 1. I say then in answer to what Mr Envy hath spoken, I never said aught but this, that what rule, or laws, or custom, or people, were flat against the Word of God, are diametrically opposite to Christianity. If I have said amiss in this, convince me of my error, and I am ready here before you to make my recantation.

2. As to the second, to wit, Mr Superstition, and his charge against me, I said only this, that in the worship of God there is required a divine faith; but there can be no divine faith without a divine revelation of the will of God: therefore whatever is thrust into the worship of God that is not agreeable to divine revelation, cannot be done but by an human faith, which faith will not profit to eternal life.

3. As to what Mr Pickthank hath said, I say (avoiding terms, as that I am said to rail, and the like), that the Prince of this town, with all the rabblement his attendants by this gentleman named, are more fit for a being in Hell than in this town and country; *The Judge his speech to the jury* and so the Lord have mercy upon me.

Then the Judge called to the jury (who all this

while stood by, to hear and observe), 'Gentlemen of the jury, you see this man about whom so great an uproar hath been made in this town: you have also heard what these worthy gentlemen have witnessed against him; also you have heard his reply and confession: it lieth now in your breasts to hang him, or save his life. But yet I think meet to instruct you into our law.

'There was an act made in the days of Pharaoh the Great, servant to our prince, that lest those of a contrary religion should multiply and grow too strong for him, their males should be thrown into the river. There was also an act made in the days of Nebuchadnezzar the Great, another of his servants, that whoever would not fall down and worship his golden image, should be thrown into a fiery furnace. There was also an act made in the days of Darius, that who so, for some time, called upon any god but his, should be cast into the lions' den. Now the substance of these laws this rebel has broken, not only in thought (which is not to be borne), but also in word and deed, which must therefore needs be intolerable.

'For that of Pharaoh, his law was made upon a supposition, to prevent mischief, no crime being yet apparent; but here is a crime apparent. For the second and third, you see he disputeth against our religion; and for the treason he hath confessed he deserveth to die the death.'

Then went the jury out, whose names were Mr Blind-man, Mr No-good, Mr Malice, Mr Love-lust, Mr Live-loose, Mr Heady, Mr High-mind, Mr Enmity, Mr Liar, Mr Cruelty, Mr Hate-light, and Mr Implacable, who every one gave in his private verdict against him among themselves, and afterwards unanimously concluded to bring him in guilty before the Judge. And first Mr Blind-man, *The jury and their names*

Everyone's private verdict

145

the foreman, said, 'I see clearly that this man is an heretic.' Then said Mr No-good, 'Away with such a fellow from the earth.' 'Ay,' said Mr Malice, 'for I hate the very looks of him.' Then said Mr Love-lust, 'I could never endure him.' 'Nor I,' said Mr Live-loose, 'for he would always be condemning my way.' 'Hang him, hang him,' said Mr Heady. 'A sorry scrub,' said Mr High-mind. 'My heart riseth against him,' said Mr Enmity. 'He is a rogue,' said Mr Liar. 'Hanging is too good for him,' said Mr Cruelty. 'Let's dispatch him out of the way,' said Mr Hate-light. Then said Mr Implacable, 'Might I have all the world given me, I could not be reconciled to him, therefore let us forthwith bring him in guilty of death.' And so they did, therefore he was presently condemned to be had from the place where he was,[81] to the place from whence he came, and there to be put to the most cruel death that could be invented.

They conclude to bring him in guilty of death

They therefore brought him out to do with him according to their law; and first they scourged him, then they buffeted him, then they lanced his flesh with knives; after that they stoned him with stones, then pricked him with their swords; and last of all they burned him to ashes at the stake. Thus came Faithful to his end. Now, I saw that there stood behind the multitude a chariot[82] and a couple of horses, waiting for Faithful, who (so soon as his adversaries had dispatched him) was taken up into it, and straightway was carried up through the clouds, with sound of trumpet, the nearest way to the Celestial Gate. But as for Christian, he had some respite, and was remanded back to prison; so he there remained for a space: but he that over-rules all things, having the power of their rage in his own hand, so wrought it about that Christian for that time escaped them, and went his way.

The cruel death of Faithful

A chariot and horses wait to take away Faithful

Christian is still alive

And as he went he sang.

> Well Faithful, thou hast faithfully professed
> Unto thy Lord: with him thou shalt be blest;
> When faithless ones with all their vain delights
> Are crying out under their hellish plights,
> Sing, Faithful, sing, and let thy name survive,
> For though they killed thee, thou art yet alive.

The song that Christian made of Faithful after his death

Now I saw in my dream, that Christian went not forth alone, for there was one whose name was Hopeful (being made so by the beholding of Christian and Faithful in their words and behaviour, in their sufferings at the Fair) who joined himself unto him, and entering into a brotherly covenant, told him that he would be his companion. Thus one died to make testimony to the truth, and another rises out of his ashes to be a companion with Christian. This Hopeful also told Christian that there were many more of the men in the Fair that would take their time and follow after. *Christian has another companion*

There is more of the men of the Fair will follow

So I saw that quickly after they were got out of the Fair they overtook one that was going before them, whose name was By-ends;[83] so they said to him, 'What countryman, sir, and how far go you this way?' He told them that he came from the town of Fair-speech, and he was going to the Celestial City (but told them not his name). *They overtake By-ends*

'From Fair-speech,' said Christian; 'is there any that be good live there?'

By-ends. Yes, said By-ends, I hope.

Christian. Pray sir, what may I call you? said Christian.

By-ends. I am a stranger to you, and you to me; if you be going this way, I shall be glad of your company; if not, I must be content. *By-ends loth to tell his name*

Christian. This town of Fair-speech, said Christian,

I have heard of it, and, as I remember, they say it's a wealthy place.

By-ends. Yes, I will assure you that it is, and I have very many rich kindred there.

Christian. Pray who are your kindred there, if a man may be so bold?

By-ends. Almost the whole town; and in particular, my Lord Turn-about, my Lord Time-server, my Lord Fair-speech (from whose ancestors that town first took its name), also Mr Smooth-man, Mr Facing-bothways, Mr Any-thing, and the parson of our parish, Mr Two-tongues, was my mother's own brother by father's side: and to tell you the truth, I am become a gentleman of good quality; yet my great-grandfather was but a waterman, looking one way and rowing another: and I got most of my estate by the same occupation.

Christian. Are you a married man?

By-ends. Yes, and my wife is a very virtuous woman, the daughter of a virtuous woman. She was my Lady Faining's daughter, therefore she came of a very honourable family, and is arrived to such a pitch of breeding that she knows how to carry it to all, even to prince and peasant. 'Tis true, we somewhat differ in religion from those of the stricter sort, yet but in two small points: first, we never strive against wind and tide; secondly, we are always most zealous when religion goes in his silver slippers; we love much to walk with him in the street if the sun shines and the people applaud it.

The wife and kindred of By-ends

Where By-ends differs from others in religion

Then Christian stepped a little atoside[84] to his fellow Hopeful, saying, 'It runs in my mind that this is one By-ends, of Fair-speech, and if it be he, we have as very a knave in our company as dwelleth in all these parts.' Then said Hopeful, 'Ask him: methinks he should not be ashamed of his name.' So Christian came up with him again; and said, 'Sir, you talk as if you knew something more than all the world doth, and if I take not my mark amiss, I deem I have half a guess of you: is not your name Mr By-ends of Fair-speech?'

By-ends. That is not my name, but indeed it is a nickname that is given me by some that cannot abide me, and I must be content to bear it as a reproach, as other good men have borne theirs before me.

Christian. But did you never give an occasion to men to call you by this name?

How By-ends got his name

By-ends. Never, never! The worst that ever I did to give them an occasion to give me this name was that I had always the luck to jump in my judgement with the present way of the times, whatever it was, and my chance was to get thereby; but if things are thus cast upon me, let me count them a blessing, but let not the malicious load me therefore with reproach.

Christian. I thought indeed that you was the man that I had heard of, and to tell you what I think I fear this name belongs to you more properly than you are willing we should think it doth.

By-ends. Well, if you will thus imagine, I cannot help it. You shall find me a fair company-keeper, if you will still admit me your associate.

He desires to keep company with Christian

Christian. If you will go with us you must go against wind and tide, the which I perceive is against your opinion; you must also own religion in his rags, as well as when in his silver slippers, and stand by him too when bound in irons, as well as when he walketh the streets with applause.

By-ends. You must not impose, nor lord it over my faith; leave me to my liberty, and let me go with you.

Christian. Not a step further, unless you will do in what I propound, as we.

Then said By-ends, 'I shall never desert my old principles, since they are harmless and profitable. If I may not go with you, I must do as I did before you overtook me, even go by myself, until some overtake me that will be glad of my company.'

Now I saw in my dream, that Christian and Hopeful forsook him, and kept their distance before him, but one of them looking back saw three men following Mr By-ends, and behold, as they came up with him, he made them a very low conjee,[85] and they also gave him a compliment. The men's names were Mr Hold-the-world, Mr Money-love, and Mr Save-all;[86] men that Mr By-ends had formerly been acquainted with; for in their minority they were schoolfellows, and were taught by one Mr Gripeman, a schoolmaster in Love-gain, which is a market town in the country of Coveting in the north.[87] This schoolmaster taught them the art of getting, either by violence, cozenage, flattery, lying or by putting on a guise of religion, and these four gentlemen had attained much of the art of their master, so that they could each of them have kept such a school themselves.

Well, when they had, as I said, thus saluted each other, Mr Money-love said to Mr By-ends, 'Who are they upon the road before us?' For Christian and Hopeful were yet within view.

By-ends. They are a couple of far countrymen, that, after their mode, are going on pilgrimage.

Mr Money-love. Alas, why did they not stay that we might have had their good company, for they, and we, and you Sir, I hope, are all going on pilgrimage.

By-ends. We are so indeed, but the men before us are so rigid, and love so much their own notions, and do also so lightly esteem the opinions of others, that let a man be never so godly, yet if he jumps not with them in all things they thrust him quite out of their company.

Mr Save-all. That's bad; But we read of some, that are righteous over-much, and such men's rigidness prevails with them to judge and condemn all but themselves. But I pray what and how many, were the things wherein you differed?

By-ends. Why, they after their headstrong manner conclude that it is duty to rush on their journey all weathers, and I am for waiting for wind and tide. They are for hazarding all for God at a clap, and I am for taking all advantages to secure my life and estate. They are for holding their notions, though all other men are against them, but I am for religion in what and so far as the times and my safety will bear it. They are for religion, when in rags and contempt, but I am for him when he walks in his golden slippers in the sunshine, and with applause.

Mr Hold-the-world. Ay, and hold you there still, good Mr By-ends, for, for my part, I can count him but a fool that having the liberty to keep what he has, shall be so unwise as to lose it. Let us be wise as serpents, 'tis best to make hay when the sun shines; you see how the bee lieth still all winter and bestirs her then only when she can have profit with pleasure. God sends sometimes rain and sometimes sunshine; if they be such fools to go through the first, yet let us be content to take fair weather along with us. For my part I like that religion best that will stand with the security of God's good blessings unto us; for who can imagine that is ruled by his reason since God has bestowed upon us the good things of this life, but that he would have us keep them for his sake. Abraham and Solomon grew rich in religion. And Job says that a good man *shall lay up gold as dust*. He must not be such as the men before us, if they be as you have described them.

Mr Save-all. I think that we are all agreed in this matter, and therefore there needs no more words about it.

Mr Money-love. No, there needs no more words about this matter indeed, for he that believes neither Scripture nor reason (and you see we have both on our side) neither knows his own liberty, nor seeks his own safety.

Mr By-ends. My brethren, we are, as you see, going all on pilgrimage, and for our better diversion from things that are bad, give me leave to propound unto you this question:

Suppose a man, a minister, or a tradesman, etc., should have an advantage lie before him to get the good blessings of this life, yet so as that he can by no means come by them except in appearance at least he becomes extraordinary zealous in some points of religion that he meddled not with before: may he not use this means to attain his end, and yet be a right honest man?

Mr Money-love. I see the bottom of your question, and with these gentlemen's good leave I will endeavour to shape you an answer. And first to speak to your question, as it concerns a minister himself. Suppose a minister, a worthy man, possessed but of a very small benefice, and has in his eye a greater, more fat and plump by far; he has also now an opportunity of getting of it; yet so as by being more studious, by preaching more frequently and zealously, and because the temper of the people requires it, by altering of some of his principles, for my part I see no reason but a man may do this (provided he has a call). Ay, and more a great deal besides, and yet be an honest man. For why,

1. His desire of a greater benefice is lawful (this cannot be contradicted) since 'tis set before him by providence; so then, he may get it if he can, making no question for conscience sake.

2. Besides, his desire after that benefice makes him more studious, a more zealous preacher, etc., and so makes him a better man. Yea, makes him better improve his parts, which is according to the mind of God.

3. Now as for his complying with the temper of his people, by deserting, to serve them, some of his principles, this argueth, 1. That he is of a self-denying temper. 2. Of a sweet and winning deportment. 3. And so more fit for the ministerial function.

4. I conclude then that a minister that changes a small for a great, should not for so doing be judged as covetous, but rather, since he is improved in his parts and industry thereby, be counted as one that pursues his call and the opportunity put into his hand to do good.

And now to the second part of the question which concerns the tradesman you mentioned: suppose such an one to have but a poor employ in the world, but by becoming religious he may mend his market, perhaps get a rich wife or more and far better customers to his shop, for my part I see no reason but that this may be lawfully done. For why,

1. To become religious is a virtue, by what means soever a man becomes so.

2. Nor is it unlawful to get a rich wife or more custom to my shop.

3. Besides the man that gets these by becoming religious, gets that which is good, of them that are good, by becoming good himself; so then here is a good wife and good customers, and good gain, and all these by becoming religious, which is good.

Therefore to become religious to get all these is a good and profitable design.

This answer, thus made by this Mr Money-love, to Mr By-ends' question, was highly applauded by them all; wherefore they concluded upon the whole, that it was most wholesome and advantageous. And because, as they thought, no man was able to contradict it, and because Christian and Hopeful was yet within call, they joyfully agreed to assault them with the question as soon as they overtook them, and the rather because they had opposed Mr By-ends before. So they called after them, and they stopped and stood still till they came up to them, but they concluded as they went that not By-ends, but old Mr Hold-the-world should propound the question to them, because, as they supposed, their answer to him would be without the remainder of that heat that was kindled betwixt Mr By-ends and them at their parting a little before.

So they came up to each other and after a short salutation Mr Hold-the-world propounded the question to Christian and his fellow, and bid them to answer it if they could.

Christian. Then said Christian, Even a babe in religion may answer ten thousand such questions. For if it be unlawful to follow Christ for loaves, as it is, how much more abominable is it to make of him and religion a stalking horse to get and enjoy the world. Nor do we find any other than heathens, hypocrites, devils and witches that are of this opinion.

1. Heathens, for when Hamor and Shechem had a mind to the daughter and cattle of Jacob, and saw that there was no ways for them to come at them but by becoming circumcised, they say to their companions: 'If every male of us be circumcised, as they

are circumcised, shall not their cattle, and their substance, and every beast of theirs be ours?' Their daughters and their cattle were that which they sought to obtain, and their religion the stalking horse they made use of to come at them. Read the whole story.[88]

2. The hypocritical Pharisees were also of this religion, long prayers were their pretence, but to get widows' houses were their intent, and greater damnation was from God their judgement.[89]

3. Judas the devil was also of this religion, he was religious for the bag,[90] that he might be possessed of what was therein, but he was lost, cast away, and the very son of perdition.

4. Simon the witch[91] was of this religion too, for he would have had the Holy Ghost that he might have got money therewith, and his sentence from Peter's mouth was according.[92]

5. Neither will it out of my mind but that that man that takes up religion for the world will throw away religion for the world; for so surely as Judas designed the world in becoming religious, so surely did he also sell religion and his master for the same. To answer the question therefore affirmatively as I perceive you have done, and to accept of as authentic such answer, is both heathenish, hypocritical and devilish, and your reward will be according to your works. Then they stood staring one upon another, but had not wherewith to answer Christian. Hopeful also approved of the soundness of Christian's answer, so there was a great silence among them. Mr By-ends and his company also staggered, and kept behind, that Christian and Hopeful might outgo them. Then said Christian to his fellow, If these men cannot stand before the sentence of men, what will they do

with the sentence of God? And if they are mute when dealt with by vessels of clay, what will they do when they shall be rebuked by the flames of a devouring fire?

Then Christian and Hopeful outwent them again, and went till they came at a delicate Plain, called *The ease that pilgrims have is but little in this life* Ease, where they went with much content; but that Plain was but narrow, so they were quickly got over it. Now at the further side of that Plain was a little *Lucre Hill a dangerous Hill* Hill called Lucre, and in that Hill a silver-mine, which some of them that had formerly gone that way, because of the rarity of it, had turned aside to see; but going too near the brink of the pit, the ground being deceitful under them broke, and they were slain; some also had been maimed there, and could not to their dying day be their own men again.

Then I saw in my dream that a little off the road, *Demas at the Hill Lucre* over against the silver-mine, stood Demas[93] (gentleman-like), to call to passengers to come and see: who *He calls to Christian and Hopeful to come to him* said to Christian and his fellow, 'Ho, turn aside hither, and I will show you a thing'.

Christian. What thing so deserving as to turn us out of the way?

Demas. Here is a silver-mine, and some digging in it for treasure; if you will come, with a little pains you may richly provide for yourselves.

Hopeful tempted to go but Christian holds him back *Hopeful.* Then said Hopeful, Let us go see.

Christian. Not I, said Christian; I have heard of this place before now, and how many have there been slain; and besides, that treasure is a snare to those that seek it, for it hindreth them in their pilgrimage. Then Christian called to Demas, saying, Is not the place dangerous? hath it not hindered many in their pilgrimage?

Demas. Not very dangerous, except to those that are careless. But withal, he blushed as he spake.

Christian. Then said Christian to Hopeful, Let us not stir a step, but still keep on our way.

Hopeful. I will warrant you, when By-ends comes up, if he hath the same invitation as we, he will turn in thither to see.

Christian. No doubt thereof, for his principles lead him that way, and a hundred to one but he dies there.

Demas. Then Demas called again, saying, But will you not come over and see?

Christian. Then Christian roundly answered, saying, Demas, Thou art an enemy to the right ways of the Lord of this way, and hast been already condemned for thine own turning aside, by one of his Majesty's judges; and why seekest thou to bring us into the like condemnation? Besides, if we at all turn aside our Lord the King will certainly hear thereof; and will there put us to shame where we would stand with boldness before him.

Demas cried again that he also was one of their fraternity and that if they would tarry a little, he also himself would walk with them.

Christian. Then said Christian, What is thy name? Is it not the same by the which I have called thee?

Demas. Yes, my name is Demas, I am the son of Abraham.

Christian. I know you, Gehazi was your great grandfather, and Judas your father, and you have trod their steps. It is but a devilish prank that thou usest: thy father was hanged for a traitor and thou deservest no better reward. Assure thyself, that when we come to the King we will do him word of this thy behaviour. Thus they went their way.

By this time By-ends and his companions was come again within sight, and they at the first beck went over to Demas. Now whether they fell into the pit by looking over the brink thereof, or whether they

(margin note, right) *Christian roundeth up rebukes Demas*

(margin note, right) *By-ends goes over to Demas*

went down to dig, or whether they was smothered in the bottom by the damps that commonly arise, of these things I am not certain: but this I observed, that they never was seen again in the way.

Then sang Christian;

> By-ends, and Silver-Demas, both agree;
> One calls, the other runs, that he may be
> A sharer in his lucre: so these two
> Take up in this world, and no further go.

They see a strange monument Now I saw that just on the other side of this Plain, the pilgrims came to a place where stood an <u>old monument, hard by the highway-side,</u> at the sight of which they were both concerned because of the strangeness of the form thereof; for it seemed to them as if it had been a woman transformed into the shape of a pillar: here therefore they stood looking and looking upon it, but could not for a time tell what they should make thereof. At last Hopeful espied written above upon the head thereof a writing in an unusual hand; but he being no scholar called to Christian (for he was learned) to see if he could pick out the meaning: so he came, and after a little laying of letters together he found the same to be this, *Remember Lot's wife*. So he read it to his fellow, after which they both concluded that that was the <u>Pillar of Salt</u>[95] into which Lot's wife was turned for her looking back with a covetous heart when she was going from Sodom for safety. Which sudden and amazing sight gave them occasion of this discourse.

Christian. Ah, my brother, this is a seasonable sight, it came opportunely to us after the invitation which Demas gave us to come over to view the Hill Lucre: and had we gone over as he desired us, and as thou wast inclining to do (my brother) we had, for aught

I know, been made ourselves a spectacle for those that shall come after to behold.

Hopeful. I am sorry that I was so foolish, and am made to wonder that I am not now as Lot's wife; for wherein was the difference 'twixt her sin and mine? She only looked back, and I had a desire to go see; let grace be adored, and let me be ashamed, that ever such a thing should be in mine heart.

Christian. Let us take notice of what we see here for our help for time to come: this woman escaped one judgement; for she fell not by the destruction of Sodom, yet she was destroyed by another; as we see, she is turned into a Pillar of Salt.

Hopeful. True, and she may be to us both caution, and example; caution that we should shun her sin, or a sign of what judgement will overtake such as shall not be prevented by this caution. So Korah, Dathan, and Abiram,[96] with the two hundred and fifty men that perished in their sin, did also become a sign, or example to others to beware: but above all, I muse at one thing, to wit, how Demas and his fellows can stand so confidently yonder to look for that treasure, which this woman, but for looking behind her (for we read not that she stepped one foot out of the way), after was turned into a Pillar of Salt; specially since the judgement which overtook her did make her an example within sight of where they are: for they cannot choose but see her, did they but lift up their eyes.

Christian. It is a thing to be wondered at, and it argueth that their heart is grown desperate in the case; and I cannot tell who to compare them to so fitly, as to them that pick pockets in the presence of the judge, or that will cut purses under the gallows. It is said of the men of Sodom, that they were sinners exceedingly, because they were sinners before the

Lord, that is, in his eyesight; and notwithstanding the kindnesses that he had showed them, for the land of Sodom was now like the Garden of Eden heretofore. This therefore provoked him the more to jealousy, and made their plague as hot as the fire of the Lord out of Heaven could make it. And it is most rationally to be concluded that such, even such as these are, that shall sin in the sight, yea, and that too in despite of such examples that are set continually before them to caution them to the contrary, must be partakers of severest judgements.

Hopeful. Doubtless thou hast said the truth, but what a mercy is it, that neither thou, but especially I, am not made myself, this example: this ministreth occasion to us to thank God, to fear before him, and always to remember Lot's wife.

I saw then that they went on their way to a *A river* pleasant river, which David the King called the River of God; but, John, The River of the Water of Life. Now their way lay just upon the bank of the River: here therefore Christian and his companion walked with great delight; they drank also of the water of the River which was pleasant and enlivening to their weary spirits; besides, on the banks of this *Trees by the* River, on either side, were green trees that bore all *river* manner of fruit; and the leaves of the trees were good *The fruit and* for medicine; with the fruit of these trees they were *leaves of the* also much delighted, and the leaves they eat to prevent *trees* surfeits, and other diseases that are incident to those that heat their blood by travels. On either side of the *A meadow in* River was also a meadow, curiously beautified with *which they* lilies; and it was green all the year long. In this *lie down to* meadow they lay down and slept, for here they might *sleep* lie down safely. When they awoke, they gathered again of the fruit of the trees, and drank again of the water of the River, and then lay down again to sleep.

160

Thus they did several days and nights. Then they sang,

> Behold ye how these crystal streams do glide
> (To comfort pilgrims) by the highway side;
> The meadows green besides their fragrant smell,
> Yield dainties for them; and he that can tell
> What pleasant fruit, yea leaves, these trees do yield,
> Will soon sell all, that he may buy this field.

So when they were disposed to go on (for they were not as yet at their journey's end) they eat and drank and departed.

Now I beheld in my dream that they had not journeyed far but the River and the way for a time parted. At which they were not a little sorry, yet they durst not go out of the way. Now the way from the River was rough, and their feet tender by reason of their travels; so the soul of the pilgrims was much discouraged, because of the way. Wherefore still as they went on they wished for better way. Now a little before them there was on the left hand of the road, a meadow, and a stile to go over into it, and that meadow is called <u>By-Path</u> Meadow. Then said *By-Path* Christian to his fellow, 'If this Meadow lieth along *Meadow.* by our wayside, let's go over into it.' Then he went *temptation* to the stile to see, and behold a path lay along by the *does make way* way on the other side of the fence. "Tis according to *for another* my wish,' said Christian, 'here is the easiest going; come, good Hopeful, and let us go over.'

Hopeful. But how if this path should lead us out of *Strong* the way? *Christians may lead weak ones out*

Christian. That's not like, said the other, look, doth *of the way* it not go along by the wayside? So Hopeful, being persuaded by his fellow, went after him over the stile. When they were gone over and were got into the path, they found it very easy for their feet; and withal, they, looking before them, espied a man walking as they did (and his name was <u>Vain-confidence</u>): so they called after him, and asked him whither that way led. He said, 'To the Celestial Gate.' Look, said Christian, did not I tell you so? by this you may see we are right. So they followed, and he went before them. But behold the night came on, and it grew very dark; so that they that were behind lost the sight of him that went before.

See what it is too suddenly to fall in with strangers

He therefore that went before (Vain-confidence by name) not seeing the way before him, fell into a deep pit, which was on purpose there made by the prince of those grounds to catch vain-glorious fools withal, and was dashed in pieces with his fall.

A pit to catch the vainglorious in

Now Christian and his fellow heard him fall. So they called to know the matter but there was none to answer, only they heard a groaning. Then said Hopeful, 'Where are we now?' Then was his fellow silent, as mistrusting that he had led him out of the way. And now it began to rain, and thunder, and lighten in a very dreadful manner, and the water rose amain.

Reasoning between Christian and Hopeful

Then Hopeful groaned in himself, saying, 'Oh that I had kept on my way!'

Christian. Who could have thought that this path should have led us out of the way?

Hopeful. I was afraid on't at very first, and therefore gave you that gentle caution. I would have spoke plainer, but that you are older than I.

Christian. Good brother, be not offended, I am sorry I have brought thee out of the way, and that I have put thee into such eminent danger; pray, my brother, forgive me, I did not do it of an evil intent.

Christian's repentance for leading of his brother out of the way

Hopeful. Be comforted my brother, for I forgive thee; and believe too, that this shall be for our good.

Christian. I am glad I have with me a merciful

brother; but we must not stand thus, let's try to go back again.

Hopeful. But, good brother, let me go before.

Christian. No, if you please let me go first; that if there be any danger I may be first therein, because by my means we are both gone out of the way.

Hopeful. No, said Hopeful, you shall not go first, for your mind being troubled may lead you out of the way again. Then for their encouragement, they heard the voice of one, saying, *Let thine heart be towards the high-way, even the way that thou wentest, turn again.* But by this time the waters were greatly risen, by reason of which the way of going back was very dangerous. (Then I thought that it is easier going out of the way when we are in, than going in when we are out.) Yet they adventured to go back; but it was so dark, and the flood was so high, that in their going back, they had like to have been drowned nine or ten times.

They are in danger of drowning as they go back

Neither could they, with all the skill they had, get again to the stile that night. Wherefore at last, lighting under a little shelter, they sat down there till the day brake; but being weary, they fell asleep. Now there was not far from the place where they lay, a castle, <u>called Doubting-Castle</u>,[97] the owner whereof was <u>Giant Despair</u>,[98] and it was in his grounds they now were sleeping; wherefore he getting up in the morning early and walking up and down in his fields, caught Christian and Hopeful asleep in his grounds. Then with a grim and surly voice he bid them awake, and asked them whence they were and what they did in his grounds. They told him they were pilgrims, and that they had lost their way. Then said the Giant, 'You have this night trespassed on me, by trampling in, and lying on my grounds, and therefore you must go along with me.' So they

They sleep in the grounds of Giant Despair

He finds them in his ground, and carries them to Doubting-Castle

163

were forced to go, because he was stronger than they. They also had but little to say, for they knew themselves in a fault. The Giant therefore drove them before him and put them into his castle, into a very dark dungeon, nasty and stinking to the spirit of these two men. Here then they lay from Wednesday morning till Saturday night, without one bit of bread or drop of drink, or any light, or any to ask how they did. They were therefore here in evil case, and were far from friends and acquaintance. Now in this place, Christian had double sorrow, because 'twas through his unadvised haste that they were brought into this distress.

The grievousness of their imprisonment

Now Giant Despair had a wife, and her name was Diffidence: so when he was gone to bed, he told his wife what he had done; to wit, that he had taken a couple of prisoners, and cast them into his dungeon, for trespassing on his grounds. Then he asked her also what he had best to do further to them. So she asked him what they were, whence they came, and whither they were bound; and he told her; then she counselled him, that when he arose in the morning, he should beat them without any mercy. So when he arose, he getteth him a grievous crab-tree cudgel and goes down into the dungeon to them; and there, first falls to rating of them as if they were dogs, although they gave him never a word of distaste; then he falls upon them, and beats them fearfully, in such sort, that they were not able to help themselves, or to turn them upon the floor. This done, he withdraws and leaves them there to condole their misery, and to mourn under their distress, so all that day they spent the time in nothing but sighs and bitter lamentations. The next night she, talking with her husband about them further, and understanding that they were yet alive, did advise him to counsel them

On Thursday Giant Despair beats his prisoners

to make away themselves. So when morning was come, he goes to them in a surly manner, as before, and perceiving them to be very sore with the stripes that he had given them the day before, he told them that since they were never like to come out of that place their only way would be forthwith to make an end of themselves, either with knife, halter or poison. 'For why,' said he, 'should you choose life, seeing it is attended with so much bitterness?' But they desired him to let them go; with that he looked ugly upon them, and rushing to them, had doubtless made an end of them himself, but that he fell into one of his fits; (for he sometimes in sunshine weather fell into fits) and lost (for a time) the use of his hand: wherefore he withdrew, and left them (as before) to consider what to do. Then did the prisoners consult between themselves, whether 'twas best to take his counsel or no: and thus they began to discourse.

On Friday giant Despair counsels them to kill themselves

The Giant sometimes has fits

Christian. Brother, said Christian, what shall we do? The life that we now live is miserable;[99] for my part, I know not whether is best to live thus or to die out of hand? *My soul chooseth strangling rather than life*; and the grave is more easy for me than this dungeon: shall we be ruled by the Giant?

Christian crushed

Hopeful. Indeed our present condition is dreadful, and death would be far more welcome to me than thus for ever to abide: but yet let us consider, the Lord of the country to which we are going hath said, *Thou shalt do no murther*, no not to another man's person; much more then are we forbidden to take his counsel to kill ourselves. Besides, he that kills another can but commit murder upon his body; but for one to kill himself is to kill body and soul at once. And moreover, my brother, thou talkest of ease in the grave; but hast thou forgotten the Hell

Hopeful comforts him

whither, for certain, the murderers go? For no murderer hath eternal life, etc. And, let us consider again, that all the law is not in the hand of Giant Despair: others, so far as I can understand, have been taken by him, as well as we, and yet have escaped out of his hand: who knows, but that God that made the world may cause that Giant Despair may die; or that, at some time or other he may forget to lock us in; or but he may in short time have another of his fits before us, and may lose the use of his limbs? And if ever that should come to pass again, for my part I am resolved to pluck up the heart of a man and to try my utmost to get from under his hand. I was a fool that I did not try to do it before, but however, my brother, let's be patient, and endure a while; the time may come that may give us a happy release: but let us not be our own murderers. With these words, Hopeful, at present did moderate the mind of his brother; so they continued together (in the dark) that day, in their sad and doleful condition.

Well, towards evening the Giant goes down into the dungeon again, to see if his prisoners had taken his counsel; but when he came there he found them alive, and truly, alive was all: for now, what for want of bread and water, and by reason of the wounds they received when he beat them, they could do little but breathe. But, I say, he found them alive, at which he fell into a grievous rage, and told them, that seeing they had disobeyed his counsel, it should be worse with them than if they had never been born.

At this they trembled greatly, and I think that Christian fell into a swound; but coming a little to himself again, they renewed their discourse about the Giant's counsel; and whether yet they had best to *Christian still dejected* take it or no. Now Christian again seemed to be for

166

doing it, but Hopeful made his second reply as followeth:

Hopeful. My brother, said he, rememberest thou not how valiant thou hast been heretofore; Apollyon could not crush thee, nor could all that thou didst hear, or see, or feel in the Valley of the Shadow of Death; what hardship, terror, and amazement hast thou already gone through, and art thou now nothing but fear? Thou seest that I am in the dungeon with thee, a far weaker man by nature than thou art: also this Giant has wounded me as well as thee; and hath also cut off the bread and water from my mouth; and with thee I mourn without the light: but let's exercise a little more patience. Remember how thou playedst the man at Vanity-Fair, and wast neither afraid of the chain nor cage, nor yet of bloody death: wherefore let us (at least to avoid the shame that becomes not a Christian to be found in) bear up with patience as well as we can.

Hopeful comforts him again, by calling former things to remembrance

Now night being come again, and the Giant and his wife being in bed, she asked him concerning the prisoners, and if they had taken his counsel: to which he replied, 'They are sturdy rogues, they choose rather to bear all hardship, than to make away themselves.' Then said she, 'Take them into the castle-yard tomorrow, and show them the bones and skulls of those that thou hast already dispatched; and make them believe ere a week comes to an end thou also wilt tear them in pieces as thou hast done their fellows before them.'

So when the morning was come the Giant goes to them again, and takes them into the castle-yard, and shows them as his wife had bidden him. 'These,' said he, 'were pilgrims as you are, once, and they trespassed in my grounds as you have done; and when I thought fit, I tore them in pieces; and so

On Saturday the Giant threatened that shortly he would pull them in pieces

167

within ten days I will do you. Go, get you down to your den again; and with that he beat them all the way thither: they lay therefore all day on Saturday in a lamentable case, as before. Now when night was come, and when Mrs Diffidence, and her husband, the Giant, were got to bed, they began to renew their discourse of their prisoners: and withal, the old Giant wondered that he could neither by his blows nor counsel bring them to an end. And with that his wife replied, 'I fear,' said she, 'that they live in hope that some will come to relieve them, or that they have pick-locks about them; by the means of which they hope to escape.' 'And, sayest thou so, my dear,' said the Giant, 'I will therefore search them in the morning.'

Well, on Saturday about midnight they began to pray, and continued in prayer till almost break of day.

Now a little before it was day, good Christian, as one half amazed, brake out in this passionate speech, 'What a fool,' quoth he, 'am I, thus to lie in a stinking dungeon, when I may as well walk at liberty. I have a key in my bosom, called promise,[100] that will (I am persuaded) open any lock in Doubting-Castle.' Then said Hopeful, 'That's good news; good brother, pluck it out of thy bosom, and try.' Then Christian pulled it out of his bosom, and began to try at the dungeon door, whose bolt (as he turned the key) gave back, and the door flew open with ease, and Christian and Hopeful both came out. Then he went to the outward door that leads into the castle-yard, and with his key opened the door also. After he went to the iron gate, for that must be opened too, but that lock went damnable hard,[101] yet the key did open it; then they thrust open the gate to make their escape with speed; but that gate, as it opened, made

A key in Christian's bosom, called Promise, opens any lock in Doubting-Castle

such a creaking that it waked Giant Despair, who hastily rising to pursue his prisoners felt his limbs to fail, for his fits took him again, so that he could by no means go after them. Then they went on, and came to the King's highway again, and so were safe, because they were out of his jurisdiction.

Now when they were gone over the stile, they began to contrive with themselves what they should do at that stile to prevent those that should come after from falling into the hands of Giant Despair. So they consented to erect there a pillar, and to engrave upon the side thereof: _Over this stile is the way to Doubting-Castle, which is kept by Giant Despair, who despiseth the King of the Celestial Country, and seeks to destroy his holy pilgrims._ Many therefore that followed after, read what was written, and escaped the danger. This done, they sang as follows:

A pillar erected by Christian and his fellow

> *Out of the way we went, and then we found*
> *What 'twas to tread upon forbidden ground;*
> *And let them that come after have a care,*
> *Lest heedlessness makes them as we to fare,*
> *Lest they for trespassing his prisoners are,*
> *Whose castle's Doubting, and whose name's Despair.*

They went then till they came to the Delectable Mountains, which Mountains belong to the Lord of that Hill of which we have spoken before; so they went up to the Mountains to behold the gardens, and orchards, the vineyards, and fountains of water, where also they drank, and washed themselves, and did freely eat of the vineyards. Now there was on the tops of these Mountains, shepherds feeding their flocks, and they stood by the highway side. The pilgrims therefore went to them, and leaning upon their staves (as is common with weary pilgrims, when they stand to talk with any by the way), they asked,

The Delectable Mountains

They are refreshed in the Mountains

Talk with the shepherds 'Whose Delectable Mountains are these? And whose be the sheep that feed upon them?'

Shepherds. These Mountains are Immanuel's Land, and they are within sight of his City, and the sheep also are his, and he laid down his life for them.

Christian. Is this the way to the Celestial City?

Shepherds. You are just in your way.

Christian. How far is it thither?

Shepherds. Too far for any but those that shall get thither indeed.

Christian. Is the way safe or dangerous?

Shepherds. Safe for those for whom it is to be safe, *but transgressors shall fall therein.*

Christian. Is there in this place any relief for pilgrims that are weary and faint in the way?

Shepherds. The Lord of these Mountains hath given us a charge *Not to be forgetful to entertain strangers*: therefore the good of the place is before you.

I saw also in my dream that when the shepherds perceived that they were wayfaring men they also put questions to them to which they made answer as in other places, as, 'Whence came you?' and, 'How got you into the way?' and, 'By what means have you so persevered therein? For but few of them that begin to come hither, do show their face on these Mountains.' But when the shepherds heard their answers, being pleased therewith, they looked very *The shepherds welcome them* lovingly upon them, and said, 'Welcome to the Delectable Mountains.'

The shepherds, I say, whose names were, Know= *The names of the shepherds* ledge, Experience, Watchful, and Sincere, took them by the hand, and had them to their tents, and made them partake of that which was ready at present. They said moreover, 'We would that you should stay here a while, to acquaint with us, and yet more to solace yourselves with the good of these Delectable Mountains.' They then told them that they were content to stay; and so they went to their rest that night, because it was very late.

Then I saw in my dream that in the morning the shepherds called up Christian and Hopeful to walk with them upon the Mountains. So they went forth with them, and walked a while, having a pleasant prospect on every side. Then said the shepherds one to another, 'Shall we show these pilgrims some wonders?' So when they had concluded to do it, *They are* they had them first to the top of an Hill called *sure wonders* Error, which was very steep on the furthest side, and *The Mountain* bid them look down to the bottom. So Christian *of Error* and Hopeful looked down and saw at the bottom several men dashed all to pieces by a fall that they had from the top. Then said Christian, 'What meaneth this?' The shepherds answered, 'Have you not heard of them that were made to err by hearkening to Hymeneus and Philetus,[102] as concerning the faith of the resurrection of the body?' They answered, 'Yes.' Then said the shepherds, 'Those that you see lie dashed in pieces at the bottom of this Mountain are they; and they have continued to this day unburied (as you see) for an example to others to take heed how they clamber too high, or how they come too near the brink of this Mountain.'

Then I saw that they had them to the top of another mountain, and the name of that is Caution, and bid *Mount* them look afar off; which when they did, they *Caution* perceived, as they thought, several men walking up and down among the tombs that were there. And they perceived that the men were blind, because they stumbled sometimes upon the tombs,[103] and because they could not get out from among them. Then said Christian, 'What means this?'

The shepherds then answered, 'Did you not see a

little below these Mountains a stile that led into a meadow on the left hand of this way? They answered, 'Yes.' Then said the shepherds, 'From that stile there goes a path that leads directly to Doubting-Castle, which is kept by Giant Despair; and these men (pointing to them among the tombs) came once on pilgrimage, as you do now, even till they came to that same stile. And because the right way was rough in that place, they chose to go out of it into that meadow, and there were taken by Giant Despair, and cast into Doubting-Castle; where, after they had a while been kept in the dungeon, he at last did put out their eyes, and led them among those tombs, where he has left them to wander to this very day, that the saying of the wise man might be fulfilled, *He that wandereth out of the way of understanding, shall remain in the congregation of the dead.*' Then Christian and Hopeful looked one upon another, with tears gushing out, but yet said nothing to the shepherds.

Then I saw in my dream that the shepherds had them to another place, in a bottom, where was a door in the side of an hill; and they opened the door, and bid them look in. They looked in therefore, and saw that within it was very dark and smoky; they also thought that they heard there a lumbering[104] noise as of fire, and a cry of some tormented, and that they smelt the scent of brimstone. Then said Christian, 'What means this?' The shepherds told them, saying, *A by-way to Hell* 'This is a by-way to Hell, a way that hypocrites go in at, namely, such as sell their birthright with Esau, such as sell their master with Judas, such as blaspheme the Gospel with Alexander, and that lie, and dissemble with Ananias and Sapphira his wife.

Hopeful. Then said Hopeful to the shepherds, I perceive that these had on them, even every one, a show of pilgrimage as we have now, had they not?

Shepherd. Yes, and held it a long time too.

Hopeful. How far might they go on pilgrimage in their day, since they notwithstanding were thus miserably cast away?

Shepherd. Some further, and some not so far as these Mountains.

Then said the pilgrims one to another, 'We had need cry to the strong for strength.'

Shepherd. Ay, and you will have need to use it when you have it, too.

By this time the pilgrims had a desire to go forwards, and the shepherds a desire they should; so they walked together towards the end of the Mountains. Then said the shepherds one to another, 'Let us here show to the pilgrims the Gates of the Celestial City, if they have skill to look through our perspective glass.[105] The pilgrims then lovingly *The shepherds* accepted the motion: so they had them to the top *perspective* of an high Hill called Clear, and gave them their *glass.* glass to look. Then they essayed to look, but the *Clear* remembrance of that last thing that the shepherds had showed them made their hands shake; by means of which impediment they could not look steadily through the glass; yet they thought they *The fruit of* saw something like the Gate, and also some of the *slavish fear* glory of the place. Then they went away and sang

> *Thus by the shepherds, secrets are revealed,*
> *Which from all other men are kept concealed:*
> *Come to the shepherds then, if you would see*
> *Things deep, things hid, and that mysterious be.*

When they were about to depart, one of the shepherds gave them a note of the way. Another of them bid them 'Beware of the flatterer.' The third bid them *A two-fold* 'Take heed that they sleep not upon the Enchanted *caution*

Ground.' And the fourth bid them 'Godspeed.' So I awoke from my dream.[106]

And I slept and dreamed again, and saw the same two pilgrims going down the Mountains along the highway towards the City. Now a little below these *The country* Mountains, on the left hand, lieth the country of *of Conceit,* Conceit; from which country there comes into the *out of which* way in which the pilgrims walked a little crooked *came* lane. Here therefore they met with a very brisk *Ignorance* lad,[107] that came out of that country; and his name was Ignorance.[108] So Christian asked him from what parts he came and whither he was going.

Christian and *Ignorance.* Sir, I was born in the country that lieth *Ignorance* off there, a little on the left hand; and I am going to *hath some* the Celestial City. *talk*

Christian. But how do you think to get in at the Gate, for you may find some difficulty there?

Ignorance. As other good people do, said he.

Christian. But what have you to show at that Gate, that may cause that the Gate should be opened unto you?

Ignorance. I know my Lord's will, and I have been a good liver, I pay every man his own; I pray, fast, pay tithes, and give alms, and have left my country, for whither I am going.

Christian. But thou camest not in at the Wicket Gate that is at the head of this way: thou camest in hither through that same crooked lane, and therefore I fear, however thou mayest think of thyself, when the reckoning day shall come thou wilt have laid to thy charge that thou art a thief and a robber instead of getting admittance into the City.

He saith to *Ignorance.* Gentlemen, ye be utter strangers to me, *every one,* I know you not, be content to follow the religion of *that he is a* your country, and I will follow the religion of mine. *fool* I hope all will be well. And as for the Gate that you talk of, all the world knows that that is a great way off of our country. I cannot think that any man in all our parts doth so much as know the way to it; nor need they matter whether they do or no, since we have, as you see, a fine, pleasant, green lane, that comes down from our country the next way into it.

When Christian saw that the man was wise in his own conceit, he said to Hopeful, whisperingly, 'There is more hopes of a fool than of him.' And said moreover, 'When he that is a fool walketh by the way, his wisdom faileth him, and he saith to every one that he is a fool. What, shall we talk further with him? Or out-go him at present, and so leave him to think of what he hath heard already, and then stop again for him afterwards, and see if by degrees we can do any good of him?' Then said Hopeful, *How to carry it to a fool*

> Let Ignorance a little while now muse
> On what is said, and let him not refuse
> Good counsel to embrace, lest he remain
> Still ignorant of what's the chiefest gain.
> God saith those that no understanding have,
> (Although he made them) them he will not save.

Hopeful. He further added, It is not good, I think, to say all to him at once; let us pass him by, if you will, and talk to him anon, even as he is able to bear it.

So they both went on, and Ignorance he came after. Now when they had passed him a little way, they entered into a very dark lane where they met a man whom seven devils had bound with seven strong cords, and were carrying of him back to the door that they saw in the side of the hill. Now good Christian began to tremble, and so did Hopeful his companion. Yet as the devils led away the man, Christian looked to see if he knew him, and he thought it might be one *The* Turn-away that dwelt in the town of Apostacy. *destruction* But he did not perfectly see his face, for he did hang *of one* his head like a thief that is found: but being gone past, *Turn-away* Hopeful looked after him, and espied on his back a paper with this inscription, *Wanton professor, and damnable apostate.* Then said Christian to his fellow, *Christian* 'Now I call to remembrance that which was told me *telleth his* of a thing that happened to a good man hereabout. *companion a* The name of the man was Little-faith, but a good *story of* *Little-faith* man, and he dwelt in the town of Sincere. The thing was this: at the entering in of this passage there *Broad-way-* comes down from Broad-way-gate a lane, called *gate.* Dead-man's Lane; so called because of the murders *Dead-man's* *Lane* that are commonly done there. And this Little-faith, going on pilgrimage as we do now, chanced to sit down there and slept. Now there happened at that time to come down that lane from Broad-way-gate, three sturdy rogues, and their names were Faint-heart, Mistrust, and Guilt (three brothers), and they, espying Little-faith where he was, came galloping up with speed. Now the good man was just awaked from his sleep, and was getting up to go on his journey. So they came all up to him, and with *Little-faith* threatening language bid him stand. At this Little- *robbed by* faith looked as white as a clout, and had neither power *Faint-heart,* *Mistrust,* to fight, nor fly. Then said Faint-heart, "Deliver thy *and Guilt* purse," but he making no haste to do it (for he was loth to lose his money), Mistrust ran up to him, and thrusting his hand into his pocket, pulled out thence a bag of silver. Then he cried out, "Thieves, thieves." *They got* With that Guilt with a great club that was in his *away his* hand struck Little-faith on the head, and with that *silver, and* *knocked him* blow felled him flat to the ground where he lay *down* bleeding as one that would bleed to death. All this while the thieves stood by. But at last, they hearing that some were upon the road, and fearing lest it should be one Great-grace that dwells in the city of Good-confidence, they betook themselves to their heels, and left this good man to shift for himself. Now after a while Little-faith came to himself, and getting up, made shift to scrabble[109] on his way. This was the story.'

Hopeful. But did they take from him all that ever he had?

Christian. No: the place where his jewels[110] were, they never ransacked, so those he kept still; but as I was told, the good man was much afflicted for his loss. For the thieves got most of his spending money. That which they got not (as I said) were jewels, also he had a little odd money left, but scarce enough to bring him to his journey's end; nay (if I was not misinformed), he was forced to beg as he went, to keep himself alive (for his jewels he might not sell). But beg and do what he could, he went (as we say) with many a hungry belly the most part of the rest of the way.

Little-faith lost not his best things

Little-faith forced to beg to his journey's end

Hopeful. But is it not a wonder they got not from him his certificate, by which he was to receive his admittance at the Celestial Gate?

Christian. 'Tis a wonder, but they got not that; though they missed it not through any good cunning of his, for he being dismayed with their coming upon him, had neither power nor skill to hide anything, so 'twas more by good providence than by his endeavour that they missed of that good thing.

He kept not his best things by his own cunning

Hopeful. But it must needs be a comfort to him that they got not this jewel from him.

Christian. It might have been great comfort to him, had he used it as he should; but they that told me the story said that he made but little use of it all the rest of the way; and that because of the dismay that he had in their taking away his money, indeed he forgot it a great part of the rest of the journey; and besides, when at any time it came into his mind, and he began to be comforted therewith, then would fresh thoughts of his loss come again upon him, and those thoughts would swallow up all.

Hopeful. Alas poor man! This could not but be a great grief unto him.

He is pitied by both

Christian. Grief! Ay, a grief indeed! Would it not a been so to any of us, had we been used as he, to be robbed and wounded too, and that in a strange place as he was? 'Tis a wonder he did not die with grief, poor heart! I was told that he scattered almost all the rest of the way with nothing but doleful and bitter complaints, telling also to all that overtook him, or that he overtook in the way as he went, where he was robbed, and how, who they were that did it, and what he lost, how he was wounded, and that he hardly escaped with life.

Hopeful. But 'tis a wonder that his necessities did not put him upon selling, or pawning some of his jewels, that he might have wherewith to relieve himself in his journey.

Christian snibbeth his fellow for unadvised speaking

Christian. Thou talkest like one upon whose head is the shell to this very day: for what should he pawn them? Or to whom should he sell them? In all that country where he was robbed his jewels were not accounted of, nor did he want that relief which could from thence be administered to him. Besides, had his jewels been missing at the gate of the Celestial City, he had (and that he knew well enough) been excluded from an inheritance there; and that would have been worse to him than the appearance and villainy of ten thousand thieves.

Hopeful. Why art thou so tart, my brother? Esau sold his birth-right, and that for a mess of pottage, and that birth-right was his greatest jewel; and if he, why might not Little-faith do so too?

Christian. Esau did sell his birth-right indeed, and so do many besides; and by so doing exclude themselves from the chief blessing, as also that caitiff did. But you must put a difference betwixt Esau and Little-faith, and also betwixt their estates. Esau's birth-right was typical, but Little-faith's jewels were not so. Esau's belly was his god, but Little-faith's belly was not so. Esau's want lay in his fleshly appetite, Little-faith's did not so. Besides, Esau could see no further than to the fulfilling of his lusts; '*For I am at the point to die,*' said he, '*and what good will this birth-right do me?*' But Little-faith, though it was his lot to have but a little faith, was by his little faith kept from such extravagancies; and made to see and prize his jewels more than to sell them, as Esau did his birth-right. You read not anywhere that Esau had faith, no not so much as a little: therefore no marvel if where the flesh only bears sway (as it will in that man where no faith is to resist) if he sells his birth-right, and his soul and all, and that to the Devil of Hell; for it is with such, as it is with the ass, *Who in her occasions cannot be turned away.* When their minds are set upon their lusts, they will have them whatever they cost. But Little-faith was of another temper, his mind was on things divine; his livelihood was upon things that were spiritual and from above; therefore to what end should he that is of such a temper sell his jewels (had there been any that would have bought them) to fill his mind with empty things? Will a man give a penny to fill his belly with hay? Or can you persuade the turtle-dove to live upon carrion like the crow? Though faithless ones can for carnal lusts, pawn, or mortgage, or sell what they have, and themselves outright to boot; yet they that have faith,

A discourse about Esau and Little-faith

Esau was ruled by his lusts

Essau never had faith

Little-faith could not live upon Esau's pottage

A comparison between the turtle-dove and the crow

saving faith, though but a little of it, cannot do so. Here therefore, my brother, is thy mistake.

Hopeful. I acknowledge it; but yet your severe reflection had almost made me angry.

Christian. Why, I did but compare thee to some of the birds that are of the brisker sort who will run to and fro in untrodden paths with the shell upon their heads: but pass by that and consider the matter under debate, and all shall be well betwixt thee and me.

Hopeful. But Christian, these three fellows, I am persuaded in my heart, are but a company of cowards: would they have run else, think you, as they did, at the noise of one that was coming on the road? Why did not Little-faith pluck up a greater heart? He might, methinks, have stood one brush with them, and have yielded when there had been no remedy.

Christian. That they are cowards many have said, but few have found it so in the time of trial. As for a great heart, Little-faith had none; and I perceive by thee, my brother, hadst thou been the man concerned, thou art but for a brush and then to yield. And verily, since this is the height of thy stomach now they are at a distance from us, should they appear to thee as they did to him, they might put thee to second thoughts.

But consider again, they are but journeymen thieves, they serve under the King of the Bottomless Pit; who if need be will come in to their aid himself, and his voice is as the roaring of a lion. I myself have been engaged as this Little-faith was, and I found it a terrible thing. These three villains set upon me, and I beginning like a Christian to resist, they gave but a call and in came their master: I would, as the saying is, have given my life for a penny; but that, as God would have it, I was clothed with armour of proof.

Hopeful swaggers

No great heart for God, where there is but little faith. We have more courage when out, than when we are in

Christian tells his own experience in this case

Ay, and yet, though I was so harnessed, I found it hard work to quit myself like a man; no man can tell what in that combat attends us but he that hath been in the battle himself.

Hopeful. Well, but they ran, you see, when they did but suppose that one Great-grace was in the way.

Christian. True, they often fled, both they and their master, when Great-grace hath but appeared; and no marvel, for he is the King's champion: but I trow you will put some difference between Little-faith and the King's champion; all the King's subjects are not his champions: nor can they, when tried, do such feats of war as he. Is it meet to think that a little child should handle Goliah as David did? Or that there should be the strength of an ox in a wren? Some are strong, some are weak, some have great faith, some have little: this man was one of the weak, and therefore he went to the walls. *The King's champion*

Hopeful. I would it had been Great-grace for their sakes.

Christian. If it had been he, he might have had his hands full: for I must tell you, that though Great-grace is excellent good at his weapons, and has and can, so long as he keeps them at sword's point, do well enough with them: yet if they get within him, even Faint-heart, Mistrust, or the other, it shall go hard but they will throw up his heels. And when a man is down, you know, what can he do?

Whoso looks well upon Great-grace's face, shall see those scars and cuts there that shall easily give demonstration of what I say. Yea, once I heard he should say (and that when he was in the combat), *'We despaired even of life.'* How did these sturdy rogues and their fellows make David groan, mourn, and roar? Yea, Heman and Hezekiah[111] too, though champions in their day, were forced to bestir them when by these assaulted; and yet that notwithstanding they had their coats soundly brushed by them. Peter upon a time would go try what he could do; but though some do say of him that he is the Prince of the Apostles, they handled him so that they made him at last afraid of a sorry girl.[112]

Besides, their King is at their whistle, he is never out of hearing; and if at any time they be put to the worst, he, if possible, comes in to help them: and of him it is said, *The sword of him that layeth at him cannot hold: the spear, the dart, nor the habergeon; he* *Leviathan's* *esteemeth iron as straw, and brass as rotten wood. The* *sturdiness* *arrow cannot make him fly, sling-stones are turned with him into stubble, darts are counted as stubble, he laugheth at the shaking of a spear.* What can a man do in this case? 'Tis true, if a man could at every turn have Job's horse, and had skill and courage to ride him, he *The excellent* might do notable things. *For his neck is clothed with* *mettle that is* *thunder, he will not be afraid as the grasshopper, the glory* *in Job's horse* *of his nostrils is terrible, he paweth in the valley, rejoiceth in his strength, and goeth out to meet the armed men. He mocketh at fear, and is not affrighted, neither turneth back from the sword. The quiver rattleth against him, the glittering spear, and the shield. He swalloweth the ground with fierceness and rage, neither believeth he that it is the sound of the trumpet. He saith among the trumpets, Ha, ha; and he smelleth the battle afar off, the thundering of the captains, and the shoutings.*

But for such footmen as thee and I are, let us never desire to meet with an enemy, nor vaunt as if we could do better, when we hear of others that they have been foiled, nor be tickled at the thoughts of our own manhood, for such commonly come by the worst when tried. Witness Peter, of whom I made mention before. He would swagger, ay he would: he would, as his vain mind prompted him to say, do better, and stand more for his master, than all men: but who so foiled, and run down with these villains as he?

When therefore we hear that such robberies are done on the King's highway, two things become us to do: first to go out harnessed, and to be sure to take a shield with us, for it was for want of that, that he that laid so lustily at Leviathan could not make him yield. For indeed, if that be wanting, he fears us not at all. Therefore he that had skill, hath said, *Above all take the shield of faith, wherewith ye shall be able to quench all the fiery darts of the wicked.*

'Tis good also that we desire of the King a convoy, yea, that he will go with us himself. This made David rejoice when in the Valley of the Shadow of Death; and Moses was rather for dying where he stood, than to go one step without his God. O my brother, if he will but go along with us, what need we be afraid of ten thousands that shall set themselves against us, but without him, *the proud helpers fall under the slain.*[113]

'Tis good to have a convoy

I for my part have been in the fray before now, and though (through the goodness of him that is best) I am as you see alive, yet I cannot boast of my manhood. Glad shall I be if I meet with no more such brunts, though I fear we are not got beyond all danger. However, since the lion and the bear hath not as yet devoured me, I hope God will also deliver us from the next uncircumcised Philistine. Then sang Christian:

> *Poor Little-faith! Hast been among the thieves?*
> *Wast robbed? Remember this, whoso believes*
> *And gets more faith shall then a victor be*
> *Over ten thousand, else scarce over three.*

So they went on, and Ignorance followed. They went then till they came at a place where they saw a

A way and way put itself into their way, and seemed withal to
a way lie as straight as the way which they should go; and
here they knew not which of the two to take, for
both seemed straight before them, therefore here
they stood still to consider. And as they were thinking about the way, behold, a man black of flesh,[114]
but covered with a very light robe, came to them, and
asked them why they stood there. They answered
they were going to the Celestial City, but knew not
which of these ways to take. 'Follow me,' said the
man, 'it is thither that I am going.' So they followed
him in the way that but now came into the road,
Christian which by degrees turned, and turned them so from
and his the City that they desired to go to, that in little time
fellow their faces were turned away from it; yet they
deluded followed him. But by and by, before they were
They are aware, he led them both within the compass of a
taken in a net, in which they were both so entangled that they
net knew not what to do; and with that, the white robe
fell off the black man's back: then they saw where
they were. Wherefore there they lay crying sometime, for they could not get themselves out.

They bewail *Christian.* Then said Christian to his fellow, Now
their do I see myself in an error; did not the shepherds bid
conditions us beware of the flatterers? As is the saying of the
wise man, so we have found it this day: *A man that
flattereth his neighbour, spreadeth a net for his feet.*

Hopeful. They also gave us a note of directions
about the way for our more sure finding thereof:
but therein we have also forgotten to read, and have
not kept ourselves from the paths of the destroyer.
Here David was wiser than we; for saith he, 'Con-
A Shining One cerning the works of men, by the word of thy lips, I have
comes to them kept me from the paths of the destroyer.'[115] Thus they lay
with a whip bewailing themselves in the net. At last they espied
in his hand a Shining One coming towards them with a whip of

small cord in his hand. When he was come to the place where they were, he asked them whence they came and what they did there. They told him that they were poor pilgrims going to Sion, but were led out of their way by a black man, clothed in white; 'who bid us,' said they, 'follow him; for he was going thither too.' Then said he with the whip, 'it is Flatterer, a false apostle, that hath transformed himself into an angel of light.' So he rent the net and let the men out. Then said he to them, 'Follow me, that I may set you in your way again'; so he led them back to the way, which they had left to follow the Flatter- *They are examined, and convicted of forgetfulness* er. Then he asked them, saying, 'Where did you lie the last night?' They said, 'With the shepherds upon the Delectable Mountains.' He asked them then if they had not of them shepherds a note of direction for the way. They answered, 'Yes.' 'But did you,' said he, 'when you was at a stand, pluck out and read your note?' They answered, 'No.' He asked them why. They said they forgot. He asked moreover, if *Deceivers fine spoken* the shepherds did not bid them beware of the Flatterer. They answered, 'Yes. But we did not imagine,' said they, 'that this fine-spoken man had been he.'

Then I saw in my dream, that he commanded them to lie down; which when they did, he chastised them sore, to teach them the good way wherein they should walk; and as he chastised them, he said, '*As many as I love, I rebuke and chasten; be zealous therefore and repent.*' This done, he bids them go on their way, *They are whipped and sent on their way* and take good heed to the other directions of the shepherds. So they thanked him for all his kindness, and went softly along the right way, singing,

> Come hither, you that walk along the way,
> See how the pilgrims fare, that go astray!

They catched are in an entangling net,
'Cause they good counsel lightly did forget:
'Tis true, they rescued were, but yet you see
They're scourged to boot: let this your caution be.

Now after a while they perceived afar off, one coming softly and alone all along the highway to meet them. Then said Christian to his fellow, 'Yonder is a man with his back toward Sion, and he is coming to meet us.'

Hopeful. I see him, let us take heed to ourselves now, lest he should prove a Flatterer also. So he drew nearer and nearer, and at last came up unto them.

The Atheist meets them His name was <u>Atheist</u>, and he asked them whither they were going.

Christian. We are going to the Mount Sion.

He laughs at them Then Atheist fell into a very great laughter.

Christian. What is the meaning of your laughter?

Atheist. I laugh to see what ignorant persons you are, to take upon you so tedious a journey; and yet are like to have nothing but your travel for your pains.

They reason together *Christian.* Why man? Do you think we shall not be received?

Atheist. Received! There is no such place as you dream of in all this world.

Christian. But there is in the world to come.

Atheist. When I was at home in mine own country, I heard as you now affirm, and from that hearing went out to see, and have been seeking this City this twenty years, but find no more of it, than I did the first day I set out.

Christian. We have both heard and believe that there is such a place to be found.

The Atheist takes up his content in this world *Atheist.* Had not I, when at home, believed, I had not come thus far to seek: but finding none (and yet I should, had there been such a place to be found, for

I have gone to seek it further than you), I am going back again, and will seek to refresh myself with the things that I then cast away for hopes of that which I now see is not.

Christian. Then said Christian to Hopeful his fellow, Is it true which this man hath said? *Christian proveth his brother.*

Hopeful. Take heed, he is one of the Flatterers; remember what it hath cost us once already for our hearkening to such kind of fellows. What! No Mount Sion? Did we not see from the Delectable Mountains the Gate of the City? Also, are we not now to walk by faith? Let us go on, said Hopeful, lest the man with the whip overtakes us again. *Hopeful's gracious answer*

You should have taught me that lesson, which I will round you in the ears withal; *Cease, my son, to hear the instruction that causeth to err from the words of knowledge.* I say my brother, cease to hear him, and let us believe to the saving of the soul. *A remembrance of former chastisements is an help against present temptations*

Christian. My brother, I did not put the question to thee, for that I doubted of the truth of our belief myself. But to prove thee, and to fetch from thee a fruit of the honesty of thy heart. As for this man, I know that he is blinded by the god of this world. Let thee and I go on knowing that we have belief of the truth, and no lie is of the truth. *A fruit of an honest heart*

Hopeful. Now do I rejoice in hope of the glory of God. So they turned away from the man, and he, laughing at them, went his way.

I saw then in my dream that they went till they came into a certain country, whose air naturally tended to make one drowsy, if he came a stranger into it. And here Hopeful began to be very dull and heavy of sleep, wherefore he said unto Christian, 'I do now begin to grow so drowsy that I can scarcely hold up mine eyes; let us lie down here and take one nap.' *They are come to the Enchanted Ground*

Hopeful begins to be drowsy

Christian keeps him awake

Christian. By no means, said the other, lest sleeping, we never awake more.

Hopeful. Why my brother? Sleep is sweet to the labouring man; we may be refreshed if we take a nap.

Christian. Do you not remember, that one of the shepherds bid us beware of the Enchanted Ground? He meant by that that we should beware of sleeping; wherefore let us not sleep as do others, but let us watch and be sober.

He is thankful

Hopeful. I acknowledge myself in a fault, and had I been here alone, I had by sleeping run the danger of death. I see it is true that the wise man saith, *Two are better than one.* Hitherto hath thy company been my mercy; and thou shalt have a good reward for thy labour.

To prevent drowsiness, they fall to good discourse. Good discourse prevents drowsiness

Christian. Now then, said Christian, to prevent drowsiness in this place, let us fall into good discourse.

Hopeful. With all my heart, said the other.

Christian. Where shall we begin?

Hopeful. Where God began with us.[116] But do you begin if you please.

The Dreamer's note

> When saints do sleepy grow, let them come hither,
> And hear how these two pilgrims talk together:
> Yea, let them learn of them, in any wise
> Thus to keep ope their drowsy slumbering eyes.
> Saints' fellowship, if it be managed well,
> Keeps them awake, and that in spite of Hell.

They begin at the beginning of their conversion

Christian. Then Christian began and said, I will ask you a question. How came you to think at first of doing as you do now?

Hopeful. Do you mean, How came I at first to look after the good of my soul?

Christian. Yes, that is my meaning.

Hopeful. I continued a great while in the delight of

those things which were seen and sold at our Fair; things which, as I believe now, would have (had I continued in them still) drownded me in perdition and destruction.

Christian. What things were they?

Hopeful. All the treasures and riches of the world. Also I delighted much in rioting, revelling, drinking, swearing, lying, uncleanness, sabbath-breaking, and what not, that tended to destroy the soul. But I found at last, by hearing and considering of things that are divine, which indeed I heard of you, as also of beloved Faithful that was put to death for his faith and good-living in Vanity-Fair, *That the end of these things is death.* And that for these things' sake the wrath of God cometh upon the children of disobedience. *Hopeful's life before conversion*

Christian. And did you presently fall under the power of this conviction?

Hopeful. No, I was not willing presently to know the evil of sin, nor the damnation that follows upon the commission of it, but endeavoured, when my mind at first began to be shaken with the Word, to shut mine eyes against the light thereof. *Hopeful at first shuts his eyes against the light*

Christian. But what was the cause of your carrying of it thus to the first workings of God's blessed spirit upon you?

Hopeful. The causes were: 1. I was ignorant that this was the work of God upon me. I never thought that by awakenings for sin, God at first begins the conversion of a sinner. 2. Sin was yet very sweet to my flesh, and I was loath to leave it. 3. I could not tell how to part with mine old companions, their presence and actions were so desirable unto me. 4. The hours in which convictions were upon me were such troublesome and such heart-affrighting hours that I could not bear, no, not so much as the remembrance of them upon my heart. *Reasons of his resisting of light*

Christian. Then as it seems, sometimes you got rid of your trouble.

Hopeful. Yes verily, but it would come into my mind again; and then I should be as bad, nay, worse than I was before.

Christian. Why, what was it that brought your sins to mind again?

Hopeful. Many things, as,

When he had lost his sense of sin, what brought it again

1. If I did but meet a good man in the streets, or,
2. If I have heard any read in the Bible, or,
3. If mine head did begin to ache, or,
4. If I were told that some of my neighbours were sick, or,
5. If I heard the bell toll for some that were dead, or,
6. If I thought of dying myself, or,
7. If I heard that sudden death happened to others.
8. But especially, when I thought of myself that I must quickly come to judgement.

Christian. And could you at any time with ease get off the guilt of sin when by any of these ways it came upon you?

Hopeful. No, not latterly, for then they got faster hold of my conscience. And then, if I did but think of going back to sin (though my mind was turned against it) it would be double torment to me.

Christian. And how did you do then?

When he could no longer shake off his guilt by sinful courses, then he endeavours to mend

Hopeful. I thought I must endeavour to mend my life, for else, thought I, I am sure to be damned.

Christian. And did you endeavour to mend?

Hopeful. Yes, and fled from, not only my sins, but sinful company too; and betook me to religious duties, as praying, reading, weeping for sin, speaking truth to my neighbours, etc. These things I did, with many others, too much here to relate.

Christian. And did you think yourself well then?

Hopeful. Yes, for a while; but at the last my trouble came tumbling upon me again, and that over the neck of all my reformations. *Then he thought himself well*

Christian. How came that about, since you was now reformed?

Hopeful. There were several things brought it upon me, especially such sayings as these: *All our righteousnesses are as filthy rags. By the works of the law no man shall be justified. When you have done all things, say, We are unprofitable*; with many more the like: from whence I began to reason with myself thus: if all my righteousnesses are filthy rags, if by the deeds of the law no man can be justified, and if when we have done all, we are yet unprofitable, then 'tis but a folly to think of Heaven by the law. I further thought thus: If a man runs a hundred pound into the shop-keeper's debt, and after that shall pay for all that he shall fetch, yet his old debt stands still in the book uncrossed for the which the shop-keeper may sue him, and cast him into prison till he shall pay the debt. *Reformation at last could not help, and why*

His being a debtor by the law troubled him

Christian. Well, and how did you apply this to yourself?

Hopeful. Why, I thought thus with myself; I have by my sins run a great way into God's book, and that my now reforming will not pay off that score; therefore I should think still under all my present amendments. But how shall I be freed from that damnation that I have brought myself in danger of by my former transgressions?

Christian. A very good application: but pray go on.

Hopeful. Another thing that hath troubled me, even since my late amendments, is, that if I look narrowly into the best of what I do now, I still see sin, new sin, mixing itself with the best of that I do. So that now I am forced to conclude that notwith- *His espying bad things in his best duties, troubled him* standing my former fond conceits of myself and duties, I have committed sin enough in one duty to send me to Hell though my former life had been faultless.

Christian. And what did you do then?

Hopeful. Do! I could not tell what to do till I brake my mind to Faithful; for he and I were well acquainted. And he told me that unless I could obtain the righteousness of a man that never had sinned, neither mine own nor all the righteousness of the world could save me.

This made him break his mind to Faithful, who told him the way to be saved

Christian. And did you think he spake true?

Hopeful. Had he told me so when I was pleased and satisfied with mine own amendments, I had called him fool for his pains: but now, since I see my own infirmity, and the sin that cleaves to my best performance, I have been forced to be of his opinion.

Christian. But did you think, when at first he suggested it to you, that there was such a man to be found of whom it might justly be said, that he never committed sin?

Hopeful. I must confess the words at first sounded strangely, but after a little more talk and company with him I had full conviction about it.

At which he started at present

Christian. And did you ask him what man this was and how you must be justified by him?

Hopeful. Yes, and he told me it was the Lord Jesus, that dwelleth on the right hand of the Most High: 'and thus,' said he, 'you must be justified by him, even by trusting to what he hath done by himself in the days of his flesh, and suffered when he did hang on the tree.' I asked him further, how that man's righteousness could be of that efficacy to justify another before God. And he told me he was the mighty God, and did what he did, and died the death also, not for himself, but for me; to whom his doings,

A more particular discovery of the way to be saved

and the worthiness of them should be imputed, if I believed on him.

Christian. And what did you do then?

Hopeful. I made my objections against my believ- *He doubts of* ing, for that I thought he was not willing to save me. *acceptation*

Christian. And what said Faithful to you then?

Hopeful. He bid me go to him and see: then I said it was presumption; but he said, 'No: for I was invited to come'. Then he gave me a book of Jesus *He is better* his inditing, to encourage me the more freely to *instructed* come. And he said, concerning that book, that every jot and tittle thereof stood firmer than Heaven and earth. Then I asked him what I must do when I came and he told me I must entreat upon my knees with all my heart and soul, the Father to reveal him to me. Then I asked him further, how I must make my supplication to him? And he said, 'Go, and thou shalt find him upon a mercy-seat, where he sits all the year long to give pardon and forgiveness to them that come. I told him that I knew not what to say when I came: and he bid me say to this effect, God *He is bid to* be merciful to me a sinner, and make me to know *pray* and believe in Jesus Christ; for I see that if his righteousness had not been, or I have not faith in that righteousness, I am utterly cast away: Lord, I have heard that thou art a merciful God, and hast ordained that thy Son Jesus Christ should be the Saviour of the world; and moreover, thou art willing to bestow him upon such a poor sinner as I am (and I am a sinner indeed), Lord take therefore this opportunity, and magnify thy grace in the salvation of my soul, through thy Son Jesus Christ. Amen.

Christian. And did you do as you were bidden?

Hopeful. Yes, over and over and over.

Christian. And did the Father reveal his Son to you?

He prays

Hopeful. Not at the first, nor second, nor third, nor fourth, nor fifth, no, nor at the sixth time neither.

Christian. What did you do then?

Hopeful. What! Why I could not tell what to do.

Christian. Had you not thoughts of leaving off praying?

He thought to leave off praying.
He durst not leave off praying, and why

Hopeful. Yes, an hundred times, twice told.

Christian. And what was the reason you did not?

Hopeful. I believed that that was true which had been told me, to wit, that without the righteousness of this Christ, all the world could not save me; and therefore thought I with myself, if I leave off, I die, and I can but die at the throne of grace. And withal, this came into my mind, *If it tarry, wait for it, because it will surely come, and will not tarry.* So I continued praying until the Father showed me his Son.

Christian. And how was he revealed unto you?

Hopeful. I did not see him with my bodily eyes, but with the eyes of mine understanding; and thus it was. One day I was very sad, I think sadder than at any one time in my life; and this sadness was through a fresh sight of the greatness and vileness of my sins: and as I was then looking for nothing but Hell, and the everlasting damnation of my soul, suddenly, as I thought, I saw the Lord Jesus look down from Heaven upon me, and saying, *'Believe on the Lord Jesus Christ, and thou shalt be saved.'*

Christ is revealed to him, and how

But I replied, 'Lord, I am a great, a very great sinner'; and he answered, *'My grace is sufficient for thee.'* Then I said 'But Lord, what is believing?' And then I saw from that saying *He that cometh to me shall never hunger, and he that believeth on me shall never thirst* that believing and coming was all one, and that he that came, that is, run out in his heart and affections after salvation by Christ, he indeed believed in Christ. Then the water stood in mine eyes, and I asked further, 'But Lord, may such a great sinner as I am be indeed accepted of thee, and be saved by thee?' And I heard him say, '*And him that cometh to me, I will in no wise cast out.*' Then I said, 'But how, Lord, must I consider of thee in my coming to thee, that my faith may be placed aright upon thee?' Then he said, '*Christ Jesus came into the world to save sinners. He is the end of the law for righteousness to every one that believes. He died for our sins, and rose again for our justification. He loved us, and washed us from our sins in his own blood. He is mediator between God and us. He ever liveth to make intercession for us.*' From all which I gathered that I must look for righteousness in his person, and for satisfaction for my sins by his blood; that what he did in obedience to his Father's law, and in submitting to the penalty thereof, was not for himself, but for him that will accept it for his salvation, and be thankful. And now was my heart full of joy, mine eyes full of tears, and mine affections running over with love, to the name, people, and ways of Jesus Christ.

Christian. This was a revelation of Christ to your soul indeed: but tell me particularly what effect this had upon your spirit?

Hopeful. It made me see that all the world, notwithstanding all the righteousness thereof, is in a state of condemnation. It made me see that God the Father, though he be just, can justly justify the coming sinner. It made me greatly ashamed of the vileness of my former life, and confounded me with the sense of mine own ignorance; for there never came thought into mine heart before now that showed me so the beauty of Jesus Christ. It made me love a holy life, and long to do something for the honour and glory of the name of the Lord Jesus. Yea, I thought, that had I now a thousand gallons of blood in my body, I could spill it all for the sake of the Lord Jesus.

I then saw in my dream, that Hopeful looked back and saw Ignorance, whom they had left behind, coming after. 'Look,' said he, to Christian, 'how far yonder youngster loitereth behind.'

Christian. Ay, ay, I see him; he careth not for our company.

Hopeful. But I trow, it would not have hurt him, had he kept pace with us hitherto.

Christian. That's true, but I warrant you he thinketh otherwise.

Young Ignorance comes up again

Hopeful. That I think he doth, but however let us tarry for him. So they did.

Then Christian said to him, 'Come away man, why do you stay so behind?'

Their talk

Ignorance. I take my pleasure in walking alone, even more a great deal than in company, unless I like it the better.

Then said Christian to Hopeful (but softly), 'Did I not tell you he cared not for our company? But however, come up and let us talk away the time in this solitary place.' Then directing his speech to Ignorance, he said, 'Come, how do you? How stands it between God and your soul now?'

Ignorance's hope, and the ground of it

Ignorance. I hope well, for I am always full of good motions, that come into my mind to comfort me as I walk.

Christian. What good motions? Pray tell us.

Ignorance. Why, I think of God and Heaven.

Christian. So do the devils and damned souls.

Ignorance. But I think of them and desire them.

Christian. So do many that are never like to come there: *The soul of the sluggard desires and hath nothing.*[117]

Ignorance. But I think of them, and leave all for them.

Christian. That I doubt, for leaving of all is an hard matter, yea, a harder matter than many are aware of. But why or by what art thou persuaded that thou hast left all for God and Heaven?

Ignorance. My heart tells me so.

Christian. The wise man says, *He that trusts his own heart is a fool.*

Ignorance. That is spoken of an evil heart, but mine is a good one.

Christian. But how dost thou prove that?

Ignorance. It comforts me in the hopes of Heaven.

Christian. That may be through its deceitfulness, for a man's heart may minister comfort to him in the hopes of that thing for which he yet has no ground to hope.

Ignorance. But my heart and life agree together, and therefore my hope is well grounded.

Christian. Who told thee that thy heart and life agrees together?

Ignorance. My heart tells me so.

Christian. Ask my fellow if I be a thief; thy heart tells thee so! Except the Word of God beareth witness in this matter, other testimony is of no value.

Ignorance. But is it not a good heart that has good thoughts? And is not that a good life, that is according to God's commandments?

Christian. Yes, that is a good heart that hath good thoughts, and that is a good life that is according to God's commandments. But it is one thing indeed to have these, and another thing only to think so.

Ignorance. Pray, what count you good thoughts, and a life according to God's commandments?

Christian. There are good thoughts of divers kinds, some respecting ourselves, some God, some Christ, and some other things.

Ignorance. What be good thoughts respecting ourselves?

What are good thoughts

Christian. Such as agree with the Word of God.

Ignorance. When does our thoughts of ourselves agree with the Word of God?

Christian. When we pass the same judgement upon ourselves which the Word passes. To explain myself, the Word of God saith of persons in a natural condition, *There is none righteous, there is none that doth good.* It saith also, *That every imagination of the heart of man is only evil, and that continually.* And again, *The imagination of man's heart is evil from his youth.* Now then, when we think thus of ourselves, having sense thereof, then are our thoughts good ones, because according to the Word of God.

Ignorance. I will never believe that my heart is thus bad.

Christian. Therefore thou never hadst one good thought concerning thyself in thy life. But let me go on: as the Word passeth a judgement upon our HEART, so it passeth a judgement upon our WAYS; and when our thoughts of our HEARTS and WAYS agree with the judgement which the Word giveth of both, then are both good because agreeing thereto.

Ignorance. Make out your meaning.

Christian. Why, the Word of God saith that man's ways are crooked ways, not good, but perverse: it saith, *They are naturally out of the good way, that they have not known it.* Now when a man thus thinketh of his ways, I say when he doth sensibly, and with heart-humiliation thus think, then hath he good thoughts of his own ways, because his thoughts now agree with the judgement of the Word of God.

Ignorance. What are good thoughts concerning God?

Christian. Even (as I have said concerning ourselves)

when our thoughts of God do agree with what the Word saith of him. And that is when we think of his being and attributes as the Word hath taught: of which I cannot now discourse at large. But to speak of him with reference to us, then we have right thoughts of God, when we think that he knows us better than we know ourselves, and can see sin in us when and where we can see none in ourselves; when we think he knows our inmost thoughts, and that our heart, with all its depths is always open unto his eyes: also when we think that all our righteousness stinks in his nostrils, and that therefore he cannot abide to see us stand before him in any confidence, even of all our best performances.

Ignorance. Do you think that I am such a fool as to think God can see no further than I? Or that I would come to God in the best of my performances?

Christian. Why, how dost thou think in this matter?

Ignorance. Why, to be short, I think I must believe in Christ for justification.

Christian. How! Think thou must believe in Christ, when thou seest not thy need of him! Thou neither seest thy original, nor actual infirmities, but hast such an opinion of thyself, and of what thou doest as plainly renders thee to be one that did never see a necessity of Christ's personal righteousness to justify thee before God. How then dost thou say, 'I believe in Christ?'

Ignorance. I believe well enough for all that.

Christian. How doest thou believe?

Ignorance. I believe that Christ died for sinners, and that I shall be justified before God from the curse through his gracious acceptance of my obedience to his law: or thus, Christ makes my duties that are religious, acceptable to his Father by virtue of his merits; and so shall I be justified.

Christian. Let me give an answer to this confession of thy faith.

The faith of 1. Thou believest with a fantastical faith, for this
Ignorance faith is nowhere described in the Word.

2. Thou believest with a false faith, because it taketh justification from the personal righteousness of Christ and applies it to thy own.

3. This faith maketh not Christ a justifier of thy person, but of thy actions; and of thy person for thy actions' sake, which is false.

4. Therefore this faith is deceitful,[118] even such as will leave thee under wrath, in the day of God Almighty. For true justifying faith puts the soul (as sensible of its lost condition by the law) upon flying for refuge unto Christ's righteousness (which righteousness of *his* is not an act of grace by which he maketh for justification *thy* obedience accepted with God, but *his* personal obedience to the law in doing and suffering for us what that required at our hands). This righteousness I say true faith accepteth, under the skirt of which the soul being shrouded, and by it presented as spotless before God, it is accepted, and acquit from condemnation.

Ignorance. What! Would you have us trust to what Christ in his own person has done without us? This conceit would loosen the reins of our lust, and tolerate us to live as we list: for what matter how we live if we may be justified by Christ's personal righteousness from all, when we believe it?

Christian. Ignorance is thy name, and as thy name is, so art thou; even this thy answer demonstrateth what I say. Ignorant thou art of what justifying righteousness is, and as ignorant how to secure thy soul through the faith of it from the heavy wrath of God. Yea, thou also art ignorant of the true effects of saving faith in this righteousness of Christ, which is to bow and win over the heart to God in Christ to love his name, his word, ways and people, and not as thou ignorantly imaginest.

Hopeful. Ask him if ever he had Christ revealed to him from Heaven?

Ignorance. What! You are a man for revelations! I believe that what both you, and all the rest of you say about that matter, is but the fruit of distracted brains. *Ignorance angles with them*

Hopeful. Why man! Christ is so hid in God from the natural apprehensions of all flesh, that he cannot by any man be savingly known, unless God the Father reveals him to them.

Ignorance. That is your faith, but not mine; yet mine I doubt not, is as good as yours, though I have not in my head so many whimsies as you. *He speaks reproachfully of what he knows not*

Christian. Give me leave to put in a word: you ought not so slightly to speak of this matter: for this I will boldly affirm (even as my good companion hath done), that no man can know Jesus Christ but by the revelation of the Father: yea, and faith too, by which the soul layeth hold upon Christ (if it be right) must be wrought by the exceeding greatness of his mighty power, the working of which faith, I perceive, poor Ignorance, thou art ignorant of. Be awakened then, see thine own wretchedness, and fly to the Lord Jesus, and by his righteousness, which is the righteousness of God (for he himself is God), thou shalt be delivered from condemnation.

Ignorance. You go so fast, I cannot keep pace with you; do you go on before, I must stay a while behind. *The talk broke up*

Then they said,

> *Well, Ignorance, wilt thou yet foolish be,*
> *To slight good counsel ten times given thee?*
> *And if thou yet refuse it, thou shalt know*
> *Ere long the evil of thy doing so:*

Remember man in time, stoop, do not fear,
Good counsel taken well, saves; therefore hear:
But if thou yet shalt slight it, thou wilt be
The loser, Ignorance, I'll warrant thee.

Then Christian addressed thus himself to his fellow.

Christian. Well, come my good Hopeful, I perceive that thou and I must walk by ourselves again.

So I saw in my dream, that they went on a pace before, and Ignorance he came hobbling after. Then said Christian to his companion, 'It pities me much for this poor man, it will certainly go ill with him at last.'

Hopeful. Alas, there are abundance in our town in his condition, whole families, yea, whole streets (and that of pilgrims too), and if there be so many in our parts, how many, think you, must there be in the place where he was born?

Christian. Indeed the Word saith, *He hath blinded their eyes, lest they should see*, etc. But now we are by ourselves, what do you think of such men? Have they at no time, think you, convictions of sin, and so consequently fears that their state is dangerous?

Hopeful. Nay, do you answer that question yourself, for you are the elder man.

Christian. Then, I say, sometimes (as I think) they may, but they being naturally ignorant, understand not that such convictions tend to their good; and therefore they do desperately seek to stifle them, and presumptuously continue to flatter themselves in the way of their own hearts.

The good use of fear

Hopeful. I do believe as you say that fear tends much to men's good, and to make them right at their beginning to go on pilgrimage.

Christian. Without all doubt it doth, if it be right:

for so says the Word, *The fear of the Lord is the beginning of wisdom.*

Hopeful. How will you describe right fear?

Christian. True, or right fear, is discovered by three things: *Right fear*

1. By its rise: it is caused by saving convictions for sin.

2. It driveth the soul to lay fast hold of Christ[119] for salvation.

3. It begetteth and continueth in the soul a great reverence of God, his Word, and ways, keeping it tender and making it afraid to turn from them, to the right hand, or to the left, to any thing that may dishonour God, break its peace, grieve the Spirit, or cause the enemy to speak reproachfully.

Hopeful. Well said, I believe you have said the truth. Are we now almost got past the Enchanted Ground?

Christian. Why, are you weary of this discourse?

Hopeful. No verily, but that I would know where we are.

Christian. We have not now above two miles further to go thereon. But let us return to our matter. Now the ignorant know not that such convictions that tend to put them in fear are for their good, and therefore they seek to stifle them. *Why ignorant persons stifle convictions. 1. In general*

Hopeful. How do they seek to stifle them?

Christian. 1. They think that those fears are wrought by the Devil (though indeed they are wrought of God) and thinking so, they resist them, as things that directly tend to their overthrow. 2. They also think that these fears tend to the spoiling of their faith when, alas for them, poor men that they are! they have none at all), and therefore they harden their hearts against them. 3. They presume they ought not to fear, and therefore, in despite of them, wax *2. In particular* presumptuously confident. 4. They see that these fears tend to take away from them their pitiful old self-holiness, and therefore they resist them with all their might.

Hopeful. I know something of this myself; for before I knew myself it was so with me.

Christian. Well, we will leave at this time our neighbour Ignorance by himself, and fall upon another profitable question.

Talk about one Temporary

Hopeful. With all my heart, but you shall still begin.

Christian. Well then, did you not know about ten years ago, one <u>Temporary</u> in your parts, who was a forward man in religion then?

Hopeful. Know him! Yes, he dwelt in Graceless, a town about two miles off of Honesty, and he dwelt next door to one Turn-back.

Where he dwelt

Christian. Right, he dwelt under the same roof with him. Well, that man was much awakened once; I believe that then he had some sight of his sins, and of the wages that was due thereto.

He was towardly once

Hopeful. I am of your mind, for (my house not being above three miles from him) he would oft times come to me, and that with many tears. Truly I pitied the man, and was not altogether without hope of him; but one may see, *it is not every one that cries, Lord, Lord.*

Christian. He told me once that he was resolved to go on pilgrimage, as we do now; but all of a sudden he grew acquainted with one Save-self, and then he became a stranger to me.

Hopeful. Now since we are talking about him, let us a little inquire into the reason of the sudden back-sliding of him and such others.

Christian. It may be very profitable, but do you begin.

Hopeful. Well then, there are in my judgement four reasons for it.

1. Though the consciences of such men are awakened, yet their minds are not changed: therefore when the power of guilt weareth away, that which provoked them to be religious ceaseth. Wherefore they naturally turn to their own course again: even as we see the dog that is sick of what he hath eaten, so long as his sickness prevails, he vomits and casts up all; not that he doth this of a free mind (if we may say a dog has a mind) but because it troubleth his stomach; but now when his sickness is over, and so his stomach eased, his desires being not at all alienate from his vomit, he turns him about, and licks up all. And so it is true which is written, *The dog is turned to his own vomit again*. Thus, I say, being hot for Heaven, by virtue only of the sense and fear of the torments of Hell, as their sense of Hell, and the fears of damnation chills and cools, so their desires for Heaven and salvation cool also. So then it comes to pass, that when their guilt and fear is gone, their desires for Heaven and happiness die; and they return to their course again.

Reason why towardly ones go back

2. Another reason is, they have slavish fears that do over-master them. I speak now of the fears that they have of men: *For the fear of men bringeth a snare*. So then, though they seem to be hot for Heaven so long as the flames of Hell are about their ears, yet when that terror is a little over, they betake themselves to second thoughts, namely, that 'tis good to be wise, and not to run (for they know not what) the hazard of losing all; or at least, of bringing themselves into unavoidable and unnecessary troubles: and so they fall in with the world again.

3. The shame that attends religion lies also as a block in their way; they are proud and haughty, and

religion in their eye is low and contemptible: therefore when they have lost their sense of Hell and wrath to come, they return again to their former course.

4. Guilt, and to meditate terror, are grievous to them, they like not to see their misery before they come into it, though perhaps the sight of it first, if they loved that sight, might make them fly whither the righteous fly and are safe. But because they do as I hinted before, even shun the thoughts of guilt and terror, therefore, when once they are rid of their awakenings about the terrors and wrath of God they harden their hearts gladly, and choose such ways as will harden them more and more.

Christian. You are pretty near the business, for the bottom of all is for want of a change in their mind and will. And therefore they are but like the felon that standeth before the judge; he quakes and trembles, and seems to repent most heartily; but the bottom of all is the fear of the halter, not of any detestation of the offence, as is evident, because, let but this man have his liberty, and he will be a thief, and so a rogue still, whereas, if his mind was changed, he would be otherwise.

Hopeful. Now I have showed you the reasons of their going back, do you show me the manner thereof.

Christian. So I will willingly.

How the apostate goes back

1. They draw off their thoughts all that they may from the remembrance of God, death, and judgement to come.

2. Then they cast off by degrees private duties, as closet-prayer, curbing their lusts, watching, sorrow for sin, and the like.

3. Then they shun the company of lively and warm Christians.

4. After that, they grow cold to public duty, as hearing, reading, godly conference, and the like.

5. Then they begin to pick holes, as we say; in the coats of some of the godly, and that devilishly that they may have a seeming colour to throw religion (for the sake of some infirmity they have spied in them) behind their backs.

6. Then they begin to adhere to and associate themselves with carnal, loose, and wanton men.

7. Then they give way to carnal and wanton discourses in secret; and glad are they if they can see such things in any that are counted honest, that they may the more boldly do it through their example.

8. After this, they begin to play with little sins openly.

9. And then, being hardened, they show themselves as they are. Thus being launched again into the gulf of misery, unless a miracle of grace prevent it they everlastingly perish in their own deceivings.

Now I saw in my dream that by this time the pilgrims were got over the Enchanted Ground, and entering into the country of Beulah,[120] whose air was very sweet and pleasant; the way lying directly through it, they solaced themselves there for a season. Yea, here they heard continually the singing of birds, and saw every day the flowers appear in the earth, and heard the voice of the turtle in the land.[121] In this country the sun shineth night and day; wherefore this was beyond the Valley of the Shadow of Death, and also out of the reach of Giant Despair; neither could they from this place so much as see Doubting-Castle. Here they were within sight of the City they were going to, also here met them some of the inhabitants thereof. For in this land the Shining *Angels* Ones commonly walked, because it was upon the borders of Heaven. In this land also the contract between the bride and the bridegroom was renewed: Yea here, *as the bridegroom rejoiceth over the bride, so did their God rejoice over them.* Here they had no want of corn and wine; for in this place they met with abundance of what they had sought for in all their pilgrimage. Here they heard voices from out of the City, loud voices, saying, *Say ye to the daughter of Sion, Behold thy salvation cometh, behold his reward is with him.* Here all the inhabitants of the country called them, *The holy people, the redeemed of the Lord, sought out,* etc.

Now as they walked in this land they had more rejoicing than in parts more remote from the Kingdom, to which they were bound; and drawing near to the City, they had yet a more perfect view thereof. It was builded of pearls and precious stones, also the street thereof was paved with gold, so that by reason of the natural glory of the City, and the reflection of the sunbeams upon it, Christian with desire fell sick, Hopeful also had a fit or two of the same disease: wherefore here they lay by it a while, crying out because of their pangs, 'If you see my Beloved, tell him that I am sick of love.'[122]

But being a little strengthened, and better able to bear their sickness, they walked on their way, and came yet nearer and nearer, where were orchards, vineyards, and gardens, and their gates opened into the highway. Now as they came up to these places, behold the gardener stood in the way; to whom the pilgrims said, 'Whose goodly vineyards and gardens are these?' He answered, 'They are the King's, and are planted here for his own delights, and also for the solace of pilgrims.' So the gardener had them into the vineyards, and bid them refresh themselves with the dainties; he also showed them there the King's walks and the arbours where he delighted to be. And here they tarried and slept.

Now I beheld in my dream, that they talked more in their sleep at this time, then ever they did in all their journey; and being in a muse thereabout, the gardener said even to me, 'Wherefore musest thou at the matter? It is the nature of the fruit of the grapes of these vineyards to go down so sweetly as to cause the lips of them that are asleep to speak.'

So I saw that when they awoke, they addressed themselves to go up to the City.[123] But, as I said, the reflections of the sun upon the City (for the City was pure gold) was so extremely glorious that they could not, as yet, with open face behold it, but through an instrument made for that purpose. So I saw that as they went on, there met them two men in raiment that shone like gold, also their faces shone as the light.

These men asked the pilgrims whence they came, and they told them; they also asked them where they had lodged, what difficulties and dangers, what comforts and pleasures they had met in the way, and they told them. Then said the men that met them, 'You have but two difficulties more to meet with, and then you are in the City.'

Christian then and his companion asked the men to go along with them, so they told them they would; 'But,' said they, 'you must obtain it by your own faith.' So I saw in my dream that they went on together till they came within sight of the Gate.

Now I further saw that betwixt them and the Gate was a River, but there was no bridge to go over; the River was very deep; at the sight therefore of this River, the pilgrims were much stounded, but the men that went with them, said, 'You must go through, or you cannot come at the Gate.'

Death is not welcome to nature though by it we pass out of this world into glory

The pilgrims then began to inquire if there was no other way to the Gate; to which they answered, 'Yes, but there hath not any, save two, to wit, Enoch and Elijah,[124] been permitted to tread that path, since the foundation of the world, nor shall, until the last trumpet shall sound.' The pilgrims then, especially Christian, began to despond in his mind, and looked this way and that, but no way could be found by them by which they might escape the River. Then they asked the men if the waters were all of a depth.

Angels help us not comfortably through death

They said no; yet they could not help them in that case; for said they, 'You shall find it deeper or shallower, as you believe in the King of the place.'

They then addressed themselves to the water; and entering, Christian began to sink, and crying out to his good friend Hopeful, he said, 'I sink in deep waters, the billows go over my head, all his waves go over me, Selah.'

Christian's conflict at the hour of death

Then said the other, 'Be of good cheer, my brother, I feel the bottom, and it is good.' Then said Christian, 'Ah my friend, the sorrows of death have compassed me about, I shall not see the land that flows with milk and honey.' And with that, a great darkness and horror fell upon Christian, so that he could not see before him; also here he in great measure lost his senses, so that he could neither remember nor orderly talk of any of those sweet refreshments that he had met with in the way of his pilgrimage. But all the words that he spake still tended to discover that he had horror of mind and hearty fears that he should die in that River, and never obtain entrance in at the Gate. Here also, as they that stood by perceived, he was much in the troublesome thoughts of the sins that he had committed both since and before he began to be a pilgrim. 'Twas also observed that he was troubled with apparitions of hobgoblins and evil spirits, for ever and anon he would intimate so much by words. Hopeful therefore here had much ado to keep his brother's head above water, yea, sometimes he would be quite gone down, and then ere a while he would rise up again half dead. Hopeful also would endeavour to comfort him, saying, 'Brother, I see the Gate, and men standing by it to receive us.' But Christian would answer, ''Tis you, 'tis you they wait for, you have been Hopeful ever since I knew you.' 'And so have you,' said he to Christian. 'Ah brother,' said he, 'surely if I was right, he would now arise to help me; but for my sins he hath brought me into the snare and hath left me.' Then said Hopeful, 'My brother, you have quite forgot the text where it's said of the wicked, *There is no band in their death, but their strength is firm, they are not troubled as other men, neither are they plagued like other men.*[125] These troubles and distresses that you go through in these waters are no sign that God hath forsaken you, but are sent to try you whether you will call to mind that which heretofore you have received of his goodness, and live upon him in your distresses.'

Then I saw in my dream that Christian was as in a muse a while; to whom also Hopeful added this word, 'Be of good cheer, Jesus Christ maketh thee whole.' And with that, Christian brake out with a loud voice, 'Oh I see him again! And he tells me, *When thou passest through the waters, I will be with thee, and through the rivers, they shall not overflow thee.*' Then they both took courage, and the enemy was after that as still as a stone, until they were gone over. Christian therefore presently found ground to stand upon; and so it followed that the rest of the River was but shallow. Thus they got over. Now upon the bank of the River, on the other side, they saw the

Christian delivered from his fears in death

two shining men again who there waited for them.
Wherefore being come up out of the river they saluted
them, saying, 'We are ministering Spirits, sent forth
to minister for those that shall be heirs of salvation.'
Thus they went along towards the Gate; now you
must note that the City stood upon a mighty hill,
but the pilgrims went up that hill with ease, because
they had these two men to lead them up by the arms;
also they had left their mortal garments behind them
in the River: for though they went in with them,
they came out without them. They therefore went
up here with much agility and speed, though the
foundation upon which the City was framed was
higher than the clouds. They therefore went up
through the regions of the air, sweetly talking as they
went, being comforted because they safely got over
the River, and had such glorious companions to
attend them.

The angels do wait for them so soon as they are passed out of this world

They have put off mortality

The talk that they had with the Shining Ones, was
about the glory of the place, who told them, that the
beauty, and glory of it was inexpressible. 'There,'
said they, 'is the Mount Sion, the heavenly Jerusalem,
the innumerable company of angels, and the spirits of
just men made perfect; you are going now,' said
they, 'to the Paradise of God, wherein you shall see
the Tree of Life, and eat of the never-fading fruits
thereof; and when you come there you shall have
white robes given you, and your walk and talk shall
be every day with the King, even all the days of
eternity. There you shall not see again such things as
you saw when you were in the lower region upon
the earth, to wit, sorrow, sickness, affliction, and
death, *for the former things are passed away.* You are
going now to Abraham, to Isaac, and Jacob, and to
the prophets, men that God hath taken away from
the evil to come, and that are now resting upon their

beds, each one walking in his righteousness.' The men then asked, 'What must we do in the holy place?' To whom it was answered, 'You must there receive the comfort of all your toil, and have joy for all your sorrow; you must reap what you have sown, even the fruit of all your prayers, and tears, and sufferings for the King by the way. In that place you must wear crowns of gold, and enjoy the perpetual sight and visions of the Holy One, *for there you shall see him as he is.* There also you shall serve him continually with praise, with shouting and thanksgiving, whom you desired to serve in the world, though with much difficulty, because of the infirmity of your flesh. There your eyes shall be delighted with seeing and your ears with hearing the pleasant voice of the Mighty One. There you shall enjoy your friends again, that are got thither before you; and there you shall with joy receive, even every one that follows into the holy place after you. There also you shall be clothed with glory and majesty, and put into an equipage fit to ride out with the King of Glory. When he shall come with sound of trumpet in the clouds, as upon the wings of the wind, you shall come with him; and when he shall sit upon the Throne of Judgement, you shall sit by him; yea, and when he shall pass sentence upon all the workers of iniquity, let them be angels or men, you also shall have a voice in that judgement, because they were his and your enemies. Also when he shall again return to the City, you shall go too, with sound of trumpet, and be ever with him.'

Now while they were thus drawing towards the Gate, behold a company of the heavenly host came out to meet them, to whom it was said, by the other two Shining Ones, 'These are the men that have loved our Lord, when they were in the world, and that have left all for his holy name, and he hath sent us to fetch them, and we have brought them thus far on their desired journey, that they may go in and look their Redeemer in the face with joy. Then the Heavenly Host gave a great shout, saying, '*Blessed are they that are called to the marriage supper of the Lamb.*'

There came out also at this time to meet them, several of the King's trumpeters, clothed in white and shining raiment, who with melodious noises and loud, made even the heavens to echo with their sound. These trumpeters saluted Christian[126] and his fellow with ten thousand welcomes from the world: and this they did with shouting and sound of trumpet.

This done, they compassed them round on every side; some went before, some behind, and some on the right hand, some on the left (as 'twere to guard them through the upper regions) continually sounding as they went with melodious noise in notes on high; so that the very sight was to them that could behold it as if Heaven itself was come down to meet them. Thus therefore they walked on together and as they walked, ever and anon these trumpeters, even with joyful sound would, by mixing their music, with looks and gestures, still signify to Christian and his brother how welcome they were into their company and with what gladness they came to meet them. And now were these two men, as 'twere, in Heaven, before they came at it; being swallowed up with the sight of angels, and with hearing of their melodious notes. Here also they had the City itself in view, and they thought they heard all the bells therein to ring, to welcome them thereto; but above all the warm and joyful thoughts that they had about their own dwelling there with such company, and that for ever and ever. Oh, by what tongue or pen can their glorious joy be expressed! And thus they came up to the Gate.

Now when they were come up to the Gate, there was written over it, in letters of gold, *Blessed are they that do his commandments, that they may have right to the Tree of Life; and may enter in through the Gates into the City.*

Then I saw in my dream that the shining men bid them call at the Gate, the which when they did, some from above looked over the Gate; to wit, Enoch, Moses, and Elijah, etc. to whom it was said, 'These pilgrims are come from the City of Destruction, for the love that they bear to the King of this place': and then the pilgrims gave in unto them each man his certificate, which they had received in the beginning; those therefore were carried into the King, who, when he had read them, said, 'Where are the men?' to whom it was answered, 'They are standing without the Gate.' The King then commanded to open the Gate; '*That the righteous nation*,' said he, '*that keepeth truth may enter in.*'

Now I saw in my dream, that these two men went in at the Gate; and lo, as they entered they were transfigured, and they had raiment put on that shone like gold. There was also that met them with harps and crowns, and gave them to them, the harp to praise withal, and the crowns in token of honour. Then I heard in my dream, that all the bells in the City rang again for joy; and that it was said unto them, '*Enter ye into the joy of your Lord.*' I also heard the men themselves, that they sang with a loud voice, saying, '*Blessing, honour, glory, and power, be to him that sitteth upon the throne, and to the Lamb for ever and ever.*'

Now just as the Gates were opened to let in the

men, I looked in after them; and behold, the City shone like the sun, the streets also were paved with gold, and in them walked many men with crowns on their heads, palms in their hands, and golden harps to sing praises withal.

There were also of them that had wings, and they answered one another without intermission, saying, *Holy, Holy, Holy, is the Lord*. And after that, they shut up the Gates: which when I had seen, I wished myself among them.

Now while I was gazing upon all these things, I turned my head to look back and saw Ignorance come up to the River side: but he soon got over, and that without half that difficulty which the other two men met with. For it happened, that there was then in that place one Vain-hope a ferry-man, that with his boat helped him over: so he, as the other I saw, did ascend the hill to come up to the Gate, only he came alone, neither did any man meet him with the least encouragement. When he was come up to the Gate he looked up to the writing that was above, and then began to knock, supposing that entrance should have been quickly administered to him. But he was asked by the men that looked over the top of the Gate, 'Whence came you, and what would you have?' He answered, 'I have eat and drank in the presence of the King, and he has taught in our streets.' Then they asked him for his certificate, that they might go in and show it to the King. So he fumbled in his bosom for one and found none. Then said they, 'Have you none?' But the man answered never a word. So they told the King, but he would not come down to see him; but commanded the two Shining Ones that conducted Christian and Hopeful to the City to go out and take Ignorance and bind him hand and foot, and have him away. Then they took him up, and carried him through the air to the door that I saw in the side of the hill, and put him in there. Then I saw that there was a way to Hell, even from the Gates of Heaven, as well as from the City of Destruction. So I awoke, and behold it was a dream.

FINIS

THE CONCLUSION

Now reader, I have told my dream to thee,
See if thou canst interpret it to me,
Or to thyself or neighbour: but take heed
Of misinterpreting: for that instead
Of doing good, will but thyself abuse:
By misinterpreting evil ensues.

Take heed also that thou be not extreme,
In playing with the outside of my dream:
Nor let my figure or similitude
Put thee into a laughter or a feud;
Leave this for boys and fools; but as for thee,
Do thou the substance of my matter see.

Put by the curtains, look within my veil;
Turn up my metaphors, and do not fail:
There if thou seekest them such things to find,
As will be helpful to an honest mind.

What of my dross thou findest there, be bold
To throw away, but yet preserve the gold.
What if my gold be wrapped up in ore?
None throws away the apple for the core:
But if thou shalt cast all away as vain,
I know not but 'twill make me dream again.[127]

THE END

THE
Pilgrim's Progress.
FROM
THIS WORLD
TO
That which is to come
The Second Part.

Delivered under-the Similitude of a

DREAM

Wherein is set forth

The manner of the setting out of *Chri
stian's* Wife and Children, their
Dangerous JOURNEY,
AND
Safe Arrival at the Desired Country.

By *JOHN BUNYAN,*

I have used Similitudes, Hos. 12 10

LONDON,
Printed for *Nathaniel Ponder* at the *Peacock*
in the *Poultry,* near the Church, 1684

THE AUTHOR'S WAY OF SENDING FORTH
HIS SECOND PART OF THE
PILGRIM

Go, now my little book to every place,
Where my first *Pilgrim* has but shown his face,
Call at their door: if any say, 'Who's there?'
Then answer thou, 'Christiana is here.'
If they bid thee 'Come in,' then enter thou
With all thy boys. And then, as thou know'st how,
Tell who they are, also from whence they came,
Perhaps they'll know them by their looks or name:
But if they should not, ask them yet again
If formerly they did not entertain
One Christian a pilgrim; if they say
They did, and was delighted in his way,
Then let them know that those related were
Unto him, yea, his wife and children are.

Tell them that they have left their house and
    home,
Are turned pilgrims, seek a world to come,
That they have met with hardships in the way,
That they do meet with troubles night and day;
That they have trod on serpents, fought with
    devils,
Have also overcome a many evils.
Yea, tell them also of the rest, who have
Of love to pilgrimage been stout and brave
Defenders of that way, and how they still
Refuse this world to do their Father's will.

Go, tell them also of those dainty things
That pilgrimage unto the pilgrim brings,
Let them acquainted be, too, how they are
Beloved of their King, under his care,
What goodly mansions for them he provides.

Tho' they meet with rough winds and swelling
    tides,
How brave a calm they will enjoy at last,
Who to their Lord, and by his ways hold fast.
    Perhaps with heart and hand they will embrace
Thee as they did my firstling,[1] and will grace
Thee and thy fellows with such cheer and fair,
As show will, they of pilgrims lovers are.

I. OBJECTION

But how if they will not believe of me
That I am truly thine, 'cause some there be
That counterfeit the pilgrim, and his name,
Seek by disguise to seem the very same.
And by that means have wrought themselves into,
The hands and houses of I know not who?

ANSWER

'Tis true, some have of late, to counterfeit
My pilgrim,[2] to their own my title set;
Yea others, half my name and title too
Have stitched to their book to make them do;
But yet they by their features do declare
Themselves not mine to be, whose ere they are.
    If such thou meet'st with, then thine only way
Before them all is to say out thy say,
In thine own native language,[3] which no man
Now useth, nor with ease dissemble can.
    If after all, they still of you shall doubt,
Thinking that you like gipsies go about,
In naughty-wise the country to defile,
Or that you seek good people to beguile
With things unwarrantable; send for me
And I will testify, you pilgrims be;
Yea, I will testify that only you
My pilgrims are, and that alone will do.

2. OBJECTION

But yet, perhaps, I may inquire for him,
Of those that wish him damned life and limb,
What shall I do, when I at such a door,
For pilgrims ask, and they shall rage the more?

ANSWER

Fright not thyself, my book, for such bugbears
Are nothing else but ground for groundless fears,
My pilgrim's book has travelled sea and land,
Yet could I never come to understand,
That it was slighted, or turned out of door
By any kingdom, were they rich or poor.
 In France and Flanders where men kill each other
My pilgrim is esteemed a friend, a brother.
 In Holland too, 'tis said, as I am told,
My pilgrim is with some, worth more than gold.
 Highlanders, and wild-Irish can agree,
My pilgrim should familiar with them be.
 'Tis in New England[4] under such advance,
Receives there so much loving countenance,
As to be trimmed, new clothed and decked with
    gems,
That it might show its features, and its limbs,
Yet more; so comely doth my pilgrim walk,
That of him thousands daily sing and talk.
 If you draw nearer home, it will appear
My pilgrim knows no ground of shame, or fear;
City and country will him entertain,
With welcome pilgrim, yea, they can't refrain
From smiling, if my pilgrim be but by,
Or shows his head in any company.
 Brave gallants[5] do my pilgrim hug and love,
Esteem it much, yea value it above
Things of a greater bulk, yea, with delight

Say my lark's leg is better than a kite.

  Young ladies, and young gentlewomen too,
Do no small kindness to my pilgrim show;
Their cabinets, their bosoms, and their hearts
My pilgrim has, 'cause he to them imparts
His pretty riddles in such wholesome strains
As yields them profit double to their pains
Of reading. Yea, I think I may be bold
To say some prize him far above their gold.

  The very children that do walk the street,
If they do but my holy pilgrim meet,
Salute him will, will wish him well and say,
He is the only stripling of the day.

  They that have never seen him yet admire
What they have heard of him, and much desire
To have his company, and hear him tell
Those pilgrim stories which he knows so well.

  Yea, some who did not love him at the first,
But called him Fool, and Noddy, say they must
Now they have seen and heard him, him commend,
And to those whom they love, they do him send.

  Wherefore my Second Part, thou needst not be
Afraid to show thy head: none can hurt thee
That wish but well to him that went before,
'Cause thou com'st after with a second store
Of things as good, as rich, as profitable,
For young, for old, for staggering and for stable.

3. OBJECTION

But some there be that say he laughs too loud;
And some do say his head is in a cloud.
Some say his words and stories are so dark
They know not how by them to find his mark.

ANSWER

  One may (I think) say both his laughs and cries,
May well be guessed at by his wat'ry eyes.

Some things are of that nature as to make
One's fancy checkle[6] while his heart doth ache,
When Jacob saw his Rachel with the sheep,
He did at the same time both kiss and weep.

    Whereas some say a cloud is in his head,
That doth but show how wisdom's covered
With its own mantles, and to stir the mind
To a search after what it fain would find,
Things that seem to be hid in words obscure,
Do but the godly mind the more allure;
To study what those sayings should contain,
That speak to us in such a cloudy strain.

    I also know, a dark similitude
Will on the fancy more itself intrude,
And will stick faster in the heart and head,
Than things from similes not borrowed.

    Wherefore, my book, let no discouragement
Hinder thy travels. Behold, thou art sent
To friends, not foes: to friends that will give place
To thee, thy pilgrims, and thy words embrace.

    Besides, what my first pilgrim left concealed,
Thou my brave second pilgrim hast revealed;
What Christian left locked up and went his way,
Sweet Christiana opens with her key.

4. OBJECTION

But some love not the method of your first,
Romance they count it, throw't away as dust,
If I should meet with such, what should I say?
Must I slight them as they slight me, or nay?

ANSWER

My Christiana, if with such thou meet,
By all means in all loving-wise, them greet;
Render them not reviling for revile:

But if they frown, I prithee on them smile.
Perhaps 'tis nature, or some ill report
Has made them thus despise, or thus retort.
  Some love no cheese, some love no fish, and
    some
Love not their friends, nor their own house or
    home;
Some start at pig, slight chicken, love not fowl,
More than they love a cuckoo or an owl.
Leave such, my Christiana, to their choice,
And seek those who to find thee will rejoice;
By no means strive, but in all humble wise,
Present thee to them in thy pilgrim's guise.
  Go then, my little book and show to all
That entertain, and bid thee welcome shall,
What thou shalt keep close, shut up from the rest,
And wish what thou shalt show them may be blest
To them for good, may make them choose to be
Pilgrims, better by far, than thee or me.
  Go then, I say, tell all men who thou art,
Say, I am Christiana, and my part
Is now with my four sons, to tell you what
It is for men to take a pilgrim's lot.
  Go also tell them who, and what they be,
That now do go on pilgrimage with thee;
Say, here's my neighbour Mercy, she is one,
That has longtime with me a pilgrim gone:
Come see her in her virgin face, and learn
Twixt idle ones, and pilgrim's to discern.
Yea let young damsels learn of her to prize
The world which is to come, in any wise;
When little tripping maidens follow God,
And leave old doting sinners to his rod,
'Tis like those days wherein the young ones cried
Hosannah to whom old ones did deride.
  Next tell them of old Honest, who you found

With his white hairs treading the pilgrim's ground,
Yea, tell them how plain-hearted this man was,
How after his good Lord he bare his cross:
Perhaps with some grey head this may prevail,
With Christ to fall in love and sin bewail.

Tell them also how Master Fearing went
On pilgrimage, and how the time he spent
In solitariness with fears and cries,
And how at last, he won the joyful prize.
He *was* a good man, though much down in spirit,
He *is* a good man, and doth life inherit.

Tell them of Master Feeblemind also,
Who not before, but still behind would go;
Show them also how he had like been slain,
And how one Great-heart did his life regain:
This man was true of heart, though weak in grace,
One might true godliness read in his face.

Then tell them of Master Ready-to-Halt,
A man with crutches, but much without fault:
Tell them how Master Feeblemind, and he
Did love, and in opinions much agree.
And let all know, though weakness was their
    chance,
Yet sometimes one could sing, the other dance.

Forget not Master Valiant-for-the-Truth,
That man of courage, though a very youth.
Tell everyone his spirit was so stout,
No man could ever make him face about,
And how Great-heart and he could not forbear
But put down Doubting-Castle, slay Despair.

Overlook not Master Despondency.
Nor Much-afraid, his daughter, though they lie
Under such mantles as may make them look
(With some) as if their God had them forsook.
They softly went, but sure, and at the end,
Found that the Lord of pilgrims was their friend.

When thou hast told the world of all these things,
Then turn about, my book, and touch these strings,
Which, if but touched will such music make,
They'll make a cripple dance, a giant quake.
Those riddles that lie couched within thy breast,
Freely propound, expound: and for the rest
Of thy mysterious lines, let them remain,
For those whose nimble fancies shall them gain.
  Now may this little book a blessing be,
To those that love this little book and me,
And may its buyer have no cause to say,
His money is but lost or thrown away.
Yea may this second pilgrim yield that fruit,
As may with each good pilgrim's fancy suit,
And may it persuade some that go astray,
To turn their foot and heart to the right way.

                    Is the Hearty Prayer
                      of the Author
                    JOHN BUNYAN

THE PILGRIM'S PROGRESS
in the similitude of a
DREAM

THE SECOND PART

COURTEOUS companions, sometime since, to tell you my dream that I had of Christian the pilgrim, and of his dangerous journey toward the Celestial Country, was pleasant to me and profitable to you. I told you then also what I saw concerning his wife and children, and how unwilling they were to go with him on pilgrimage, insomuch that he was forced to go on his progress without them, for he durst not run the danger of that destruction which he feared would come by staying with them, in the City of Destruction, wherefore, as I then showed you, he left them and departed.

Now it hath so happened through the multiplicity of business,[7] that I have been much hindered, and kept back from my wonted travels into those parts whence he went, and so could not till now obtain an opportunity to make further inquiry after whom he left behind that I might give you an account of them. But having had some concerns that way of late, I went down again thitherward. Now, having taken up my lodgings in a wood about a mile off the place, as I slept I dreamed again.

And as I was in my dream, behold, an aged gentleman came by where I lay; and because he was to go some part of the way that I was travelling, methought I got up and went with him. So as we walked, and as travellers usually do, it was as if we fell into discourse, and our talk happened to be about Christian and his travels: for thus I began with the old man.

'Sir,' said I, 'what town is that there below, that lieth on the left hand of our way?'

Then said Mr Sagacity,[8] for that was his name, 'It is the City of Destruction, a populous place, but possessed with a very ill-conditioned, and idle sort of people.'

'I thought that was that City,' quoth I, 'I went once myself through that town, and therefore know that this report you give of it is true.'

Sagacity. Too true, I wish I could speak truth in speaking better of them that dwell therein.

'Well, Sir,' quoth I, 'then I perceive you to be a well-meaning man: and so one that takes pleasure to hear and tell of that which is good; pray did you never hear what happened to a man some time ago in this town whose name was Christian, that went on pilgrimage up towards the higher regions?'

Sagacity. Hear of him! Aye, and I also heard of the molestations, troubles, wars, captivities, cries, groans, frights and fears that he met with, and had in his journey. Besides, I must tell you, all our country rings of him, there are but few houses that have heard of him and his doings, but have sought after and got the records of his pilgrimage; yea, I think I may say that that his hazardous journey has got a many well-wishers to his ways: for though when he was here, he was fool in every man's mouth, yet now he is gone, he is highly commended of all. For 'tis said he lives bravely where he is: yea, many of them that are resolved never to run his hazards, yet have their mouths water at his gains.

Christians are well spoken of when gone, though called fools while they are here

'They may,' quoth I, 'well think, if they think anything that is true, that he liveth well where he is, for he now lives at and in the fountain of life, and has what he has without labour and sorrow, for there is no grief mixed therewith.

Sagacity. Talk! The people talk strangely about him. Some say that he now walks in white, that he has a chain of gold about his neck, that he has a crown of gold beset with pearls upon his head. Others say that the Shining Ones that sometimes showed themselves to him in his journey are become his companions, and that he is as familiar with them in the place where he is as here one neighbour is with another. Besides, 'tis confidently affirmed concerning him, that the King of the place where he is, has bestowed upon him already a very rich and pleasant dwelling at court, and that he every day eateth and drinketh, and walketh, and talketh with him, and receiveth of the smiles and favours of him that is Judge of all there. Moreover, it is expected of some that his Prince, the Lord of that country, will shortly come into these parts,[9] and will know the reason, if they can give any, why his neighbours set so little by him, and had him so much in derision when they perceived that he would be a pilgrim. For they say that now he is so in the affections of his Prince, and that his sovereign is so much concerned with the indignities that was cast upon Christian when he became a pilgrim, that he will look upon all as if done unto himself; and no marvel, for 'twas for the love that he had to his Prince, that he ventured as he did.

Christian's King will take Christian's part

'I dare say,' quoth I, 'I am glad on't, I am glad for the poor man's sake, for now that he has rest from his labour, and for that he now reapeth the benefit of his tears with joy, and for that he is got beyond the gun-shot of his enemies, and is out of the reach of them that hate him. I also am glad for that a rumour of these things is noised abroad in this country; who can tell but that it may work some good effect on some that are left behind? But, pray sir, while it is fresh in my mind, do you hear anything of his wife and children? Poor hearts, I wonder in my mind what they do.'

Good tidings of Christian's wife and children

Sagacity. Who! Christiana and her sons! They are like to do as well as did Christian himself, for though they all played the fool at the first, and would by no means be persuaded by either the tears or entreaties of Christian, yet second thoughts have wrought wonderfully with them so they have packed up and are also gone after him.

'Better, and better,' quoth I, 'But what! Wife and children and all?'

Sagacity. 'Tis true: I can give you an account of the matter, for I was upon the spot at the instant, and was throughly acquainted with the whole affair.

'Then,' said I, 'a man it seems may report it for a truth?'

Sagacity. You need not fear to affirm it, I mean that they are all gone on pilgrimage, both the good woman and her four boys. And being we are as I perceive going some considerable way together, I will give you an account of the whole of the matter.

This Christiana (for that was her name from the day that she with her children betook themselves to a pilgrim's life), after her husband was gone over the River, and she could hear of him no more, her thoughts began to work in her mind; first, for that she had lost her husband, and for that the loving bond of that relation was utterly broken betwixt them. For you know, said he to me, nature can do no less but entertain the living with many a heavy cogitation in the remembrance of the loss of loving relations. This therefore of her husband did cost her many a tear. But this was not all, for Christiana did also

Mark this, you that are churls to your godly relations

234

begin to consider with herself, whether her unbecoming behaviour towards her husband was not one cause that she saw him no more, and that in such sort he was taken away from her. And upon this came into her mind by swarms all her unkind, unnatural, and ungodly carriages to her dear friend, which also clogged her conscience and did load her with guilt. She was moreover much broken with recalling to remembrance the restless groans, brinish tears and self-bemoanings of her husband, and how she did harden her heart against all his entreaties, and loving persuasions (of her and her sons) to go with him, yea, there was not anything that Christian either said to her or did before her all the while that his burden did hang on his back, but it returned upon her like a flash of lightning, and rent the caul of her heart in sunder, specially that bitter outcry of his, 'What shall I do to be saved', did ring in her ears most dolefully.

Then said she to her children, 'Sons, we are all undone. I have sinned away your father, and he is gone; he would have had us with him; but I would not go myself; I also have hindered you of life.' With that the boys fell all into tears, and cried out to go after their father. 'Oh!' said Christiana, 'that it had been but our lot to go with him, then had it fared well with us beyond what 'tis like to do now. For though I formerly foolishly imagined concerning the troubles of your father that they proceeded of a foolish fancy that he had, or for that he was overrun with melancholy humours, yet now 'twill not out of my mind but that they sprang from another cause, to wit, for that the light of light was given him by the help of which, as I perceive, he has escaped the snares of death.' Then they all wept again, and cried out 'Oh, woe worth the day.'

Christiana's dream

The next night Christiana had a dream, and behold she saw as if a broad parchment was opened before her in which were recorded the sum of her ways, and the times, as she thought, looked very black upon her. Then she cried out aloud in her sleep, 'Lord have mercy upon me a sinner,' and the little children heard her.

After this she thought she saw two very ill-favoured ones standing by her bed-side, and saying, *Mark this, this is the quintessence of hell* 'What shall we do with this woman? For she cries out for mercy waking and sleeping: if she be suffered to go on as she begins, we shall lose her as we have lost her husband. Wherefore we must by one way or other seek to take her off from the thoughts of what shall be hereafter: else all the world cannot help it, but she will become a pilgrim.'

Now she awoke in a great sweat, also a trembling was upon her, but after a while she fell to sleeping *Help against discouragement* again. And then she thought she saw Christian her husband in a place of bliss among many immortals, with an harp in his hand, standing and playing upon it before one that sat on a throne with a rainbow about his head. She saw also as if he bowed his head with his face to the paved-work that was under the Prince's feet, saying, 'I heartily thank my Lord and King for bringing of me into this place.' Then shouted a company of them that stood round about, and harped with their harps: but no man living could tell what they said, but Christian and his companions.

Next morning when she was up, had prayed to *Convictions seconded with fresh tidings of God's readiness to pardon* God, and talked with her children awhile, one knocked hard at the door; to whom she spake out saying, 'If thou comest in God's name, come in.' So he said 'Amen,' and opened the door, and saluted her with 'Peace be to this House'. The which when he

236

had done, he said, 'Christiana, knowest thou wherefore I am come?' Then she blushed and trembled, also her heart began to wax warm with desires to know whence he came, and what was his errand to her. So he said unto her, 'My name is Secret, I dwell with those that are high. It is talked of where I dwell, as if thou had'st a desire to go thither; also there is a report that thou art aware of the evil thou hast formerly done to thy husband in hardening of thy heart against his way, and in keeping of these thy babes in their ignorance. Christiana, the Merciful One has sent me to tell thee that he is a God ready to forgive, and that he taketh delight to multiply pardon to offences. He also would have thee know that he inviteth thee to come into his presence, to his table, and that he will feed thee with the fat of his house, and with the heritage of Jacob thy father.

'There is Christian thy husband that was, with legions more his companions, ever beholding that face that doth minister life to beholders: and they will all be glad when they shall hear the sound of thy feet step over thy Father's threshold.'

Christiana at this was greatly abashed in herself, and bowing her head to the ground, this visitor proceeded and said, 'Christiana! Here is also a letter for thee which I have brought from thy husband's King.' So she took it and opened it, but it smelt after he manner of the best perfume, also it was written in letters of gold. The contents of the letter was that the King would have her do as did Christian her husband; for that was the way to come to his City, and to dwell in his presence with joy forever. At this the good woman was quite overcome: so she *Christiana* cried out to her visitor, 'Sir, will you carry me and *quite* my children with you, that we also may go and wor- *overcome* ship this King?'

237

Then said the visitor, 'Christiana! The bitter is before the sweet.' Thou must through troubles as did he that went before thee enter this Celestial City. *Further instruction to Christiana* Wherefore I advise thee to do as did Christian thy husband: go to the Wicket Gate yonder, over the plain, for that stands in the head of the way up which thou must go, and I wish thee all good speed. Also I advise that thou put this letter in thy bosom. That thou read therein to thyself and to thy children, until you have got it by root-of-heart. For it is one of the songs that thou must sing while thou art in this house of thy pilgrimage. Also this thou must deliver in at the further Gate.'

Now I saw in my dream that this old gentleman, as he told me this story, did himself seem to be greatly affected therewith. He moreover proceeded and said: So Christiana called her sons together, and *Christiana prays well for her journey* began thus to address herself unto them. 'My sons, I have, as you may perceive, been of late under much exercise in my soul about the death of your father, not for that I doubt at all of his happiness, for I am satisfied now that he is well. I have also been much affected with the thoughts of mine own state and yours, which I verily believe is by nature miserable; my carriages also to your father in his distress, is a great load to my conscience. For I hardened both mine own heart and yours against him, and refused to go with him on pilgrimage.

'The thoughts of these things would now kill me outright, but that for a dream which I had last night, and but that for the encouragement that this stranger has given me this morning. Come, my children, let us pack up, and be gone to the Gate that leads to the Celestial Country, that we may see your father and be with him and his companions in peace according to the laws of that land.'

Then did her children burst out into tears for joy that the heart of their mother was so inclined. So their visitor bid them farewell, and they began to prepare to set out for their journey.

But while they were thus about to be gone, two of the women that were Christiana's neighbours came up to her house and knocked at her door. To whom she said as before, 'If you come in God's name, come in.' At this the women were stunned, for this kind of language they used not to hear or to perceive to drop from the lips of Christiana. Yet they came in; but behold they found the good woman a preparing to be gone from her house. *Christiana's new language stunds[10] her old neighbours*

So they began[11] and said, 'Neighbour, pray what is your meaning by this?'

Christiana answered and said to the eldest of them, whose name was Mrs Timorous, 'I am preparing for a journey.' (This Timorous was daughter to him that met Christian upon the Hill Difficulty; and would a had him gone back for fear of the lions.)

Timorous. For what journey I pray you?

Christiana. Even to go after my good husband, and with that she fell aweeping. *Timorous comes to visit Christiana, with Mercy one of her neighbours*

Timorous. I hope not so, good neighbour, pray for your poor children's sake, do not so unwomanly cast away yourself.

Christiana. Nay, my children shall go with me; not one of them is willing to stay behind.

Timorous. I wonder in my very heart what, or who, has brought you into this mind.

Christiana. Oh, neighbour, knew you but as much as I do I doubt not but that you would go with me.

Timorous. Prithee, what new knowledge hast thou got that so worketh off thy mind from thy friends, and that tempteth thee to go nobody knows where?

Christiana. Then Christiana replied, I have been

sorely afflicted since my husband's departure from *Death* me; but specially since he went over the River. But that which troubleth me most is my churlish carriages to him when he was under his distress. Besides, I am now as he was then; nothing will serve me but going on pilgrimage. I was a dreamed[12] last night that I saw him. O, that my soul was with him. He dwelleth in the presence of the King of the Country, he sits and eats with him at his table, he is become a companion of immortals, and has a house now given him to dwell in to which the best palaces on earth, if compared, seems to me to be but as a dunghill. The Prince of the place has also sent for me with promise of entertainment if I shall come to him; his messenger was here even now, and has brought me a letter which invites me to come. And with that she plucked out her letter, and read it, and said to them, What now will you say to this?

Timorous. Oh, the madness that has possessed thee and thy husband, to run yourselves upon such difficulties! You have heard, I am sure, what your husband did meet with, even in a manner at the first step, that he took on his way, as our neighbour Obstinate yet can testify; for he went along with him, yea and Pliable too, until they, like wise men, were afraid to go any further. We also heard over and above, how he met with the lions, Apollyon, the Shadow of Death, and many other things: nor is the danger he met *The* with at Vanity-Fair to be forgotten by thee. For if he, *reasonings of* though a man, was so hard put to it, what canst thou *the flesh* being but a poor woman do? Consider also that these four sweet babes are thy children, thy flesh and thy bones. Wherefore, though thou shouldest be so rash as to cast away thyself, yet for the sake of the fruit of thy body, keep thou at home.

But Christiana said unto her, 'Tempt me not, my

neighbour: I have now a price put into mine hand to get gain, and I should be a fool of the greatest size, if I should have no heart to strike in with the opportunity. And for that you tell me of all these troubles that I am like to meet with in the way, they are so *A pertinent* far off from being to me a discouragement that they *reply to fleshly* show I am in the right. The bitter must come before *reasonings* the sweet, and that also will make the sweet the sweeter. Wherefore, since you came not to my house in God's name, as I said, I pray you to be gone and not to disquiet me further.'

Then Timorous all to reviled her, and said to her fellow, 'Come neighbour Mercy, let's leave her in her own hands since she scorns our counsel and company.' But Mercy was at a stand, and could not so readily comply with her neighbour, and that for a twofold reason. First, her bowels yearned[13] over *Mercy's* Christiana; so she said within herself, 'If my neigh- *bowels yearn* bour will needs be gone, I will go a little way with *over* her, and help her.' Secondly, her bowels yearned over *Christiana* her own soul (for what Christiana had said had taken some hold upon her mind). Wherefore she said within herself again, 'I will yet have more talk with this Christiana, and if I find truth and life in what she shall say, myself with my heart shall also go with her.' Wherefore Mercy began thus to reply to her neighbour Timorous.

Mercy. Neighbour, I did indeed come with you to *Timorous* see Christiana this morning, and since she is, as you *forsakes her;* see, a taking of her last farewell of her country, I *but Mercy* think to walk this sun-shine morning a little way with *cleaves to her* her to help her on the way. But she told her not of her second reason, but kept that to herself.

Timorous. Well, I see you have a mind to go a fooling too; but take heed in time, and be wise: while we are out of danger we are out, but when we are in, we are in. So Mrs Timorous returned to her house, and Christiana betook herself to her journey.

Timorous acquaints her friends what the good Christiana intends to do

But when Timorous was got home to her house, she sends for some of her neighbours, to wit, Mrs Bats-eyes, Mrs Inconsiderate, Mrs Light-mind, and Mrs Know-nothing. So when they were come to her house she falls to telling of the story of Christiana, and of her intended journey. And thus she began her tale.

Timorous. Neighbours, having had little to do this morning I went to give Christiana a visit, and when I came at the door I knocked, as you know 'tis our custom; and she answered, 'If you come in God's name, come in.' So in I went, thinking all was well: But when I came in, I found her preparing herself to depart the town, she and also her children. So I asked her what was her meaning by that, and she told me in short that she was now of a mind to go on pilgrimage as did her husband. She told me also of a dream that she had, and how the King of the Country where her husband was, had sent her an inviting letter to come thither.

Mrs Know-nothing

Then said Mrs Know-nothing, 'And what! Do you think she will go?'

Timorous. Aye, go she will, whatever come on't; and methinks I know it by this; for that which was my great argument to persuade her to stay at home (to wit, the troubles she was like to meet with in the way) is one great argument with her to put her forward on her journey. For she told me in so many words, 'The bitter goes before the sweet. Yea, and for as much as it so doth, it makes the sweet the sweeter.'

Mrs Bats-eyes

Mrs Bats-eyes. Oh this blind and foolish woman, said she, will she not take warning by her husband's afflictions? For my part, I say if he was here again he would rest him content in a whole skin, and never run so many hazards for nothing.

Mrs Inconsiderate also replied, saying, 'Away with such fantastical fools from the town; a good riddance, for my part, I say of her. Should she stay where she dwells, and retain this her mind, who could live quietly by her? For she will either be dumpish or un-neighbourly, or talk of such matters as no wise body can abide: wherefore, for my part, I shall never be sorry for her departure; let her go, and let better come in her room: 'twas never a good world since these whimsical fools dwelt in it.' *Mrs Inconsiderate*

Then Mrs Light-mind added as followeth, 'Come put this kind of talk away. I was yesterday at Madam Wanton's, where we were as merry as the maids.[14] For who do you think should be there, but I, and Mrs Love-the-flesh and three or four more, with Mr Lechery, Mrs Filth, and some others. So there we had music and dancing and what else was meet to fill up the pleasure. And I dare say my lady herself is an admirably well-bred gentlewoman, and Mr Lechery is as pretty a fellow.' *Mrs Light-mind. Madam Wanton, she that had like to a been too hard for Faithful in time past*

By this time Christiana was got on her way, and Mercy went along with her. So as they went, her children being there also, Christiana began to discourse. 'And, Mercy,' said Christiana, 'I take this as an unexpected favour that thou shouldest set foot out of doors with me to accompany me a little in my way. *Discourse betwixt Mercy and good Christiana*

Mercy. Then said young Mercy (for she was but young), If I thought it would be to purpose to go with you, I would never go near the town any more. *Mercy inclines to go*

Christiana. Well Mercy, said Christiana, cast in thy lot with me. I well know what will be the end of our pilgrimage; my husband is where he would not but be for all the gold in the Spanish mines. Nor shalt thou be rejected, though thou goest but upon my invitation. The King who hath sent for me and my children is one that delighteth in mercy. Besides, if

Christiana would have her neighbour with her

thou wilt, I will hire thee, and thou shalt go along with me as my servant. Yet we will have all things in common betwixt thee and me, only go along with me.

Mercy doubts of acceptance

Mercy. But how shall I be ascertained that I also shall be entertained? Had I but this hope from one that can tell, I would make no stick at all but would go, being helped by him that can help, though the way was never so tedious.

Christian allures her to the gate which is Christ, and promiseth there to inquire for her

Christiana. Well, loving Mercy, I will tell thee what thou shalt do, go with me to the Wicket Gate, and there I will further inquire for thee, and if there thou shalt not meet with encouragement, I will be content that thou shalt return to thy place. I also will pay thee for thy kindness which thou showest to me and my children in thy accompanying of us in our way as thou doest.

Mercy prays

Mercy. Then will I go thither, and will take what shall follow, and the Lord grant that my lot may there fall even as the King of Heaven shall have his heart upon me.

Christiana glad of Mercy's company

Christiana then was glad at her heart, not only that she had a companion, but also for that she had prevailed with this poor maid to fall in love with her own salvation. So they went on together, and Mercy began to weep. Then said Christiana, 'Wherefore weepeth my sister so?'

Mercy grieves for her carnal relations

Mercy. Alas! said she, who can but lament that shall but rightly consider what a state and condition my poor relations are in, that yet remain in our sinful town: and that which makes my grief the more heavy is because they have no instructor nor any to tell them what is to come.

Christian's prayers were answered for his relations after he was dead

Christiana. Bowels[15] becometh pilgrims. And thou dost for thy friends as my good Christian did for me when he left me; he mourned for that I would not

244

heed nor regard him, but his Lord and ours did gather up his tears and put them into his bottle, and now both I, and thou, and these my sweet babes, are reaping the fruit and benefit of them. I hope, Mercy, these tears of thine will not be lost,[16] for the truth hath said, *That they that sow in tears shall reap in joy, in singing. And he that goeth forth and weepeth, bearing precious seed, shall doubtless come again with rejoicing, bringing his sheaves with him.*[17]

Then said Mercy,

> *Let the most blessed be my guide,*
> *If't be his blessed will,*
> *Unto his Gate, into his fold,*
> *Up to his Holy Hill.*

> *And let him never suffer me*
> *To swerve, or turn aside*
> *From his free grace, and holy ways,*
> *What e'er shall me betide.*

> *And let him gather them of mine,*
> *That I have left behind.*
> *Lord make them pray they may be thine,*
> *With all their heart and mind.*

Now my old friend proceeded, and said, but when Christiana came up to the Slough of Despond, she began to be at a stand. 'For,' said she, 'this is the place in which my dear husband had like to a been smothered with mud.' She perceived also, that notwithstanding the command of the King to make this place for pilgrims good; yet it was rather worse than formerly.[18] So I asked if that was true. 'Yes,' said the old gentleman, 'too true. For that many there be that pretend to be the King's labourers; and that say they are for mending the King's highway, that bring *Their own carnal conclusions, instead of the Word of Life*

245

dirt and dung instead of stones, and so mar, instead of mending.' Here Christiana therefore, with her boys, did make a stand. 'But,' said Mercy, 'come let us venture, only let us be wary.' Then they looked well to the steps, and made a shift to get staggeringly over. Yet Christiana had like to a been in, and that not once nor twice. Now they had no sooner got over, but they thought they heard words that said unto them, *Blessed is she that believeth, for there shall be a performance of the things that have been told her from the Lord.*

Mercy the boldest at the Slough of Despond

Then they went on again; and said Mercy to Christiana, 'Had I as good ground to hope for a loving reception at the Wicket Gate as you, I think no Slough of Despond would discourage me.'

'Well,' said the other, 'you know your sore, and I know mine; and, good friend, we shall all have enough evil before we come at our journey's end.

'For can it be imagined that the people that design to attain such excellent glories as we do, and that are so envied that happiness as we are, but that we shall meet with what fears and scares, with what troubles and afflictions they can possibly assault us with that hate us?'

Prayer should be made with consideration, and fear: as well as in faith and hope

And now Mr Sagacity left me to dream out my dream by myself. Wherefore methought I saw Christiana, and Mercy and the boys go all of them up to the Gate. To which when they were come, they betook themselves to a short debate about how they must manage their calling at the Gate, and what should be said to him that did open to them. So it was concluded, since Christiana was the eldest, that she should knock for entrance, and that she should speak to him that did open for the rest. So Christiana began to knock, and as her poor husband did, she knocked and knocked again. But instead of any that answered, they all thought that they heard as if a dog came barking upon them. A dog, and a great one too, and this made the women and children afraid. Nor durst they for a while dare to knock any more, for fear the mastiff should fly upon them. Now therefore they were greatly tumbled up and down in their minds, and knew not what to do. Knock they durst not, for fear of the dog: go back they durst not, for fear that the keeper of that Gate should espy them as they so went and should be offended with them. At last they thought of knocking again and knocked more vehemently than they did at the first. Then said the keeper of the Gate, 'Who is there?' So the dog left off to bark, and he opened unto them. *The dog, the Devil, an enemy to prayer. Christiana and her companions perplexed about prayer*

Then Christiana made low obeisance, and said, 'Let not our Lord be offended with his handmaidens, for that we have knocked at his princely Gate.' Then said the keeper, 'Whence come ye, and what is that you would have?'

Christiana answered, 'We are come from whence Christian did come, and upon the same errand as he; to wit, to be, if it shall please you, graciously admitted by this Gate, into the way that leads to the Celestial City. And I answer, my Lord, in the next place, that I am Christiana, once the wife of Christian, that now is gotten above.'

With that the keeper of the Gate did marvel, saying, 'What, is she become now a pilgrim, that but awhile ago abhorred that life?' Then she bowed her head, and said, 'Yes; and so are these my sweet babes also.'

Then he took her by the hand, and led her in, and said also, '*Suffer the little children to come unto me*', and with that he shut up the Gate. This done, he called to a trumpeter that was above over the Gate to entertain Christiana with shouting and sound of trumpet for *How Christiana is entertained at the Gate* joy. So he obeyed and sounded, and filled the air with his melodious notes.

Now all this while, poor Mercy did stand without, trembling and crying for fear that she was rejected. But when Christiana had gotten admittance for herself and her boys, then she began to make intercession for Mercy.

Christiana. And she said, my Lord, I have a companion of mine that stands yet without, that is come *Christiana's* hither upon the same account as myself. One that is *prayer for her* much dejected in her mind, for that she comes as she *friend Mercy* thinks without sending for, whereas I was sent to by my husband's King to come.

The delays Now Mercy began to be very impatient, for each *make the* minute was as long to her as an hour, wherefore she *hungering* prevented Christiana from a fuller interceding for her *soul the* prevented Christiana from a fuller interceding for her *fervent* by knocking at the Gate herself. And she knocked then so loud that she made Christiana to start. Then said the keeper of the Gate, 'Who is there?' And said Christiana, 'It is my friend.'

So he opened the Gate, and looked out; but *Mercy faints* Mercy was fallen down without in a swoon, for she fainted and was afraid that no Gate should be opened to her.

Then he took her by the hand, and said, 'Damsel, I bid thee arise.'

'O Sir,' said she, 'I am faint, there is scarce life left in me.' But he answered that one once said, '*When my soul fainted within me, I remembered the Lord, and my prayer came in unto thee, into thy holy temple.* Fear not, but stand upon thy feet, and tell me wherefore thou art come.'

Mercy. I am come, for that unto which I was never *The cause of* invited, as my friend Christiana was. Hers was from *her fainting* the King, and mine was but from her,[19] wherefore I fear I presume.

'Did she desire thee to come with her to this place?'

Mercy. Yes. And as my Lord sees, I am come. And if there is any grace and forgiveness of sins to spare, I beseech that I thy poor handmaid may be partaker thereof.

Then he took her again by the hand, and led her gently in, and said: 'I pray for all them that believe on me, by what means soever they come unto me.' *Mark this* Then said he to those that stood by, 'Fetch something, and give it Mercy to smell on thereby to stay her fainting.' So they fetched her a bundle of myrrh and a while after she was revived.

And now was Christiana, and her boys, and Mercy, received of the Lord at the head of the way and spoke kindly unto by him.

Then said they yet further unto him, 'We are sorry for our sins, and beg of our Lord his pardon and further information what we must do.'

'I grant pardon,' said he, 'by word and deed; by word in the promise of forgiveness, by deed in the way I obtained it. Take the first from my lips with a kiss, and the other as it shall be revealed.'

Now I saw in my dream that he spake many good words unto them, whereby they were greatly gladded. He also had them up to the top of the Gate and showed them by what deed they were saved, and told them withal that that sight they would have again as they went along in the way, to their comfort. *Christ crucified seen afar off*

So he left them a while in a summer-parlour below, where they entered into talk by themselves. And thus Christiana began, 'O Lord! How glad am I that we are got in hither!' *Talk between the Christians*

Mercy. So you well may; but I of all have cause to leap for joy.

Christiana. I thought one time as I stood at the Gate (because I had knocked and none did answer) that all our labour had been lost: specially when that ugly cur made such a heavy barking against us.

Mercy. But my worst fears was after I saw that you was taken into his favour, and that I was left behind: Now thought I, 'tis fulfilled which is written, *Two women shall be grinding together; the one shall be taken, and the other left.* I had much ado to forbear crying out, 'Undone, undone'.

And afraid I was to knock any more; but when I looked up, to what was written over the Gate, I took courage. I also thought that I must either knock again or die. So I knocked; but I cannot tell how, for my spirit now struggled betwixt life and death.

Christiana. Can you not tell how you knocked? I am sure your knocks were so earnest, that the very sound of them made me start. I thought I never heard such knocking in all my life. I thought you would a come in by violent hand, or a took the Kingdom by storm.

Mercy. Alas, to be in my case, who that so was could but a done so? You saw that the door was shut upon me, and that there was a most cruel dog[20] thereabout. Who, I say, that was so faint hearted as I, that would not a knocked with all their might? But pray what said my Lord to my rudeness, was he not angry with me?

Christiana. When he heard your lumbering noise he gave a wonderful innocent smile. I believe what you did pleased him well enough, for he showed no sign to the contrary. But I marvel in my heart why he keeps such a dog; had I known that afore I fear I should not have had heart enough to a ventured myself in this manner. But now we are in we are in, and I am glad with all my heart.

Mercy. I will ask if you please next time he comes down why he keeps such a filthy cur in his yard. I hope he will not take it amiss.

Christiana thinks her companion prays better than she

Christ pleased with loud and restless praises

'Ay do,' said the children, 'and persuade him to *The children*
hang him for we are afraid that he will bite us when *are afraid of*
we go hence.'   *the dog*

So at last he came down to them again, and Mercy
fell to the ground on her face before him and wor-
shipped, and said, 'Let my Lord accept of the sacrifice
of praise which I now offer unto him, with the calves
of my lips.'

So he said to her, 'Peace be to thee, stand up.'

But she continued upon her face and said, 'Righteous art thou O Lord when I plead with thee, yet let
me talk with thee of thy judgements: wherefore dost *Mercy*
thou keep so cruel a dog in thy yard at the sight of *expostulates*
which such women and children as we are ready to *about the dog*
fly from thy Gate for fear?'

He answered, and said: 'That dog has another
owner, he also is kept close in an other man's ground; *Devil*
only my pilgrims hear his barking. He belongs to the
castle which you see there at a distance: but can come
up to the walls of this place. He has frighted many an
honest pilgrim from worse to better by the great
voice of his roaring. Indeed he that oweth[21] him, doth
not keep him of any good will to me or mine; but
with intent to keep the pilgrims from coming to me,
and that they may be afraid to knock at this Gate for
entrance. Sometimes also he has broken out and has
worried some that I love; but I take all at present
patiently; I also give my pilgrims timely help so they
are not delivered up to his power to do to them what
his doggish nature would prompt him to. But what! *A check to*
My purchased one, I trow, hadst thou known never *the carnal fear*
so much beforehand thou wouldst not a been afraid *of the pilgrims*
of a dog.

'The beggars that go from door to door, will,
rather than they will lose a supposed alms, run the

251

hazard of the bawling, barking, and biting too of a dog; and shall a dog, a dog in an other man's yard, a dog, whose barking I turn to the profit of pilgrims, keep any from coming to me? *I deliver them from the lions, their darling from the power of the dog.*'

Christians when wise enough acquiesce in the wisdom of their Lord

Mercy. Then said Mercy, I confess my ignorance: I spake what I understood not: I acknowledge that thou doest all things well.

Christiana. Then Christiana began to talk of their journey, and to inquire after the way. So he fed them, and washed their feet, and set them in the way of his steps according as he had dealt with her husband before.

So I saw in my dream that they walked on in their way and had the weather very comfortable to them. Then Christiana began to sing, saying,

> *Blessed be the day that I began*
> *A pilgrim for to be;*
> *And blessed also be that man*
> *That thereto moved me.*
>
> *'Tis true, 'twas long ere I began*
> *To seek to live for ever:*
> *But now I run fast as I can,*
> *'Tis better late than never.*
>
> *Our tears to joy, our fears to faith*
> *Are turned, as we see:*
> *Thus our beginning (as one saith),*
> *Shows what our end will be.*[22]

Now there was, on the other side of the wall that fenced in the way up which Christiana and her companions was to go, a Garden; and that Garden belonged to him whose was that barking dog, of whom mention was made before. And some of the fruit-trees that grew in that Garden shot their

The Devil's Garden

branches over the wall, and being mellow, they that found them did gather them up and oft eat of them to their hurt. So Christiana's boys, as boys are apt to do, being pleased with the trees, and with the fruit that did hang thereon, did plash[23] them, and began to eat. Their mother did also chide them for so doing, but still the boys went on. *The children eat of the enemy's fruit*

'Well,' said she, 'my sons, you transgress, for that fruit is none of ours.' But she did not know that they did belong to the enemy; I'll warrant you if she had, she would a been ready to die for fear. But that passed, and they went on their way. Now by that they were gone about two bows-shot from the place that let them into the way: they espied two very ill-favoured ones coming down apace to meet them. With that Christiana, and Mercy her friend covered themselves with their veils, and so kept on their journey; the children also went on before, so at last they met together. Then they that came down to meet them, came just up to the women as if they would embrace them; but Christiana said, 'Stand back, or go peaceably by as you should.' Yet these two as men that are deaf regarded not Christiana's words; but began to lay hands upon them; at that Christiana waxing very wroth spurned at them with her feet. Mercy also, as well as she could, did what she could to shift them. Christiana again, said to them, 'Stand back and be gone, for we have no money to lose being pilgrims as ye see, and such too as live upon the charity of our friends.' *Two ill-favoured ones* *They assault Christiana* *The pilgrims struggle with them*

Ill-favoured ones. Then said one of the two of the men, We make no assault upon you for money but are come out to tell you that if you will but grant one small request which we shall ask, we will make women of you for ever.

Christiana. Now Christiana, imagining what they should mean, made answer again, We will neither hear nor regard, nor yield to what you shall ask. We are in haste, cannot stay, our business is a business of life and death. So again she and her companions made a fresh assay to go past them. But they letted them in their way.

Ill-favoured ones. And they said, We intend no hurt to your lives, 'tis an other thing we would have.

Christiana. Ay, quoth Christiana, you would have us body and soul, for I know 'tis for that you are come; but we will die rather upon the spot than suffer ourselves to be brought into such snares as shall hazard our well being hereafter. And with that they *She cries out* both shrieked out, and cried 'Murder, murder': and so put themselves under those laws that are provided for the protection of women. But the men still made their approach upon them with design to prevail against them: they therefore cried out again.

'Tis good Now they being, as I said, not far from the Gate in *to cry out* at which they came, their voice was heard from *when we are* where they was, thither. Wherefore some of the *assaulted* house came out, and knowing that it was Christiana's tongue: they made haste to her relief. But by that they was got within sight of them, the women was in a very great scuffle, the children also stood crying by. *The Reliever* Then did he that came in for their relief, call out to *comes* the ruffians saying, 'What is that thing that you do? Would you make my Lord's people to transgress?' *The Ill-* He also attempted to take them; but they did make *ones fly to* their escape over the wall into the Garden of the *the Devil for* man to whom the great dog belonged, so the dog *relief* became their protector. This Reliever then came up to the women and asked them how they did. So they answered, 'We thank thy Prince, pretty well, only we have been somewhat affrighted; we thank thee also

for that thou camest in to our help, for otherwise we had been overcome.'

Reliever. So after a few more words, this Reliever said as followeth: I marvelled much when you was entertained at the Gate above, being ye knew that ye were but weak women, that you petitioned not the Lord there for a conductor. Then might you have avoided these troubles, and dangers, for he would have granted you one. *The Reliever talks to the women*

Christiana. Alas, said Christiana, we were so taken with our present blessing that dangers to come were forgotten by us; besides, who could have thought that so near the King's Palace there should have lurked such naughty ones: indeed it had been well for us had we asked our Lord for one; but since our Lord knew 'twould be for our profit, I wonder he sent not one along with us. *Mark this*

Reliever. It is not always necessary to grant things not asked for lest by so doing they become of little esteem; but when the want of a thing is felt, it then comes under in the eyes of him that feels it that estimate that properly is its due, and so consequently will be thereafter used. Had my Lord granted you a conductor, you would not neither so have bewailed that oversight of yours in not asking for one as now you have occasion to do. So all things work for good, and tend to make you more wary. *We lose for want of asking for*

Christiana. Shall we go back again to my Lord, and confess our folly and ask one?

Reliever. Your confession of your folly, I will present him with: to go back again, you need not. For in all places where you shall come you will find no want at all, for in every of my Lord's lodgings which he has prepared for the reception of his pilgrims there is sufficient to furnish them against all attempts whatsoever. But, as I said, he will be inquired of by them to do it for them, and 'tis a poor thing that is not worth asking for. When he had thus said, he went back to his place, and the pilgrims went on their way.

The mistake of Mercy *Mercy.* Then said Mercy, What a sudden blank is here! I made account we had now been past all danger, and that we should never see sorrow more.

Christiana's guilt *Christiana.* Thy innocency, my sister, said Christiana to Mercy, may excuse thee much; but as for me, my fault is so much the greater, for that I saw this danger before I came out of the doors, and yet did not provide for it where provision might a been had. I am therefore much to be blamed.

Mercy. Then said Mercy, How knew you this before you came from home? Pray open to me this riddle.

Christiana. Why, I will tell you. Before I set foot out of doors, one night as I lay in my bed, I had a dream about this. For methought I saw two men, as like these as ever the world they could look, stand at my beds-feet, plotting how they might prevent my salvation. I will tell you their very words. They said *Christiana's* ('twas when I was in my troubles), 'What shall we do *dream repeated* with this woman? for she cries out waking and sleeping for forgiveness; if she be suffered to go on as she begins, we shall lose her as we have lost her husband.' This you know might a made me take heed, and have provided when provision might a been had.

Mercy makes good use of their neglect of duty *Mercy.* Well, said Mercy, as by this neglect we have an occasion ministered unto us to behold our own imperfections: so our Lord has taken occasion thereby, to make manifest the riches of his grace. For he, as we see, has followed us with unasked kindness, and has delivered us from their hands that were stronger than we, of his mere good pleasure.

Thus now when they had talked away a little more time, they drew nigh to an House which stood in the way, which House was built for the relief of pilgrims as you will find more fully related in the first part of these records of the *Pilgrim's Progress*. So they drew on towards the House (the House of the Interpreter) and when they came to the door they heard a great talk in the House; they then gave ear, and heard, as they thought, Christiana mentioned by name. For you must know that there went along, even before her, a talk of her and her children's going on pilgrimage. And this thing was the more pleasing to them, because they had heard that she was Christian's wife, that woman who was sometime ago so unwilling to hear of going on pilgrimage. Thus therefore they stood still and heard the good people within commending her, who they little thought stood at the door. At last Christiana knocked as she had done at the Gate before. Now when she had knocked, there came to the door a young damsel and opened the door and looked, and behold two women was there.

Talk in the Interpreter's House about Christiana's going on pilgrimage

She knocks at the door

The door is opened to them by Innocent

Damsel. Then said the damsel to them, With whom would you speak in this place?

Christiana. Christiana answered, We understand that this is a privileged place for those that are become pilgrims, and we now at this door are such. Wherefore we pray that we may be partakers of that for which we at this time are come; for the day, as thou seest, is very far spent, and we are loth tonight to go any further.

Damsel. Pray what may I call your name, that I may tell it to my Lord within?

Christiana. My name is Christiana; I was the wife of that pilgrim that some years ago did travel this way, and these be his four children. This maiden also is my companion, and is going on pilgrimage too.

Innocent. Then ran Innocent in (for that was her name) and said to those within, Can you think who is at the door? There is Christiana and her children, and her companion, all waiting for entertainment here. Then they leaped for joy, and went and told their master. So he came to the door, and looking upon her, he said, 'Art thou that Christiana whom Christian, the good man, left behind him, when he betook himself to a pilgrim's life?'

Joy in the House of the Interpreter that Christiana is turned pilgrim

Christiana. I am that woman that was so hard-hearted as to slight my husband's troubles, and that left him to go on in his journey alone, and these are his four children; but now I also am come, for I am convinced that no way is right but this.

Interpreter. Then is fulfilled that which also is written of the man that *said to his son, go work today in my vineyard, and he said to his father, I will not; but afterwards repented and went.*

Christiana. Then said Christiana, So be it, amen, God make it a true saying upon me, and grant that I may be found at the last of him in peace without spot and blameless.

Interpreter. But why standest thou thus at the door, come in thou daughter of Abraham,²⁴ we were talking of thee but now: for tidings have come to us before, how thou art become a pilgrim. Come children, come in; come maiden, come in; so he had them all into the House.

So when they were within, they were bidden sit down and rest them, the which when they had done, those that attended upon the pilgrims in the House, came into the room to see them. And one smiled, and another smiled, and they all smiled for joy that Christiana was become a pilgrim. They also looked upon the boys, they stroked them over the faces with the hand in token of their kind reception of them: they also carried it lovingly to Mercy, and bid them all welcome into their Master's House.

Old saints glad to see the young ones walk in God's ways

After a while, because supper was not ready, the Interpreter took them into his significant rooms, and showed them what Christian, Christiana's husband had seen sometime before. Here therefore they saw the man in the cage, the man and his dream, the man that cut his way through his enemies, and the picture of the biggest of them all, together with the rest of those things that were then so profitable to Christian. *The significant rooms*

This done, and after these things had been somewhat digested by Christiana, and her company: the Interpreter takes them apart again: and has them first into a room, where was a man that could look no way but downwards, with a muck-rake[25] in his hand. There stood also one over his head with a celestial crown in his hand, and proffered to give him that crown for his muck-rake; but the man did neither look up, nor regard, but raked to himself the straws, the small sticks, and dust of the floor. *The man with the muck-rake expounded*

Then said Christiana, I persuade myself that I know somewhat the meaning of this: for this is a figure of a man of this world, is it not, good sir?

Interpreter. Thou hast said the right, said he, and his muck-rake doth show his carnal mind. And whereas thou seest him rather give heed to rake up straws and sticks, and the dust of the floor, than to what he says that calls to him from above with the celestial crown in his hand, it is to show that Heaven is but as a fable to some, and that things here are counted the only things substantial. Now whereas it was also showed thee that the man could look no way but downwards, it is to let thee know that earthly things when they are with power upon men's minds quite carry their hearts away from God.

Christiana. Then said Christiana, O! deliver me from this muck-rake. *Christiana's prayer against the muck-rake*

Interpreter. That prayer, said the Interpreter, has

lain by till 'tis almost rusty: 'Give me not riches' is scarce the prayer of one of ten thousand. Straws and sticks and dust with most are the great things now looked after.

With that Mercy and Christiana wept, and said, 'It is alas! too true.'

When the Interpreter had showed them this, he has them into the very best room in the house (a very brave room it was), so he bid them look round about, and see if they could find anything profitable there. Then they looked round and round: for there was nothing there to be seen but a very great spider[26] on the wall: and that they overlooked.

Mercy. Then said Mercy, Sir, I see nothing; but Christiana held her peace.

Interpreter. But said the Interpreter, look again: she *Of the spider* therefore looked again and said, Here is not any thing, but an ugly spider who hangs by her hands upon the wall. Then said he, Is there but one spider in all this spacious room? Then the water stood in Christiana's eyes, for she was a woman quick of apprehension, and she said, 'Yes, Lord, there is more here than one. *Talk about* Yea, and spiders whose venom is far more destructive *the spider* than that which is in her.' The Interpreter then looked pleasantly upon her, and said, Thou hast said the truth. This made Mercy blush, and the boys to cover their faces. For they all began now to understand the riddle.

Then said the Interpreter again, *The spider taketh hold with her hands, as you see, and is in Kings' palaces.* And wherefore is this recorded but to show you that *The* how full of the venom of sin soever you be, yet you *interpretation* may by the hand of faith lay hold of, and dwell in the best room that belongs to the King's House above?

Christiana. I thought, said Christiana, of something

of this; but I could not imagine it all. I thought that we were like spiders, and that we looked like ugly creatures, in what fine room soever we were: but that by this spider, this venomous and ill-favoured creature, we were to learn how to act faith, that came not into my mind. And yet she has taken hold with her hands as I see, and dwells in the best room in the House. God has made nothing in vain.

Then they seemed all to be glad; but the water stood in their eyes: yet they looked one upon another, and also bowed before the Interpreter.

He had them then into another room where was a hen and chickens, and bid them observe a while. So *Of the hen* one of the chickens went to the trough to drink, and *and chickens* every time she drank she lift up her head and her eyes towards Heaven. 'See,' said he, 'what this little chick doth, and learn of her to acknowledge whence your mercies come, by receiving them with looking up. Yet again,' said he, 'observe and look.' So they gave heed, and perceived that the hen did walk[27] in a fourfold method towards her chickens. 1. She had a common call, and that she hath all day long. 2. She had a special call, and that she had but sometimes. 3. She had a brooding note. And 4. she had an out-cry.[28]

'Now,' said he, 'compare this hen to your King, and these chickens to his obedient ones. For answerable to her, himself has his methods which he walketh in towards his people. By his common call he gives nothing, by his special call, he always has something to give, he has also a brooding voice for them that are under his wing. And he has an out-cry, to give the alarm when he seeth the enemy come. I chose, my darlings, to lead you into the room where such things are, because you are women, and they are easy for you.'

Christiana. And sir, said Christiana, pray let us see some more. So he had them into the slaughter-house, where was a butcher a killing of a sheep: and behold the sheep was quiet, and took her death patiently. Then said the Interpreter: 'You must learn of this sheep to suffer, and to put up wrongs without murmurings and complaints. Behold how quietly she takes her death, and without objecting she suffereth her skin to be pulled over her ears. Your King doth call you his sheep.'

Of the butcher and the sheep

After this he led them into his garden where was great variety of flowers: and he said, 'Do you see all these?' So Christiana said, 'Yes.' Then said he again, 'Behold the flowers are divers in stature, in quality, and colour, and smell, and virtue, and some are better than some: also where the gardener has set them, there they stand, and quarrel not one with another.'[29]

Of the garden

Again he had them into his field, which he had sowed with wheat and corn: but when they beheld, the tops of all was cut off, only the straw remained. He said again, this ground was dunged, and ploughed, and sowed; but what shall we do with the crop? Then said Christiana, 'Burn some and make muck of the rest.' Then said the Interpreter again, 'Fruit you see is that thing you look for, and for want of that you condemn it to the fire, and to be trodden under foot of men: beware that in this you condemn not yourselves.'

Of the field

Then, as they were coming in from abroad, they espied a little robin with a great spider in his mouth. So the Interpreter said, 'Look here.' So they looked, and Mercy wondered; but Christiana said, 'What a disparagement is it to such a little pretty bird as the robin-redbreast is, he being also a bird above many that loveth to maintain a kind of sociableness with man. I had thought they had lived upon crumbs of

Of the robin and the spider

bread, or upon other such harmless matter. I like him worse than I did.'

The Interpreter then replied, 'This robin is an emblem very apt to set forth some professors by; for to sight they are as this robin, pretty of note, colour and carriages, they seem also to have a very great love for professors that are sincere, and above all other to desire to sociate with, and to be in their company, as if they could live upon the good man's crumbs. They pretend also that therefore it is that they frequent the House of the Godly and the appointments of the Lord: but when they are by themselves, as the robin, they can catch and gobble up spiders, they can change their diet, drink iniquity, and swallow down sin like water.'

So when they were come again into the House, because supper as yet was not ready, Christiana again desired that the Interpreter would either show or tell of some other things that are profitable.

Pray, and you will get at that which yet lies unrevealed

Then the Interpreter began and said, 'The fatter the sow is, the more she desires the mire;[30] the fatter the ox is, the more gamesomely he goes to the slaughter; and the more healthy the lusty man is, the more prone he is unto evil.

'There is a desire in women to go neat and fine, and it is a comely thing to be adorned with that that in God's sight is of great price.

''Tis easier watching a night or two, than to sit up a whole year together: So 'tis easier for one to begin to profess well, than to hold out as he should to the end.

'Every ship-master, when in a storm, will willingly cast that overboard that is of the smallest value in the vessel; but who will throw the best out first? None but he that feareth not God.

'One leak will sink a ship, and one sin will destroy a sinner.

'He that forgets his friend, is ungrateful unto him; but he that forgets his Saviour is unmerciful to himself.

'He that lives in sin, and looks for happiness hereafter, is like him that soweth cockle and thinks to fill his barn with wheat or barley.

'If a man would live well, let him fetch his last day to him, and make it always his company-keeper.

'Whispering and change of thoughts proves that sin is in the world.

'If the world which God sets light by is counted a thing of that worth with men: what is Heaven which God commendeth?

'If the life that is attended with so many troubles is so loth to be let go by us, what is the life above?

'Everybody will cry up the goodness of men; but who is there that is, as he should, affected with the goodness of God?

'We seldom sit down to meat; but we eat and leave. So there is in Jesus Christ more merit and righteousness than the whole world has need of.'

Of the tree that is rotten at heart When the Interpreter had done, he takes them out into his garden again, and had them to a tree[31] whose inside was all rotten, and gone, and yet it grew and had leaves. Then said Mercy, 'What means this?' 'This tree,' said he, 'whose outside is fair, and whose inside is rotten, is it to which many may be compared that are in the Garden of God, who with their mouths speak high in behalf of God, but indeed will do nothing for him, whose leaves are fair; but their heart good for nothing but to be tinder for the Devil's tinder-box.'

They are at supper Now supper was ready, the table spread, and all things set on the board; so they sat down and did eat when one had given thanks. And the Interpreter did usually entertain those that lodged with him with music at meals, so the minstrels played. There was also one that did sing. And a very fine voice he had. His song was this:

> The Lord is only my support,
> And he that doth me feed:
> How can I then want any thing
> Whereof I stand in need?

When the song and music was ended, the Interpreter asked Christiana what it was that at first did move her to betake herself to a pilgrim's life.

Christiana answered, 'First, the loss of my husband *Talk at* came into my mind, at which I was heartily grieved: *supper* but all that was but natural affection. Then after that came the troubles and pilgrimage of my husband *A repetition* into my mind, and also how like a churl I had carried *of Christiana's* it to him as to that. So guilt took hold of my mind, *experience* and would have drawn me into the pond; but that opportunely I had a dream of the well-being of my husband, and a letter sent me by the King of that Country where my husband dwells, to come to him. The dream and the letter together so wrought upon my mind, that they forced me to this way.'

Interpreter. But met you with no opposition afore you set out of doors?

Christiana. Yes, a neighbour of mine, one Mrs Timorous. (She was akin to him that would have persuaded my husband to go back for fear of the lions.) She all-to-be-fooled me for, as she called it, my intended desperate adventure; she also urged what she could, to dishearten me to it, the hardships and troubles that my husband met with in the way; but all this I got over pretty well. But a dream that I had, of two ill-looked ones, that I thought did plot how to make me miscarry in my journey, that hath troubled me much: yea, it still runs in my mind, and makes me afraid of everyone that I meet, lest they should meet me to do me a mischief, and to turn me out of the way. Yea, I may tell my Lord, tho' I would not have everybody know it, that between this and the Gate by which we got into the way, we were both so sorely assaulted, that we were made to cry out murder, and the two that made this assault upon us, were like the two that I saw in my dream.

A question put to Mercy   Then said the Interpreter, 'Thy beginning is good, thy latter end shall greatly increase.' So he addressed himself to Mercy: and said unto her, 'And what moved thee to come hither, sweetheart?'

Mercy. Then Mercy blushed and trembled, and for a while continued silent.

Interpreter. Then said he, be not afraid, only believe, and speak thy mind.

Mercy's answer   *Mercy*. So she began and said, Truly, sir, my want of experience is that that makes me covet to be in silence, and that also that fills me with fears of coming short at last. I cannot tell of visions and dreams as my friend Christiana can, nor know I what it is to mourn for my refusing of the counsel of those that were good relations.

Interpreter. What was it then, dear heart, that hath prevailed with thee to do as thou hast done?

Mercy. Why, when our friend here, was packing up to be gone from our town, I and another went accidentally to see her. So we knocked at the door and went in. When we were within, and seeing what she was doing, we asked what was her meaning. She said she was sent for to go to her husband, and then she up and told us, how she had seen him in a dream, dwelling in a curious place among immortals wearing a crown, playing upon a harp, eating and drinking at his Prince's table, and singing praises to him for bringing him thither, etc. Now methought, while she was telling these things unto us, my heart burned within me. And I said in my heart, if this be true, I will leave my father and my mother, and the land of my nativity, and will, if I may, go along with Christiana.

So I asked her further of the truth of these things, and if she would let me go with her: for I saw now that there was no dwelling but with the danger of ruin any longer in our town. But yet I came away with a heavy heart, not for that I was unwilling to come away; but for that so many of my relations were left behind. And I am come with all the desire of my heart, and will go if I may with Christiana unto her husband and his King.

Interpreter. Thy setting out is good, for thou hast given credit to the truth. Thou art a Ruth, who did for the love that she bore to Naomi, and to the Lord her God, leave father and mother, and the land of her nativity to come out and go with a people that she knew not heretofore. The Lord recompense thy work, and a full reward be given thee of the Lord God of Israel, under whose wings thou art come to trust.

Now supper was ended, and preparations was made for bed, the women were laid singly alone, and the boys by themselves. Now when Mercy was in bed, she could not sleep for joy, for that now her doubts of missing at last, were removed further from her than ever they were before. So she lay blessing and praising God who had had such favour for her. *They address themselves for bed*

Mercy's good night's rest

In the morning they arose with the sun, and the prepared themselves for their departure: but the Interpreter would have them tarry a while, 'For,' said he, 'you must orderly go from hence.' Then said he to the damsel that at first opened unto them, 'Take them and have them into the garden, to the Bath,[32] *The Bath Sanctification* and there wash them, and make them clean from the soil which they have gathered by travelling.' Then Innocent the damsel took them and had them into the *They wash* garden, and brought them to the Bath, so she told *in it* them that there they must wash and be clean, for so her Master would have the women to do that called at his House as they were going on pilgrimage. They then went in and washed, yea they and the boys and all, and they came out of that Bath not only sweet and clean; but also much enlivened and strengthened in their joints. So when they came in, they looked fairer a deal than when they went out to the washing.

When they were returned out of the garden from the Bath, the Interpreter took them and looked upon them and said unto them, 'Fair as the moon.' Then *They are* he called for the seal[33] wherewith they used to be *sealed* sealed that were washed in his Bath. So the seal was brought, and he set his mark upon them that they might be known in the places whither they were yet to go. Now the seal was the contents and sum of the Passover which the Children of Israel did eat when they came out from the land of Egypt: and the mark was set between their eyes. This seal greatly added to their beauty, for it was an ornament to their faces. It also added to their gravity, and made their countenances more like them of angels.

Then said the Interpreter again to the damsel that waited upon these women, 'Go into the vestry and fetch out garments for these people.' So she went and fetched out white raiment, and laid it down before him; so he commanded them to put it on. It was *They are* fine linen, white and clean. When the women were *clothed* thus adorned they seemed to be a terror one to the other, for that they could not see that glory each one on herself which they could see in each other. Now *True humility* therefore they began to esteem each other better than themselves. For, 'You are fairer than I am,' said one, and, 'You are more comely than I am,' said another. The children also stood amazed to see into what fashion they were brought.

The Interpreter then called for a man-servant of his, one Great-heart,[34] and bid him take sword, and helmet and shield, and, 'Take these my daughters,' said he, 'and conduct them to the House called Beautiful, at which place they will rest next.' So he took his weapons, and went before them, and the Interpreter said, 'God speed.' Those also that belonged to the family sent them away with many a good wish. So they went on their way, and sung,

> *This place has been our second stage,*
> *Here we have heard and seen*
> *Those good things that from age to age,*
> *To others hid have been.*

> *The dunghill-raker, spider, hen,*
> *The chicken too to me*
> *Hath taught a lesson, let me then*
> *Conformed to it be.*

> *The butcher, garden and the field,*
> *The robin and his bait,*
> *Also the rotten tree doth yield*
> *Me argument of weight*

> *To move me for to watch and pray,*
> *To strive to be sincere,*
> *To take my Cross up day by day,*
> *And serve the Lord with fear.*

Now I saw in my dream that they went on, and Great-heart went before them, so they went and came to the place where Christian's burthen fell off his back and tumbled into a sepulchre. Here then they made a pause, and here also they blessed God. Now said Christiana, 'It comes to my mind what was said to us at the Gate, to wit, that we should have pardon, by word and deed;[35] by word, that is, by the promise; by deed, to wit, in the way it was obtained. What the promise is, of that I know something: but what is it to have pardon by deed, or in the way that it was obtained, Mr Great-heart, I suppose you know; wherefore if you please let us hear you discourse thereof.'

A comment upon what was said at the Gate, or a discourse of our being justified by Christ   *Great-heart.* Pardon by the deed done, is pardon obtained by some one, for another that hath need thereof: not by the person pardoned, but in the way, saith another, in which I have obtained it. So then to speak to the question more large, the pardon that you and Mercy and these boys have attained was obtained by another, to wit, by him that let you in at the Gate: and he hath obtained it in this double way. He has performed righteousness to cover you, and spilt blood to wash you in.

Christiana. But if he parts with his righteousness to us: what will he have for himself?

Great-heart. He has more righteousness than you have need of, or than he needeth himself.

Christiana. Pray make that appear.

Great-heart. With all my heart, but first I must premise that he of whom we are now about to speak, is one that has not his fellow. He has two natures in one person, plain to be distinguished, impossible to be divided. Unto each of these natures a righteousness belongeth, and each righteousness is essential to that nature. So that one may as easily cause the nature to be extinct, as to separate its justice or righteousness from it. Of these righteousnesses therefore, we are not made partakers so as that they or any of them should be put upon us that we might be made just, and live thereby. Besides these there is a righteousness which this person has, as these two natures are joined in one. And this is not the righteousness of the Godhead, as distinguished from the manhood; nor the righteousness of the manhood, as distinguished from the Godhead; but a righteousness which standeth in the union of both natures, and may properly be called the righteousness that is essential to his being prepared of God to the capacity of the mediatory office which he was to be entrusted with. If he parts with his first righteousness, he parts with his Godhead; if he parts with his second righteousness, he parts with the purity of his manhood; if he parts with this third, he parts with that perfection that capacitates him to the office of mediation. He has therefore another righteousness which standeth in performance, or obedience to a revealed will: and that is it that he puts upon sinners, and that by which their sins are covered. Wherefore he saith, *as by one man's disobedience many were made sinners, so by the obedience of one shall many be made righteous.*

Christiana. But are the other righteousnesses of no use to us?

Great-heart. Yes, for though they are essential to his natures and office, and so cannot be communicated unto another, yet it is by virtue of them that the righteousness that justifies is for that purpose efficacious. The righteousness of his Godhead gives virtue to his obedience; the righteousness of his manhood giveth capability to his obedience to justify, and the righteousness that standeth in the union of these two natures to his office, giveth authority to that righteousness to do the work for which it is ordained.

So then, here is a righteousness that Christ, as God, has no need of, for he is God without it; here is a righteousness that Christ, as man, has no need of to make him so, for he is perfect man without it. Again, here is a righteousness that Christ as God-man has no need of, for he is perfectly so without it. Here then is a righteousness that Christ, as God, as man, as God-man has no need of, with reference to himself, and therefore he can spare it, a justifying righteousness, that he for himself wanteth not, and therefore he giveth it away. Hence 'tis called the gift of righteousness. This righteousness, since Christ Jesus the Lord has made himself under the law, must be given away: for the law doth not only bind him that is under it to do justly; but to use charity: wherefore he must, he ought by the law, if he hath two coats, to give one to him that has none. Now our Lord hath indeed two coats, one for himself, and one to spare: wherefore he freely bestows one upon those that have none. And thus Christiana, and Mercy, and the rest of you that are here, doth your pardon come by deed, or by the work of another man. Your Lord Christ is he that has worked and given away what he wrought for to the next poor beggar he meets.

But again, in order to pardon by deed, there must something be paid to God as a price, as well as something prepared to cover us withal. Sin has delivered us up to the just curse of a righteous law: now from this curse we must be justified by way of redemption, a price being paid for the harms we have done, and this is by the blood of your Lord, who came and stood in your place, and stead, and died your death for your transgressions. Thus has he ransomed you from your transgressions by blood, and covered your polluted and deformed souls with righteousness, for the sake of which, God passeth by you and will not *Christiana* hurt you when he comes to judge the world.

affected with
this way of   *Christiana.* This is brave. Now I see that there was
Redemption something to be learnt by our being pardoned by

word and deed. Good Mercy, let us labour to keep this in mind, and my children do you remember it also. But, Sir, was not this it that made my good Christian's burden fall from off his shoulder and that made him give three leaps for joy?

Great-heart. Yes, 'twas the belief of this, that cut *How the* those strings that could not be cut by other means, *strings that* and 'twas to give him a proof of the virtue of this *Christian's* that he was suffered to carry his burden to the Cross. *burden to him were cut*

Christiana. I thought so, for though my heart was lightful and joyous before, yet it is ten times more lightsome and joyous now. And I am persuaded by what I have felt, though I have felt but little as yet, that if the most burdened man in the world was here, and did see and believe, as I now do, 'twould make his heart the more merry and blithe.

Great-heart. There is not only comfort, and the *How* ease of a burden brought to us, by the sight and *affection to* consideration of these, but an endeared affection begot *in the soul* in us by it: for who can, if he doth but once think that pardon comes, not only by promise, but thus, but be affected with the way and means of his redemption, and so with the man that hath wrought it for him?

Christiana. True, methinks it makes my heart bleed *Cause of* to think that he should bleed for me. Oh! thou *admiration* loving one, Oh! thou blessed one. Thou deservest to have me all, thou hast paid for me ten thousand times more than I am worth. No marvel that this made the water stand in my husband's eyes, and that it made him trudge so nimbly on, I am persuaded he wished me with him, but vile wretch that I was, I let him come all alone. O Mercy, that thy father and mother were here, yea, and Mrs Timorous also. Nay I wish now with all my heart, that here was Madam Wanton too. Surely, surely, their hearts would be affected, nor could the fear of the one, nor the powerful lusts of the other prevail with them to go home again, and to refuse to become good pilgrims.

Great-heart. You speak now in the warmth of your affections; will it, think you, be always thus with you? Besides, this is not communicated to every one, nor *To be affected* to every one that did see your Jesus bleed. There was *with Christ* that stood by, and that saw the blood run from his *and with* heart to the ground, and yet was so far off this, that *what he has* instead of lamenting, they laughed at him, and in- *done is a* stead of becoming his disciples, did harden their *thing special* hearts against him. So that all that you have, my daughters, you have by a peculiar impression made by a divine contemplating upon what I have spoken to you. Remember that 'twas told you, that the hen by her common call, gives no meat to her chickens. This you have therefore by a special grace.

Simple and Now I saw still in my dream that they went on *Sloth and* until they were come to the place that Simple, and *Presumption* Sloth and Presumption lay and slept in, when Chris- *hanged, and* tian went by on pilgrimage. And behold they were *why* hanged up in irons a little way off on the other side.

Mercy. Then said Mercy to him that was their guide and conductor, What are those three men? And for what are they hanged here?

Great-heart. These three men were men of very bad qualities, they had no mind to be pilgrims them- selves, and whosoever they could they hindered; they were for sloth and folly themselves, and who- ever they could persuade with, they made so too, and withal taught them to presume that they should do well at last. They were asleep when Christian went by, and now you go by they are hanged.

Mercy. But could they persuade any to be of their opinion?

Great-heart. Yes, they turned several out of the *Their crimes* way. There was Slow-pace that they persuaded to do as they. They also prevailed with one Short-wind, with one No-heart, with one Linger-after-lust, and with one Sleepy-head, and with a young woman, her name was Dull, to turn out of the way and become as they. Besides, they brought up an ill report of your Lord, persuading others that he was a task-master. They also brought up an evil report of the good land, saying, "Twas not half so good as some pretend it was.' They also began to vilify his servants, and to count the very best of them meddlesome, troublesome busy-bodies. Further, they would call the bread of God, husks, the comforts of his children, fancies, the travail and labour of pilgrims, things to no purpose. *Who they prevailed upon to turn out of the way*

Christiana. Nay, said Christiana, if they were such, they shall never be bewailed by me; they have but what they deserve, and I think it is well that they hang so near the highway that others may see and take warning. But had it not been well if their crimes had been engraven in some plate of iron or brass, and left here even where they did their mischiefs for a caution to other bad men?

Great-heart. So it is, as you well may perceive if you will go a little to the wall.

Mercy. No, no, let them hang and their names rot, and their crimes live for ever against them; I think it a high favour that they were hanged afore we came hither; who knows else what they might a done to such poor women as we are? Then she turned it into a song, saying,

> Now then, you three, hang there and be a sign
> To all that shall against the truth combine:
> And let him that comes after, fear this end,
> If unto pilgrims he is not a friend.
> And thou my soul of all such men beware
> That unto holiness opposers are.

Thus they went on till they came at the foot of the Hill Difficulty. Where again their good friend, Mr Great-heart, took an occasion to tell them of what happened there when Christian himself went by. So *'Tis difficult* he had them first to the spring. 'Lo,' saith he, 'this is *getting of* the spring that Christian drank of, before he went up *good* this Hill, and then 'twas clear and good; but now 'tis *doctrine in* this Hill, and then 'twas clear and good; but now 'tis *erroneous* dirty with the feet of some that are not desirous that *times* pilgrims here should quench their thirst.' Thereat Mercy said, 'And why so envious, tro?'[36] But said their guide, 'It will do, if taken up, and put into a vessel that is sweet and good; for then the dirt will sink to the bottom, and the water come out by itself more clear.' Thus therefore Christiana and her companions were compelled to do. They took it up and put it into an earthen-pot and so let it stand till the dirt was gone to the bottom, and then they drank thereof.

Next he showed them the two by-ways that were at the foot of the Hill, where Formality and Hypocrisy lost themselves. 'And,' said he, 'these are dangerous paths: two were here cast away when Christian came by. And although, as you see, these ways *By-paths* are since stopped up[37] with chains, posts, and a ditch, *though barred* yet there are that will choose to adventure here, *up will not* rather than take the pains to go up this Hill. *keep all from* *going in them*

Christiana. The way of transgressors is hard. 'Tis a wonder that they can get into those ways, without danger of breaking their necks.

Great-heart. They will venture, yea, if at any time any of the King's servants doth happen to see them, and doth call unto them, and tell them that they are in the wrong ways, and do bid them beware the danger. Then they will railingly return them answer and say, *As for the word that thou hast spoken unto us in the name of the King, we will not hearken unto thee; but we will certainly do whatsoever thing goeth out of our own mouths,* etc. Nay if you look a little farther you shall see that these ways are made cautionary enough, not only by these posts and ditch and chain; but also by being hedged up. Yet they will choose to go there.

Christiana. They are idle, they love not to take pains, up-hill-way is unpleasant to them. So it is fulfilled unto them as it is written, *The way of the slothful man is a hedge of thorns. Yea, they will rather choose to walk upon a snare than to go up this Hill, and the rest of this way to the City.*[38] *The reason why some do choose to go in by-ways*

Then they set forward and began to go up the Hill, and up the Hill they went; but before they got to the top, Christiana began to pant, and said, 'I dare say this is a breathing Hill, no marvel if they that love their ease more than their souls choose to themselves a smoother way.' Then said Mercy, 'I must sit down.' Also the least of the children began to cry. 'Come, come,' said Great-heart, 'sit not down here, for a little above is the Prince's Arbour.' Then took he the little boy by the hand, and led him up thereto. *The Hill puts the pilgrims to it*

They sit in the Arbour

When they were come to the Arbour they were very willing to sit down, for they were all in a pelting heat. Then said Mercy, '*How sweet is rest to them that labour!* And how good is the Prince of pilgrims to provide such resting places for them! Of this Arbour I have heard much, but I never saw it before. But here let us beware of sleeping, for as I have heard, for that it cost poor Christian dear.'

Then said Mr Great-heart to the little ones, 'Come my pretty boys, how do you do? What think you now of going on pilgrimage?' 'Sir,' said the least, 'I was almost beat out of heart; but I thank you for lending me a hand at my need. And I remember now *The little boys answer to the guide, and also to Mercy* what my mother has told me, namely, that the way to Heaven is as up a ladder, and the way to Hell is as down a hill. But I had rather go up the ladder to life, than down the hill to death.

Which is hardest uphill or downhill? Then said Mercy, 'But the proverb is, *To go down the hill is easy.*' But James said (for that was his name), 'The day is coming when in my opinion, going down-hill will be the hardest of all.' ''Tis a good boy,' said his master, 'thou hast given her a right answer.' Then Mercy smiled, but the little boy did blush.

They refresh themselves *Christiana.* Come, said Christiana, will you eat a bit, a little to sweeten your mouths, while you sit here to rest your legs? For I have here a piece of pomegranate which Mr Interpreter put in my hand, just when I came out of his doors; he gave me also a piece of an honeycomb, and a little bottle of spirits. 'I thought he gave you something,' said Mercy, 'because he called you a-to-side.' Yes, so he did, said the other. But Mercy, it shall still be as I said it should, when at first we came from home, thou shalt be a sharer in all the good that I have, because thou so willingly didst become my companion. Then she gave to them, and they did eat, both Mercy, and the boys. And said Christiana to Mr Great-heart, Sir, will you do as we? But he answered, 'You are going on pilgrimage, and presently I shall return; much good may what you have, do to you. At home I eat the same every day.' Now when they had eaten and drank, and had chatted a little longer, their guide said to them, 'The day wears away, if you think good, let us prepare to be going.' So they got up to go, and the little boys went before; but Christiana forgat to take her bottle of spirits with her, so she sent her little boy back to fetch *Christiana forgets her bottle of spirits* it. Then said Mercy, 'I think this is a losing place. Here Christian lost his roll, and here Christiana left her bottle behind her. Sir, what is the cause of this?'

So their guide made answer and said, 'The cause is sleep, or forgetfulness; some sleep, when they should keep awake and some forget, when they should remember; and this is the very cause why often at the resting places some pilgrims in some things come off losers. Pilgrims should watch and remember what *Mark this* they have already received under their greatest enjoyments; but for want of doing so, oft times their rejoicing ends in tears, and their sunshine in a cloud: witness the story of Christian at this place.'

When they were come to the place where Mistrust and Timorous met Christian to persuade him to go back for fear of the lions, they perceived as it were a stage, and before it towards the road, a broad plate with a copy of verses written thereon, and underneath, the reason of the raising up of that stage in that place rendered: the verses were these:

> Let him that sees this stage take heed,
> Unto his heart and tongue,
> Lest if he do not, here he speed
> As some have long agone.

The words underneath the verses were: 'This stage was built to punish such upon, who through timorousness, or mistrust shall be afraid to go further on pilgrimage. Also on this stage both Mistrust and Timorous were burned thorough the tongue with and hot iron for endeavouring to hinder Christian in his journey.'

Then said Mercy, 'This is much like to the saying *An emblem of* of the beloved, *What shall be given unto thee? or what* *those that go* *shall be done unto thee thou false tongue? sharp arrows* *on bravely,* *of the mighty with coals of juniper.'* *when there is* *no danger;*
So they went on till they came within sight of the *but shrink* lions. Now Mr Great-heart was a strong man, so he *when troubles* *come*

was not afraid of a lion. But yet when they were come up to the place where the lions were, the boys that went before were now glad to cringe behind, for they were afraid of the lions, so they stepped back and went behind. At this their guide smiled, and said, 'How now my boys, do you love to go before when no danger doth approach and love to come behind so soon as the lions appear?'

Of Grim the giant, and of his backing the lions Now as they went up, Mr Great-heart drew his sword with intent to make a way for the pilgrims in spite of the lions. Then there appeared one that it seems had taken upon him to back the lions. And he said to the pilgrims' guide, 'What is the cause of your coming hither?' Now the name of that man was Grim or Bloody-man,[39] because of his slaying of pilgrims, and he was of the race of the giants.

Great-heart. Then said the pilgrims' guide, These women and children are going on pilgrimage, and this is the way they must go, and go it they shall in spite of thee and the lions.

Grim. This is not their way, neither shall they go therein. I am come forth to withstand them, and to that end will back the lions.

Now to say truth, by reason of the fierceness of the lions, and of the grim carriage of him that did back them, this way had of late lain much unoccupied, and was almost all grown over with grass.

Christiana. Then said Christiana, Though the high-ways have been unoccupied heretofore, and though the travellers have been made in time past to walk through by-paths, it must not be so now I am risen, *Now I am risen a mother in Israel.*

Grim. Then he swore by the lions, but it should; and therefore bid them turn aside, for they should not have passage there.

Great-heart. But their guide made first his approach

unto Grim, and laid so heavily at him with his sword, that he forced him to a retreat.

Grim. Then said he (that attempted to back the lions), Will you slay me upon mine own ground?

Great-heart. 'Tis the King's highway that we are in, *A fight* and in this way it is that thou hast placed thy lions; *betwixt Grim* but these women and these children, though weak, *Great-heart* shall hold on their way in spite of thy lions. And with that he gave him again a down-right blow, and brought him upon his knees. With this blow he also broke his helmet, and with the next he cut off an arm. Then did the giant roar so hideously that his voice frighted the women, and yet they were glad to *The victory* see him lie sprawling upon the ground. Now the lions were chained, and so of themselves could do nothing. Wherefore when old Grim that intended to back them was dead, Mr Great-heart said to the pilgrims, Come now and follow me, and no hurt shall happen to you from the lions. They therefore *They pass by* went on; but the women trembled as they passed by *the lions* them, the boys also looked as if they would die, but they all got by without further hurt.

Now then they were within sight of the porter's *They come to* lodge, and they soon came up unto it; but they made *the porter's* the more haste after this to go thither, because 'tis *lodge* dangerous travelling there in the night. So when they were come to the Gate, the guide knocked, and the porter cried, 'Who is there?' But as soon as the guide had said 'It is I,' he knew his voice and came down. (For the guide had oft before that came thither as a conductor of pilgrims.) When he was came down, he opened the Gate, and seeing the guide standing just before it (for he saw not the women, for they were behind) he said unto him, 'How now Mr Great-heart, what is your business here so late to-night?' 'I have brought,' said he, 'some pilgrims hither, where by my Lord's commandment they must lodge. I had been here some time ago, had I not been opposed by the giant that did use to back the lions. But I after a long and tedious combat with him have cut him off, and have brought the pilgrims hither in safety.

Porter. Will you not go in, and stay till morning?

Great-heart. No, I will return to my Lord tonight.

Christiana. Oh sir, I know not how to be willing you should leave us in our pilgrimage, you have been so faithful, and so loving to us, you have fought so stoutly for us, you have been so hearty in counselling of us, that I shall never forget your favour towards us.

Mercy. Then said Mercy, O that we might have thy company to our journey's end! How can such poor women as we hold out in a way so full of troubles as this way is without a friend and defender?

James. Then said James, the youngest of the boys, Pray sir be persuaded to go with us and help us, because we are so weak, and the way so dangerous as it is.

Great-heart. I am at my Lord's commandment. If he shall allot me to be your guide quite through, I will willingly wait upon you; but here you failed at first; for when he bid me come thus far with you, then you should have begged me of him to have gone quite through with you, and he would have granted your request. However, at present I must withdraw, and so good Christiana, Mercy, and my brave children, adieu.

Then the porter, Mr Watchful, asked Christiana of her country, and of her kindred, and she said, 'I came from the City of Destruction, I am a widow woman, and my husband is dead, his name was Christian the pilgrim.' 'How,' said the porter, 'was he your husband?' 'Yes,' said she, 'and these are his children,

[margin notes:]
Great-heart attempts to go back. The pilgrims implore his company still

Help lost for want of asking for

Christiana makes herself known to the porter, he tells it to a damsel and this,' pointing to Mercy, 'is one of my towns-women.' Then the porter rang his bell, as at such times he is wont, and there came to the door one of the damsels, whose name was Humble-mind. And to her the porter said, 'Go tell it within that Christiana the wife of Christian and her children are come hither on pilgrimage.' She went in therefore and told it. But oh what a noise for gladness was there within *Joy at the* when the damsel did but drop that word out of her *noise of the* mouth! *pilgrims' coming*

So they came with haste to the porter, for Christiana stood still at the door; then some of the most grave said unto her, 'Come in Christiana, come in thou wife of that good man, come in thou blessed woman, come in with all that are with thee.' So she went in, and they followed her that were her children and her companions. Now when they were gone in, they were had into a very large room, where they were bidden to sit down: so they sat down, and the chief of the House was called to see, and welcome the guests. Then they came in, and understanding who *Christians'* they were, did salute each one with a kiss, and *love is* said, 'Welcome ye vessels of the grace of God, *sight of one* welcome to us your friends.' *another*

Now because it was somewhat late, and because the pilgrims were weary with their journey, and also made faint with the sight of the fight, and of the terrible lions, therefore they desired as soon as might be, to prepare to go to rest. 'Nay,' said those of the family, 'refresh yourselves first with a morsel of meat.' For they had prepared for them a lamb with the accustomed sauce belonging thereto. For the porter had heard before of their coming, and had told it to them within. So when they had supped, and ended their prayer with a psalm they desired they might go to rest. 'But let us,' said Christiana, 'if we may be so bold as to choose, be in that chamber that was my husband's, when he was here. So they had them up thither, and they lay all in a room. When they were at rest, Christiana and Mercy entered into discourse about things that were convenient.

Christiana. Little did I think once that when my husband went on pilgrimage I should ever a followed.

Mercy. And you as little thought of lying in his bed, and in his chamber to rest as you do now.

Christiana. And much less did I ever think of seeing his face with comfort, and of worshipping the Lord the King with him, and yet now I believe I shall.

Christ's bosom is for all pilgrims

Mercy. Hark, don't you hear a noise?

Music

Christiana. Yes, 'tis as I believe a noise of music,[40] for joy that we are here.

Mercy. Wonderful! Music in the house, music in the heart, and music also in heaven, for joy that we are here.

Thus they talked a while, and then betook themselves to sleep; so in the morning, when they were awake, Christiana said to Mercy,

Christiana. What was the matter that you did laugh in your sleep tonight? I suppose you was in a dream?

Mercy did laugh in her sleep

Mercy. So I was, and a sweet dream it was; but are you sure I laughed?

Christiana. Yes, you laughed heartily; But prithee, Mercy, tell me thy dream?

Mercy. I was a dreamed[41] that I sat all alone in a solitary place, and was bemoaning of the hardness of my heart. Now I had not sat there long, but methought many were gathered about me to see me, and to hear what it was that I said. So they hearkened, and I went on bemoaning the hardness of my heart. At this, some of them laughed at me, some called me fool, and some began to thrust me about. With that, methought I looked up, and saw one coming with

Mercy's dream

What her dream was

wings towards me. So he came directly to me, and said 'Mercy, what aileth thee?' Now when he had heard me make my complaint, he said, 'Peace be to thee.' He also wiped mine eyes with his handkerchief, and clad me in silver and gold; he put a chain about my neck, and ear-rings in mine ears and a beautiful crown upon my head. Then he took me by my hand, and said, 'Mercy, come after me.' So he went up, and I followed, till we came at a golden Gate. Then he knocked, and when they within had opened, the man went in and I followed him up to a throne, upon which one sat, and he said to me, 'Welcome, daughter.' The place looked bright, and twinkling like the stars, or rather like the sun, and I thought that I saw your husband there, so I awoke from my dream. But did I laugh?

Christiana. Laugh! Ay, and well you might to see yourself so well. For you must give me leave to tell you, that I believe it was a good dream, and that as you have begun to find the first part true, so you shall find the second at last. *God speaks once, yea twice, yet man perceiveth it not. In a dream, in a vision of the night, when deep sleep falleth upon men, in slumbering upon the bed.* We need not, when a-bed, lie awake to talk with God; he can visit us while we sleep, and cause us then to hear his voice. Our heart oft times wakes when we sleep, and God can speak to that, either by words, by proverbs, by signs, and similitudes, as well as if one was awake.

Mercy. Well, I am glad of my dream, for I hope ere long to see it fulfilled to the making of me laugh again. *Mercy glad of her dream*

Christiana. I think it is now time to rise and to know what we must do.

Mercy. Pray, if they invite us to stay a while, let us willingly accept of the proffer. I am the willinger to stay awhile here, to grow better acquainted with these maids; methinks Prudence, Piety and Charity, have very comely and sober countenances.

Christiana. We shall see what they will do. So when they were up and ready, they came down. And they asked one another of their rest, and if it was comfortable, or not.

Mercy. Very good, said Mercy. It was one of the best night's lodging that ever I had in my life.

They stay here some time Then said Prudence and Piety, 'If you will be persuaded to stay here a while, you shall have what the house will afford.'

Charity. Ay, and that with a very good will, said Charity. So they consented, and stayed there about a month or above, and became very profitable one to *Prudence desires to catechize Christiana's children* another. And because Prudence would see how Christiana had brought up her children, she asked leave of her to catechize them: so she gave her free consent. Then she began at the youngest whose name was James.

James catechized *Prudence.* And she said, Come, James, canst thou tell who made thee?

James. God the Father, God the Son, and God the Holy Ghost.

Prudence. Good boy. And canst thou tell who saves thee?

James. God the Father, God the Son, and God the Holy Ghost.

Prudence. Good boy still. But how doth God the Father save thee?

James. By his grace.

Prudence. How doth God the Son save thee?

James. By his righteousness, death, and blood, and life.

Prudence. And how doth God the Holy Ghost save thee?

James. By his illumination, by his renovation, and by his preservation.

Then said Prudence to Christiana, 'You are to be commended for thus bringing up your children. I suppose I need not ask the rest these questions, since the youngest of them can answer them so well. I will therefore now apply myself to the youngest next.'

Prudence. Then she said, Come Joseph (for his name was Joseph), will you let me catechize you? *Joseph catechized*

Joseph. With all my heart.

Prudence. What is man?

Joseph. A reasonable creature, so made by God, as my brother said.

Prudence. What is supposed by this word saved?

Joseph. That man by sin has brought himself into a state of captivity and misery.

Prudence. What is supposed by his being saved by the Trinity?

Joseph. That sin is so great and mighty a tyrant that none can pull us out of its clutches but God, and that God is so good and loving to man as to pull him indeed out of this miserable state.

Prudence. What is God's design in saving of poor men?

Joseph. The glorifying of his name, of his grace, and justice, etc. And the everlasting happiness of his creature.

Prudence. Who are they that must be saved?

Joseph. Those that accept of his salvation.

'Good boy, Joseph, thy mother has taught thee well, and thou hast hearkened to what she has said unto thee.'

Then said Prudence to Samuel, who was the eldest but one,

Prudence. Come Samuel, are you willing that I should catechize you also? *Samuel catechized*

Samuel. Yes, forsooth, if you please.

Prudence. What is Heaven?

Samuel. A place, and state most blessed, because God dwelleth there.

Prudence. What is Hell?

Samuel. A place and state most woeful, because it is the dwelling place of sin, the Devil, and death.

Prudence. Why wouldest thou go to Heaven?

Samuel. That I may see God, and serve him without weariness; that I may see Christ, and love him everlastingly; that I may have that fullness of the Holy Spirit in me, that I can by no means here enjoy.

Prudence. A very good boy also, and one that has learned well.

Matthew catechized Then she addressed herself to the eldest, whose name was Matthew, and she said to him, 'Come Matthew, shall I also catechize you?'

Matthew. With a very good will.

Prudence. I ask then, if there was ever any thing that had a being, antecedent to, or before God?

Matthew. No, for God is eternal, nor is there any thing excepting himself that had a being until the beginning of the first day. *For in six days the Lord made Heaven and earth, the sea and all that in them is.*

Prudence. What do you think of the Bible?

Matthew. It is the Holy Word of God.

Prudence. Is there nothing written therein but what you understand?

Matthew. Yes, a great deal.

Prudence. What do you do when you meet with such places therein, that you do not understand?

Matthew. I think God is wiser than I. I pray also that he will please to let me know all therein that he knows will be for my good.

Prudence. How believe you as touching the resurrection of the dead?

Matthew. I believe they shall rise, the same that was buried: the same in nature, though not in corruption. And I believe this upon a double account: first, because God has promised it; secondly, because he is able to perform it.

Then said Prudence to the boys, 'You must still hearken to your mother, for she can learn you more. You must also diligently give ear to what good talk you shall hear from others, for for your sakes do they speak good things. Observe also and that with carefulness, what the heavens and the earth do teach you; but especially be much in the meditation of that book that was the cause of your father's becoming a pilgrim. I for my part, my children, will teach you what I can while you are here, and shall be glad if you will ask me questions that tend to godly edifying.' *Prudence's conclusion upon the catechizing of the boys*

Now by that these pilgrims had been at this place a week, Mercy had a visitor that pretended some good will unto her, and his name was Mr Brisk,[42] a man of some breeding, and that pretended to religion, but a man that stuck very close to the world. So he came once or twice, or more to Mercy, and offered love unto her. Now Mercy was of a fair countenance, and therefore the more alluring. *Mercy has a sweet heart*

Her mind also was to be always busying of herself in doing, for when she had nothing to do for herself, she would be making of hose and garments for others, and would bestow them upon them that had need. And Mr Brisk not knowing where or how she disposed of what she made, seemed to be greatly taken, for that he found her never idle. 'I will warrant her a good housewife,' quoth he to himself. *Mercy's temper*

Mercy then revealed the business to the maidens that were of the House, and inquired of them concerning him: for they did know him better than she. So they told her that he was a very busy young man, *Mercy inquires of the maids concerning Mr Brisk* and one that pretended to religion, but was as they feared, a stranger to the power of that which was good.

'Nay then,' said Mercy, 'I will look no more on him, for I purpose never to have a clog to my soul.'

Prudence then replied that there needed no great matter of discouragement to be given to him, her continuing so as she had began to do for the poor would quickly cool his courage.

So the next time he comes, he finds her at her old work, a making of things for the poor. Then said he, *Talk betwixt* 'What always at it?' 'Yes,' said she, 'either for myself, *Mercy and* or for others.' 'And what canst thee earn a day?' *Mr Brisk* quoth he. 'I do these things,' said she, *'that I may be rich in good works, laying up in store a good foundation against the time to come, that I may lay hold on eternal life.'* 'Why prithee what dost thou with them?' said *He forsakes* he. 'Clothe the naked,' said she. With that his coun- *her, and why* tenance fell. So he forbore to come at her again. And when he was asked the reason why, he said that Mercy was a pretty lass; but troubled with ill con- ditions.[43]

Mercy in the When he had left her, Prudence said, 'Did I not tell *practice of* thee that Mr Brisk would soon forsake thee? Yea, he *mercy* will raise up an ill report of thee: for notwithstanding *rejected;* his pretence to religion, and his seeming love to *While Mercy in the name* Mercy, yet Mercy and he are of tempers so different, *of Mercy is* that I believe they will never come together.' *liked*

Mercy. I might a had husbands afore now, though I spake not of it to any; but they were such as did not like my conditions, though never did any of them find fault with my person: so they and I could not agree.

Prudence. Mercy in our days is little set by, any further than as to its name: the practice which is set forth by thy conditions there are but few that can abide.

Mercy. Well, said Mercy, if nobody will have me, *Mercy's*
I will die a maid, or my conditions shall be to me as a *resolution*
husband. For I cannot change my nature, and to have
one that lies cross to me in this, that I purpose never to
admit of, as long as I live. I had a sister named Bounti- *How Mercy's*
ful that was married to one of these churls; but he *sister was*
and she could never agree;[44] but because my sister *husband*
was resolved to do as she had began, that is, to
show kindness to the poor, therefore her husband
first cried her down at the cross,[45] and then turned
her out of his doors.

Prudence. And yet he was a professor, I warrant
you?

Mercy. Yes, such a one as he was, and of such as he,
the world is now full; but I am for none of them all.

Now Matthew the eldest son of Christiana fell sick, *Matthew*
and his sickness was sore upon him, for he was much *falls sick*
pained in his bowels, so that he was with it at times
pulled as 'twere both ends together. There dwelt also
not far from thence, one Mr Skill, an ancient and
well approved physician. So Christiana desired it, and
they sent for him, and he came. When he was entered
the room, and had a little observed the boy, he concluded that he was sick of the gripes. Then he said to *Gripes of*
his mother, 'What diet has Matthew of late fed upon?' *conscience*
'Diet,' said Christiana, 'nothing but that which is
wholesome.' The physician answered, 'This boy has *The*
been tampering with something which lies in his *physician's*
maw undigested, and that will not away without *judgement*
means. And I tell you he must be purged or else he
will die.'

Samuel. Then said Samuel, Mother, Mother, what *Samuel puts*
was that which my brother did gather up and eat, so *his mother in*
soon as we were come from the Gate that is at the *fruit his*
head of this way? You know that there was an *brother did eat*
orchard on the left hand, on the other side of the

wall, and some of the trees hung over the wall, and my brother did plash and did eat.

Christiana. True my child, said Christiana, he did take thereof and did eat; naughty boy as he was, I did chide him, and yet he would eat thereof.

Skill. I knew he had eaten something that was not wholesome food. And that food, to wit, that fruit[46] is even the most hurtful of all. It is the fruit of Beelzebub's orchard. I do marvel that none did warn you of it; many have died thereof.

Christiana. Then Christiana began to cry, and she said, O naughty boy, and O careless mother, what shall I do for my son?

Skill. Come, do not be too much dejected; the boy may do well again; but he must purge and vomit.

Christiana. Pray sir, try the utmost of your skill with him whatever it costs.

Skill. Nay, I hope I shall be reasonable. So he made him a purge; but it was too weak. 'Twas said it was made of the blood of a goat, the ashes of an heifer, *Potion* and with some of the juice of hyssop, etc.[47] When Mr *prepared* Skill had seen that that purge was too weak, he made him one to the purpose. 'Twas made *ex carne et* *The Latin sanguine Christi*[48] (you know physicians give strange *I borrow* medicines to their patients) and it was made up into pills with a promise or two, and a proportionable quantity of salt. Now he was to take them three at a time fasting in half a quarter of a pint of the tears of repentance. When this potion was prepared, and *The boy loth* brought to the boy, he was loth to take it, though *to take the* torn with the gripes as if he should be pulled in *physic* pieces. 'Come, come,' said the physician, 'you must take it.' 'It goes against my stomach,' said the boy. 'I must have you take it,' said his mother. 'I shall vomit it up again,' said the boy. 'Pray, sir,' said

Christiana to Mr Skill, 'how does it taste?' 'It has no ill taste,' said the doctor, and with that she touched one of the pills with the tip of her tongue. 'Oh Matthew,' said she, 'this potion is sweeter than honey. If thou lovest thy mother, if thou lovest thy brothers, if thou lovest Mercy, if thou lovest thy life, take it.' So with much ado, after a short prayer for the blessing of God upon it, he took it, and it wrought kindly with him. It caused him to purge, it caused him to sleep and rest quietly, it put him into a fine heat and breathing sweat, and did quite rid him of his gripes. *The mother tastes it, and persuades him*

So in little time he got up, and walked about with a staff, and would go from room to room, and talk with Prudence, Piety, and Charity of his distemper and how he was healed. *A Word of God in the hand of his faith*

So when the boy was healed, Christiana asked Mr Skill, saying, 'Sir, what will content you for your pains and care to and of my child?' And he said, 'You must pay the Master of the College of Physicians, according to rules made, in that case, and provided.'

Christiana. But sir, said she, what is this pill good for else?

Skill. It is an universal pill; 'tis good against all the diseases that pilgrims are incident to, and when it is well prepared it will keep good time out of mind. *This pill an universal remedy*

Christiana. Pray, sir, make me up twelve boxes of them: for if I can get these, I will never take other physic.

Skill. These pills are good to prevent diseases, as well as to cure when one is sick. Yea, I dare say it, and stand to it, that if a man will but use this physic as he should, it will make him live for ever. But, good Christiana, thou must give these pills, no other way but as I have prescribed: for if you do they will do *In a glass of the tears of repentance* no good. So he gave unto Christiana physic for herself, and her boys, and for Mercy: and bid Matthew take heed how he eat any more green plums, and kissed them and went his way.

It was told you before that Prudence bid the boys, that if at any time they would, they should ask her some questions that might be profitable, and she would say something to them.

Of physic *Matthew.* Then Matthew who had been sick, asked her, Why for the most part physic should be bitter to our palates?

Prudence. To show how unwelcome the Word of God and the effects thereof are to a carnal heart.

Of the effects of physic *Matthew.* Why does physic, if it does good, purge, and cause that we vomit?

Prudence. To show that the Word when it works effectually, cleanseth the heart and mind. For look what the one doth to the body, and other doth to the soul.

Of fire and of the sun *Matthew.* What should we learn by seeing the flame of our fire go upwards? and by seeing the beams and sweet influences of the sun strike downwards?

Prudence. By the going up of the fire, we are taught to ascend to heaven by fervent and hot desires. And by the sun his sending his heat, beams, and sweet influences downwards; we are taught that the Saviour of the world, though high, reaches down with his grace and love to us below.

Of the clouds *Matthew.* Where have the clouds their water?

Prudence. Out of the sea.

Matthew. What may we learn from that?

Prudence. That ministers should fetch their doctrine from God.

Matthew. Why do they empty themselves upon the earth?

Prudence. To show that ministers should give out what they know of God to the world.

Matthew. Why is the rainbow caused by the sun? *Of the rainbow*

Prudence. To show that the Covenant of God's Grace is confirmed to us in Christ.

Matthew. Why do the springs come from the sea to us, through the earth?

Prudence. To show that the grace of God comes to us through the Body of Christ.

Matthew. Why do some of the springs rise out of the tops of high hills? *Of the springs*

Prudence. To show that the Spirit of Grace shall spring up in some that are great and mighty, as well as in many that are poor and low.

Matthew. Why doth the fire fasten upon the candle-wick? *Of the candle*[49]

Prudence. To show that unless grace doth kindle upon the heart, there will be no true light of life in us.

Matthew. Why is the wick and tallow and all spent to maintain the light of the candle?

Prudence. To show that body and soul and all, should be at the service of, and spend themselves to maintain in good condition that Grace of God that is in us.

Matthew. Why doth the pelican pierce her own breast with her bill?[50] *Of the pelican*

Prudence. To nourish her young ones with her blood, and thereby to show that Christ the blessed so loveth his young, his people, as to save them from death by his blood.

Matthew. What may one learn by hearing the cock to crow? *Of the cock*

Prudence. Learn to remember Peter's sin, and Peter's repentance. The cock's crowing shows also that day is coming on, let then the crowing of the cock put thee in mind of that last and terrible Day of Judgement.

The weak may sometimes call the strong to prayers

Now about this time their month was out, wherefore they signified to those of the House that 'twas convenient for them to up and be going. Then said Joseph to his mother, 'It is convenient that you forget not to send to the House of Mr Interpreter, to pray him to grant that Mr Great-heart should be sent unto us, that he may be our conductor the rest of our way.' 'Good boy,' said she, 'I had almost forgot.' So she drew up a petition, and prayed Mr Watchful the porter to send it by some fit man to her good friend Mr Interpreter; who when it was come, and he had seen the contents of the petitions, said to the messenger, 'Go tell them that I will send him.'

They provide to be gone on their way

When the family where Christiana was saw that they had a purpose to go forward, they called the whole house together to give thanks to their King, for sending of them such profitable guests as these. Which done, they said to Christiana, 'And shall we not show thee something according as our custom is to do to pilgrims, on which thou mayest meditate when thou art upon the way?' So they took Christiana, her children and Mercy into the closet, and

Eve's apple

showed them one of the apples that Eve did eat of, and that she also did give to her husband, and that for the eating of which they both were turned out of Paradise, and asked her what she thought that was.

A sight of sin is amazing

Then Christiana said, ''Tis food, or poison, I know not which,' so they opened the matter to her, and she held up her hands and wondered.

Jacob's ladder

Then they had her to a place, and showed her Jacob's ladder. Now at that time there were some angels ascending upon it. So Christiana looked and looked, to see the angels go up, and so did the rest of the company. Then they were going into another place to show them something else: but James said to his mother, 'Pray bid them stay here a little longer, for this is a curious sight.' So they turned again, and stood feeding their eyes with this so pleasant a prospect. After this they had them into a place where *A sight of Christ is taking* did hang up a golden anchor, so they bid Christiana *Golden anchor* take it down; 'For,' said they, 'you shall have it with you, for 'tis of absolute necessity that you should, that you may lay hold of that within the veil, and stand steadfast, in case you should meet with turbulent weather.' So they were glad thereof. Then they took them, and had them to the mount upon which Abraham our father had offered up Isaac his son, and *Of Abraham offering up Isaac* showed them the altar, the wood, the fire, and the knife, for they remain to be seen to this very day. When they had seen it, they held up their hands and blest themselves, and said, 'Oh! What a man, for love to his Master and for denial to himself, was Abraham!' After they had showed them all these things, Prudence took them into the dining-room, where stood a pair[51] of excellent virginals, so she *Prudence's virginals* played upon them, and turned what she had showed them into this excellent song, saying,

> *Eve's apple we have showed you,*
> *Of that be you aware:*
> *You have seen Jacob's ladder too,*
> *Upon which angels are.*

> *An anchor you received have;*
> *But let not these suffice,*
> *Until with Abra'm you have gave,*
> *Your best, a sacrifice.*

Now about this time one knocked at the door, so the porter opened, and behold Mr Great-heart was *Mr Great-heart come again* there; but when he was come in, what joy was there?

For it came now fresh again into their minds, how but a while ago he had slain old Grim Bloody-man, the giant, and had delivered them from the lions.

He brings a token from his Lord with him

Then said Mr Great-heart to Christiana, and to Mercy, 'My Lord has sent each of you a bottle of wine, and also some parched corn, together with a couple of pomegranates. He has also sent the boys some figs, and raisins to refresh you in your way.'

Then they addressed themselves to their journey, and Prudence and Piety went along with them. When they came at the gate, Christiana asked the porter, if any of late went by. He said, 'No, only one some time since: who also told me that of late there

Robbery

had been a great robbery committed on the King's highway, as you go: but,' he saith, 'the thieves are taken, and will shortly be tried for their lives.' Then Christiana, and Mercy, was afraid; but Matthew said, 'Mother fear nothing, as long as Mr Great-heart is to go with us, and to be our conductor.'

Christiana takes her leave of the porter

Then said Christiana to the porter, 'Sir, I am much obliged to you for all the kindnesses that you have showed me since I came hither, and also for that you have been so loving and kind to my children. I know not how to gratify your kindness, wherefore pray as a token of my respects to you, accept of this small mite.' So she put a gold angel[52] in his hand, and he

The porter's blessing

made her a low obeisance, and said, 'Let thy garments be always white, and let thy head want no ointment. Let Mercy live and not die, and let not her works be few.' And to the boys he said, 'Do you fly youthful lusts, and follow after godliness with them that are grave, and wise, so shall you put gladness into your mother's heart, and obtain praise of all that are sober minded.' So they thanked the porter and departed.

Now I saw in my dream that they went forward until they were come to the brow of the hill, where

Piety bethinking herself cried out, 'Alas! I have forgot what I intended to bestow upon Christiana, and her companions. I will go back and fetch it.' So she ran, and fetched it. While she was gone, Christiana thought she heard in a grove a little way off, on the right-hand, a most curious melodious note, with words much like these,

> Through all my life thy favour is
> So frankly showed to me,
> That in thy House for evermore
> My dwelling place shall be.[53]

And listening still she thought she heard another answer it, saying,

> For why, the Lord our God is good,
> His mercy is forever sure:
> His truth at all times firmly stood:
> And shall from age to age endure.

So Christiana asked Prudence, what 'twas that made those curious notes. 'They are,' said she, 'our country birds: they sing these notes but seldom, except it be at the spring, when the flowers appear, and the sun shines warm, and then you may hear them all day long. I often,' said she, 'go out to hear them, we also oft times keep them tame in our house. They are very fine company for us when we are melancholy, also they make the woods and groves, and solitary places, places desirous to be in.'

By this time Piety was come again. So she said to *Piety* Christiana, 'Look here, I have brought thee a scheme[54] *bestoweth something on* of all those things that thou hast seen at our House, *them at* upon which thou mayest look when thou findest thy- *parting* self forgetful, and call those things again to remembrance for thy edification, and comfort.'

Now they began to go down the Hill into the Valley of Humiliation. It was a steep Hill, and the way was slippery; but they were very careful, so they got down pretty well. When they were down in the Valley, Piety said to Christiana, 'This is the place where Christian your husband met with the foul fiend Apollyon, and where they had that dreadful fight that they had. I know you cannot but have heard thereof. But be of good courage, as long as you have here Mr Great-heart to be your guide and conductor, we hope you will fare the better.' So when these two had committed the pilgrims unto the conduct of their guide, he went forward, and they went after.

Mr Great-heart at the Valley of Humiliation   *Great-heart.* Then said Mr Great-heart, We need not be so afraid of this Valley: for here is nothing to hurt us, unless we procure it to ourselves. 'Tis true, Christian did here meet with Apollyon, with whom he also had a sore combat; but that fray, was the fruit of those slips that he got in his going down the Hill. For they that get slips there, must look for combats here. And hence it is that this Valley has got so hard a name. For the common people when they hear that some frightful thing has befallen such an one in such a place, are of an opinion that that place is haunted with some foul fiend, or evil spirit; when alas it is for the fruit of their doing, that such things do befall them there.

The reason why Christian was so beset here   This Valley of Humiliation is of itself as fruitful a place, as any the crow flies over; and I am persuaded if we could hit upon it, we might find somewhere hereabouts something that might give us an account why Christian was so hardly beset in this place.

A pillar with an inscription on it   Then James said to his mother, 'Lo, yonder stands a pillar, and it looks as if something was written thereon: let us go and see what it is.' So they went, and found there written, *Let Christian's slips*[55] *before he came hither, and the battles that he met with in this place, be a warning to those that come after.* 'Lo,' said their guide, 'did not I tell you, that there was something hereabouts that would give intimation of the reason why Christian was so hard beset in this place?' Then turning himself to Christiana, he said: 'No disparagement to Christian more than to many others whose hap and lot his was. For 'tis easier going up, than down this Hill; and that can be said but of few hills in all these parts of the world. But we will leave the good man, he is at rest, he also had a brave victory over his enemy; let him grant that dwelleth above, that we fare no worse when we come to be tried than he.

'But we will come again to this Valley of Humiliation. It is the best, and most fruitful piece of ground in all those parts. It is fat ground, and as you see, consisteth much in meadows: and if a man was to come here in the summer-time, as we do now, if he knew not any thing before thereof, and if he also delighted himself in the sight of his eyes, he might see that that would be delightful to him. Behold, how green this Valley is, also how beautified with lilies. I have also known many labouring men that have got good estates in this Valley of Humiliation (for God resisteth the proud but gives more, more grace to the humble); for indeed it is a very fruitful soil, and doth bring forth by handfuls. Some also have wished that the next way to their Father's House were here, that they might be troubled no more with either hills or mountains to go over; but the way is the way, and there's an end.'

This Valley a brave place

Men thrive in the Valley of Humiliation

Now as they were going along and talking, they espied a boy feeding his father's sheep. The boy was in very mean clothes, but of a very fresh and well-favoured countenance, and as he sat by himself he sung. 'Hark,' said Mr Great-heart, 'to what the shepherd's boy saith.' So they hearkened, and he said,

> *He that is down, needs fear no fall,*
> *He that is low, no pride:*
> *He that is humble, ever shall*
> *Have God to be his guide.*
>
> *I am content with what I have,*
> *Little be it, or much:*
> *And, Lord, contentment still I crave,*
> *Because thou savest such.*
>
> *Fullness to such a burden is*
> *That go on pilgrimage:*
> *Here little, and hereafter bliss,*
> *Is best from age to age.*

Then said their guide, 'Do you hear him? I will dare to say, that this boy lives a merrier life, and wears more of that herb called hearts-ease in his bosom, than he that is clad in silk and velvet; but we will proceed in our discourse.

Christ, when in the flesh, had his country-house in the Valley of Humiliation 'In this Valley our Lord formerly had his country-house, he loved much to be here; he loved also to walk these meadows, for he found the air was pleasant. Besides, here a man shall be free from the noise, and from the hurryings of this life; all states are full of noise and confusion, only the Valley of Humiliation is that empty and solitary place. Here a man shall not be so let and hindered[56] in his contemplation, as in other places he is apt to be. This is a Valley that nobody walks in, but those that love a pilgrim's life. And though Christian had the hard hap to meet here with Apollyon, and to enter with him a brisk encounter yet I must tell you that in former times men have met with angels here, have found pearls here, and have in this place found the words of life.

'Did I say, our Lord had here in former days his country-house, and that he loved here to walk? I will add, in this place, and to the people that live and trace these grounds, he has left a yearly revenue to be faithfully paid them at certain seasons, for their maintenance by the way, and for their further encouragement to go on in their pilgrimage.'

Samuel. Now as they went on, Samuel said to Mr Great-heart: Sir, I perceive that in this Valley, my Father and Apollyon had their battle; but whereabout was the fight, for I perceive this Valley is large?

Great-heart. Your father had that battle with Apollyon at a place yonder, before us, in a narrow passage just beyond Forgetful-Green. And indeed that place is the most dangerous place in all these parts. For if at any time the pilgrims meet with any brunt, it is when they forget what favours they have received, and how unworthy they are of them. This was the place also where others have been hard put to it. But more of the place when we are come to it; for I persuade myself that to this day there remains either some sign of the battle, or some monument to testify that such a battle there was fought. *Forgetful-Green*

Mercy. Then said Mercy, I think I am as well in this Valley as I have been anywhere else in all our journey: the place methinks suits with my spirit. I love to be in such places where there is no rattling with coaches, nor rumbling with wheels: methinks here one may without much molestation be thinking what he is, whence he came, what he has done, and to what the King has called him. Here one may think, and break at heart, and melt in one's spirit, until one's eyes become like the fish pools of Heshbon. They *Humility a sweet grace* that go rightly through this Valley of Baca make it a well, the rain that God sends down from Heaven upon them that are here also filleth the pools. This Valley is that from whence also the King will give to his their vineyards, and they that go through it shall sing, as Christian did, for all he met with Apollyon.

An experiment of it   *Great-heart*. 'Tis true, said their guide, I have gone through this Valley many a time, and never was better than when here.

I have also been a conduct to several pilgrims, and they have confessed the same; *To this man will I look, saith the King, even to him that is poor, and of a contrite spirit, and that trembles at my word.*

The place where Christian and the Fiend did fight; some signs of the battle remains   Now they were come to the place where the afore-mentioned battle was fought. Then said the guide to Christiana, her children, and Mercy: 'This is the place, on this ground Christian stood, and up there came Apollyon against him. And look, did not I tell you, here is some of your husband's blood upon these stones to this day: behold also how here and there are yet to be seen upon the place, some of the shivers of Apollyon's broken darts: see also how they did beat the ground with their feet as they fought, to make good their places against each other, how also with their by-blows they did split the very stones in pieces. Verily Christian did here play the man, and showed himself as stout, as could, had he been here, even Hercules himself. When Apollyon was beat, he made his retreat to the next Valley, that is called the Valley of the Shadow of Death, unto which we shall come anon.

A monument of the battle   'Lo yonder also stands a monument, on which is engraven this battle, and Christian's victory to his fame throughout all ages.' So because it stood just on the wayside before them, they stepped to it and read the writing, which word for word was this:

Hard by, here was a battle fought,
Most strange, and yet most true.
Christian and Apollyon sought
Each other to subdue.

The man so bravely played the man,
He made the fiend to fly:
Of which a monument I stand,
The same to testify.

A monument of Christian's victory

When they had passed by this place, they came upon the borders of the Shadow of Death, and this Valley was longer than the other, a place also most strangely haunted with evil things, as many are able to testify. But these women and children went the better through it, because they had daylight, and because Mr Great-heart was their conductor.

When they were entered upon this Valley, they thought that they heard a groaning as of dead men: a very great groaning. They thought also they did hear words of lamentation spoken, as of some in extreme torment. These things made the boys to quake, the women also looked pale and wan; but their guide bid them be of good comfort. *Groanings heard*

So they went on a little further, and they thought that they felt the ground begin to shake under them, as if some hollow place was there; they heard also a kind of a hissing as of serpents; but nothing as yet appeared. Then said the boys, 'Are we not yet at the end of this doleful place?' But the guide also bid them be of good courage, and look well to their feet, 'Lest haply,' said he, 'you be taken in some snare.' *The ground shakes*

Now James began to be sick; but I think the cause thereof was fear, so his mother gave him some of that glass of spirits that she had given her at the Interpreter's House, and three of the pills that Mr Skill had prepared, and the boy began to revive. Thus they *James sick with fear*

305

went on till they came to about the middle of the
The Fiend Valley, and then Christiana said, 'Methinks I see
appears something yonder upon the road before us, a thing of
a shape such as I have not seen.' Then said Joseph,
The pilgrims 'Mother, what is it?' 'An ugly thing, child; an ugly
are afraid thing,' said she. 'But mother, what is it like?' said he.
''Tis like I cannot tell what,' said she. And now it was
but a little way off. Then said she, 'It is nigh.'

Great-heart 'Well, well,' said Mr Great-heart, 'let them that are
encourages most afraid keep close to me.' So the fiend came on,
them and the conductor met it; but when it was just come
to him, it vanished to all their sights. Then remembered they what had been said sometime ago. 'Resist
the Devil, and he will fly from you.'

They went therefore on, as being a little refreshed;
but they had not gone far, before Mercy looking
behind her, saw as she thought, something most like
A lion a lion, and it came a great padding pace after; and it
had a hollow voice of roaring, and at every roar that
it gave, it made all the Valley echo, and their hearts
to ache, save the heart of him that was their guide.
So it came up, and Mr Great-heart went behind, and
put the pilgrims all before him. The lion also came
on apace, and Mr Great-heart addressed himself to
give him battle. But when he saw that it was deter-
mined that resistance should be made, he also drew
back and came no further.

A pit and Then they went on again, and their conductor did
darkness go before them, till they came at a place where was
cast up a pit the whole breadth of the way, and before
they could be prepared to go over that a great mist
and a darkness fell upon them so that they could not
see. Then said the pilgrims, 'Alas! now what shall
we do?' But their guide made answer; 'Fear not, stand
still and see what an end will he put to this also.' So
they stayed there because their path was marred. They

then also thought that they did hear more apparently the noise and rushing of the enemies, the fire also and the smoke of the pit was much easier to be discerned. Then said Christiana to Mercy, 'Now I see what my poor husband went through. I have heard much of this place, but I never was here afore now; poor man, he went here all alone in the night; he had night almost quite through the way, also these fiends were busy about him, as if they would have torn him in pieces. Many have spoke of it, but none can tell what the Valley of the Shadow of Death should mean, until they come in it themselves. *The heart knows its own bitterness, and a stranger intermeddleth not with its joy.* To be here is a fearful thing.' *Christiana now knows what her husband felt*

Great-heart. This is like doing business in great waters, or like going down into the deep; this is like being in the heart of the sea, and like going down to the bottoms of the mountains: now it seems as if the earth with its bars were about us for ever. *But let them that walk in darkness and have no light, trust in the name of the Lord, and stay upon their God.* For my part, as I have told you already, I have gone often through this Valley, and have been much harder put to it than now I am, and yet you see I am alive. I would not boast, for that I am not mine own saviour. But I trust we shall have a good deliverance. Come, let us pray for light to him that can lighten our darkness, and that can rebuke, not only these, but all the Satans in Hell. *Great-heart's reply*

So they cried and prayed, and God sent light and deliverance, for there was now no let in their way, no not there, where but now they were stopped with a pit. *They pray*

Yet they were not got through the Valley; so they went on still, and behold great stinks and loathsome smells, to the great annoyance of them. Then said

Mercy to Christiana Mercy to Christiana, 'There is not such pleasant being here as at the Gate, or at the Interpreter's, or at the House where we lay last.'

One of the boys' reply 'O but,' said one of the boys, 'it is not so bad to go through here, as it is to abide here always, and for aught I know, one reason why we must go this way to the House prepared for us, is, that our home might be made the sweeter to us.'

'Well said, Samuel,' quoth the guide, 'thou hast now spoke like a man.' 'Why, if ever I get out here again,' said the boy, 'I think I shall prize light and good way better than ever I did in all my life.' Then said the guide, 'We shall be out by and by.'

So on they went, and Joseph said, 'Cannot we see to the end of this Valley as yet?' Then said the guide, 'Look to your feet, for you shall presently be among the snares.' So they looked to their feet and went on; but they were troubled much with the snares. Now when they were come among the snares, they espied *Heedless is slain, and Takeheed preserved* a man cast into the ditch on the left hand, with his flesh all rent and torn. Then said the guide, 'That is one Heedless that was agoing this way; he has lain there a great while. There was one Takeheed with him, when he was taken and slain, but he escaped their hands. You cannot imagine how many are killed here about, and yet men are so foolishly venturous, as to set out lightly on pilgrimage, and to come without a guide. Poor Christian, it was a wonder that he here escaped, but he was beloved of his God, also he had a good heart of his own, or else he could never a done it. Now they drew towards the end of the way, and just there where Christian had seen the cave when he went by, out thence *Maul a Giant* came forth Maul, a Giant.[57] This Maul did use to spoil young pilgrims with sophistry, and he called Greatheart by his name, and said unto him, 'How many times have you been forbidden to do these things?' Then said Mr Great-heart, 'What things?' 'What things?' quoth the Giant, 'you know what things; but I will put an end to your trade'. 'But pray,' said Mr Great-heart, 'before we fall to it, let us understand wherefore we must fight' (now the women and children stood trembling, and knew not what to do); quoth the Giant, 'You rob the country, and rob it with the worst of thefts'. 'These are but generals,' said Mr Great-heart, 'come to particulars, man.' *He quarrels with Great-heart*

Then said the Giant, 'Thou practises the craft of a kidnapper, thou gatherest up women and children, and carriest them into a strange country, to the weakening of my master's kingdom.' But now Great-heart replied, 'I am a servant of the God of Heaven, my business is to persuade sinners to repentance, I am commanded to do my endeavour to turn men, women and children, from darkness to light, and from the power of Satan to God, and if this be indeed the ground of thy quarrel, let us fall to it as soon as thou wilt.' *God's ministers counted as kidnappers*

Then the Giant came up, and Mr Great-heart went to meet him, and as he went, he drew his sword, but the Giant had a club: so without more ado they fell to it, and at the first blow the Giant stroke Mr Great-heart down upon one of his knees; with that the women and children cried out. So Mr Great-heart recovering himself, laid about him in full lusty manner, and gave the Giant a wound in his arm; thus he fought for the space of an hour to that height of heat that the breath came out of the Giant's nostrils, as the heat doth out of a boiling cauldron. *The Giant and Mr Great-heart must fight* *Weak folk's prayers do sometimes help strong folk's cries*

Then they sat down to rest them, but Mr Great-heart betook him to prayer; also the women and children did nothing but sigh and cry all the time that the battle did last.

When they had rested them, and taken breath, they both fell to it again, and Mr Great-heart with a full *The Giant* blow fetched the Giant down to the ground. 'Nay *struck down* hold, and let me recover,' quoth he. So Mr Great-heart fairly let him get up; so to it they went again; and the Giant missed but little of all-to-breaking Mr Great-heart's skull with his club.

Mr Great-heart seeing that, runs to him in the full heat of his spirit, and pierceth him under the fifth rib; with that the Giant began to faint, and could hold up *He is slain,* his club no longer. Then Mr Great-heart seconded *and his head* his blow, and smit the head of the Giant from his *disposed of* shoulders. Then the women and children rejoiced, and Mr Great-heart also praised God for the deliverance he had wrought.

When this was done, they amongst them erected a pillar, and fastened the Giant's head thereon, and wrote underneath in letters that passengers might read,

> He that did wear this head, was one
> That pilgrims did misuse;
> He stopped their way, he spared none,
> But did them all abuse;
> Until that I, Great-heart, arose,
> The pilgrims' guide to be;
> Until that I did him oppose,
> That was their enemy.

Now I saw that they went to the ascent that was a little way off cast up to be a prospect for pilgrims. (That was the place from whence Christian had the first sight of Faithful his brother.) Wherefore here they sat down, and rested, they also here did eat and drink, and make merry, for that they had gotten deliverance from this so dangerous an enemy. As they sat thus and did eat, Christiana asked the guide if he had caught no hurt in the battle. Then said Mr Great-heart, 'No, save a little on my flesh; yet that also shall be so far from being to my determent, that it is at present a proof of my love to my Master and you, and shall be a means by grace to increase my reward at last.'

'But *was* you not afraid, good sir, when you see him come with his club?' *Discourse of the fight*

'It is my duty,' said he, 'to distrust mine own ability, that I may have reliance on him that is stronger than all.' 'But what did you think when he fetched you down to the ground at the first blow?' 'Why I thought,' quoth he, 'that so my Master himself was served, and yet he it was that conquered at the last.'

Matthew. When you all have thought what you please, I think God has been wonderful good unto us both in bringing us out of this Valley and in delivering us out of the hand of this enemy; for my part I see no reason why we should distrust our God any more, since he has now and in such a place as this given us such testimony of his love as this. *Matthew here admires goodness*

Then they got up and went forward; now a little before them stood an oak, and under it when they came to it, they found an old pilgrim fast asleep; they knew that he was a pilgrim by his clothes, and his staff, and his girdle. *Old Honest asleep under an oak*

So the guide Mr Great-heart awaked him, and the old gentleman, as he lift up his eyes cried out; 'What's the matter? who are you? and what is your business here?'

Great-heart. Come man, be not so hot, here is none but friends; yet the old man gets up and stands upon his guard, and will know of them what they were. Then said the guide, My name is Great-heart, I am the guide of these pilgrims which are going to the Celestial Country.

One saint sometimes takes another for his enemy

Honest. Then said Mr Honest, I cry you mercy; I feared that you had been of the company of those that some time ago did rob Little-faith of his money; but now I look better about me, I perceive you are honester people.

Talk between Great-heart and he

Great-heart. Why what would or could you a done, to a helped yourself, if we indeed had been of that company?

Honest. Done! Why I would a fought as long as breath had been in me; and had I so done, I am sure you could never have given me the worst on't, for a Christian can never be overcome, unless he shall yield of himself.

Great-heart. Well said, Father Honest, quoth the guide, for by this I know that thou art a cock of the right kind, for thou hast said the truth.

Honest. And by this also I know that thou knowest what true pilgrimage is, for all others do think that we are the soonest overcome of any.

Whence Mr Honest came

Great-heart. Well, now we are so happily met, pray let me crave your name, and the name of the place you came from?

Honest. My name I cannot, but I came from the Town of Stupidity; it lieth about four degrees beyond the City of Destruction.

Great-heart. Oh! Are you that countryman then? I deem I have half a guess of you, your name is old Honesty, is it not? So the old gentleman blushed, and said, 'Not Honesty in the abstract, but Honest is my name, and I wish that my nature shall agree to what I am called.'

Honest. But sir, said the old gentleman, how could you guess that I am such a man, since I came from such a place?

Great-heart. I had heard of you before, by my Master, for he knows all things that are done on the earth: but I have often wondered that any should *Stupified* come from your place; for your town is worse than *ones are* is the City of Destruction itself. *worse than those merely*

Honest. Yes, we lie more off from the sun, and so *carnal* are more cold and senseless; but was a man in a mountain of ice, yet if the sun of righteousness will arise upon him, his frozen heart shall feel a thaw; and thus it hath been with me.

Great-heart. I believe it, Father Honest, I believe it, for I know the thing is true.

Then the old gentleman saluted all the pilgrims with a holy kiss of charity, and asked them of their names and how they had fared since they set out on their pilgrimage.

Christiana. Then said Christiana, My name I sup- *Old Honest* pose you have heard of; good Christian was my *and Christiana* husband, and these four were his children. But can *talk* you think how the old gentleman was taken, when she told him who she was? He skipped, he smiled, and blessed them with a thousand good wishes, saying,

Honest. I have heard much of your husband, and of his travels and wars which he underwent in his days. Be it spoken to your comfort, the name of your husband rings all over these parts of the world; his faith, his courage, his enduring, and his sincerity under all has made his name famous. Then he turned *He also talks* him to the boys, and asked them of their names, which *with the boys* they told him. And then said he unto them, Matthew, *Old Mr* be thou like Matthew the publican, not in vice, but *Honest's* virtue. Samuel, said he, be thou like Samuel the *blessing on* prophet, a man of faith and prayer. Joseph, said he, *them* be thou like Joseph in Potiphar's house, chaste, and one that flies from temptation. And, James, be thou like James the just, and like James the brother of our Lord.

He blesseth Mercy   Then they told him of Mercy, and how she had left her town and her kindred to come along with Christiana, and with her sons. At that the old honest man said 'Mercy, is thy name? By mercy shalt thou be sustained, and carried through all those difficulties that shall assault thee in thy way, till thou come thither where thou shalt look the Fountain of Mercy in the face with comfort.'

All this while the guide Mr Great-heart was very much pleased, and smiled upon his companion.

Talk of one Mr Fearing   Now as they walked along together, the guide asked the old gentleman if he did not know one Mr Fearing,[58] that came on pilgrimage out of his parts.

Honest. Yes, very well, said he, he was a man that had the root of the matter in him, but he was one of the most troublesome pilgrims that ever I met with in all my days.

Great-heart. I perceive you knew him, for you have given a very right character of him.

Honest. Knew him! I was a great companion of his, I was with him most an end; when he first began to think of what would come upon us hereafter, I was with him.

Great-heart. I was his guide from my Master's House, to the Gates of the Celestial City.

Honest. Then you knew him to be a troublesome one?

Great-heart. I did so, but I could very well bear it: for men of my calling are often times entrusted with the conduct of such as he was.

Honest. Well then, pray let us hear a little of him, and how he managed himself under your conduct.

Mr Fearing's troublesome pilgrimage   *Great-heart.* Why, he was always afraid that he should come short of whither he had a desire to go. Every thing frightened him that he heard anybody speak of, that had the least appearance of opposition in it. I heard that he lay roaring at the Slough of *His behaviour* Despond, for above a month together, nor durst he, *at the Slough* for all he saw several go over before him, venture, *of Despond* though they, many of them, offered to lend him their hand. He would not go back again neither. The Celestial City, he said he should die if he came not to it, and yet was dejected at every difficulty, and stumbled at every straw that anybody cast in his way. Well, after he had lain at the Slough of Despond a great while, as I have told you; one sunshine morning, I do not know how, he ventured, and so got over. But when he was over, he would scarce believe it. He had, I think, a Slough of Despond in his mind, a slough that he carried everywhere with him, or else he could never have been as he was. So he came up to the Gate, you know what I mean, that stands at the head of this way, and there also he stood a good while before he would adventure to knock. When the *His behaviour* Gate was opened he would give back, and give place *at the Gate* to others, and say that he was not worthy. For, for all he gat before some to the Gate, yet many of them went in before him. There the poor man would stand shaking and shrinking; I dare say it would have pitied one's heart to have seen him: nor would he go back again. At last he took the hammer that hanged on the Gate in his hand, and gave a small rap or two; then one opened to him, but he shrunk back as before. He that opened, stepped out after him, and said, 'Thou trembling one, what wantest thou?' With that he fell to the ground. He that spoke to him wondered to see him so faint. So he said to him, 'Peace be to thee; up, for I have set open the door to thee; come in, for thou art blest.' With that he gat up, and went in trembling, and when he was in, he was ashamed to show his face. Well, after he had been entertained there a while, as you know how the manner is, he was bid go on his way, and also told the way he should take. So he came till he came to our house, *His behaviour* but as he behaved himself at the Gate, so he did at *at the* my master the Interpreter's door. He lay thereabout *Interpreter's* *door* in the cold a good while, before he would adventure to call; yet he would not go back. And the nights were long and cold then. Nay he had a note of necessity in his bosom to my Master, to receive him, and grant him the comfort of his House, and also to allow him a stout and valiant conduct, because he was himself so chicken-hearted a man; and yet for all that he was afraid to call at the door. So he lay up and down thereabouts till, poor man, he was almost starved; yea, so great was his dejection, that though he saw several others for knocking got in, yet he was afraid to venture. At last, I think I looked out of the window, and perceiving a man to be up and down about the door, I went out to him, and asked what he was; but poor man, the water stood in his eyes. So I perceived what he wanted. I went therefore in, and told it in the House, and we showed the thing to our Lord; so he sent me out again, to entreat him to come in, but I dare say I had hard work to do it. At last he came in, and I will say that for my Lord, *How he was* he carried it wonderful lovingly to him. There were *entertained* but a few good bits at the table, but some of it was *there* laid upon his trencher. Then he presented the note, and my Lord looked thereon and said his desire should be granted. So when he had been there a *He is a little* good while, he seemed to get some heart, and to be *encouraged at* a little more comfortable. For my Master, you must *the* *Interpreter's* know, is one of very tender bowels, especially to *House* them that are afraid, wherefore he carried it so towards him, as might tend most to his encouragement. Well, when he had had a sight of the things of the place, and was ready to take his journey to go to

316

the City, my Lord, as he did to Christian before, gave him a bottle of spirits, and some comfortable things to eat. Thus we set forward, and I went before him; but the man was but of few words, only he would sigh aloud.

When we were come to where the three fellows were hanged, he said that he doubted that that would be his end also. Only he seemed glad when he saw the Cross and the Sepulchre. There I confess he desired to stay a little, to look; and he seemed for a while after to be a little cheery. When we came at the Hill Difficulty he made no stick at that, nor did he much fear the lions. For you must know that his trouble was not about such things as those, his fear was about his acceptance at last. *He was greatly afraid when he saw the gibbet, cheery when he saw the Cross*

I got him in at the House Beautiful, I think before he was willing; also when he was in, I brought him acquainted with the damsels that were of the place, but he was ashamed to make himself much for company, he desired much to be alone, yet he always loved good talk, and often would get behind the screen to hear it; he also loved much to see ancient things, and to be pondering them in his mind. He told me afterwards, that he loved to be in those two Houses from which he came last, to wit, at the Gate, and that of the Interpreter's, but that he durst not be so bold to ask. *Dumpish at the House Beautiful*

When we went also from the House Beautiful, down the Hill into the Valley of Humiliation, he went down as well as ever I saw man in my life, for he cared not how mean he was, so he might be happy at last. Yea, I think there was a kind of a sympathy betwixt that Valley and him. For I never saw him better in all his pilgrimage than when he was in that Valley. *He went down into, and was very pleasant in the Valley of Humiliation*

Here he would lie down, embrace the ground, and

317

kiss the very flowers that grew in this Valley. He would now be up every morning by break of day, tracing and walking to and fro in this Valley.

Much perplexed in the Valley of the Shadow of Death
But when he was come to the entrance of the Valley of the Shadow of Death, I thought I should have lost my man; not for that he had any inclination to go back, that he always abhorred, but he was ready to die for fear. 'O, the hobgoblins will have me, the hobgoblins will have me,' cried he; and I could not beat him out on't. He made such a noise, and such an outcry here, that, had they but heard him, 'twas enough to encourage them to come and fall upon us.

But this I took very great notice of, that this Valley was as quiet while he went through it, as ever I knew it before or since. I suppose those enemies here had now a special check from our Lord, and a command not to meddle until Mr Fearing was passed over it.

It would be too tedious to tell you of all; we will therefore only mention a passage or two more. *His behaviour at Vanity-Fair* When he was come at Vanity-Fair, I thought he would have fought with all the men in the Fair; I feared there we should both have been knocked o'the head, so hot was he against their fooleries; upon the Enchanted Ground, he also was very wakeful. But when he was come at the River where was no bridge, there again he was in a heavy case; 'Now, now,' he said, he should be drowned for ever, and so never see that face with comfort, that he had come so many miles to behold.

And here also I took notice of what was very remarkable, the water of that River was lower at this time than ever I saw it in all my life; so he went over at last not much above wet-shod. When he was going up to the Gate, Mr Great-heart began to take his leave of him, and to wish him a good reception above; so he said, 'I shall, I shall.' Then parted we *His boldness* asunder, and I saw him no more. *at last*

Honest. Then it seems he was well at last.

Great-heart. Yes, yes, I never had doubt about him, he was a man of a choice spirit, only he was always kept very low, and that made his life so burthensome to himself, and so troublesome to others. He was above many, tender of sin; he was so afraid of doing injuries to others that he often would deny himself of that which was lawful, because he would not offend.

Honest. But what should be the reason that such a good man should be all his days so much in the dark?

Great-heart. There are two sorts of reasons for it; *Reason why* one is, The wise God will have it so. Some must pipe, *good men are* and some must weep: now Mr Fearing was one that *so in the* played upon this base. He and his fellows sound the *dark* sackbut,[59] whose notes are more doleful than the notes of other music are. Though indeed some say, the base is the ground of music. And for my part, I care not at all for that profession that begins not in heaviness of mind. The first string that the musician usually touches, is the base when he intends to put all in tune; God also plays upon this string first when he sets the soul in tune for himself. Only here was the imperfection of Mr Fearing, he could play upon no other music but this, till towards his latter end.

I make bold to talk thus[60] metaphorically, for the ripening of the wits of young readers, and because in the Book of the Revelations the saved are compared to a company of musicians that play upon their trumpets and harps and sing their songs before the throne.

Honest. He was a very zealous man, as one may see by what relation you have given of him. Difficulties, lions, or Vanity-Fair, he feared not at all:

'twas only sin, death and hell that was to him a terror; because he had some doubts about his interest in that Celestial Country.

A close about him **Great-heart.** You say right. Those were the things that were his troublers, and they, as you have well observed, arose from the weakness of his mind thereabout, not from weakness of spirit as to the practical part of a pilgrim's life. I dare believe that as the proverb is he could have bit a firebrand[61] had it stood in his way: but the things with which he was oppressed, no man ever yet could shake off with ease.

Christiana's sentence **Christiana.** Then said Christiana, This relation of Mr Fearing has done me good. I thought nobody had been like me, but I see there was some semblance 'twixt this good man and I, only we differed in two things. His troubles were so great they brake out, but mine I kept within. His also lay so hard upon him, they made him that he could not knock at the houses provided for entertainment; but my trouble was always such as made me knock the louder.

Mercy's sentence **Mercy.** If I might also speak my heart, I must say that something of him has also dwelt in me. For I have ever been more afraid of the lake and the loss of a place in Paradise, than I have been of the loss of other things. Oh, thought I, may I have the happiness to have a habitation there, 'tis enough, though I part with all the world to win it.

Matthew's sentence **Matthew.** Then said Matthew, Fear was one thing that made me think that I was far from having that within me that accompanies salvation, but if it was so with such a good man as he, why may it not also go well with me?

James's sentence **James.** No fears, no grace, said James. Though there is not always grace where there is the fear of Hell; yet to be sure there is no grace where there is no fear of God.

Great-heart. Well said, James, thou hast hit the mark, *For the fear of God is the beginning of wisdom;* and to be sure they that want the beginning, have neither middle nor end. But we will here conclude our discourse of Mr Fearing, after we have sent after him this farewell,

> *Well, Master Fearing, thou didst fear*
> *Thy God, and wast afraid*
> *Of doing anything, while here,*
> *That would have thee betrayed.*
> *And didst thou fear the lake and pit?*
> *Would others did so too,*
> *For, as for them that want thy wit,*
> *They do themselves undo.*

Their farewell about him

Now I saw that they still went on in their talk. For after Mr Great-heart had made an end with Mr Fearing, Mr Honest began to tell them of another, but his name was Mr Self-will. 'He pretended himself to be a pilgrim,' said Mr Honest; 'but I persuade myself, he never came in at the Gate that stands at the head of the way.'

Of Mr Self-will

Great-heart. Had you ever any talk with him about it?

Honest. Yes, more than once or twice; but he would always be like himself, self-willed. He neither cared for man, nor argument, nor yet example; what his mind prompted him to, that he would do, and nothing else could he be got to.

Old Honest had talked with him

Great-heart. Pray what principles did he hold, for I suppose you can tell?

Honest. He held that a man might follow the vices[62] as well as the virtues of the pilgrims, and that if he did both, he should be certainly saved.

Self-will's opinions

Great-heart. How! If he had said, 'tis possible for the best to be guilty of the vices, as well as to partake of the virtues of pilgrims, he could not much a been blamed: for indeed we are exempted from no vice absolutely, but on condition that we watch and strive. But this I perceive is not the thing: but if I understand you right, your meaning is, that he was of that opinion, that it was allowable so to be.

Honest. Ay, ay, so I mean, and so he believed and practised.

Great-heart. But what ground had he for his so saying?

Honest. Why, he said he had the Scripture for his warrant.

Great-heart. Prithee, Mr Honest, present us with a few particulars.

Honest. So I will. He said to have to do with other men's wives had been practised by David, God's beloved, and therefore he could do it. He said to have more women than one was a thing that Solomon practised, and therefore he could do it. He said that Sarah and the godly midwives of Egypt lied, and so did saved Rahab, and therefore he could do it. He said that the Disciples went at the bidding of their Master, and took away the owner's ass, and therefore he could do so too. He said that Jacob got the inheritance of his father in a way of guile and dissimulation, and therefore he could do so too.

Great-heart. High base! indeed, and you are sure he was of this opinion?

Honest. I have heard him plead for it, bring Scripture for it, bring argument for it, etc.

Great-heart. An opinion that is not fit to be with any allowance in the world.

Honest. You must understand me rightly: he did not say that any man might do this; but, that those that had the virtues of those that did such things might also do the same.

Great-heart. But what more false than such a conclusion? For this is as much as to say that because good men heretofore have sinned of infirmity, therefore he had allowance to do it of a presumptuous mind. Or if because a child, by the blast of the wind, or for that it stumbled at a stone, fell down and so defiled itself in mire, therefore he might wilfully lie down and wallow like a boar therein. Who could a thought that any one could so far a been blinded by the power of lust? But what is written must be true: they stumble at the Word, being disobedient, whereunto also they were appointed.

His supposing that such may have the godly man's virtues who addict themselves to their vices is also a delusion as strong as the other. 'Tis just as if the dog should say, I have, or may have the qualities of the child, because I lick up its stinking excrements. To eat up the sin of God's people is no sign of one that is possessed with their virtues. Nor can I believe that one that is of this opinion, can at present have faith or love in him. But I know you have made strong objections against him, prithee what can he say for himself?

Honest. Why, he says, to do this by way of opinion, seems abundance more honest than to do it, and yet hold contrary to it in opinion.

Great-heart. A very wicked answer, for though to let loose the bridle to lusts while our opinions are against such things is bad; yet to sin, and plead a toleration so to do, is worse; the one stumbles beholders accidentally, the other pleads them into the snare.

Honest. There are many of this man's mind that have not this man's mouth, and that makes going on pilgrimage of so little esteem as it is.

Great-heart. You have said the truth, and it is to

be lamented. But he that feareth the King of Paradise, shall come out of them all.

Christiana. There are strange opinions in the world. I know one that said 'twas time enough to repent when they came to die.

Great-heart. Such are not over wise. That man would a been loath, might he have had a week to run twenty mile in for his life, to have deferred that journey to the last hour of that week.

Honest. You say right, and yet the generality of them that count themselves pilgrims do indeed do thus. I am, as you see, an old man, and have been a traveller in this road many a day; and I have taken notice of many things.

I have seen some that have set out as if they would drive all the world afore them, who yet have in few days, died as they in the wilderness, and so never gat sight of the Promised Land.

I have seen some that have promised nothing at first setting out to be pilgrims, and that one would a thought could not have lived a day, that have yet proved very good pilgrims.

I have seen some that have run hastily forward, that again have after a little time run just as fast back again.

I have seen some who have spoke very well of a pilgrim's life at first, that after a while have spoken as much against it.

I have heard some, when they first set out for Paradise say positively, there is such a place, who when they have been almost there have come back again, and said there is none.

I have heard some vaunt what they would do in case they should be opposed, that have even at a false alarm fled faith, the pilgrim's way, and all.

Now as they were thus in their way there came one

running to meet them, and said, 'Gentlemen, and *Fresh news* you of the weaker sort, if you love life, shift for your- *of trouble* selves, for the robbers are before you.'

Great-heart. Then said Mr Great-heart, They be the *Great-heart's* three that set upon Little-faith heretofore. Well, said *resolution* he, we are ready for them; so they went on their way. Now they looked at every turning when they should a met with the villains. But whether they heard of Mr Great-heart, or whether they had some other game, they came not up to the pilgrims.

Christiana. Christiana then wished for an inn for *Christiana* herself and her children, because they were weary. *wisheth for* Then said Mr Honest, 'There is one a little before us, *an inn* where a very honourable disciple, one Gaius,[63] dwells.' *Gaius* So they all concluded to turn in thither; and the rather, because the old gentleman gave him so good a report. So when they came to the door they went *They enter* in, not knocking, for folks use not to knock at the *into his house* door of an inn. Then they called for the master of the house, and he came to them. So they asked if they might lie there that night.

Gaius. Yes gentlemen, if you be true men, for my *Gaius* house is for none but pilgrims. Then was Christiana, *entertains* Mercy, and the boys, the more glad, for that the *them, and* innkeeper was a lover of pilgrims. So they called for *how* rooms, and he showed them one for Christiana, and her children, and Mercy, and another for Mr Great-heart and the old gentleman.

Great-heart. Then said Mr Great-heart, Good Gaius, what hast thou for supper? For these pilgrims have come far today, and are weary.

Gaius. It is late, said Gaius; so we cannot conveni-ently go out to seek food; but such as we have you shall be welcome to, if that will content.

Great-heart. We will be content with what thou hast in the house, for as much as I have proved thee;

thou art never destitute of that which is convenient.

Gaius his cook   Then he went down, and spake to the cook, whose name was Taste-that-which-is-good, to get ready supper for so many pilgrims. This done, he comes up again, saying, 'Come my good friends, you are welcome to me, and I am glad that I have an house to entertain you; and while supper is making ready, if you please, let us entertain one another with some good discourse.' So they all said, 'Content.'

Talk between Gaius and his guests   *Gaius.* Then said Gaius, Whose wife is this aged matron? and whose daughter is this young damsel?

Great-heart. The woman is the wife of one Christian, a pilgrim of former times, and these are his four children. The maid is one of her acquaintance; one that she hath persuaded to come with her on pilgrimage. The boys take all after their father, and covet to *Mark this* tread in his steps. Yea, if they do but see any place where the old pilgrim hath lain, or any print of his foot, it ministereth joy to their hearts, and they covet to lie, or tread in the same.

Of Christian's ancestors   *Gaius.* Then said Gaius, Is this Christian's wife, and are these Christian's children? I knew your husband's father, yea, also his father's father. Many have been good of this stock, their ancestors dwelt first at Antioch.[64] Christian's progenitors (I supose you have heard your husband talk of them) were very worthy men. They have above any that I know, showed themselves men of great virtue and courage, for the Lord of the pilgrims, his ways, and them that loved him. I have heard of many of your husband's relations that have stood all trials for the sake of the truth. Stephen that was one of the first of the family from whence your husband sprang, was knocked o' the head with stones. James, another of this generation, was slain with the edge of the sword. To say nothing of Paul and Peter, men anciently of the family from whence your husband came. There was Ignatius, who was cast to the lions. Romanus, whose flesh was cut by pieces from his bones; and Policarp,[65] that played the man in the fire. There was he that was hanged up in a basket[66] in the sun for the wasps to eat; and he who they put into a sack and cast him into the sea, to be drowned. 'Twould be impossible, utterly to count up all of that family that have suffered injuries and death, for the love of a pilgrim's life. Nor can I but be glad, to see that thy husband has left behind him four such boys as these. I hope they will bear up their father's name, and tread in their father's steps, and come to their father's end.

Great-heart. Indeed sir, they are likely lads, they seem to choose heartily their father's ways.

Gaius. That is it that I said, wherefore Christian's family is like still to spread abroad upon the face of the ground, and yet to be numerous upon the face of the earth. Wherefore let Christiana look out some damsels for her sons, to whom they may be betrothed, etc. that the name of their father and the house of his progenitors may never be forgotten in the world. *Advice to Christiana about her boys*

Honest. 'Tis pity this family should fall and be extinct.

Gaius. Fall[67] it cannot, but be diminished it may; but let Christiana take my advice, and that's the way to uphold it.

And Christiana, said this inn-keeper, I am glad to see thee and thy friend Mercy together here, a lovely couple. And may I advise, take Mercy into a nearer relation to thee. If she will, let her be given to Matthew thy eldest son. 'Tis the way to preserve you a posterity in the earth. So this match was concluded, and in process of time they were married. But more of that hereafter. *Mercy and Matthew marry*

Gaius also proceeded, and said, 'I will now speak on

the behalf of women[68] to take away their reproach. For as death and the curse came into the world by a woman, so also did life and health; *God sent forth his Son, made of a woman.* Yea, to show how much those that came after did abhor the act of their mother, this sex, in the Old Testament, coveted children if happily this or that woman might be the mother of the Saviour of the world. I will say again, that when the Saviour was come, women rejoiced in him before either man or angel. I read not that ever any man did give unto Christ so much as one groat, but the women followed him and ministered to him of their substance. 'Twas a woman that washed his feet with tears, and a woman that anointed his body to the burial. They were women that wept when he was going to the Cross, and women that followed him from the Cross, and that sat by his sepulchre when he was buried. They were women that was first with him at his resurrection morn, and women that brought tidings first to his disciples that he was risen from the dead. Women therefore are highly favoured, and show by these things that they are sharers with us in the grace of life.

Why women of old so much desired children

Now the cook sent up to signify that supper was almost ready, and sent one to lay the cloth, the trenchers, and to set the salt and bread in order.

Supper ready

Then said Matthew, 'The sight of this cloth, and of this forerunner of the supper, begetteth in me a greater appetite to my food than I had before.'

Gaius. So let all ministering doctrines to thee in this life beget in thee a greater desire to sit at the supper of the great King in his Kingdom; for all preaching, books, and ordinances here, are but as the laying of the trenchers, and as setting of salt upon the board, when compared with the feast that our Lord will make for us when we come to his House.

What to be gathered from laying of the board with the cloth and trenchers

So supper came up, and first a heave-shoulder and a wave-breast[69] was set on the table before them: to show that they must begin their meal with prayer and praise to God. The heave-shoulder David lifted his heart up to God with, and with the wave-breast, where his heart lay, with that he used to lean upon his harp when he played. These two dishes were very fresh and good, and they all eat heartily-well thereof.

The next they brought up, was a bottle of wine, red as blood. So Gaius said to them, 'Drink freely, this is the juice of the true vine, that makes glad the heart of God and man.' So they drank and were merry.

The next was a dish of milk well crumbed. But Gaius said, 'Let the boys have that, that they may grow thereby.' *A dish of milk*

Then they brought up in course a dish of butter and honey. Then said Gaius, 'Eat freely of this, for this is good to cheer up and strengthen your judgements and understandings. This was our Lord's dish when he was a child; *Butter and honey shall he eat, that he may know to refuse the evil, and choose the good.*'[70] *Of honey and butter*

Then they brought them up a dish of apples, and they were very good-tasted fruit. Then said Matthew, 'May we eat apples, since they were such by and with which the Serpent beguiled our first mother?' *A dish of apples*

Then said Gaius,

Apples were they with which we were beguiled,
Yet sin, not apples hath our souls defiled.
Apples forbid, if eat, corrupts the blood:
To eat such, when commanded, does us good.
Drink of his flagons then, thou, Church, his dove,
And eat his apples, who art sick of love.

Then said Matthew, 'I made the scruple, because I a while since was sick with eating of fruit.'

Gaius. Forbidden fruit will make you sick, but not what our Lord has tolerated.

A dish of nuts While they were thus talking, they were presented with another dish; and 'twas a dish of nuts. Then said some at the table, 'Nuts spoil tender teeth; especially the teeth of children.' Which when Gaius heard, he said,

> *Hard texts are nuts (I will not call them cheaters),*
> *Whose shells do keep their kernels from the eaters.*
> *Ope then the shells, and you shall have the meat,*
> *They here are brought, for you to crack and eat.*

Then were they very merry, and sat at the table a long time, talking of many things. Then said the old gentleman, 'My good landlord, while we are cracking your nuts, if you please do you open this riddle:

A riddle put forth by old Honest
> *A man there was, though some did count him mad,*
> *The more he cast away, the more he had.'*

Then they all gave good heed, wondering what good Gaius would say, so he sat still a while, and then thus replied:

Gaius opens it
> *He that bestows his goods upon the poor,*
> *Shall have as much again, and ten times more.*

Joseph wonders Then said Joseph, 'I dare say, sir, I did not think you could a found it out.'

'Oh!' said Gaius, 'I have been trained up in this way a great while: nothing teaches like experience; I have learned of my Lord to be kind, and have found by experience that I have gained thereby: *There is that scattereth, yet increaseth, and there is that with-holdeth more than is meet, but it tendeth to poverty. There is that maketh himself rich, yet hath nothing; there is that maketh himself poor, yet hath great riches.'*

Then Samuel whispered to Christiana his mother,

and said, 'Mother, this is a very good man's house, let us stay here a good while, and let my brother Matthew be married here to Mercy, before we go any further.'

The which Gaius the host overhearing, said, 'With a very good will my child.'

So they stayed there more than a month, and Mercy was given to Matthew to wife. *Matthew and Mercy are married*

While they stayed here, Mercy as her custom was, would be making coats and garments to give to the poor, by which she brought up a very good report upon the pilgrims.

But to return again to our story. After supper the lads desired a bed, for that they were weary with travelling. Then Gaius called to show them their chamber, but said Mercy, 'I will have them to bed.' So she had them to bed, and they slept well, but the rest sat up all night. For Gaius and they were such suitable company that they could not tell how to part. Then after much talk of their Lord, themselves, and their journey, old Mr Honest, he that put forth the riddle to Gaius, began to nod. Then said Great-heart, 'What sir, you begin to be drowsy, come rub up, now here's a riddle for you.' Then said Mr Honest, 'Let's hear it.' *The boys go to bed, the rest sit up*

Old Honest nods

Then said Mr Great-heart,

> He that will kill, must first be overcome: *A riddle*
> Who live abroad would, first must die at home.

'Huh,' said Mr Honest, 'it is a hard one, hard to expound, and harder to practise. But come, Landlord,' said he, 'I will, if you please, leave my part to you, do you expound it, and I will hear what you say.'

'No,' said Gaius, ''twas put to you, and 'tis expected that you should answer it.'

Then said the old gentleman,

The riddle
opened

> *He first by grace must conquered be,*
> *That sin would mortify.*
> *And who that lives would convince me,*
> *Unto himself must die.*

'It is right,' said Gaius; 'good doctrine and experience teaches this. For first, until grace displays itself and overcomes the soul with its glory, it is altogether without heart to oppose sin. Besides, if sin is Satan's cords, by which the soul lies bound, how should it make resistance, before it is loosed from that infirmity?

'Secondly, nor will any that knows either reason or grace, believe that such a man can be a living monument of grace that is a slave to his own corruptions.

A question
worth the
minding

'And now it comes in my mind, I will tell you a story, worth the hearing. There were two men that went on pilgrimage, the one began when he was young, the other when he was old. The young man had strong corruptions to grapple with, the old man's were decayed with the decays of nature. The young man trod his steps as even as did the old one, and was every way as light as he; who now, or which of them had their graces shining clearest, since both seemed to be alike?'

A comparison

Honest. The young man's, doubtless. For that which heads it against the greatest opposition, gives best demonstration that it is strongest, specially when it also holdeth pace with that that meets not with half so much: as to be sure old age does not.

A mistake

Besides, I have observed that old men have blessed themselves with this mistake; namely, taking the decays of nature for a gracious conquest over corruptions, and so have been apt to beguile themselves.

Indeed old men that are gracious are best able to give advice to them that are young, because they have seen most of the emptiness of things. But yet, for an old and a young to set out both together, the young one has the advantage of the fairest discovery of a work of grace within him, though the old man's corruptions are naturally the weakest.

Thus they sat talking till break of day. Now when the family was up, Christiana bid her son James that he should read a chapter; so he read the fifty-third of Isaiah. When he had done, Mr Honest asked why it was said that the Saviour is said to come out of a dry ground, and also that he had no form nor comeliness in him? *Another question*

Great-heart. Then said Mr Great-heart, To the first I answer, because the Church of the Jews, of which Christ came, had then lost almost all the sap and spirit of religion. To the second I say, the words are spoken in the person of the unbelievers, who because they want that eye that can see into our Prince's heart, therefore they judge of him by the meanness of his outside.

Just like those that know not that precious stones are covered over with a homely crust; who when they have found one, because they know not what they have found, cast it again away as men do a common stone.

'Well,' said Gaius, 'Now you are here, and since, as I know, Mr Great-heart is good at his weapons, if you please, after we have refreshed ourselves, we will walk into the fields, to see if we can do any good. About a mile from hence, there is one Slay-good,[71] a giant, that doth much annoy the King's highway in these parts. And I know whereabout his haunt is, he is master of a number of thieves; 'twould be well if we could clear these parts of him.' *Giant Slay-good assaulted and slain*

So they consented and went, Mr Great-heart with his sword, helmet, and shield; and the rest with spears and staves.

He is found with one Feeble-mind in his hands

When they came to the place where he was, they found him with one Feeble-mind in his hands, whom his servants had brought unto him, having taken him in the way; now the Giant was rifling of him with a purpose after that to pick his bones. For he was of the nature of flesh-eaters.

Well, so soon as he saw Mr Great-heart, and his friends, at the mouth of his cave with their weapons, he demanded what they wanted.

Great-heart. We want thee; for we are come to revenge the quarrel of the many that thou hast slain of the pilgrims, when thou hast dragged them out of the King's highway; wherefore come out of thy cave. So he armed himself and came out, and to a battle they went, and fought for above an hour, and then stood still to take wind.

Slay-good. Then said the Giant, Why are you here on my ground?

Great-heart. To revenge the blood of pilgrims, as I also told thee before; so they went to it again, and the Giant made Mr Great-heart give back, but he came up again, and in the greatness of his mind, he let fly with such stoutness at the Giant's head and sides, that he made him let his weapon fall out of his hand. So he smote him, and slew him, and cut off his head,

One Feeble-mind rescued from the Giant

and brought it away to the inn. He also took Feeble-mind the pilgrim, and brought him with him to his lodgings. When they were come home, they showed his head to the family, and then set it up as they had done others before for a terror to those that should attempt to do as he hereafter.

Then they asked Mr Feeble-mind how he fell into his hands.

Feeble-mind. Then said the poor man, I am a sickly man, as you see, and because death did usually once a day knock at my door, I thought I should never be well at home. So I betook myself to a pilgrim's life; and have travelled hither from the town of Uncertain, where I and my father were born. I am a man of no strength at all, of body, nor yet of mind, but would, if I could, though I can but crawl, spend my life in the pilgrim's way. When I came at the Gate that is at the head of the way, the lord of that place did entertain me freely. Neither objected he against my weakly looks, nor against my feeble mind; but gave me such things that were necessary for my journey, and bid me hope to the end. When I came to the House of the Interpreter, I received much kindness there, and because the Hill Difficulty was judged too hard for me, I was carried up that by one of his servants. Indeed I have found much relief from pilgrims, though none was willing to go so softly as I am forced to do. Yet still as they came on, they bid me be of good cheer, and said that it was the will of their Lord that comfort should be given to the feeble-minded, and so went on their own pace. When I was come up to Assault-Lane, then this Giant met with me, and bid me prepare for an encounter; but alas, feeble one that I was, I had more need of a cordial. So he came up and took me, I conceited he should not kill me; also when he had got me into his den, since I went not with him willingly, I believed I should come out alive again. For I have heard, that not any pilgrim that is taken captive by violent hands, if he keeps heart-whole towards his Master, is by the laws of providence to die by the hand of the enemy. Robbed, I looked to be, and robbed to be sure I am; but I am as you see escaped with life, for the which I thank my King as author, and you as the means.

How Feeble-mind came to be a pilgrim

Mark this

335

Other brunts I also look for, but this I have resolved
Mark this on, to wit, to run when I can, to go when I cannot
run, and to creep when I cannot go. As to the main,
I thank him that loves me, I am fixed; my way is
before me, my mind is beyond the River that has no
bridge, though I am as you see, but of a feeble mind.

Honest. Then said old Mr Honest, Have not you
some time ago been acquainted with one Mr Fearing,
a pilgrim?

Mr Fearing   *Feeble-mind.* Acquainted with him, yes. He came
Mr from the town of Stupidity, which lieth four degrees
Feeble-mind's to the northward of the City of Destruction, and as
Uncle many off of where I was born; yet we were well
acquainted, for indeed he was mine uncle, my
father's brother; he and I have been much of a
temper, he was a little shorter than I, but yet we
were much of a complexion.

Feeble-mind   *Honest.* I perceive you knew him, and I am apt to
has some of believe also that you were related one to another;
Mr Fearing's for you have his whitely look, a cast like his with your
features eye, and your speech is much alike.

Feeble-mind. Most have said so that have known us
both, and besides, what I have read in him I have for
the most part found in myself.

Gaius   *Gaius.* Come, sir, said good Gaius, be of good
comforts him cheer, you are welcome to me, and to my house; and
what thou hast a mind to, call for freely; and what
thou would'st have my servants do for thee, they
will do it with a ready mind.

Notice to   *Feeble-mind.* Then said Mr Feeble-mind, This is
be taken of unexpected favour, and as the sun shining out of a
providence very dark cloud. Did Giant Slay-good intend me this
favour when he stopped me, and resolved to let me
go no further? Did he intend that after he had rifled
my pockets, I should go to Gaius mine host? Yet so
it is.

Now, just as Mr Feeble-mind and Gaius was thus in talk; there comes one running, and called at the door, and told that about a mile and an half off, there was one Mr Not-right a pilgrim, struck dead upon the place where he was, with a thunder-bolt. *Tidings how one Not-right was slain with a thunderbolt and Mr Feeble-mind's comment upon it*

Feeble-mind. Alas! said Mr Feeble-mind, is he slain? He overtook me some days before I came so far as hither, and would be my company-keeper. He also was with me when Slay-good the Giant took me, but he was nimble of his heels, and escaped. But it seems he escaped to die and I was took to live.

> What, one would think, doth seek to slay outright,
> Oft-times, delivers from the saddest plight.
> That very providence, whose face is death,
> Doth oft-times to the lowly life bequeath.
> I taken was, he did escape and flee,
> Hands crossed, gives death to him and life to me.

Now about this time Matthew and Mercy was married; also Gaius gave his daughter Phoebe to James, Matthew's brother, to wife; after which time, they yet stayed above ten days at Gaius's house, spending their time and the seasons like as pilgrims use to do.

When they were to depart, Gaius made them a feast, and they did eat and drink, and were merry. *The pilgrim's prepare to go forward* Now the hour was come that they must be gone, wherefore Mr Great-heart called for a reckoning. But Gaius told him that at his house it was not the custom for pilgrims to pay for their entertainment. He boarded them by the year, but looked for his pay from the good Samaritan, who had promised him at *How they greet one another at parting* his return, whatsoever charge he was at with them, faithfully to repay him. Then said Mr Great-heart to him,

Great-heart. Beloved, thou dost faithfully, whatsoever

thou dost, to the brethren and to strangers, which have borne witness of thy charity before the Church. Whom if thou yet bring forward on their journey after a godly sort, thou shalt do well.[72]

Gaius his last kindness to Feeble-mind Then Gaius took his leave of them all, and of his children, and particularly of Mr Feeble-mind. He also gave him something to drink by the way.

Now Mr Feeble-mind, when they were going out of the door, made as if he intended to linger. The which, when Mr Great-heart espied, he said, come Mr Feeble-mind, pray do you go along with us, I will be your conductor, and you shall fare as the rest.

Feeble-mind for going behind *Feeble-mind.* Alas, I want a suitable companion, you are all lusty and strong, but I, as you see, am weak; I choose therefore rather to come behind, lest, by reason of my many infirmities, I should be both a burthen to myself, and to you. I am, as I said, a man of a weak and feeble mind, and shall be offended and made weak at that which others can bear. I shall like *His excuse for it* no laughing, I shall like no gay attire, I shall like no unprofitable questions. Nay, I am so weak a man, as to be offended with that which others have a liberty to do. I do not yet know all the truth; I am a very ignorant Christian man; sometimes if I hear some rejoice in the Lord, it troubles me because I cannot do so too. It is with me, as it is with a weak man among the strong, or as with a sick man among the healthy, or as a lamp despised. (*He that is ready to slip with his feet, is as a lamp despised, in the thought of him that is at ease.*) So that I know not what to do.

Great-heart's commission *Great-heart.* But brother, said Mr Great-heart. I have it in commission, to comfort the feeble-minded,[73] and to support the weak. You must needs go along with us; we will wait for you, we will lend you our *A Christian Spirit* help, we will deny ourselves of some things, both opinionative and practical, for your sake; we will not enter into doubtful disputations before you, we will be made all things to you, rather than you shall be left behind.

Now, all this while they were at Gaius's door; and behold as they were thus in the heat of their discourse, Mr Ready-to-halt came by, with his crutches in his *Promises* hand, and he also was going on pilgrimage.

Feeble-mind. Then said Mr Feeble-mind to him, *Feeble-mind* Man! how camest thou hither? I was but just now *glad to see* complaining that I had not a suitable companion, but *come by* thou art according to my wish. Welcome, welcome, good Mr Ready-to-halt, I hope thee and I may be some help.

Ready-to-halt. I shall be glad of thy company, said the other; and good Mr Feeble-mind, rather than we will part, since we are thus happily met, I will lend thee one of my crutches.

Feeble-mind. Nay, said he, though I thank thee for thy good will, I am not inclined to halt before I am lame. How be it, I think when occasion is, it may help me against a dog.

Ready-to-halt. If either myself, or my crutches, can do thee a pleasure, we are both at thy command, good Mr Feeble-mind.

Thus therefore they went on, Mr Great-heart and Mr Honest went before, Christiana and her children went next, and Mr Feeble-mind and Mr Ready-to-halt came behind with his crutches. Then said Mr Honest,

Honest. Pray Sir, now we are upon the road, tell us *New talk* some profitable things of some that have gone on pilgrimage before us.

Great-heart. With a good will. I suppose you have heard how Christian of old did meet with Apollyon in the Valley of Humiliation, and also what hard work he had to go through the Valley of the Shadow of Death. Also I think you cannot but have heard how Faithful was put to it with Madam Wanton, with Adam the first, with one Discontent, and Shame, four as deceitful villains as a man can meet with upon the road.

Honest. Yes, I have heard of all this; but indeed, good Faithful was hardest put to it with Shame, he was an unwearied one.

Great-heart. Ay, for as the pilgrim well said, he of all men had the wrong name.

Honest. But pray Sir, where was it that Christian and Faithful met Talkative? That same was also a notable one.

Great-heart. He was a confident fool, yet many follow his ways.

Honest. He had like to a beguiled Faithful?

Great-heart. Ay, But Christian put him into a way quickly to find him out. Thus they went on till they came at the place where Evangelist met with Christian and Faithful, and prophesied to them of what should befall them at Vanity-Fair.

Great-heart. Then said their guide, Hereabouts did Christian and Faithful meet with Evangelist, who prophesied to them of what troubles they should meet with at Vanity-Fair.

Honest. Say you so! I dare say it was a hard chapter that then he did read unto them.

Great-heart. 'Twas so, but he gave them encouragement withal. But what do we talk of them, they were a couple of lion-like men; they had set their faces like flint.[74] Don't you remember how undaunted they were when they stood before the judge?

Honest. Well Faithful bravely suffered!

Great-heart. So he did, and as brave things came on't: For Hopeful and some others, as the story relates it, were converted by his death.

Honest. Well, but pray go on; for you are well acquainted with things.

Great-heart. Above all that Christian met with after he had passed through Vanity-Fair, one By-ends was the arch one.

Honest. By-ends; what was he?

Great-heart. A very arch fellow, a downright hypocrite; one that would be religious which way ever the world went, but so cunning that he would be sure neither to lose, nor suffer for it.

He had his mode of religion for every fresh occasion, and his wife was as good at it as he. He would turn and change from opinion to opinion; yea, and plead for so doing too. But so far as I could learn, he came to an ill end with his by-ends, nor did I ever hear that any of his children were ever of any esteem with any that truly feared God.

Now by this time they were come within sight of the town of Vanity, where Vanity-Fair is kept. So when they saw that they were so near the town they consulted with one another how they should pass through the town, and some said one thing, and some another. At last Mr Great-heart said, 'I have, as you may understand, often been a conductor of pilgrims through this town; now I am acquainted with one Mr Mnason, a Cyprusian[75] by nation, an old disciple, at whose house we may lodge. If you think good,' said he, 'we will turn in there.' *They are come within sight of Vanity*

They enter into one Mr Mnason's to lodge

'Content,' said old Honest; 'Content,' said Christiana; 'Content,' said Mr Feeble-mind; and so they said all. Now you must think it was eventide, by that they got to the outside of the town, but Mr Great-heart knew the way to the old man's house. So thither they came; and he called at the door, and the old man within knew his tongue so soon as ever he heard it; so he opened, and they all came in. Then said Mnason their host, 'How far have ye come to-day?' So they said, 'From the house of Gaius our friend.' 'I promise you,' said he, 'you have gone a good stitch, you may well be a-weary; sit down.' So they sat down.

Great-heart. Then said their guide, Come, what cheer, sirs, I dare say you are welcome to my friend.

They are glad of entertainment

Mnason. I also, said Mr Mnason, do bid you welcome; and whatever you want, do but say, and we will do what we can to get it for you.

Honest. Our great want, a while since, was harbour, and good company, and now I hope we have both.

Mnason. For harbour, you see what it is, but for good company, that will appear in the trial.

Great-heart. Well, said Mr Great-heart, will you have the pilgrims up into their lodging?

Mnason. I will, said Mr Mnason. So he had them to their respective places; and also showed them a very fair dining-room where they might be and sup together until time was come to go to rest.

Now when they were set in their places, and were a little cheery after their journey, Mr Honest asked his landlord if there were any store of good people in the town.

Mnason. We have a few, for indeed they are but a few, when compared with them on the other side.

They desire to see some of the good people in the town

Honest. But how shall we do to see some of them? For the sight of good men to them that are going on pilgrimage is like to the appearing of the moon and the stars to them that are sailing upon the seas.

Some sent for

Mnason. Then Mr Mnason stamped with his foot, and his daughter Grace came up; so he said unto her, Grace, go you, tell my friends, Mr Contrite, Mr Holy-man, Mr Love-saint, Mr Dare-not-lie and Mr Penitent that I have a friend or two at my house, that have a mind this evening to see them.

So Grace went to call them, and they came, and after salutation made, they sat down together at the table.

Then said Mr Mnason their landlord, 'My neighbours, I have, as you see, a company of strangers come to my house, they are pilgrims. They come from afar, and are going to Mount Sion. But who,' quoth he, 'do you think this is?' pointing with his finger to Christiana. 'It is Christiana, the wife of Christian, that famous pilgrim, who with Faithful his brother were so shamefully handled in our town.' At that they stood amazed, saying, 'We little thought to see Christiana, when Grace came to call us, wherefore this is a very comfortable surprise.' Then they asked her of her welfare, and if these young men were her husband's sons. And when she had told them they were; they said, 'The King whom you love, and serve, make you as your father, and bring you where he is in peace.'

Honest. Then Mr Honest (when they were all sat down) asked Mr Contrite and the rest in what posture their town was at present?

Contrite. You may be sure we are full of hurry in fair time. 'Tis hard keeping our hearts and spirits in any good order, when we are in a cumbered condition. He that lives in such a place as this is, and that has to do with such as we have, has need of an item[76] to caution him to take heed every moment of the day.

Honest. But how are your neighbours for quietness?

Contrite. They are much more moderate now[77] than formerly. You know how Christian and Faithful were used at our town; but of late, I say, they have been far more moderate. I think the blood of

[margin note: Some talk betwixt Mr Honest and Contrite]

[margin note: The fruit of watchfulness]

[margin note: Persecution not so hot at Vanity-Fair as formerly]

Faithful lieth with load upon them till now; for since they burned him, they have been ashamed to burn any more: in those days we were afraid to walk the streets, but now we can show our heads. Then the name of a professor was odious, now, specially in some parts of our town (for you know our town is large) religion is counted honourable.

Then said Mr Contrite to them, 'Pray how faireth it with you in your pilgrimage, how stands the country affected towards you?'

Honest. It happens to us, as it happeneth to wayfaring men; sometimes our way is clean, sometimes foul; sometimes up-hill, sometimes down-hill; we are seldom at a certainty. The wind is not always on our backs, nor is everyone a friend that we meet with in the way. We have met with some notable rubs already; and what are yet behind we know not, but for the most part we find it true, that has been talked of of old, A good man must suffer trouble.

Contrite. You talk of rubs; what rubs have you met withal?

Honest. Nay, ask Mr Great-heart our guide, for he can give the best account of that.

Great-heart. We have been beset three or four times already: first Christiana and her children were beset with two ruffians, that they feared would a took away their lives; we was beset with Giant Bloody-man, Giant Maul, and Giant Slaygood. Indeed we did rather beset the last, than were beset of him: and thus it was. After we had been some time at the house of Gaius, mine host, and of the whole Church, we were minded upon a time to take our weapons with us, and go see if we could light upon any of those that were enemies to pilgrims (for we heard that there was a notable one thereabouts). Now Gaius knew his haunt better than I, because he dwelt thereabout, so we looked and looked till at last we discerned the mouth of his cave; then we were glad and plucked up our spirits. So we approached up to his den, and lo, when we came there, he had dragged by mere force into his net, this poor man, Mr Feeble-mind, and was about to bring him to his end. But when he saw us, supposing as we thought, he had had another prey, he left the poor man in his hole and came out. So we fell to it full sore, and he lustily laid about him; but in conclusion, he was brought down to the ground, and his head cut off, and set up by the wayside for a terror to such as should after practise such ungodliness. That I tell you the truth, here is the man himself to affirm it, who was as a lamb taken out of the mouth of the lion.

Feeble-mind. Then said Mr Feeble-mind, I found this true to my cost, and comfort; to my cost, when he threatened to pick my bones every moment; and to my comfort, when I saw Mr Great-heart and his friends with their weapons approach so near for my deliverance.

Holy-man. Then said Mr Holy-man, There are two things that they have need to be possessed with that go on pilgrimage, courage and an unspotted life. If they have not courage, they can never hold on their way; and if their lives be loose, they will make the very name of a pilgrim stink. *Mr Holy-man's speech*

Love-saint. Then said Mr Love-saint; I hope this caution is not needful amongst you. But truly there are many that go upon the road, that rather declare themselves strangers to pilgrimage, than strangers and pilgrims in the earth. *Mr Love-saint's speech*

Dare-not-lie. Then said Mr Dare-not-lie, 'Tis true; they neither have the pilgrim's weed, nor the pilgrim's courage; they go not uprightly, but all awry with their feet, one shoe goes inward, another out- *Mr Dare-not-lie his speech*

ward, and their hosen out behind, there a rag, and
there a rent, to the disparagement of their Lord.

Mr Penitent
his speech *Penitent.* These things, said Mr Penitent, they
ought to be troubled for, nor are the pilgrims like to
have that grace put upon them and their pilgrim's
progress, as they desire, until the way is cleared of
such spots and blemishes.

Thus they sat talking and spending the time, until
supper was set upon the table. Unto which they went
and refreshed their weary bodies, so they went to
rest. Now they stayed in this Fair a great while, at
the house of this Mr Mnason, who in process of time
gave his daughter Grace unto Samuel, Christiana's
son, to wife, and his daughter Martha to Joseph.

The time, as I said, that they lay here, was long (for
it was not now as in former times). Wherefore the
pilgrims grew acquainted with many of the good
people of the town, and did them what service they
could. Mercy, as she was wont, laboured much for
the poor, wherefore their bellies and backs blessed
her, and she was there an ornament to her profession.
And to say the truth, for Grace, Phoebe, and Martha,
they were all of a very good nature, and did much
good in their place. They were also all of them very
fruitful, so that Christian's name, as was said before,
was like to live in the world.

A monster While they lay here, there came a monster out of
the woods, and slew many of the people of the
town. It would also carry away their children,
and teach them to suck its whelps. Now no man
in the town durst so much as face this Monster;
but all men fled when they heard the noise of his
coming.

The Monster[78] was like unto no one beast upon
His shape the earth. Its body was like a dragon and it had
His nature seven heads and ten horns. It made great havoc of

children, and yet it was governed by a woman. This monster propounded conditions to men; and such men as loved their lives more than their souls accepted of those conditions. So they came under.

Now this Mr Great-heart, together with these that came to visit the pilgrims at Mr Mnason's house, entered into a covenant to go and engage this beast, if perhaps they might deliver the people of this town, from the paws and mouths of this so devouring a serpent.

Then did Mr Great-heart, Mr Contrite, Mr Holy- *How he is* man, Mr Dare-not-lie, and Mr Penitent, with their *engaged* weapons go forth to meet him. Now the Monster at first was very rampant and looked upon these enemies with great disdain, but they so belaboured him, being sturdy men at arms, that they made him make a retreat: so they came home to Mr Mnason's house again.

The Monster, you must know, had his certain seasons to come out in and to make his attempts upon the children of the people of the town, also these seasons did these valiant worthies watch him in and did still continually assault him, in so much that in process of time he became not only wounded, but lame; also he has not made that havoc of the townsmen's children, as formerly he has done. And it is verily believed by some, that this beast will die of his wounds.

This therefore made Mr Great-heart and his fellows of great fame in this town, so that many of the people that wanted their taste of things yet had a reverend esteem and respect for them. Upon this account therefore it was that these pilgrims got not much hurt here. True, there were some of the baser sort that could see no more than a mole, nor understand more than a beast; these had no reverence for these men, nor took they notice of their valour or adventures.

Well, the time drew on that the pilgrims must go on their way, wherefore they prepared for their journey. They sent for their friends, they conferred with them, they had some time set apart therein to commit each other to the protection of their Prince. There was again that brought them of such things as they had, that was fit for the weak and the strong, for the women and the men; and so laded them with such things as was necessary.

Then they set forwards on their way, and their friends accompanying them so far as was convenient, they again committed each other to the protection of their King, and parted.

They therefore that were of the pilgrims' company went on, and Mr Great-heart went before them; now the women and children being weakly, they were forced to go as they could bear, by this means Mr Ready-to-halt and Mr Feeble-mind had more to sympathize with their condition.

When they were gone from the townsmen, and when their friends had bid them farewell, they quickly came to the place where Faithful was put to death: There therefore they made a stand, and thanked him that had enabled him to bear his Cross so well, and the rather, because they now found that they had a benefit by such a manly suffering as his was.

They went on therefore after this, a good way further, talking of Christian and Faithful, and how Hopeful joined himself to Christian after that Faithful was dead.

Now they were come up with the Hill Lucre, where the silver-mine was, which took Demas off from his pilgrimage, and into which, as some think, By-ends fell and perished; wherefore they considered that. But when they were come to the old monument that stood over against the Hill Lucre, to wit, to the Pillar of Salt that stood also within view of Sodom, and its stinking lake, they marvelled, as did Christian before, that men of that knowledge and ripeness of wit as they was, should be so blinded as to turn aside here. Only they considered again, that nature is not affected with the harms that others have met with, specially if that thing upon which they look has an attracting virtue upon the foolish eye.

I saw now that they went on till they came at the river that was on this side of the Delectable Mountains. To the river where the fine trees grow on both sides, and whose leaves, if taken inwardly, are good against surfeits; where the meadows are green all the year long, and where they might lie down safely.

By this river side in the meadow, there were cotes and folds for sheep, an house built for the nourishing and bringing up of those lambs, the babes of those women that go on pilgrimage. Also there was here one that was entrusted with them, who could have compassion, and that could gather these lambs with his arm, and carry them in his bosom, and that could gently lead those that were with young. Now to the care of this man, Christiana admonished her four daughters[79] to commit their little ones; that by these waters they might be housed, harboured, succoured and nourished, and that none of them might be lacking in time to come. This man, if any of them go astray, or be lost, he will bring them again; he will also bind up that which was broken, and will strengthen them that are sick. Here they will never want meat, and drink and clothing, here they will be kept from thieves and robbers, for this man will die before one of those committed to his trust shall be lost. Besides, here they shall be sure to have good nurture and admonition, and shall be taught to walk in right paths, and that you know is a favour of no small account. Also here, as you see, are delicate waters, pleasant meadows, dainty flowers, variety of trees, and such as bear wholesome fruit. Fruit, not like that that Matthew eat of, that fell over the wall out of Beelzebub's Garden, but fruit that procureth health where there is none, and that continueth and increaseth it where it is.

So they were content to commit their little ones to him; and that which was also an encouragement to them so to do, was, for that all this was to be at the charge of the King, and so was an hospital to young children and orphans.

They being come to By-Path stile, have a mind to have a pluck with Giant Despair

Now they went on: and when they were come to By-Path Meadow, to the stile over which Christian went with his fellow Hopeful, when they were taken by Giant Despair, and put into Doubting-Castle, they sat down and consulted what was best to be done, to wit, now they were so strong, and had got such a man as Mr Great-heart for their conductor: whether they had not best to make an attempt upon the Giant, demolish his castle, and if there were any pilgrims in it to set them at liberty before they went any further. So one said one thing, and another said the contrary. One questioned if it was lawful to go upon unconsecrated ground, another said they might provided their end was good; but Mr Great-heart said, 'Though that assertion offered last cannot be universally true, yet I have a commandment to resist sin, to overcome evil, to fight the good fight of faith. And I pray, with whom should I fight this good fight if not with Giant Despair? I will therefore attempt the taking away of his life and the demolishing of Doubting-Castle.' Then said he, 'Who will go with me?' Then said old Honest, 'I will.' 'And so will we too,' said

Christian's four sons, Matthew, Samuel, James and Joseph, for they were young men and strong.

So they left the women in the road, and with them Mr Feeble-mind, and Mr Ready-to-halt, with his crutches, to be their guard, until they came back, for in that place though Giant Despair dwelt so near, they keeping in the road, *A little child might lead them.*

So Mr Great-heart, old Honest, and the four young men, went to go up to Doubting-Castle, to look for Giant Despair. When they came at the castle gate, they knocked for entrance with an unusual noise. At that the old Giant comes to the gate, and Diffidence his wife follows. Then said he, 'Who, and what is he, that is so hardy, as after this manner to molest the Giant Despair?' Mr Great-heart replied, 'It is I, Great-heart, one of the King of the Celestial Country's conductors of pilgrims to their place. And I demand of thee that thou open thy gates for my entrance, prepare thyself also to fight, for I am come to take away thy head, and to demolish Doubting-Castle.'

Now Giant Despair, because he was a Giant, thought no man could overcome him, and again, thought he, since heretofore I have made a conquest of angels, shall Great-heart make me afraid? So he harnessed himself and went out. He had a cap of steel upon his head, a breastplate of fire girded to him, and he came out in iron shoes, with a great club in his hand. Then these six men made up to him, and beset him behind and before; also when Diffidence, the Giantess, came up to help him, old Mr Honest cut her down at one blow. Then they fought for their lives, and Giant Despair was brought down to the ground, but was very loath to die. He struggled hard, and had, as they say, as many lives as a cat, but Great-

Despair has overcome angels

Despair is loth to die

heart was his death, for he left him not till he had severed his head from his shoulders.

Then they fell to demolishing Doubting-Castle,[80] and that you know might with ease be done, since Giant Despair was dead. They were seven days in destroying of that; and in it of pilgrims, they found one Mr Despondency, almost starved to death, and one Much-afraid his daughter; these two they saved alive. But it would a made you a wondered to have seen the dead bodies that lay here and there in the castle yard, and how full of dead men's bones the dungeon was.

When Mr Great-heart and his companions had performed this exploit, they took Mr Despondency, and his daughter Much-afraid, into their protection, for they were honest people, though they were prisoners in Doubting-Castle, to that tyrant Giant Despair. They therefore I say, took with them the head of the Giant (for his body they had buried under a heap of stones) and down to the road and to their companions they came, and showed them what they had done. Now when Feeble-mind, and Ready-to-halt saw that it was the head of Giant Despair indeed, they were very jocund and merry. Now Christiana, if need was, could play upon the vial, and her daughter Mercy upon the lute. So, since they were so merry disposed, she played them a lesson, and Ready-to-halt would dance. So he took Despondency's daughter, named Much-afraid, by the hand, and to dancing they went in the road. True, he could not dance without one crutch in his hand, but I promise you, he footed it well; also the girl was to be commended, for she answered the music handsomely.

They have music and dancing for joy

As for Mr Despondency, the music was not much to him, he was for feeding rather than dancing, for that he was almost starved. So Christiana gave him some of her bottle of spirits for present relief, and then prepared him something to eat; and in little time the old gentleman came to himself and began to be finely revived.

Now I saw in my dream when all these things were finished, Mr Great-heart took the head of Giant Despair, and set it upon a pole by the highway side, right over against the pillar that Christian erected for a caution to pilgrims that came after to take heed of entering into his grounds.

Then he writ under it upon a marble stone, these verses following:

> This is the head of him, whose name only,
> In former times, did pilgrims terrify.
> His Castle's down, and Diffidence his wife,
> Brave master Great-heart has bereft of life.
> Despondency, his daughter Much-afraid,
> Great-heart, for them, also the man has played.
> Who hereof doubts, if he'll but cast his eye,
> Up hither, may his scruples satisfy,
> This head also when doubting cripples dance,
> Doth show from fears they have deliverance.

A monument of deliverance

When these men had thus bravely showed themselves against Doubting-Castle, and had slain Giant Despair, they went forward, and went on till they came to the Delectable Mountains, where Christian and Hopeful refreshed themselves with the varieties of the place. They also acquainted themselves with the shepherds there, who welcomed them as they had done Christian before, unto the Delectable Mountains.

Now the shepherds seeing so great a train follow Mr Great-heart (for with him they were well acquainted), they said unto him, 'Good sir, you have got a goodly company here; pray where did you find all these?'

Then Mr Great-heart replied,

The guide's speech to the shepherds

First here's Christiana and her train,
Her sons, and her sons' wives, who like the wain
Keep by the pole, and do by compass steer,
From sin to grace, else they had not been here.
Next here's old Honest come on pilgrimage,
Ready-to-halt too, who I dare engage,
True-hearted is, and so is Feeble-mind,
Who willing was, not to be left behind.
Despondency, good man, is coming after,
And so also is Much-afraid, his daughter.
May we have entertainment here, or must
We further go? Let's know whereon to trust.

Their entertainment

Then said the shepherds: 'This is a comfortable company, you are welcome to us, for we have for the feeble, as for the strong; our Prince has an eye to what is done to the least of these. Therefore infirmity must not be a block to our entertainment.' So they had them to the palace door, and then said unto them, 'Come in Mr Feeble-mind, come in Mr Ready-to-halt, come in Mr Despondency, and Mrs Much-afraid his daughter. These, Mr Great-heart,' said the shepherds to the guide, 'we call in by name, for that they are most subject to draw back; but as for you, and the rest that are strong, we leave you to your wonted liberty.' Then said Mr Great-heart, 'This day I see that grace doth shine in your faces, and that you are my Lord's shepherds indeed; for that you have not pushed these diseased neither with side nor shoulder, but have rather strewed their way into the palace with flowers, as you should.'

A description of false shepherds

So the feeble and weak went in, and Mr Great-heart, and the rest did follow. When they were also set down, the shepherds said to those of the weakest sort, 'What is it that you would have? For,' said they, 'all things must be managed here, to the supporting of the weak, as well as to the warning of the unruly.'

So they made them a feast of things easy of digestion, and that were pleasant to the palate, and nourishing, the which when they had received, they went to their rest, each one respectively unto his proper place. When morning was come, because the mountains were high, and the day clear; and because it was the custom of the shepherds to show to the pilgrims, before their departure, some rarities, therefore after they were ready, and had refreshed themselves, the shepherds took them out into the fields, and showed them first what they had showed to Christian before.

Then they had them to some new places. The first was to Mount-Marvel, where they looked, and behold a man at a distance that tumbled the hills about with words. Then they asked the shepherds what that should mean. So they told him, that that man was the son of one Great-grace, of whom you read in the first part of the records of the *Pilgrim's Progress*. And he is set there to teach pilgrims how to believe down, or to tumble out of their ways, what difficulties they shall meet with, by faith. Then said Mr Great-heart, 'I know him, he is a man above many.' *Mount-Marvel*

Then they had them to another place, called Mount-Innocent. And there they saw a man clothed all in white; and two men, Prejudice and Ill-will, continually casting dirt upon him. Now behold the dirt, whatsoever they cast at him, would in little time fall off again, and his garment would look as clear as if no dirt had been cast thereat. *Mount-Innocent*

Then said the pilgrims, 'What means this?' The shepherds answered, 'This man is named Godly-man, and this garment is to show the innocency of his life. Now those that throw dirt at him are such as hate his well-doing, but as you see the dirt will not stick upon his clothes; so it shall be with him that liveth truly innocently in the world. Whoever they be that would make such men dirty, they labour all in vain; for God, by that a little time is spent, will cause that their innocence shall break forth as the light, and their righteousness as the noonday.'

Mount-Charity Then they took them, and had them to Mount-Charity, where they showed them a man that had a bundle of cloth lying before him, out of which he cut coats and garments, for the poor that stood about him; yet his bundle or roll of cloth was never the less.

Then said they, 'What should this be?' 'This is,' said the shepherds, 'to show you, that he that has a heart to give of his labour to the poor, shall never want wherewithal. He that watereth shall be watered himself. And the cake[81] that the widow gave to the prophet did not cause that she had ever the less in her barrel.'

The work of one Fool, and one Want-wit They had them also to a place where they saw one Fool and one Want-wit, washing of an Ethiopian[82] with intention to make him white, but the more they washed him, the blacker he was. They then asked the shepherds what that should mean. So they told them, saying, 'Thus shall it be with the vile person; all means used to get such an one a good name, shall in conclusion tend but to make him more abominable. Thus it was with the Pharisees, and so shall it be with all hypocrites.'

Mercy has a mind to see the hole in the hill Then said Mercy the wife of Matthew to Christiana her mother, 'Mother, I would, if it might be, see the hole in the hill; or that commonly called, the By-way to Hell.' So her mother brake her mind to the shepherds. Then they went to the door; it was in the side of an hill, and they opened it, and bid Mercy hearken awhile. So she hearkened, and heard one saying, 'Cursed be my father for holding of my feet back from the way of peace and life'; and another said, 'O that I had been torn in pieces before I had, to save my life, lost my soul'; and another said, 'If I were to live again, how would I deny myself rather than come to this place.' Then there was as if the very earth had groaned, and quaked under the feet of this young woman for fear; so she looked white, and came trembling away, saying, 'Blessed be he and she that is delivered from this place.'

Now when the shepherds had showed them all these things, then they had them back to the palace, and entertained them with what the house would afford; but Mercy being a young, and breeding *Mercy* woman, longed for something which she saw there, *longeth, and* but was ashamed to ask. Her mother-in-law then *for what* asked her what she ailed, for she looked as one not well. Then said Mercy, 'There is a looking-glass hangs up in the dining-room, off of which I cannot take my mind; if therefore I have it not, I think I shall miscarry.' Then said her mother, 'I will mention thy wants to the shepherds, and they will not deny it thee.' But she said, 'I am ashamed that these men should know that I longed.' 'Nay my daughter,' said she, 'it is no shame, but a virtue, to long for such a thing as that.' So Mercy said, 'Then mother, if you please, ask the shepherds if they are willing to sell it.'

Now the glass was one of a thousand. It would present a man, one way, with his own feature exactly, and turn it but another way, and it would show one *It was the* the very face and similitude of the Prince of pilgrims *Word of God* himself. Yea I have talked with them that can tell, and they have said, that they have seen the very crown of thorns upon his head, by looking in that glass, they have therein also seen the holes in his hands, in his feet, and his side. Yea, such an excellency is there in that glass that it will show him to one where they have a mind to see him, whether living or dead, whether in earth or heaven, whether in a state of humiliation, or in his exaltation, whether coming to suffer, or coming to reign.

Christiana therefore went to the shepherds apart (now the names of the shepherds are Knowledge, Experience, Watchful, and Sincere), and said unto them, 'There is one of my daughters, a breeding woman, that I think doth long for some thing that she hath seen in this house, and she thinks she shall miscarry if she should by you be denied.

Experience. Call her, call her, She shall assuredly *She doth* have what we can help her to. So they called her, and *not lose her* said to her, 'Mercy, what is that thing thou wouldest *longing* have?' Then she blushed and said, 'The great glass that hangs up in the dining-room.' So Sincere ran and fetched it, and with a joyful consent it was given her. Then she bowed her head, and gave thanks, and said, 'By this I know that I have obtained favour in your eyes.'

They also gave to the other young women such things as they desired, and to their husbands great commendations, for that they joined with Mr Greatheart to the slaying of Giant Despair, and the demolishing of Doubting-Castle.

How the About Christiana's neck, the shepherds put a brace- *shepherds* let, and so they did about the necks of her four *adorn the* *pilgrims* daughters, also they put ear-rings in their ears, and jewels on their foreheads.

When they were minded to go hence, they let them go in peace, but gave not to them those certain cautions which before was given to Christian and his companion. The reason was for that these had Great-heart to be their guide, who was one that was well acquainted with things, and so could give them their cautions more seasonably, to wit, even then when the danger was nigh the approaching.

What cautions Christian and his companions had received of the shepherds, they had also lost by that the time was come that they had need to put them in practice. Wherefore here was the advantage that this company had over the other.

From hence they went on singing, and they said,

> Behold, how fitly are the stages set!
> For their relief that pilgrims are become;
> And how they us receive without one let,
> That make the other life our mark and home.
> What novelties they have, to us they give,
> That we, though pilgrims, joyful lives may live.
> They do upon us too such things bestow,
> That show we pilgrims are, where'ere we go.

When they were gone from the shepherds, they quickly came to the place where Christian met with one Turn-away, that dwelt in the Town of Apostacy. Wherefore of him Mr Great-heart their guide did now put them in mind; saying, 'This is the place where Christian met with one Turn-away, who carried with him the character of his rebellion at his back. And this I have to say concerning this man, he would hearken to no counsel, but once a falling, persuasion could not stop him. When he came to the place where the cross and the sepulchre was, he did meet with one that did bid him look there, but he gnashed with his teeth and stamped, and said he was resolved to go back to his own town. Before he came to the Gate, he met with Evangelist, who offered to lay hands on him, to turn him into the way again. But this Turn-away resisted him, and having done

How one Turn-away managed his apostacy

much despite unto him, he got away over the wall and so escaped his hand.'

Then they went on, and just at the place where Little-faith formerly was robbed, there stood a man with his sword drawn, and his face all bloody. Then said Mr Great-heart, 'What art thou?' The man made *One* answer, saying, 'I am one whose name is Valiant-for-*Valiant-for-* Truth, I am a pilgrim, and am going to the Celestial *Truth beset* City. Now as I was in my way, there was three men *with thieves* did beset me, and propounded unto me these three things. Whether I would become one of them? Or go back from whence I came? Or die upon the place? To the first I answered, I had been a true man a long season, and therefore, it could not be expected that I now should cast in my lot with thieves. Then they demanded what I would say to the second. So I told them that the place from whence I came, had I not found incommodity there, I had not forsaken it at all, but finding it altogether unsuitable to me, and very unprofitable for me, I forsook it for this way. Then they asked me what I said to the third. And I told them, my life cost more dear far than that I should lightly give it away. Besides, you have nothing to do thus to put things to my choice; wherefore at your peril be it, if you meddle. Then these three, to wit, Wild-head, Inconsiderate, and Pragmatic, drew upon me, and I also drew upon them.

How he 'So we fell to it, one against three, for the space of *behaved* above three hours. They have left upon me, as you *himself, and* see, some of the marks of their valour, and have also *put them to* carried away with them some of mine. They are but *flight* just now gone. I suppose they might, as the saying is, hear your horse dash,[83] and so they betook them to flight.'

Great-heart. But here was great odds, three against one.

Valiant-for-Truth. 'Tis true, but little and more, are nothing to him that has the truth on his side. *Though an host should encamp against me, said one, my heart shall not fear. Though war should rise against me, in this will I be confident, etc.*[84] Besides, said he, I have read in some records that one man has fought an army; and how many did Sampson slay with the jaw bone of an ass?

Great-heart wonders at his valour

Great-heart. Then said the guide, Why did you not cry out, that some might a came in for your succour?

Valiant-for-Truth. So I did, to my King, who I knew could hear, and afford invisible help, and that was sufficient for me.

Great-heart. Then said Great-heart to Mr Valiant-for-Truth, Thou hast worthily behaved thyself; let me see thy sword; so he showed it him.

Has a mind to see his sword, and spends his judgement on it

When he had taken it in his hand, and looked thereon a while, he said, 'Ha! It is a right Jerusalem blade.'[85]

Valiant-for-Truth. It is so. Let a man have one of these blades, with a hand to wield it, and skill to use it, and he may venture upon an angel with it. He need not fear its holding, if he can but tell how to lay on. Its edges will never blunt. It will cut flesh, and bones, and soul, and spirit, and all.

Great-heart. But you fought a great while, I wonder you was not weary?

Valiant-for-Truth. I fought till my sword did cleave to my hand, and when they were joined together, as if a sword grew out of my arm, and when the blood run through my fingers, then I fought with most courage.

*The Word
The Faith
Blood*

Great-heart. Thou hast done well, thou hast resisted unto blood, striving against sin. Thou shalt abide by us, come in, and go out with us; for we are thy companions.

Then they took him and washed his wounds, and

gave him of what they had, to refresh him, and so they went on together. Now as they went on, because Mr Great-heart was delighted in him (for he loved one greatly that he found to be a man of his hands) and because there was with his company them that was feeble and weak, therefore he questioned with him about many things; as first, what countryman he was.

What countryman Mr Valiant was

Valiant-for-Truth. I am of Dark-land, for there I was born, and there my father and mother are still.

Great-heart. Dark-land, said the guide, doth not that lie upon the same coast with the City of Destruction?

How Mr Valiant came to go on pilgrimage

Valiant-for-Truth. Yes it doth. Now that which caused me to come on pilgrimage, was this: we had one Mr Tell-true came into our parts, and he told it about, what Christian had done, that went from the City of Destruction. Namely, how he had forsaken his wife and children and had betaken himself to a pilgrim's life. It was also confidently reported how he had killed a serpent[86] that did come out to resist him in his journey, and how he got through to whither he intended. It was also told what welcome he had at all his Lord's lodgings; specially when he came to the Gates of the Celestial City. 'For there,' said the man, 'he was received with sound of trumpet, by a company of Shining Ones.' He told it also, how all the bells in the City did ring for joy at his reception, and what golden garments he was clothed with, with many other things that now I shall forbear to relate. In a word, that man so told the story of Christian and his travels that my heart fell into a burning haste to be gone after him, nor could father or mother stay me, so I got from them, and am come thus far on my way.

He begins right

Great-heart. You came in at the Gate, did you not?

Valiant-for-Truth. Yes, yes. For the same man also told us, that all would be nothing if we did not begin to enter this way at the Gate.

Great-heart. Look you, said the guide to Christiana, the pilgrimage of your husband and what he has gotten thereby is spread abroad far and near. *Christian's name famous*

Valiant-for-Truth. Why, is this Christian's wife?

Great-heart. Yes, that it is, and these are also her four sons.

Valiant-for-Truth. What! and going on pilgrimage too?

Great-heart. Yes, verily, they are following after.

Valiant-for-Truth. It glads me at the heart! Good man! How joyful will he be when he shall see them that would not go with him, yet to enter after him in at the Gates into the City? *He is much rejoiced to see Christian's wife*

Great-heart. Without doubt it will be a comfort to him; for next to the joy of seeing himself there, it will be a joy to meet there his wife and his children.

Valiant-for-Truth. But now you are upon that, pray let me see your opinion about it. Some make a question whether we shall know one another when we are there. *Whether we shall know one another when we come to Heaven*

Great-heart. Do they think they shall know themselves then? Or that they shall rejoice to see themselves in that bliss? And if they think they shall know and do these; why not know others, and rejoice in their welfare also?

Again, since relations are our second self, though that state will be dissolved there, yet why may it not be rationally concluded that we shall be more glad to see them there than to see they are wanting?

Valiant-for-Truth. Well, I perceive whereabouts you are as to this. Have you any more things to ask me about my beginning to come on pilgrimage?

Great-heart. Yes. Was your father and mother willing that you should become a pilgrim?

Valiant-for-Truth. Oh, no. They used all means imaginable to persuade me to stay at home.

Great-heart. Why, what could they say against it?

The great stumbling-blocks that by his friends were laid in his way

Valiant-for-Truth. They said it was an idle life, and if I myself were not inclined to sloth and laziness, I would never countenance a pilgrim's condition.

Great-heart. And what did they say else?

Valiant-for-Truth. Why, they told me that it was a dangerous way, yea the most dangerous way in the world, said they, is that which the pilgrims go.

Great-heart. Did they show wherein this way is so dangerous?

Valiant-for-Truth. Yes. And that in many particulars.

Great-heart. Name some of them.

Valiant-for-Truth. They told me of the Slough of Despond, where Christian was well nigh smothered.

The first stumbling-block

They told me that there were archers standing ready in Beelzebub-Castle, to shoot them that should knock at the Wicket Gate for entrance. They told me also of the wood, and dark Mountains, of the Hill Difficulty, of the lions, and also of the three giants, Bloodyman, Maul, and Slay-good. They said moreover, that there was a foul fiend haunted the Valley of Humiliation, and that Christian was, by him, almost bereft of life. 'Besides,' said they, 'you must go over the Valley of the Shadow of Death, where the hobgoblins are, where the light is darkness, where the way is full of snares, pits, traps and gins.' They told me also of Giant Despair, of Doubting-Castle, and of the ruins that the pilgrims met with there. Further, they said I must go over the Enchanted Ground, which was dangerous. And that after all this I should find a River over which I should find no bridge, and that that River did lie betwixt me and the Celestial Country.

Great-heart. And was this all?

Valiant-for-Truth. No, they also told me that this *The second* way was full of deceivers, and of persons that laid await there to turn good men out of the path.

Great-heart. But how did they make that out?

Valiant-for-Truth. They told me that Mr Worldly- *The third* wiseman did there lie in wait to deceive. They also said that there was Formality and Hypocrisy continually on the road. They said also that By-ends, Talkative, or Demas would go near to gather me up; that the Flatterer would catch me in his net, or that with greenheaded Ignorance I would presume to go on to the Gate, from whence he always was sent back to the hole that was in the side of the Hill and made to go the By-way to Hell.

Great-heart. I promise you, this was enough to discourage. But did they make an end here?

Valiant-for-Truth. No, stay. They told me also of *The fourth* many that had tried that way of old, and that had gone a great way therein, to see if they could find something of the glory there that so many had so much talked of from time to time, and how they came back again, and befooled themselves for setting a foot out of doors in that path, to the satisfaction of all the country. And they named several that did so, as Obstinate, and Pliable, Mistrust, and Timorous, Turn-away, and old Atheist, with several more; who, they said, had some of them gone far to see if they could find, but not one of them found so much advantage by going, as amounted to the weight of a feather.

Great-heart. Said they anything more to discourage you?

Valiant-for-Truth. Yes. They told me of one Mr *The fifth*

Fearing, who was a pilgrim, and how he found this way so solitary, that he never had comfortable hour therein, also that Mr Despondency had like to been starved therein; Yea, and also, which I had almost forgot, that Christian himself about whom there has been such a noise, after all his ventures for a Celestial Crown, was certainly drowned in the black River and never went foot further, however it was smothered up.

Great-heart. And did none of these things discourage you?

Valiant-for-Truth. No. They seemed but as so many nothings to me.

Great-heart. How came that about?

How he got over these stumbling-blocks *Valiant-for-Truth.* Why, I still believed what Mr Tell-true had said, and that carried me beyond them all.

Great-heart. Then this was your victory, even your faith?

Valiant-for-Truth. It was so, I believed and therefore came out, got into the way, fought all that set themselves against me, and by believing am come to this place.

> *Who would true valour see*
> *Let him come hither;*
> *One here will constant be,*
> *Come wind, come weather.*
> *There's no discouragement,*
> *Shall make him once relent,*
> *His first avowed intent,*
> *To be a pilgrim.*
>
> *Who so beset him round,*
> *With dismal stories,*
> *Do but themselves confound;*
> *His strength the more is.*

No lion can him fright,
He'll with a giant fight,
But he will have a right,
To be a pilgrim.

Hobgoblin, nor foul fiend,
Can daunt his spirit:
He knows, he at the end,
Shall life inherit.
Then fancies fly away,
He'll fear not what men say,
He'll labour night and day,
To be a pilgrim.[87]

By this time they were got to the Enchanted Ground, where the air naturally tended to make one drowsy. And that place was all grown over with briars and thorns, excepting here and there, where was an enchanted arbour, upon which, if a man sits, or in which if a man sleeps, 'tis a question, say some, whether ever they shall rise or wake again in this world. Over this forest therefore they went, both one with another, and Mr Great-heart went before, for that he was the guide, and Mr Valiant-for-Truth, he came behind, being there a guard, for fear lest peradventure some fiend, or dragon, or giant, or thief, should fall upon their rear, and so do mischief. They went on here each man with his sword drawn in his hand; for they knew it was a dangerous place. Also they cheered up one another as well as they could. Feeble-mind, Mr Great-heart commanded should come up after him, and Mr Despondency was under the eye of Mr Valiant.

Now they had not gone far, but a great mist and a darkness fell upon them all; so that they could scarce, for a great while, see the one the other. Wherefore they were forced for some time to feel for one another by words; for they walked not by sight.

But any one must think that here was but sorry going for the best of them all, but how much worse for the women and children; who both of feet and heart were but tender. Yet so it was that through the encouraging words of he that led in the front and of him that brought them up behind they made a pretty good shift to wag along.

The way also was here very wearisome, through dirt and slabbiness. Nor was there on all this ground, so much as one inn, or victualling-house, therein to refresh the feebler sort. Here therefore was grunting, and puffing, and sighing: while one tumbleth over a bush, another sticks fast in the dirt, and the children, some of them, lost their shoes in the mire. While one cries out, 'I am down', and another, 'Ho, where are you?' and a third, 'The bushes have got such fast hold on me, I think I cannot get away from them.'

An Arbour on the Enchanting Ground Then they came at an Arbour, warm, and promising much refreshing to the pilgrims; for it was finely wrought above-head, beautified with greens, furnished with benches, and settles. It also had in it a soft couch whereon the weary might lean. This, you must think, all things considered, was tempting; for the pilgrims already began to be foiled with the badness of the way; but there was not one of them that made so much as a motion to stop there. Yea, for aught I could perceive, they continually gave so good heed to the advice of their guide, and he did so faithfully tell them of dangers, and of the nature of dangers when they were at them, that usually when they were nearest to them they did most pluck up *The name of the Arbour* their spirits and hearten one another to deny the flesh. This Arbour was called The Slothful's Friend, on purpose to allure, if it might be, some of the pilgrims there, to take up their rest when weary.

I saw then in my dream that they went on in this *The way* their solitary ground till they came to a place at which *difficult to* a man is apt to lose his way. Now, though when it *find* was light their guide could well enough tell how to miss those ways that led wrong, yet in the dark he was put to a stand: But he had in his pocket a map of *The guide has* all ways leading to or from the Celestial City; where- *a map of all* fore he strook a light (for he never goes also without *ways leading* his tinder-box) and takes a view of his book or map, *the city* which bids him be careful in that place to turn to the right-hand-way. And had he not here been careful to look in his map they had all in probability been smothered in the mud, for just a little before them, and that at the end of the cleanest way too, was a pit, none knows how deep, full of nothing but mud, there made on purpose to destroy the pilgrims in.

Then thought I with myself, who, that goeth on *God's book* pilgrimage, but would have one of these maps about him, that he may look when he is at a stand, which is the way he must take?

They went on then in this Enchanted Ground, till *An Arbour* they came to where was another Arbour, and it was *and two* built by the highway-side. And in that Arbour there *asleep therein* lay two men whose names were Heedless and Too-bold. These two went thus far on pilgrimage, but here being wearied with their journey, they sat down to rest themselves and so fell fast asleep. When the pilgrims saw them, they stood still and shook their heads; for they knew that the sleepers were in a pitiful case. Then they consulted what to do; whether to go on and leave them in their sleep, or to step to them and try to awake them. So they concluded to *The pilgrims* go to them and wake them; that is, if they could; but *try to wake* with this caution, namely, to take heed that them- *them* selves did not sit down, nor embrace the offered benefit of that Arbour.

So they went in and spake to the men, and called each by his name (for the guide, it seems, did know them), but there was no voice nor answer. Then the guide did shake them, and do what he could to disturb them. Then said one of them, 'I will pay you when I take my money.' At which the guide shook his head. 'I will fight so long as I can hold my sword in my hand,' said the other. At that, one of the children laughed.

Their endeavour is fruitless Then said Christiana, 'What is the meaning of this?' The guide said, 'They talk in their sleep. If you strike them, beat them, or whatever else you do to them, they will answer you after this fashion; or as one of them said in old time, when the waves of the sea did beat upon him, and he slept as one upon the mast of a ship, *When I awake I will seek it again.* You know when men talk in their sleeps, they say anything; but their words are not governed, either by faith or reason. There is an incoherency in their words now, as there was before betwixt their going on pilgrimage and sitting down here. This then is the mischief on't, when heedless ones go on pilgrimage, 'tis twenty to one, but they are served thus. For this Enchanted Ground is one of the last refuges that the enemy to pilgrims has; wherefore it is as you see placed almost at the end of the way, and so it standeth against us with the more advantage. For when, thinks the enemy, will these fools be so desirous to sit down as when they are weary, and when so like to be weary as when almost at their journey's end? Therefore it is, I say, that the Enchanted Ground is placed so nigh to the Land Beulah, and so near the end of their race. Wherefore let pilgrims look to themselves, lest it happen to them as it has done to these that as you see are fallen asleep and none can wake them.'

Then the pilgrims desired with trembling to go forward, only they prayed their guide to strike a light, that they might go the rest of their way by the help of the light of a lanthorn. So he strook a light, and they went by the help of that through the rest of this way, though the darkness was very great. *The light of the Word*

But the children began to be sorely weary, and they cried out unto him that loveth pilgrims, to make their way more comfortable. So by that they had gone a little further, a wind arose that drove away the fog, so the air became more clear. *The children cry for weariness*

Yet they were not off (by much) of the Enchanted Ground; only now they could see one another better, and the way wherein they should walk.

Now when they were almost at the end of this ground, they perceived that a little before them was a solemn noise, as of one that was much concerned. So they went on and looked before them, and behold, they saw, as they thought, a man upon his knees, with hands and eyes lift up, and speaking, as they thought, earnestly to one that was above. They drew nigh, but could not tell what he said; so they went softly till he had done. When he had done, he got up and began to run towards the Celestial City. Then Mr Great-heart called after him, saying, 'So-ho, friend, let us have your company, if you go, as I suppose you do, to the Celestial City.' So the man stopped, and they came up to him. But as soon as Mr Honest saw him, he said, 'I know this man.' Then said Mr Valiant-for-Truth, 'Prithee who is it?' ''Tis one,' said he, 'that comes from whereabouts I dwelt; his name is Stand-fast, he is certainly a right good pilgrim.' *Stand-fast upon his knees in the Enchanted Ground* *The story of Stand-fast*

So they came up one to another, and presently

Talk betwixt him and Mr Honest Stand-fast said to old Honest, 'Ho, Father Honest, are you there?' 'Ay,' said he, 'that I am, as sure as you are there.' 'Right glad am I,' said Mr Stand-fast, 'that I have found you on this road.' 'And as glad am I,' said the other, 'that I espied you upon your knees.' Then Mr Stand-fast blushed, and said, 'But why, did you see me?' 'Yes, that I did,' quoth the other, 'and with my heart was glad at the sight.' 'Why, what did you think?' said Stand-fast. 'Think,' said old Honest, 'what should I think? I thought we had an honest man upon the road, and therefore should have his company by and by. If you thought not amiss, how happy am I? But if I be not as I should, I alone must bear it.' 'That is true,' said the other; 'but your fear doth further confirm me that things are right betwixt the Prince of pilgrims and your soul. For he saith, *Blessed is the man that feareth always.*'

They found him at prayer *Valiant-for-Truth.* Well, but brother, I pray thee tell us what was it that was the cause of thy being upon thy knees, even now? Was it for that some special mercy laid obligations upon thee, or how?

What it was that fetched him upon his knees *Stand-fast.* Why we are as you see, upon the Enchanted Ground, and as I was coming along, I was musing with myself of what a dangerous road the road in this place was, and how many that had come even thus far on pilgrimage had here been stopped, and been destroyed. I thought also of the manner of the death with which this place destroyeth men. Those that die here die of no violent distemper; the death which such die is not grievous to them. For he that goeth away in a sleep, begins that journey with desire and pleasure. Yea, such acquiesce in the will of that disease.

Honest. Then Mr Honest interrupting of him said, Did you see the two men asleep in the Arbour?

Stand-fast. Ay, ay, I saw Heedless, and Too-bold

there; and for aught I know, there they will lie till they rot. But let me go on in my tale: As I was thus musing, as I said, there was one in very pleasant attire, but old, that presented herself unto me, and offered me three things, to wit, her body, her purse, and her bed. Now the truth is, I was both aweary, and sleepy, I am also as poor as a howlet, and that, perhaps, the witch knew. Well, I repulsed her once and twice, but she put by my repulses, and smiled. Then I began to be angry, but she mattered that nothing at all. Then she made offers again, and said if I would be ruled by her, she would make me great and happy. 'For,' said she, 'I am the mistress of the world, and men are made happy by me.' Then I asked her name, and she told me it was Madam Bubble.[88] This set me further from her; but she still followed me with enticements. Then I betook me, as you see, to my knees, and with hands lift up, and cries, I prayed to him that had said he would help. So just as you came up, the gentlewoman went her way. Then I continued to give thanks for this my great deliverance, for I verily believe she intended no good, but rather sought to make stop of me in my journey.

Madam Bubble, or this vain world

Honest. Without doubt her designs were bad. But stay, now you talk of her, methinks I either have seen her, or have read some story of her.

Stand-fast. Perhaps you have done both.

Honest. Madam Bubble! Is she not a tall comely dame, something of a swarthy complexion?

Stand-fast. Right, you hit it, she is just such an one.

Honest. Doth she not speak very smoothly, and give you a smile at the end of a sentence?

Stand-fast. You fall right upon it again, for these are her very actions.

Honest. Doth she not wear a great purse by her

side, and is not her hand often in it fingering her money as if that was her heart's delight?

Stand-fast. 'Tis just so. Had she stood by all this while, you could not more amply set her forth before me, nor have better described her features.

Honest. Then he that drew her picture was a good limner, and he that wrote of her said true.

The world   *Great-heart.* This woman is a witch, and it is by virtue of her sorceries that this Ground is enchanted; whoever doth lay their head down in her lap, had as good lay it down upon that block over which the axe doth hang; and whoever lay their eyes upon her beauty are counted the enemies of God. This is she that maintaineth in their splendour all those that are the enemies of pilgrims. Yea, this is she that has bought off many a man from a pilgrim's life. She is a great gossiper, she is always, both she and her daughters, at one pilgrim's heels or other, now commending, and then preferring the excellencies of this life. She is a bold and impudent slut; she will talk with any man. She always laugheth poor pilgrims to scorn, but highly commends the rich. If there be one cunning to get money in a place, she will speak well of him, from house to house. She loveth banqueting, and feasting mainly well; she is always at one full table or another. She has given it out in some places that she is a goddess, and therefore some do worship her. She has her times and open places of feasting, and she will say and avow it, that none can show a food comparable to hers. She promiseth to dwell with children's children if they will but love and make much of her. She will cast out of her purse gold like dust, in some places and to some persons. She loves to be sought after, spoken well of, and to lie in the bosoms of men. She is never weary of commending of her commodities, and she loves them most that think best of her. She will promise to some crowns and kingdoms if they will but take her advice, yet many has she brought to the halter, and ten thousand times more to Hell.

Stand-fast. O! said Stand-fast, What a mercy is it that I did resist her; for whither might she a drawn me?

Great-heart. Whither! Nay, none but God knows whither. But in general to be sure, she would a drawn thee *into many foolish and hurtful lusts, which drown men in destruction and perdition.*

'Twas she that set Absalom against his father, and Jeroboam against his master. 'Twas she that persuaded Judas to sell his Lord, and that prevailed with Demas to forsake the godly pilgrim's life; none can tell of the mischief that she doth. She makes variance betwixt rulers and subjects, betwixt parents and children, 'twixt neighbour and neighbour, 'twixt a man and his wife, 'twixt a man and himself, 'twixt the flesh and the heart.

Wherefore good Master Stand-fast, be as your name is, and when you have done all, stand.

At this discourse there was among the pilgrims a mixture of joy and trembling, but at length they brake out and sang:

> *What danger is the pilgrim in,*
> *How many are his foes,*
> *How many ways there are to sin,*
> *No living mortal knows.*
> *Some of the ditch shy are, yet can*
> *Lie tumbling in the mire:*
> *Some though they shun the frying-pan,*
> *Do leap into the fire.*

After this I beheld, until they were come into the Land of Beulah, where the sun shineth night and day.

Here because they was weary, they betook themselves a while to rest. And because this country was common for pilgrims, and because the orchards and vineyards that were here belonged to the King of the Celestial Country, therefore they were licensed to make bold with any of his things.

But a little while soon refreshed them here, for the bells did so ring, and the trumpets continually sound so melodiously, that they could not sleep, and yet they received as much refreshing, as if they had slept their sleep never so soundly. Here also all the noise of them that walked the streets, was, 'More pilgrims are come to town.' And another would answer, saying, 'And so many went over the water, and were let in at the Golden Gates today.' They would cry again, 'There is now a legion of Shining Ones, just come to town; by which we know that there are more pilgrims upon the road, for here they come to wait for them and to comfort them after all their sorrow.' Then the pilgrims got up and walked to and fro: but how were their ears now filled with heavenly noises, and their eyes delighted with celestial visions? In this land they heard nothing, saw nothing, felt nothing, smelt nothing, tasted nothing that was offensive to their stomach or mind; only when they *Death bitter* tasted of the water of the River over which they *to the flesh,* were to go, they thought that tasted a little bitterish *but sweet to* to the palate, but it proved sweeter when 'twas down. *the soul.*

Death has its In this place there was a record kept of the names *ebbings and* of them that had been pilgrims of old, and a history of *flowings like* all the famous acts that they had done. It was here *the tide* also much discoursed how the River to some had had its flowings, and what ebbings it has had while others have gone over. It has been in a manner dry for some, while it has overflowed its banks for others.

In this place, the children of the Town would go

into the King's gardens and gather nose-gays for the pilgrims, and bring them to them with much affection. Here also grew camphire, with spickenard, and saffron, calamus, and cinnamon, with all its trees of frankincense, myrrh, and aloes, with all chief spices. With these the pilgrims' chambers were perfumed, while they stayed here; and with these were their bodies anointed to prepare them to go over the River when the time appointed was come.

Now while they lay here and waited for the good hour; there was a noise in the town that there was a Post come[89] from the Celestial City, with matter of great importance, to one Christiana, the wife of Christian the pilgrim. So inquiry was made for her, and the house was found out where she was, so the post presented her with a letter; the contents whereof was, 'Hail, good woman, I bring thee tidings that the Master calleth for thee, and expecteth that thou shouldest stand in his presence, in clothes of immortality, within this ten days.' *A Messenger of Death sent to Christiana*

His message

When he had read this letter to her he gave her therewith a sure token that he was a true Messenger, and was come to bid her make haste to be gone. The token was an arrow with a point sharpened with love let easily into her heart, which by degrees wrought so effectually with her that at the time appointed she must be gone. *How welcome is death to them that have nothing to do but to die*

When Christiana saw that her time was come, and that she was the first of this company that was to go over, she called for Mr Great-heart her guide, and told him how matters were. So he told her he was heartily glad of the news, and could a been glad had the post came for him. Then she bid that he should give advice how all things should be prepared for her journey. *Her speech to her guide*

So he told her, saying, 'Thus and thus it must be,

and we that survive will accompany you to the riverside.'

To her children Then she called for her children, and gave them her blessing, and told them that she yet read with comfort the mark that was set in their foreheads, and was glad to see them with her there and that they had kept their garments so white. Lastly, she bequeathed to the poor that little she had, and commanded her sons and her daughters to be ready against the Messenger should come for them.

To Mr Valiant When she had spoken these words to her guide and to her children, she called for Mr Valiant-for-Truth, and said unto him, 'Sir, You have in all places showed yourself true-hearted, be faithful unto death, and my King will give you a Crown of Life. I would also entreat you to have an eye to my children, and if at any time you see them faint, speak comfortably to them. For my daughters, my sons' wives, they have been faithful, and a fulfilling of the promise upon *To Mr Stand-fast* them, will be their end.' But she gave Mr Stand-fast a ring.

To old Honest Then she called for old Mr Honest, and said of him, 'Behold an Israelite indeed, in whom is no guile.' Then said he, 'I wish you a fair day when you set out for Mount Sion, and shall be glad to see that you go over the River dry-shod.' But she answered, 'Come wet, come dry, I long to be gone; for however the weather is in my journey, I shall have time enough when I come there to sit down and rest me, and dry me.'

To Mr Ready-to-halt Then came in that good man Mr Ready-to-halt to see her. So she said to him, 'Thy travel hither has been with difficulty, but that will make thy rest the sweeter. But watch, and be ready, for at an hour when you think not, the Messenger may come.'

After him, came in Mr Despondency, and his

daughter Much-afraid. To whom she said, 'You *To*
ought with thankfulness for ever to remember your *Despondency,*
deliverance from the hands of Giant Despair, and out *and his*
of Doubting-Castle. The effect of that mercy is, that *daughter*
you are brought with safety hither. Be ye watchful,
and cast away fear; be sober, and hope to the end.'

Then she said to Mr Feeble-mind, 'Thou was deliv- *To Feeble-*
ered from the mouth of Giant Slay-good, that thou *mind*
mightest live in the light of the living for ever, and
see thy King with comfort. Only I advise thee to
repent thee of thy aptness to fear and doubt of his
goodness before he sends for thee, lest thou shouldest
when he comes be forced to stand before him for that
fault with blushing.'

Now the day drew on that Christiana must be *Her last day,*
gone. So the road was full of people to see her take *and manner of*
her journey. But behold all the banks beyond the *departure*
River were full of horses and chariots, which were
come down from above to accompany her to the
City Gate. So she came forth and entered the River
with a beckon of farewell, to those that followed her
to the riverside. The last word she was heard to say
here was, 'I come Lord, to be with thee and bless thee.'

So her children and friends returned to their place,
for that those that waited for Christiana had carried
her out of their sight. So she went and called and
entered in at the Gate with all the ceremonies of joy
that her husband Christian had done before her.

At her departure her children wept, but Mr Great-
heart, and Mr Valiant-for-Truth, played upon the
well-tuned cymbal and harp for joy. So all departed
to their respective places.

In process of time there came a Post to the town *Ready-to-halt*
again, and his business was with Mr Ready-to-halt. *summoned*
So he inquired him out, and said to him, 'I am come
to thee in the name of him whom thou hast loved and

followed, though upon crutches. And my message is to tell thee that he expects thee at his table to sup with him in his Kingdom the next day after Easter. Wherefore prepare thyself for this journey.'

Then he also gave him a token that he was a true messenger, saying, *I have broken thy golden bowl, and loosed thy silver cord.*

After this Mr Ready-to-halt called for his fellow pilgrims, and told them, saying, 'I am sent for, and God shall surely visit you also.' So he desired Mr Valiant-for-Truth to make his will. And because he had nothing to bequeath to them that should survive *Promises* him but his crutches and his good wishes, therefore *His will* thus he said: 'These crutches I bequeath to my son that shall tread in my steps with an hundred warm wishes that he may prove better than I have done.'

Then he thanked Mr Great-heart, for his conduct and kindness, and so addressed himself to his journey. When he came at the brink of the River, he said, 'Now I shall have no more need of these crutches, since yonder are chariots and horses for me to ride on.' *His last* The last words he was heard to say, was, 'Welcome *words* life.' So he went his way.

Feeble-mind After this, Mr Feeble-mind had tidings brought *summoned* him, that the Post sounded his horn at his chamber door. Then he came in and told him, saying, 'I am come to tell thee that the Master has need of thee, and that in very little time thou must behold his face in brightness. And take this as a token of the truth of my message, *Those that look out at the windows shall be darkened.*'

Then Mr Feeble-mind called for his friends, and told them what errand had been brought unto him, and what token he had received of the truth of the *He makes* message. Then he said, 'Since I have nothing to be-*no will* queath to any, to what purpose should I make a

380

will? As for my feeble mind, that I will leave behind me, for that I shall have no need of that in the place whither I go, nor is it worth bestowing upon the poorest pilgrim: wherefore when I am gone, I desire that you Mr Valiant-for-Truth, would bury it in a dunghill. This done, and the day being come in which he was to depart; he entered the River as the rest. His last words were, 'Hold out faith and pati- *His last words* ence.' So he went over to the other side.

When days had many of them passed away, Mr *Mr* Despondency was sent for. For a Post was come, and *Despondency's* brought this message to him: 'Trembling man, these *summons* are to summon thee to be ready with thy King, by the next Lord's Day, to shout for joy for thy deliverance from all thy doubtings.'

And said the Messenger, 'That my message is true, take this for a proof.' So he gave him *The Grasshopper to be a burthen unto him.* Now Mr Des- *His daughter* pondency's daughter, whose name was Much-afraid, *goes too* said, when she heard what was done, that she would go with her father. Then Mr Despondency said to his friends; 'Myself and my daughter, you know what we have been, and how troublesomely we have behaved ourselves in every company. My will and *His will* my daughter's is, that our desponds, and slavish fears, be by no man ever received from the day of our departure for ever; for I know that after my death they will offer themselves to others. For, to be plain with you, they are ghosts, the which we entertained when we first began to be pilgrims, and could never shake them off after. And they will walk about and seek entertainment of the pilgrims, but for our sakes shut ye the doors upon them.'

When the time was come for them to depart, they went to the brink of the River. The last words of *His last* Mr Despondency, were, 'Farewell night, welcome *words*

381

day.' His daughter went through the River singing, but none could understand what she said.

Then it came to pass a while after, that there was *Mr Honest summoned* a Post in the town that inquired for Mr Honest. So he came to the house where he was, and delivered to his hand these lines: 'Thou art commanded to be ready against this day seven night, to present thyself before thy Lord, at his Father's House. And for a token that my message is true, *All thy daughters of music shall be brought low.*' Then Mr Honest called for *He makes no will* his friends, and said unto them, 'I die, but shall make no will. As for my honesty, it shall go with me; let him that comes after be told of this.' When the day that he was to be gone, was come, he addressed himself to go over the River. Now the River at that time overflowed the banks in some places. But Mr Honest *Good-conscience helps Mr Honest over the river* in his life-time had spoken to one Good-conscience to meet him there, the which he also did, and lent him his hand, and so helped him over. The last words of Mr Honest were, 'Grace reigns.' So he left the world.

Mr Valiant summoned After this it was noised abroad that Mr Valiant-for-Truth was taken with a summons, by the same Post as the other; and had this for a token that the summons was true, *That his pitcher was broken at the fountain.* When he understood it, he called for his friends, and told them of it. Then said he, 'I am going to my fathers, and though with great difficulty I am got hither, yet now I do not repent me of all the trouble I have been at to arrive where I am. My *His will* sword, I give to him that shall succeed me in my pilgrimage, and my courage and skill, to him that can get it. My marks and scars I carry with me, to be a witness for me that I have fought his battles who now will be my rewarder.' When the day that he must go hence was come many accompanied him to the River side, into which, as he went, he said, 'Death, where is thy sting?' And as he went down deeper, he said, 'Grave where is thy victory?' So he passed over, and *His last words* the trumpets sounded for him on the other side.

Then there came forth a summons for Mr Stand- *Mr Stand-fast* fast. (This Mr Stand-fast was he that the rest of the *is summoned* pilgrims found upon his knees in the Enchanted Ground.) For the Post brought it him open in his hands. The contents whereof were, That he must prepare for a change of life, for his Master was not willing that he should be so far from him any longer. At this Mr Stand-fast was put into a muse; 'Nay,' said the Messenger, 'You need not doubt of the truth of my message; for here is a token of the truth thereof, *Thy wheel is broken at the cistern.*' Then he called to him Mr Great-heart, who was their guide, *He calls for* and said unto him, 'Sir, although it was not my hap *Mr* to be much in your good company in the days of my *Great-heart* pilgrimage, yet since the time I knew you, you have *His speech* been profitable to me. When I came from home, I *to him* left behind me a wife, and five small children. Let me entreat you, at your return (for I know that you will go, and return to your Master's House, in hopes that you may yet be a conductor to more of the holy pilgrims), that you send to my family, and let them be acquainted with all that hath, and shall happen unto me. Tell them moreover, of my happy arrival to this place, and of the present late blessed condition that I am in. Tell them also of Christian, and of *His errand to* Christiana his wife, and how she and her children *his family* came after her husband. Tell them also of what a happy end she made, and whither she is gone. I have little or nothing to send to my family, except it be prayers, and tears for them; of which it will suffice, if thou acquaint them, if peradventure they may pre- vail. When Mr Stand-fast had thus set things in order, and the time being come for him to haste him away; he also went down to the River. Now there was a great calm at that time in the River, wherefore Mr Stand-fast, when he was about half way in, he stood a while and talked to his companions that had waited upon him thither. And he said,

His last words 'This River has been a terror to many, yea the thoughts of it also have often frighted me. But now methinks I stand easy, my foot is fixed upon that upon which the feet of the priests that bare the Ark of the Covenant stood while Israel went over this Jordan. The waters indeed are to the palate bitter, and to the stomach cold; yet the thoughts of what I am going to, and of the conduct that waits for me on the other side, doth lie as a glowing coal at my heart.

'I see myself now at the end of my journey, my toilsome days are ended. I am going now to see that head that was crowned with thorns, and that face that was spit upon, for me.

'I have formerly lived by hear-say and faith, but now I go where I shall live by sight, and shall be with him, in whose company I delight myself.

'I have loved to hear my Lord spoken of, and wherever I have seen the print of his shoe in the earth, there I have coveted to set my foot too.

'His name has been to me as a civet-box, yea, sweeter than all perfumes. His voice to me has been most sweet, and his countenance I have more desired than they that have most desired the light of the sun. His word I did use to gather for my food, and for antidotes against my faintings. He has held me, and I have kept me from mine iniquities: yea, my steps hath he strengthened in his way.'

Now while he was thus in discourse his countenance changed, his strong men bowed under him, and after he had said, 'Take me, for I come unto thee,' he ceased to be seen of them.

But glorious it was, to see how the open region was filled with horses and chariots, with trumpeters and pipers, with singers, and players on stringed instruments, to welcome the pilgrims as they went up and followed one another in at the beautiful Gate of the City.

As for Christian's children, the four boys that Christiana brought with her, with their wives and children, I did not stay where I was, till they were gone over. Also since I came away, I heard one say that they were yet alive, and so would be for the increase of the Church in that place where they were for a time.

Shall it be my lot to go that way again, I may give those that desire it an account of what I here am silent about; mean time I bid my reader *Adieu*.

FINIS

NOTES
THE FIRST PART

1. (p. 43) *the way/And race of saints*   The book referred to is probably *The Heavenly Footman* (1698), which teaches the Christian 'so to run that he may obtain' and then passes from St Paul's metaphor of a race to that of an arduous journey; it seems less likely to have been *The Strait Gate* (1676), as suggested by Bunyan's first biographer John Brown, since that does not have the journey at all.

2. (p. 43) *Still as I pulled it came*   Like flax, when the spinner pulls the thread towards her from the distaff.

3. (p. 45) *a pearl may in a toad's head dwell*   According to popular lore a precious stone was formed in the head of the toad. See *As You Like It*, II.i.12–14.

4. (p. 46) *types, shadows and metaphors*   Types are episodes or characters in the Old Testament prefiguring what occurs in the New Testament. The animals mentioned in the following lines are the sacrificial offerings of the Jews described in the Pentateuch and they foreshadow the sacrifice of Christ.

5. (p. 47) *Sound words I know Timothy is to use*   I Timothy 6.3.

6. (p. 48) *Dialogue-wise*   Among other books teaching religion in dialogue form Bunyan must have particularly in mind Arthur Dent, *The Plain Mans Path-way to Heaven* (1601, and many subsequent editions), which his first wife brought him as part of her marriage dowry.

7. (p. 49) *Dost thou love picking-meat?*   Dainty food, or the best portions.

8. (p. 51) *The goal*   The prison. It seems likely that the First Part of *The Pilgrim's Progress* was composed during Bunyan's first imprisonment in the county jail (1660–72), probably during the later years of that period. The word in the text, 'a den', is again used for a prison in the episode of Doubting Castle: 'Get you down to your den again' (p. 168).

9. (p. 51) *friend*   Used in the seventeenth century for a close relation as well as in our sense.

10. (p. 52) *he would also walk solitarily in the fields* This recalls Bunyan himself in the time of his greatest despair: 'But one day, as I was passing in the field' (*Grace Abounding*, ed. Roger Sharrock, Oxford, 1962, p. 72).

11. (p. 52) *Evangelist* He represents the ideal Christian minister. Bunyan may be recalling the Bedford pastor John Gifford, who had helped him out of his spiritual crisis (*Grace Abounding*, p. 37).

12. (p. 52) *Tophet* Hell.

13. (p. 53) *yonder Wicket Gate* The 'strait gate' of Luke 13.24, the moment of reception of the grace of Christ, which begins the process of conversion.

14. (p. 57) *Despond* The despair caused by sin, which Bunyan had experienced at an early stage of his conversion.

15. (p. 58) *Plat* A flat, low-lying piece of ground.

16. (p. 58) *this sixteen hundred years* Since the first preaching of Christianity.

17. (p. 59) *Mr Worldly-Wiseman* Although he has most tellingly caught the features of any complacent prig, this figure may be specially intended to satirize the Latitudinarian party in the Church of England – prosperous clergymen who must have seemed to Bunyan scandalous in the liberality of their views and their defence of a purely moral Christianity. He had conducted a bitter controversy with one particular Latitudinarian, Edward Fowler, vicar of Northill, near Bedford, against whom he wrote *A Defence of the Doctrine of Justification by Faith* (1672). Fowler conformed to the Prayer Book in 1662 and thus retained his living when Puritans were ejected: his time-serving as well as his doctrine may have occasioned Bunyan's anger.

18. (p. 63) *yonder high Hill* Mount Sinai, where Moses stood to receive the ten commandments, represents the old law which condemns the sinner. Romans 7.

19. (p. 65) *Now the just shall live by faith* . . . Hebrews 10.38.

20. (p. 68) *Good Will . . . he opened the Gate* i.e. Christ accepted him into the Christian life. Since Christ himself is

the Gate, Good Will is an allegorical figure standing for divine grace.

21. (p. 69) *Beelzebub* The Old Testament 'lord of the flies': usually in later literature treated as Satan's deputy, as in Marlowe and Milton, but here the leader of the devils.

22. (p. 70) *a sought for* 'a' is the unstressed colloquial form of 'have'. Bunyan is reproducing the speech patterns with which he was familiar. There are several other instances in the first edition, but in later ones they were normalized to 'have', presumably by the printer.

23. (p. 71) *butt down upon* Issue into.

24. (p. 71) *the House of the Interpreter* This episode embodies the instruction proper for the new convert; it corresponds to Bunyan's experience early in his conversion when John Gifford took him to his own house to interpret his spiritual problems to him. Instruction takes the form of emblems or symbolical pictures. Emblem books, in which the pictures were accompanied by verses, were a popular genre in the Renaissance period, e.g. Francis Quarles, *Emblemes* (1635), which Bunyan probably knew. At the end of his career he contributed to the genre with *A Book for Boys and Girls* (1686).

25. (p. 72) *a picture of a very grave person* Evangelist depicted as the ideal pastor. Quarles in his book has an emblem of a pilgrim gazing up to heaven with the lines:

> Where shall I seek a Guide? where shall I meet
>> Some lucky hand to lead my trembling paces?
> What trusty Lanterne will direct my feet
>> To scape the danger of these dang'rous places ...

26. (p. 75) *In thy life thou received'st thy good things ...* Cf. Luke 16.25.

27. (p. 76) *This fire is the work of grace* The emblem of Jesus sweeping out the dusty room of the heart is found in Catholic emblem literature (Etienne Luzvic, *Le coeur dévot*, Douai, 1627); but imagery of the human heart before and after sanctification is frequent in Protestant emblem books also.

28. (p. 77) *a man of a very stout countenance* His sword and helmet indicate that he has put on the whole armour of God described in Ephesians 6.17.

29. (p. 77) *the three* Enoch, Moses and Elijah, who 'looked over the Gate' when Christian arrived at the Celestial City (see p. 203).

30. (p. 78) *professor* One who seriously professes religious faith.

31. (p. 78) *fair for* Set fair for, likely to reach.

32. (p. 78) *I am now a man of despair* He is an apostate who has committed the sin against the Holy Ghost and has put himself beyond God's mercy. This was a favourite preoccupation of Puritan pastoral psychology. There was the famous case of Francis Spira, which Bunyan speaks of in *Grace Abounding*, p. 49: 'A book [Spira's *Life*] that was to my troubled spirit as salt, when rubbed into a fresh wound'. Also, nearer home, there was the case of John Child, a member of the Bedford church who had gone over to the Church of England and then, in remorse, committed suicide; Bunyan may have been one of those who remonstrated with him before his defection. See *The Church Book of Bunyan Meeting 1650–1821*, facsimile edition by G. B. Harrison (1928) folios 18–22.

33. (p. 81) *upon that place stood a Cross* The Calvinist view of redemption: Christian is released from his sins by having Christ's righteousness freely imputed to him. His burden (his sins) falls off: 'He that is come to Christ has the advantage of him that is coming, in that he is eased of his burden' (Bunyan, *Come and Welcome to Jesus Christ*, 1678, published in the same year as *The Pilgrim's Progress*, First Part).

34. (p. 82) *three Shining Ones* Since the first, not the second, says 'Thy sins be forgiven', three angels rather than the Trinity.

35. (p. 82) *a bottom* Hollow, valley.

36. (p. 83) *Every fat.* Every vessel. The phrase is proverbial: cf. the form, 'Every tub must stand on its own bottom.'

37. (p. 84) *above a thousand years* This reflects the Puritan view that after the first few centuries the purity of Christian doctrine had become corrupted by formalism and the consolidation of Papal supremacy.

38. (p. 85) *the coat that is on thy back* The white dress of the elect just given to Christian by the angels, Revelation 19.8. Christian's reply states that it is his Lord's coat, as if he were a medieval retainer.

39. (p. 86) *a wide field full of dark mountains* 'Before your feet stumble upon the dark mountains', Jeremiah 13.16. The Biblical image comes out rather vaguely in Bunyan, who knew only the flat Bedfordshire countryside.

40. (p. 87) *Go to the ant* ... Proverbs 6.6.

41. (p. 88) *he felt in his bosom for his roll* The roll is his personal assurance of election from God; that he has lost it signifies a morbid doubting of the promises of election, such as Bunyan underwent after his conversion.

42. (p. 88) *fact* Action.

43. (p. 90) *palace ... Beautiful* The episode represents church-fellowship. As in a gathered church, Christian, the neophyte, has to give an account of his religious experience. Houghton House near Houghton Conquest, built by Inigo Jones for Mary Sidney, Countess of Pembroke, has been suggested as a model for the House Beautiful.

44. (p. 90) *two lions* The lions represent persecution, civil and ecclesiastical, of Nonconformists under the Clarendon Code.

45. (p. 92) *Prudence, Piety and Charity* The fact that the principal keepers of the House Beautiful are women reminds us of the important role played by women in the Bedford congregation. 'God also hath appointed, that those that come into his Royal presence, should first go to the House of the Women, the Church' (Bunyan, *The Greatness of the Soul*).

46. (p. 96) *I have a wife and four small children* At the time of his imprisonment in 1660 Bunyan had 'four small children that cannot help themselves' (*A Relation of My Imprisonment*), who were left to be looked after by his

second wife Elizabeth, his first wife having died in 1658.

47. (p. 99) *had him into the armoury* The 'whole armour of God' of Ephesians 6.13–17. The military metaphor was almost as dear to the Puritans as that of pilgrimage and Bunyan develops it at length in the sieges of his other allegory *The Holy War* (1682).

48. (p. 100) *the Delectable Mountains* In the description that follows Bunyan draws on the fertile landscapes of the Old Testament, especially those in the Psalms and the Song of Solomon.

49. (p. 102) *Apollyon* In Greek, the destroyer. 'The angel of the bottomless pit, whose name in the Hebrew tongue is Abaddon, but in the Greek tongue hath his name Apollyon', Revelation 9.11. 'Sin is the Apollyon, the destroyer', Jeremy Taylor, *Holy Dying* (1651).

50. (p. 102) *with scales like a fish* The monster is described like a dragon of the old chivalric romances, some of which Bunyan had read in their late chapbook versions. The fight also resembles a conflict in romance, with long intervals between the bouts and the champion restored by the leaves of a miraculous tree.

51. (p. 105) *stroddled* A provincial form, altered to 'straddled' in the editions subsequent to the first.

52. (p. 106) *brast* Burst.

53. (p. 107) *The children of the spies* The spies sent to search the land of Canaan 'brought up an evil report of the land . . . unto the children of Israel', Numbers 13.32.

54. (p. 108) *a very deep ditch* It has been suggested that the ditch represents reliance on works, while the 'quag' is that antinomianism which considers that the gift of grace absolves one from the moral law.

55. (p. 108) *quag* Quagmire.

56. (p. 108) *to tip over into the mire* Some Bedfordshire roads were notorious still towards the end of the seventeenth century when Celia Fiennes travelled them, and even thirty years later when Defoe wrote: 'The country people are not able to bring their corn for the mere badness of the ways' (*A Tour through the Whole Island of Great Britain*, 1724–6).

57. (p. 110) *suggested many grievous blasphemies to him* '... whole floods of blasphemies, both against God, Christ and the Scriptures, was poured upon my spirit' (*Grace Abounding*, p. 31).

58. (p. 110) *I will fear none ill* Echoing Psalm 23 in the metrical version of Sternhold and Hopkins:

> Yet though I walke in vaile of death
> Yet will I fear none ill.

59. (p. 111) *satyrs* Not classical, but Biblical satyrs: 'owls shall dwell there, and satyrs shall dance there' (Isaiah 13.21, of the desert that shall replace Babylon).

60. (p. 112) *crazy and stiff in his joints* This reference to the weakness of Papal power could hardly have been written after the Declaration of Indulgence in 1672 had occasioned renewed Protestant fears of Catholic influence.

61. (p. 113) *the avenger of blood* Deuteronomy 19.4–6.

62. (p. 114) *he leered away* To look with downcast eye as if ashamed. 'The tempter did leer and steal away from me' (*Grace Abounding*, p. 44).

63. (p. 115) *The dog is turned to his vomit again* ... 2 Peter 2.22.

64. (p. 115) *Joseph was hard put to it by her* Genesis 39.11–13. The story of Potiphar's wife.

65. (p. 116) *Adam the First* The carnal and unregenerate nature of man. 'The old man which is corrupt according to the lusts of deceit' Ephesians 4.22. Faithful is prone to the sins of the flesh (Madam Wanton), Christian to spiritual ones (the Slough of Despond). Christ, according to Paul, is the second Adam, Romans 5.12–14.

66. (p. 119) *want of understanding in all natural science* Shame appeals to intellectual snobbery in a highly topical manner: the new physical science was fashionable (e.g. at court) in the Restoration period.

67. (p. 121) *The wise shall inherit glory* Proverbs 3.35.

68. (p. 122) *Talkative* Bunyan, like other Puritans, constantly proclaims the inadequacy of a merely notional faith: 'A prating tongue will not unlock the gates of heaven' (*The Strait Gate*).

69. (p. 127) *pure religion and undefiled* ... James 1.27.

NOTES

70. (p. 128) *sounding brass, and tinkling cymbals* I Corinthians 13.1

71. (p. 129) *lie at the catch* Lie in wait to catch out in conversation.

72. (p. 130) *Give me understanding,* ... Psalm 119 1.34.

73. (p. 131) *heart-holiness* etc. These compound words for spiritual qualities are frequent in Puritan usage; cf. 'heart-work', p. 122, l. 4.

74. (p. 136) *Vanity-Fair* For this allegory of the world's pleasures Bunyan probably draws on his knowledge of the great annual fair held in Stourbridge near Cambridge; it had its own 'Court of Piepowder' (*Pieds pouldreux*, dusty feet) to try offences committed in the fair. 'Here is a court of justice always open from morning till night, where the mayor of Cambridge, or his deputy, sits as judge' (Nichols, *Bibliographia Topographica Britannica*, 1790, v.82).

75. (p. 137) *several rows and streets* Again, the naming of rows of stalls after countries might be borrowed from Stourbridge Fair, where different groups of foreign merchants were represented.

76. (p. 138) *bedlams* Lunatics: from the hospital of St Mary of Bethlehem, used as an asylum.

77. (p. 138) *the language of Canaan* The special features of Puritan speech were often ridiculed, especially by the writers of comedy (e.g. Ben Jonson in *Bartholomew Fair*).

78. (p. 139) *amuse* Surprise, bewilder.

79. (p. 141) *Lord Hategood* In this portrait Bunyan may be recalling his own harsh treatment by the Bedfordshire magistrate Sir John Kelynge when prosecuted for field preaching; but there were other judges, including the notorious Lord Chief Justice Jeffreys, whose severity towards Nonconformists was well known, and some things in Hategood's speeches and interventions recall the reported style of Jeffreys.

80. (p. 142) *Pickthank* A flatterer: 'smiling pickthanks and base newsmongers', I *Henry IV*, III.ii.25.

81. (p. 146) *to be had from the place where he was* Here and throughout the trial scene the formulae and procedure of an English criminal trial are observed; the subsequent

torments of Faithful show these being conflated with the accounts of early Christian martyrdoms Bunyan had read in John Foxe's *Acts and Monuments*.

82. (p. 146) *a chariot* This echoes the ascension into heaven of Elijah, 2 Kings 2.11.

83. (p. 147) *By-ends* The satire is directed against ministers who conform for secondary considerations of wealth or security, like those who accepted the Book of Common Prayer in 1662 and thus escaped ejection from their livings. 'Are there not many by-ends in duties?' (Flavel, *Touchstone of Sincerity*, 1679).

84. (p. 148) *atoside* Variant of 'at one side'.

85. (p. 150) *conjee* Bow (French *congée*).

86. (p. 150) *Save-all* He may be an Arminian, who believes that Christ died for all men, not only the elect; or he may simply be a miser.

87. (p. 150) *in the country of Coveting in the north* The old joke about Scottish close-fistedness.

88. (p. 155) *the whole story* Genesis 34.20–23.

89. (p. 155) *hypocritical Pharisees ...* Luke 20.46–7.

90. (p. 155) *religious for the bag* The bag in which Judas carried the thirty pieces of silver paid for betraying Jesus.

91. (p. 155) *Simon the witch* Simon Magus, Acts 8.19. The masculine usage is common: Bunyan could have met it in Foxe, *Acts and Monuments*, 'He is a witch asking counsel at soothsayers.'

92. (p. 155) *his sentence from Peter's mouth was according* Acts 20–21.

93. (p. 156) *Demas* He abandoned Paul on his missionary journey, 'having loved this present world', 2 Timothy 4.10.

94. (p. 157) *roundeth up* Rebukes.

95. (p. 158) *the Pillar of Salt* The pillar of salt into which Lot's wife had been transformed still survived according to popular superstition. The romancing Mandeville (*c.*1356) places it at the right side of the Dead Sea (*Travels of Sir John Mandeville*, Ch. ix).

96. (p. 159) *Korah, Dathan, and Abiram* Numbers 26.9–10.

97. (p. 163) *Doubting-Castle* After a period of ease by the River of the Water of Life the pilgrims are again assailed by fears of their own election and of having committed the unpardonable sin.

98. (p. 163) *Giant Despair* Though he represents the terrible guilt of Puritan moral theology, the giant behaves like those of folk-tale and popular romance.

99. (p. 165) *The life that we now live is miserable* Francis Spira and Bunyan's fellow church-member John Child had been driven to suicide by their despair.

100. (p. 168) *a key in my bosom, called promise* The theological point is made, though with some detriment to the effect of the adventure story: Christian had no need to despair of his salvation: Scripture showed that the promises of God's covenant with him prevented his repentance from being rejected.

101. (p. 168) *damnable hard* A grim pun: it is the fear of damnation that is locking them in.

102. (p. 171) *Hymeneus and Philetus* Who said that the resurrection was past already, 2 Timothy 2.17,18.

103. (p. 171) *they stumbled sometimes upon the tombs* 'Oh, the unthought of imaginations, frights, fears and terrors, that are affected by a thorough application of guilt, leading to desperation. *This is the man that hath his dwelling among the tombs, with the dead; that is always crying out, and cutting himself with stones*', Grace Abounding, p. 58. The allusion is to Proverbs 21.16, which is quoted in the following paragraph.

104. (p. 172) *lumbering* Rumbling (the word was becoming archaic in this sense).

105. (p. 173) *perspective glass* Telescope.

106. (p. 174) *I awoke from my dream* Though some critics have thought the break between two dreams artistically justifiable on the grounds that Christian has decisively overcome his despair, it seems most likely that it simply indicates the author's release from prison (the 'den'). He would then have finished the First Part after 1672.

107. (p. 174) *a very brisk lad* 'A Brisk man ... has

396

nothing in him that is properly his own but confidence', Samuel Butler, *Characters and Passages from Notebooks* (Cambridge, 1908), p. 201.

108. (p. 174) *Ignorance* He relies complacently on his outward conformity and his good deeds ('I have been a good liver'). He is like the Pharisee in the parable and is made to speak like him.

109. (p. 177) *scrabble* Scramble, stumble: a provincial frequentative form which Bunyan was fond of using.

110. (p. 177) *his jewels* His saving faith, cf. 'O, I saw my Gold was in my Trunk at home! in Christ, my Lord and Saviour!', *Grace Abounding*, p. 73.

111. (p. 181) *Heman and Hezekiah* Heman was the grandson of the prophet Samuel to whom Psalm 88 is ascribed, and Hezekiah was the King of Judah whose faith was shaken by the invasion of the Assyrians, 2 Kings, 18,19.

112. (p. 182) *a sorry girl* The servant girl to whom Peter lied that he had not been with Christ, Luke 22.54–62.

113. (p. 183) *the proud helpers fall under the slain* Isaiah 10.4.

114. (p. 184) *a man black of flesh* The only really difficult allegory in *The Pilgrim's Progress*, as is reflected in the diverse interpretations of the commentators. It looks as if the idea of false pastors with winning words has been combined with the notion of the devil as a flatterer, and popular superstitition believed that the devil appeared as a black man.

115. (p. 184) *Concerning the works of men . . .* Psalm 17.4.

116. (p. 188) *Where God began with us* They are to discuss their personal experience of God's grace, as in statements converts were often required to give before the congregation they had joined and in the published spiritual autobiographies of separatists. Hopeful's account which follows comes close to being a recapitulation of Bunyan's in *Grace Abounding*. The climax when he sees Jesus looking down from heaven upon him and saying, 'My grace is sufficient for thee' is paralleled in the autobiography, pp. 64–5. The language, and the theology, are close to that

of Luther in his *Commentary on the Epistle to the Galatians*, which Bunyan had read in the Elizabethan edition of Thomas Vautrollier (1575).

117.   (p. 196) *The soul of the sluggard* . . .   Proverbs 13.4.

118.   (p. 200) *Therefore this faith is deceitful*, etc. The exposition of true justifying faith in this paragraph resembles the arguments in *The Defence of the Doctrine of Justification by Faith* (1672), written against the moralized Christianity of the Anglican Edward Fowler. This would support the view that the *Defence* and the later part of *The Pilgrim's Progress* (First Part) were written about the same time. Ignorance replies that if we must rely solely on Christ's grace and not at all on our own righteousness, this is an invitation to immorality ('would loosen the reins of our lust'). Fowler had made the same point about the danger of antinomianism, separating morality from belief: 'That such a reliance (as that of acting faith, first, on the merits of Christ for justification) is ordinarily to be found amongst unregenerate, and even the worst of men', *The Design of Christianity*, p. 223.

119.   (p. 203) *to lay fast hold of Christ*   One of the phrases specially employed by the Baptists and other Dissenters to describe conversion experience and ridiculed by their opponents in the Church of England. For the latter, cf. Robert South, *Sermons* (6th edition, 1727) iii.165.

120.   (p. 207) *the country of Beulah*   'Thou shalt be called Hephzi-bah [my delight is in her] and thy land Beulah [married]', Isaiah 62.4.

121.   (p. 207) *heard the voice of the turtle in the land*   The description of Beulah that follows is full of echoes of the Song of Solomon.

122.   (p. 208) *If you see my Beloved* . . .   Song of Solomon 5.8.

123.   (p. 209) *the City*   The description of the Holy City relies on the traditional sources in Isaiah and Revelation. Bunyan had already treated the symbolism of the materials of heaven at length in *The Holy City* (1665) and in his poem *The Building of the House of God* (1688), in the second section on the beauty of the church.

124. (p. 210) *Enoch and Elijah* Who had been translated into heaven without experiencing death.

125. (p. 211) *There is no band in their death* ... Psalm 73.4–5. The quotation, as often with Bunyan, is from the Geneva Version, the Bible translation most approved by the Puritans, though becoming a little old-fashioned by this time.

126. (p. 214) *These trumpeters saluted Christian* One of several instances of Bunyan's love of music.

127. (p. 219) *But if thou shalt cast all away* ... These lines suggest that a second part was contemplated before the publication and success of the first.

THE SECOND PART

1. (p. 224) *my firstling* The First Part. It was phenomenally successful, going through thirteen editions before Bunyan's death in 1688, and earning its publisher, Nathaniel Ponder, the name of 'Bunyan Ponder'.

2. (p. 224) *counterfeit/My pilgrim* There were numerous imitations, spurious continuations, and unauthorized reprints made up with sheets from different editions. T.S. (Thomas Sherman) issued a stilted Second Part, which purported to give due dignity to the allegory. In 1693 there was a spurious Part III which was often reprinted.

3. (p. 224) *thine own native language* Bunyan shows himself well aware of the distinctiveness of his colloquial manner.

4. (p. 225) *France and Flanders* ... *New England* The first Dutch and French translations were published in 1682 and 1685 respectively, both at Amsterdam. The first American edition appeared at Boston in 1681. No Gaelic version prior to Bunyan's death has survived, but there is a Welsh one, *Taith y Pererin* (London, 1687).

5. (p. 225) *Brave gallants* Bunyan's style was fitting to a taste that was beginning to prefer strength of natural wit to pedantic scholarship; thus the learned Puritan John Owen told Charles II that he would relinquish his learning to have the tinker's abilities, *Life of Owen* in *Works*, 1826, i.305.

6. (p. 227) *checkle* Chuckle.

7. (p. 231) *multiplicity of business* During the years between the publication of the First and Second Parts Bunyan was pastor of the Bedford gathered church with responsibility for its outlying congregations in Bedfordshire and Cambridgeshire; he also published seven books in this period, including *Badman* and *The Holy War* (1678–84).

8. (p. 232) *Mr Sagacity* He resembles the Wiseman who tells the story in *Badman*, which had been written a few years before. But Bunyan soon tires of this device and returns by a sure instinct to the direct vision of his dream.

9. (p. 233) *come into these parts* At the Day of Judgement. The text alludes to Matthew 25.31–46.

10. (p. 239) *stunds* Astounds.

11. (p. 239) *So they began* The behaviour of interfering neighbours is also described in *Seasonable Counsel, or Advice to Sufferers*, which appeared in the same year as the Second Part: 'Now also come kindred, and relations, and acquaintance; some chide, some cry, some argue, some threaten, some promise, some flatter, and some do all, to befool him for so unadvised an act as to cast away himself, and to bring his wife and children to beggary for such a thing as religion', Bunyan, *Works*, edited by George Offor (1862) ii.733.

12. (p. 240) *I was a dreamed* Impersonal verb formed from the past participle with its old prefix y-.

13. (p. 241) *her bowels yearned* 1 Kings 3.26.

14. (p. 243) *as merry as the maids* The domesticated language of the neighbours is full of proverbial phrases.

15. (p. 244) *Bowels* Pity, compassion.

16. (p. 245) *these tears of thine will not be lost* Mercy has not received a definite call like Christian and Christiana; she goes on pilgrimage out of friendship to the latter: she is to be saved not by her deeds, but by displaying a truly Christian sensibility. Her character illustrates how much more subtle Bunyan's understanding of the working of grace had become since he wrote the First Part, which is confined to the dramatic either/or aspect of religious conversion.

17. (p. 245) *they that sow in tears* ... Psalm 126.5–6.

18. (p. 245) *rather worse than formerly* There is implied satire here on the Strict Baptists of London, with whom Bunyan had conducted a controversy in 1672–3. It is suggested that their strict conditions for church membership would have driven believers away.

19. (p. 248) *Hers was from the King, and mine was but from her* Cf. note 18 above. The response of the keeper of the Gate is surprisingly liberal ('by what means soever they come unto me').

20. (p. 250) *a most cruel dog* The devil. 'Deliver ... my darling from the power of the dog', Psalm 22.20.

21. (p. 251) *oweth* Owneth.

22. (p. 252) *Blessed be the day that I began* ... The lyrics in the Second Part are metrically derived from Sternhold and Hopkins' version of the Psalms. Bunyan's purpose in including them may have been to promote congregational singing, which had its opponents within the Open Communion Baptist churches. The Bedford congregation was divided and hymn-singing was not finally permitted until 1691.

23. (p. 253) *plash* Shake.

24. (p. 258) *daughter of Abraham* Abraham as father of the children of Israel was a type of Christ: 'they which be of faith are blessed with faithful Abraham', Galatians 3.9.

25. (p. 259) *with a muck-rake* A traditional image for avarice. Bunyan could have met it in Arthur Dent, *Plain Mans Path-Way*, or in Francis Quarles, *Emblemes*, Book II.2:

> Let not thy nobler thoughts be always raking
> The world's base Dunghill.

26. (p. 260) *a very great spider* The sinner, like the spider, contains corruption, that of original sin, and yet can possess a royal palace (heaven). 'The spider taketh hold with her hands, and is in kings' palaces', Proverbs 30.28.

27. (p. 261) *walk* Behave, conduct herself.

28. (p. 261) *a common call* ... An early-nineteenth-century Nonconformist editor of Bunyan defined the different calls of the hen to her chickens as follows:

'Common call, the invitations; brooding voice, the promises; outcry, the warnings of the gospel', Joseph Ivimey, *The Pilgrim's Progress. A New Edition* (1821), p. 297.

29. (p. 262) *Behold the flowers are divers in stature* . . . 'When Christians stand every one in their places, and do the work of their relations, then they are like the flowers in the garden', Bunyan, *Christian Behaviour* in *Works* (1862) ii.500.

30. (p. 263) *The fatter the sow is, the more she desires the mire* Cf. 'Likely lies in the mire and unlikely gets over', *Oxford Dictionary of English Proverbs* (1948) p. 369. Most of the Interpreter's sayings or variants of them can be found in the standard dictionaries of proverbs; M. P. Tilley, *A Dictionary of the Proverbs in England in the Sixteenth and Seventeenth Centuries* (Oxford University Press, 1951) is especially useful.

31. (p. 264) *a tree* The symbol of the fair tree rotten at the heart for the lapsed, hypocritical believer is a prominent element in Bunyan's preaching to which he devoted a whole treatise, *The Barren Fig-tree* (1673).

32. (p. 267) *The Bath Sanctification* Believers' baptism by immersion. There is no treatment of baptism in the First Part and Bunyan may have been under pressure from fellow Baptists; his own Bedford church was Open Communion and practised adult baptism not as a necessary condition but as an optional sign of church membership.

33. (p. 268) *the seal* The mark of election, Ephesians 1.13. It is equated with the Passover, when the Israelites escaped from Egypt, since the Passover was taken to prefigure the liberation of Christians from sin by Christ.

34. (p. 269) *one Great-heart* He is a minister of Christ armed with 'the whole armour of God', Ephesians 6.13–17. He has been thought to recall some idealized Parliamentary officer from Bunyan's Civil War service.

35. (p. 270) *pardon, by word and deed* The theology of the working of grace here proclaimed by Great-heart is more fully expounded in *The Doctrine of the Law and Grace Unfolded* (1659).

36. (p. 276) *tro* Interrogative participle formed from 'trow ye' (believe you).

37. (p. 276) *these ways are since stopped up* Possibly alluding to the vigilance against Catholic subversion after the Popish Plot.

38. (p. 277) *The way of the slothful man is a hedge of thorns . . .* Proverbs 15.19.

39. (p. 280) *Grim or Bloody-man* He represents the civil power which executed the penal laws against Nonconformists. The lions which were asleep when Faithful passed are now awake: this reflects the renewed period of persecution in 1681–4.

40. (p. 284) *a noise of music* A concert, or a company of musicians: 'see if thou canst find out Sneak's noise', *2 Henry IV*, II.iv.11.

41. (p. 284) *I was a dreamed* Cf. p. 240 note 12.

42. (p. 289) *Mr Brisk* He behaves like a Restoration gallant, and the word suggests gallantry. *O.E.D.* quotes Etherege: 'He has been, as the sparkish word is, brisk upon the ladies already' (*Man of Mode*).

43. (p. 290) *ill conditions* Bad qualities.

44. (p. 291) *could never agree* The evils of a marriage with an unreligious husband are fully explored in *The Life and Death of Mr Badman* (1680).

45. (p. 291) *cried her down at the cross* Disclaiming the responsibility for the maintenance of one's wife at the market cross was supposed to constitute a form of divorce.

46. (p. 292) *that fruit* Matthew's eating of the overhanging apples from the orchard is an allegory of original sin.

47. (p. 292) *the blood of a goat . . .* Signs of the old law of Moses, Hebrews 10.1–4.

48. (p. 292) *ex carne et sanguine Christi* The borrowed Latin imitates that of a medical prescription. There is a pun involving 'Mathew's Pills', a well-known patent remedy of the time, invented by Richard Mathew (*The Unlearned Alchymist His Antidote, or a more full and ample Explanation of the Use, Virtue and Benefit of my PILL*, 1662). This medicine too was 'a corrector of all Vegetative poysons', had to be taken in a liquid, and was effective against 'gripings'.

49. (p. 295) *Of the candle* Human life and the presence of grace are likened to a candle flame in Emblem xiv 'Meditations upon a Candle' of *A Book for Boys and Girls*, and also in one of the emblems of Francis Quarles, *Hieroglyphikes of the Life of Man* (1638).

50. (p. 295) *Why doth the pelican* ... That the pelican fed its young from its own blood was still regarded as a fact of natural history in Bunyan's time by some authorities, though Sir Thomas Browne dismissed it as a superstition in his *Pseudodoxia Epidemica*.

51. (p. 297) *a pair* A set.

52. (p. 298) *a gold angel* A gold coin, once the noble, named from its device on the obverse of St Michael killing the dragon; worth 6s. 8d.

53. (p. 299) *Through all my life* ... Each stanza is from a different psalm in the version of Sternhold and Hopkins (1562), Psalms 23.6 and 100.5.

54. (p. 299) *a scheme* Digest, summary.

55. (p. 301) *Christian's slips* Christian's difficulties in the Valley of Humiliation imply that he had succumbed to pride. 'I have also ... been often tempted to pride and liftings up of Heart', *Grace Abounding*, p.90.

56. (p. 302) *let and hindered* 'Through our sins and wickedness we are sore let and hindered', Collect for the Fourth Sunday in Advent.

57. (p. 308) *Maul, a Giant* The Roman Catholic Church. The reference to his spoiling the pilgrims with sophistry suggests the activity of the Jesuits; that to 'my master's kingdom' raises the question of the foreign allegiance of Catholics, a common charge in the age of the Popish Plot.

58. (p. 314) *Mr Fearing* The first of a group of Christians of tender conscience who appear on pilgrimage. The Bedford church held liberal principles in regard to communion: a member, Joan Cooke, who moved from Bedford to London, was permitted to join any congregation she chose 'for her edification and the furtherance of her faith' (*Church Book*, 30 March 1682).

59. (p. 319) *sackbut* Bass trumpet.

60. (p. 319) *I make bold to talk thus* Again, Bunyan's metaphor of the musician sounding the base (bass) reveals his love of music.

61. (p. 320) *he could have bit a firebrand* This phrase, and a few others, have the character of traditional proverbs but are not recorded in any of the collections.

62. (p. 321) *a man might follow the vices* Self-will is an extreme antinomian who believes that the elect are free to indulge the sins of the flesh since the covenant of grace has quite superseded the covenant of works and the Mosiac law. Such were the opinions of the Ranter sect and Bunyan as a young man had a friend who was a Ranter (*Grace Abounding*, pp. 16–17).

63. (p. 325) *one Gaius* 'The host of himself and of the whole church', Romans 16.23.

64. (p. 326) *at Antioch* 'And the disciples were called Christians first in Antioch', Acts 11.26.

65. (p. 327) *Ignatius ... Romanus ... Policarp* After Stephen, James, Paul and Peter, mention is made of these martyrs whom Bunyan knew from the first book of Foxe's *Acts and Monuments*. St Ignatius, bishop of Antioch, was martyred at Rome *c*.107; St Romanus was put to death under Diocletian *c*.304; St Polycarp, bishop of Smyrna, was burnt to death *c*.155.

66. (p. 327) *he that was hanged up in a basket* This was Marcus of Arethusa, who was thus martyred under Julian the Apostate 332–63.

67. (p. 327) *Fall* Lapse, become extinct.

68. (p. 328) *on the behalf of women* Women played an important role in the Bedford church; in the first list of members they were in a considerable majority, and in 1683 there was a demand for separate prayer-meetings for women, which was resisted: Bunyan may have felt that recognition of the feminine contribution was required to offset this rebuff.

69. (p. 329) *a heave-shoulder and a wave-breast* The meats 'heaved' or lifted in sacrifice before God: they constituted

the peace offering made by Aaron and his sons, Leviticus 7.32–4.

70.   (p. 329) *Butter and honey shall he eat . . .*   Isaiah 7.15.

71.   (p. 333) *one Slay-good*   This giant seems to have no particular allegorical significance, but he has terrorized Feeble-mind, who is one of the over-scrupulous overtaken by the pilgrims, and therefore prone to spiritual distress at small provocation.

72.   (p. 338) *Beloved, thou dost faithfully . . .*   3 John 6.

73.   (p. 338) *to comfort the feeble-minded*   'the edification of souls in the faith and holiness of the gospel, is of greater concernment than an agreement in outward things', *A Confession of My Faith* in *Works*, ii.611.

74.   (p. 340) *like flint*   Isaiah 1.7.

75.   (p. 341) *Mr Mnason, a Cyprusian*   'One Mnason of Cyprus, an old disciple with whom we should lodge', Acts 21.16.

76.   (p. 343) *an item*   A hint.

77.   (p. 343) *more moderate now*   Presumably since the Declaration of Indulgence to Nonconformists in 1672; this statement does not allow for the recurrence of persecution in the last years of Charles II's reign and may therefore have been written before that period.

78.   (p. 346) *The Monster*   The beast of Revelation 17.3, identified by Protestants as the Church of Rome.

79.   (p. 349) *daughters*   Generally used for daughters-in-law.

80.   (p. 352) *demolishing Doubting-Castle*   A recent editor, N. H. Keeble, has commented on the weakness of the allegory at this point: how can the temptation to despair be wholly removed from future believers? But Bunyan seems intent to extract every minor dramatic advantage from a sequel covering the same ground.

81.   (p. 356) *the cake*   1 Kings 17.8–16.

82.   (p. 356) *washing of an Ethiopian*   A common emblem. The previous emblem of Prejudice and Ill-wind fruitlessly casting dirt on the innocent man is this emblem in reverse.

83. (p. 360) *hear your horse dash* Another proverbial phrase not recorded in the standard collections.

84. (p. 361) *Though an host* ... Psalm 27.3.

85. (p. 361) *Jerusalem blade* On the analogy of Toledo blade.

86. (p. 362) *a serpent* A dragon: probably Apollyon.

87. (p. 367) *Who would true valour see* ... Bunyan's most celebrated lyric: it carries verbal reminiscences of Amiens's song in *As You Like It*.

88. (p. 373) *Madam Bubble* The bubble is used throughout Quarles' *Emblemes* as an image of the world's vanity.

89. (p. 377) *a Post come* The use of the imagery of death from Ecclesiastes 12 runs like a refrain through this last episode; the pitcher broken at the well, the golden bowl, the silver cord, the grasshopper. It was a familiar text at Puritan deathbeds, cf. Edward Bagshaw, *Life and Death of Mr Bolton* (3rd ed., 1635): 'The night before hee died, when the doores without began to be shut, and the daughters of Musicke to be brought low ...'

FOR THE BEST IN PAPERBACKS, LOOK FOR THE 🐧

In every corner of the world, on every subject under the sun, Penguin represents quality and variety – the very best in publishing today.

For complete information about books available from Penguin – including Puffins, Penguin Classics and Arkana – and how to order them, write to us at the appropriate address below. Please note that for copyright reasons the selection of books varies from country to country.

In the United Kingdom: Please write to *Dept E.P., Penguin Books Ltd, Harmondsworth, Middlesex, UB7 0DA.*

If you have any difficulty in obtaining a title, please send your order with the correct money, plus ten per cent for postage and packaging, to *PO Box No 11, West Drayton, Middlesex*

In the United States: Please write to *Dept BA, Penguin, 299 Murray Hill Parkway, East Rutherford, New Jersey 07073*

In Canada: Please write to *Penguin Books Canada Ltd, 2801 John Street, Markham, Ontario L3R 1B4*

In Australia: Please write to the *Marketing Department, Penguin Books Australia Ltd, P.O. Box 257, Ringwood, Victoria 3134*

In New Zealand: Please write to the *Marketing Department, Penguin Books (NZ) Ltd, Private Bag, Takapuna, Auckland 9*

In India: Please write to *Penguin Overseas Ltd, 706 Eros Apartments, 56 Nehru Place, New Delhi, 110019*

In the Netherlands: Please write to *Penguin Books Netherlands B.V., Postbus 195, NL–1380AD Weesp*

In West Germany: Please write to *Penguin Books Ltd, Friedrichstrasse 10–12, D–6000 Frankfurt/Main 1*

In Spain: Please write to *Longman Penguin España, Calle San Nicolas 15, E–28013 Madrid*

In Italy: Please write to *Penguin Italia s.r.l., Via Como 4, I-20096 Pioltello (Milano)*

In France: Please write to *Penguin Books Ltd, 39 Rue de Montmorency, F-75003 Paris*

In Japan: Please write to *Longman Penguin Japan Co Ltd, Yamaguchi Building, 2–12–9 Kanda Jimbocho, Chiyoda-Ku, Tokyo 101*

PENGUIN CLASSICS

Netochka Nezvanova   Fyodor Dostoyevsky

Dostoyevsky's first book tells the story of 'Nameless Nobody' and introduces many of the themes and issues which will dominate his great masterpieces.

Selections from the Carmina Burana   A verse translation by David Parlett

The famous songs from the *Carmina Burana* (made into an oratorio by Carl Orff) tell of lecherous monks and corrupt clerics, drinkers and gamblers, and the fleeting pleasures of youth.

Fear and Trembling   Søren Kierkegaard

A profound meditation on the nature of faith and submission to God's will which examines with startling originality the story of Abraham and Isaac.

Selected Prose   Charles Lamb

Lamb's famous essays (under the strange pseudonym of Elia) on anything and everything have long been celebrated for their apparently innocent charm; this major new edition allows readers to discover the darker and more interesting aspects of Lamb.

The Picture of Dorian Gray   Oscar Wilde

Wilde's superb and macabre novella, one of his supreme works, is reprinted here with a masterly Introduction and valuable Notes by Peter Ackroyd.

A Treatise of Human Nature   David Hume

A universally acknowledged masterpiece by 'the greatest of all British Philosophers' – A. J. Ayer

FOR THE BEST IN PAPERBACKS, LOOK FOR THE

PENGUIN CLASSICS

A Passage to India E. M. Forster

Centred on the unresolved mystery in the Marabar Caves, Forster's great work provides the definitive evocation of the British Raj.

The Republic Plato

The best-known of Plato's dialogues, *The Republic* is also one of the supreme masterpieces of Western philosophy whose influence cannot be overestimated.

The Life of Johnson James Boswell

Perhaps the finest 'life' ever written, Boswell's *Johnson* captures for all time one of the most colourful and talented figures in English literary history.

Remembrance of Things Past (3 volumes) Marcel Proust

This revised version by Terence Kilmartin of C. K. Scott Moncrieff's original translation has been universally acclaimed – available for the first time in paperback.

Metamorphoses Ovid

A golden treasury of myths and legends which has proved a major influence on Western literature.

A Nietzsche Reader Friedrich Nietzsche

A superb selection from all the major works of one of the greatest thinkers and writers in world literature, translated into clear, modern English.

PENGUIN CLASSICS

Matthew Arnold	**Selected Prose**
Jane Austen	**Emma**
	Lady Susan, The Watsons, Sanditon
	Mansfield Park
	Northanger Abbey
	Persuasion
	Pride and Prejudice
	Sense and Sensibility
Anne Brontë	**The Tenant of Wildfell Hall**
Charlotte Brontë	**Jane Eyre**
	Shirley
	Villette
Emily Brontë	**Wuthering Heights**
Samuel Butler	**Erewhon**
	The Way of All Flesh
Thomas Carlyle	**Selected Writings**
Wilkie Collins	**The Moonstone**
	The Woman in White
Charles Darwin	**The Origin of the Species**
Charles Dickens	**American Notes for General Circulation**
	Barnaby Rudge
	Bleak House
	The Christmas Books
	David Copperfield
	Dombey and Son
	Great Expectations
	Hard Times
	Little Dorrit
	Martin Chuzzlewit
	The Mystery of Edwin Drood
	Nicholas Nickleby
	The Old Curiosity Shop
	Oliver Twist
	Our Mutual Friend
	The Pickwick Papers
	Selected Short Fiction
	A Tale of Two Cities

Benjamin Disraeli	**Sybil**
George Eliot	**Adam Bede**
	Daniel Deronda
	Felix Holt
	Middlemarch
	The Mill on the Floss
	Romola
	Scenes of Clerical Life
	Silas Marner
Elizabeth Gaskell	**Cranford and Cousin Phillis**
	The Life of Charlotte Brontë
	Mary Barton
	North and South
	Wives and Daughters
Edward Gibbon	**The Decline and Fall of the Roman Empire**
George Gissing	**New Grub Street**
Edmund Gosse	**Father and Son**
Richard Jefferies	**Landscape with Figures**
Thomas Macaulay	**The History of England**
Henry Mayhew	**Selections from London Labour and The London Poor**
John Stuart Mill	**On Liberty**
William Morris	**News from Nowhere and Selected Writings and Designs**
Walter Pater	**Marius the Epicurean**
John Ruskin	**'Unto This Last' and Other Writings**
Sir Walter Scott	**Ivanhoe**
Robert Louis Stevenson	**Dr Jekyll and Mr Hyde**
William Makepeace Thackeray	**The History of Henry Esmond**
	Vanity Fair
Anthony Trollope	**Barchester Towers**
	Framley Parsonage
	Phineas Finn
	The Warden
Mrs Humphrey Ward	**Helbeck of Bannisdale**
Mary Wollstonecraft	**Vindication of the Rights of Women**

FOR THE BEST IN PAPERBACKS, LOOK FOR THE

PENGUIN CLASSICS

Arnold Bennett	The Old Wives' Tale
Joseph Conrad	Heart of Darkness
	Nostromo
	The Secret Agent
	The Shadow-Line
	Under Western Eyes
E. M. Forster	Howard's End
	A Passage to India
	A Room With a View
	Where Angels Fear to Tread
Thomas Hardy	The Distracted Preacher and Other Tales
	Far From the Madding Crowd
	Jude the Obscure
	The Mayor of Casterbridge
	The Return of the Native
	Tess of the d'Urbervilles
	The Trumpet Major
	Under the Greenwood Tree
	The Woodlanders
Henry James	The Aspern Papers and The Turn of the Screw
	The Bostonians
	Daisy Miller
	The Europeans
	The Golden Bowl
	An International Episode and Other Stories
	Portrait of a Lady
	Roderick Hudson
	Washington Square
	What Maisie Knew
	The Wings of the Dove
D. H. Lawrence	The Complete Short Novels
	The Plumed Serpent
	The Rainbow
	Selected Short Stories
	Sons and Lovers
	The White Peacock
	Women in Love

PENGUIN CLASSICS

John Aubrey	**Brief Lives**
Francis Bacon	**The Essays**
James Boswell	**The Life of Johnson**
Sir Thomas Browne	**The Major Works**
John Bunyan	**The Pilgrim's Progress**
Edmund Burke	**Reflections on the Revolution in France**
Thomas de Quincey	**Confessions of an English Opium Eater**
	Recollections of the Lakes and the Lake Poets
Daniel Defoe	**A Journal of the Plague Year**
	Moll Flanders
	Robinson Crusoe
	Roxana
	A Tour Through the Whole Island of Great Britain
Henry Fielding	**Jonathan Wild**
	Joseph Andrews
	The History of Tom Jones
Oliver Goldsmith	**The Vicar of Wakefield**
William Hazlitt	**Selected Writings**
Thomas Hobbes	**Leviathan**
Samuel Johnson/ James Boswell	**A Journey to the Western Islands of Scotland/The Journal of a Tour to the Hebrides**
Charles Lamb	**Selected Prose**
Samuel Richardson	**Clarissa**
	Pamela
Adam Smith	**The Wealth of Nations**
Tobias Smollet	**Humphry Clinker**
Richard Steele and Joseph Addison	Selections from the **Tatler** and the **Spectator**
Laurence Sterne	**The Life and Opinions of Tristram Shandy, Gentleman**
	A Sentimental Journey Through France and Italy
Jonathan Swift	**Gulliver's Travels**
Dorothy and William Wordsworth	**Home at Grasmere**

Saint Anselm	**The Prayers and Meditations**
Saint Augustine	**The Confessions**
Bede	**A History of the English Church and People**
Chaucer	**The Canterbury Tales**
	Love Visions
	Troilus and Criseyde
Froissart	**The Chronicles**
Geoffrey of Monmouth	**The History of the Kings of Britain**
Gerald of Wales	**History and Topography of Ireland**
	The Journey through Wales and **The Description of Wales**
Gregory of Tours	**The History of the Franks**
Julian of Norwich	**Revelations of Divine Love**
William Langland	**Piers the Ploughman**
Sir John Mandeville	**The Travels of Sir John Mandeville**
Marguerite de Navarre	**The Heptameron**
Christine de Pisan	**The Treasure of the City of Ladies**
Marco Polo	**The Travels**
Richard Rolle	**The Fire of Love**
Thomas à Kempis	**The Imitation of Christ**

ANTHOLOGIES AND ANONYMOUS WORKS

The Age of Bede
Alfred the Great
Beowulf
A Celtic Miscellany
The Cloud of Unknowing and Other Works
The Death of King Arthur
The Earliest English Poems
Early Christian Writings
Early Irish Myths and Sagas
Egil's Saga
The Letters of Abelard and Heloise
Medieval English Verse
Njal's Saga
Seven Viking Romances
Sir Gawain and the Green Knight
The Song of Roland